The Shattered Stars:

Breach of Contract

Book 1

By
Vance Huxley

Published by Entrada Publishing.

Printed in the United States of America.

Contents

To my Noeline and to the Joy of my life

Thank you to my editor Sharon Umbaugh,
for turning my words into a book worth reading.

My thanks to Rachel at Entrada
for all her hard work and encouragement.

Pleb

Bobby B stood in a line along the wall of the court, one of thirty defendants. Not that the defence lawyer, a lowly supervisor in the justice department, had bothered defending them. The judge banged a gavel. "Guilty. Illegal firearms were used during this attempted uprising, and a Trooper killed. An example must be made. You are all sentenced to death."

Bobby's head reeled. He'd waved goodbye to Mam this morning and gone out to add his voice to the protest about the layoffs at Britmine, not join an uprising! Bertram had promised him a few extra creds to buy food for his Mam if he'd stand in the line to make up numbers. Bertram's gang were short of muscle and even at four weeks shy of sixteen, Bobby B stood almost six feet tall.

Then all hell broke loose and the Troopers had moved in, someone a couple of streets away had started shooting, and Bertram yelled for everyone to split. Bobby did, along with a group of others. They'd run down the alley, but a big armoured vehicle swung across the entrance, a voice bellowed stop, and Troopers poured out and lined up with levelled weapons. Two men had run, and were shot, so the rest knelt while the cuffs went on. Now Bobby thought he should have run and saved time.

"Silence!" The shuffling and murmuring stopped. "You are fortunate because today there are alternatives. Recruits are needed for the army, and Britmine requires volunteers for the deep levels. Each defendant will be asked and must answer clearly. Death, Army or Britmine." He looked down and read the first name. Bobby didn't need to think about it. Da's bones were at the bottom of a Britmine shaft because sealing the shaft had been cheaper than digging out the miners, so he wasn't going down there. He didn't fancy the army much, the fighting on the news looked bloody but his chances had to be better.

The fifth man broke the one-word answers. "Can I choose navy?"

"Death." The judge gestured to the Sergeant and a Trooper grabbed the man by the scruff of the neck.

He shouted, "No, no, I'll take army," as he was dragged through the door but nobody listened.

"There are three answers and I have no time to waste on pointless argument." The judge banged his gavel. "Next."

Seven names later the judge paused. "This one is only fifteen." Bobby hoped again, briefly, as a clerk spoke into the judge's ear. "He'll be sixteen by the time they're trained? I see." He looked down at the papers again. "Bobby B? What is your full name?"

Bobby sighed. "Bobby B. Army."

The judge narrowed his eyes. "You've got a bad attitude for such a young man. The army will knock that out of you. Next." Using the B instead of a surname wasn't attitude. Bobby B didn't want his full name on the list that would go up outside the other housing blocks in the residential complex for Britmine workers. In particular, he didn't want his name put up outside housing block 12C where he'd lived since birth. His Mam still lived there and would have a hard enough time on her own without everyone knowing her son had joined up. The Plebs, the workforce, hated the Troopers, and even if Bobby wouldn't be a Trooper straight away he'd wear an army uniform. As the twenty-six men filed out, nearly all of them new army recruits, Bobby wondered about the three who chose death. Surely being in the army couldn't be that bad?

*   *   *

Similar courtroom scenes played out throughout the United Kingdoms because unknown to the defendants, the judges had been told to increase recruitment. "Pierre Stifles, you are charged with theft of corporate property, trespass, criminal damage, and use of a deadly weapon." The defendant, a scrawny nineteen-year-old just under 5' 6" tall, stared in shock. The weapon consisted of a length of thin wire with a bit of wood at each end, and he'd only ever used it to throttle deer! "Because of the weapon used, you are eligible for the death sentence, but you have alternative choices. Ten years vat-cleaning in the Chemworks, or join the army."

Pierre Stifles didn't hesitate, because he wouldn't last a year on vat-cleaning. The workers were rotated every fourteen days to stop the build-up of chemicals in their bodies. "Army." He stumbled from the dock, wondering how he'd survive the bloody chaos he saw on the news.

His Dad taught him to be a poacher, to live in shadows and move quiet enough to sneak up on a sleeping deer. But there'd be no hiding place on a battlefield and he wasn't built for fighting.

*   *   *

Kris Hellis gingerly touched his swollen cheek but the bleeding had stopped. He flexed his hands to crack his knuckles, he always did when things started to go viral, but stopped because that would be a really bad idea just now. The Troopers with shock-sticks were looking for an excuse. Instead he sucked a skinned knuckle and glared at the nearest Trooper with one eye. Only one eye because the other had swollen shut. The Trooper sneered at him, safe enough with the irons Kris wore.

"Kris Hellis, you have been found guilty of affray, riot, damage to public property, resisting arrest and attempted murder." Kris's head snapped up and he stared. Attempted murder? When the Troopers arrived to break up the gang fight, he'd stood with the others, hands on his head, because the Troopers brought guns to a fist fight. Then one slapped him for glaring, and he'd punched the basted. Well all right, he'd pulled the basted's faceplate up and smeared his nose all over his face, but the Trooper hit him first! Then the rest could be called self-defence because the Troopers had beaten the shite out of him.

"But…"

"Silence! Prisoner will not speak. Trooper, you may use a shock-stick if he does so again without permission." The judge glared and Kris fought down an urge to jump out of the dock and go for the basted, because he'd not get far with the shackles on. "One Trooper with concussion, one with a broken arm and two more unfit for duty? You are lucky none died because that means you have a choice. Usually someone guilty of a serious crime has the option to undertake unpleasant work for a corporation, but with your violent tendencies that would be unwise. The sentence is death, or you may volunteer for the army."

Kris Hellis sighed in relief. He didn't mind the army because he liked fighting, or fighting liked him since trouble found him all the time. He'd still get women because the black market vids always showed that they liked the uniform. "Army." He grinned at the Trooper as he shuffled out because next time he met the shite, Kris Hellis would have a gun as well.

* * *

Rokur Fenton stood quietly in the dock, patiently waiting as the defence lawyer explained why the defendant had a weapon. Not really a weapon, it certainly wouldn't scratch a Trooper jacket or helmet but it killed pigeons and seagulls well enough. The little pellets the compressed-air rifle fired were unlikely to seriously injure anyone, and Fenton never aimed it at a person even in fun. Instead he killed the birds and sometimes rats, to help his family get by.

He sold pigeons for food if his parents didn't use them to feed everyone at home, and some people bought the seagulls and rats for animal food. He hoped so, there'd been rumours and Fenton wouldn't buy burgers or fishcakes from the cheaper stalls in the market. Now someone had turned him in for having the weapon, probably jealous, and Fenton expected to get a few years hard labour in the quarry. A burly 6' 2" twenty-year old, he didn't mind hard labour though he would miss that rifle. Susan wouldn't wait but they really weren't that serious about each other anyway.

"Guilty. Because you were found with an illegal deadly weapon, a rifle, the sentence should be death or thirty years hard labour." Fenton stared. He opened his mouth but the judge carried on. "Your expertise with the rifle allows me to offer another option, joining the army. You may speak, but only to say death, quarry or army."

Fenton thought quickly. He wouldn't get paid doing hard labour as a convict, but he would in the army, and they'd give him a real rifle. He stifled any qualms about aiming it at people. "Army." He shuffled out of the courtroom, the chains between his ankles rattling. Because of his size everyone treated him as a bruiser, heavy muscle, and he already expected the same reaction from the other recruits.

* * *

A hundred new recruits stumbled off the buses and milled about in the middle of a wide expanse of concrete as the transport left. "Form lines, you bloody idjeets. You're soldiers now, not a flock of bledrin sheep!" The man with three stripes on his arm glared, and the pair with two stripes brandished shock-sticks.

"Give us a bleedin' chance." The big man stuck out his chest and sneered as the smaller uniformed figure marched towards him. Instead of arguing, the approaching soldier raised a knee, quickly, accurately, and with considerable force. The speaker screamed, dropped, and rolled about whimpering with both hands cradling his groin.

"I am a Sergeant, and you may call me Sarge but not because you are my friends. These two are Corporals, or Corps. You will not answer back, or give any of us that civvie shite, because we will hurt you." He looked around the group, contempt in his look and voice. "The sooner you incompetent basteds all die, the sooner I can go back to real soldiering. Now get in lines." The crowd did their best.

"Sergeant?"

"There's always one bigmouth. Hellfire, did the Ultimate CEO lose a minion? Where did the other half of you go, to the navy for fish bait?" The sergeant looked Stifles down, and down. "What's your name?"

"Pierre Stifles."

"What do you want, Siflis?"

The small man considered arguing about his name, but the first victim hadn't stopped whimpering yet. "Don't we get uniforms, and guns and all that?"

"Not yet, Siflis. First we make you fit and healthy, or kill you. Then we'll fit the survivors with uniforms, and introduce you to the serious part of soldiering, and kill some more of you. Then the Frogs, Krauts or Russ kill some more. With luck you'll all cark it within a year and I'll be done with you."

"But aren't we soldiers, don't we get to fight back?" Bobby fought a sudden impulse to step back a bit as the sergeant's glare moved onto him.

"No, you aren't soldiers. You are Timers, first-timers, and as a hint of how much we think of you, your unit of one hundred is called a Mob. If you survive your first ten years, you'll turn into Troopers, which are nearly soldiers. Another ten years of that and if by some miracle you haven't carked it by then you'll be a real soldier, a Squaddie." The sergeant frowned. "Who are you?"

"Bobby B. Sarge."

"What does the B stand for?"

"B. Sarge."

"Goody, we have a comedian. Since you spoke up you must like volunteering, so go and stand at that end. You, Siflis, go to the back so nobody trips over you. Beebi, lead off towards those huts and do not try to march. That will make me angry because you'll make a bledrin shambles of it, and you won't like me when I'm angry." The sergeant glared at the Timers. "Move it!" The recruits did, most of them reflecting that they didn't like Sarge much even when he wasn't angry.

Then they all tried to come to terms with the wooden huts and sparse facilities that were home for the foreseeable future. Within days they also started to realise just how far down the army shite-heap a Timer stood. Their Mob of one hundred had a Supervisor in charge, but a trainee Supervisor because it didn't matter if he made a mistake and Timers ended up dead. Everyone below Supervisors seemed to be disposable, though Sarge might not be easy to dispose of.

* * *

Within a week everyone could march, or near enough not to be beaten or shocked by the Corporals for screwing up. They'd also learned to never, ever, really make Sarge angry. The poor basted who found that out left on a stretcher and didn't come back, because Sarge stripped down to his skivvies and kicked the man around the parade ground until he lay still. The kicking wasn't so bad, most of them had seen that in whatever housing complex they'd grown up in. What scared them were the shiny steel kneecaps that Sarge used to do a lot of the damage.

"That's called metal." Bobby leaned closer, listening, because this recruit seemed to know more than most. "The only way to get that is to be a good fighter, good enough so the army thinks you are worth the expense of the repairs. If not, you'll go home a cripple."

"Feckin hell, Google, I don't fancy that. How do you know?"

"My father works in an office, he hears things." Google, already called that because he seemed to know everything, sighed. "Didn't keep me out of the army." Nobody asked, because not prying into another Timer's past life had already become an unofficial rule. They were all in the shite together now.

The army gave them an explanation about metal during one of the lectures that started soon afterwards. Google had the gist of it right. If the army thought the man worth the expense, he would be repaired. The use of Kwikheal and the fitting of a permanent bio-steel interface between the new metal and the flesh meant the additions could be clipped on and off, and few interfaces were rejected. Google explained that Kwikheal had been developed so the rich basteds could have their new hearts up and running in no time. The bio-steel interface came from the last gasps of the space programme before the corporations closed the lot down as uneconomic.

More official lectures followed on army regulations, politics in both the UKs and the wider world, weapons, and a plethora of seemingly unrelated subjects. Though some subjects didn't need an official lecture. "Timers will refrain from using the usual filthy language civvies think is normal." Sarge stood above yet another moaning Timer. "You will use less objectionable terms such as bledrin or sodit. You will refer to women of loose morals or those you'd like to have loose morals as Divas. The usual terms for carnal knowledge are not allowed. Because you are Timers and think with your nuts, it is impossible for you to just stop talking about sex, so you will say Pooch."

"Even in the barracks, Sarge?" Bobby frowned. "Most of us don't talk dirty anyway, its mainly the gangs that use the worst words." He stopped, because the chances were a good few of the Timers were from gangs.

"The gangs use those sorts of words to pretend they are big rough types. The army doesn't use them because we don't need to prove anything. We don't spout filth because the Supervisors and higher officers are not Plebs. Our Supervisor has been raised far from the housing complexes, with a nanny and three nurses, and will probably break out in a rash if you use bad language within a thousand metres."

"The gangs use pooch as well, but I don't see why."

Sarge laughed. "It's to make them look tough like Troopers."

Bobby was still lost. "So why pooch, isn't that a dog?"

"Pooch as in screw the pooch, because we can't expect you to remember a long posh word like fornicate. You will Pooch the Diva instead of spouting the filth that comes naturally to you, so that none of you sully the ears of your Supervisor. Though you won't be doing that until you've had your first taste of action."

"When is that, Sarge?"

"Hells Bells, I should have known it would be you wanting to know about Divas. When you finally learn all the really interesting shite in those lectures you'll learn to hurt people, and then actually go and try to do it. Eventually, Bells, you will go to a palace and meet the Divas, and hopefully cut down on the self-abuse." Sarge smiled at Hellis and the rest tensed but the lesson had finally gone in and Hellis accepted Hells Bells, or Bells, as a name. Since Sarge had already beaten him up four times for objecting, that was overdue. "Now since everyone has so much spare breath, thirty push-ups and yes, you as well, Siflis. It'll be easier for you because a decent breeze will do most of the lifting."

*   *   *

Bobby hated lectures, not just because of the boring drone of the voices but because the training meant all the Timers were always tired, and sitting comfortably meant he usually drifted off to sleep. "You, that Timer, third in, sixth row. Yes, you. Name?"

"Bobby B, sir."

"What does the B stand for?"

Bobby winced inside. "B, Sir."

"Your sergeant is supposed to knock that sort of insolence out of you. I will encourage him to try harder. Now, since you find my explanation boring, perhaps you can find a more interesting way to tell the others how the United Kingdoms came about?" The Line Supervisor's mocking voice stirred a worm of resentment because the snide basted hadn't been marching all morning, but Bobby squashed it. The last Timer to get snotty with a Supervisor had been lashed bloody.

"Sorry sir."

"Sergeant, three stripes with the strap to help this Timer stay awake." That would sting, but the strap didn't cut the skin and scar like the lash did. Bobby stood and stripped off his shirt, then braced against the wall with his hands up and legs spread while the Corporal administered the punishment. "Now if everyone is awake, I'll start again?" A round of muffled complaints followed that because the time would come out of their meal break. Several glares were directed at Bobby, then all the

Timers tried to look as wide-eyed as possible as the Line Supervisor turned back to his screen and pointer.

"Until one hundred and thirty-seven years ago, the world used to be split into national blocs. These divisions were arbitrary, inefficient, and uneconomic, and squandered vast sums simply to curry favour with the electorate or fight for political beliefs or almost worthless land. The world periodically descended into depression and these countries would borrow vast sums, which were never repaid. The corporations developed into multinationals, and began to combine into conglomerates with more wealth and power than the countries themselves. Finally, when the national bodies once more came with their begging bowl, the actual creators of wealth said no. Since then the world has been run efficiently."

Nobody spoke during the pause, which was supposed to be for any questions. "The elected representatives ceded the mechanisms of government and all government owned assets, in return for which the corporations cancelled the national debts. Portions of conglomerates recombined to concentrate on econo-geographical areas. The old countries of Germany, Austria, Greece, Poland, and a several smaller countries, for instance, became the Mid-European Economic Consortium or MEEC."

The Line Manager sneered at the Timers. "You will never need to know all this unless any of you survive long enough to become Squaddies, so I will not list them all. You only need to know that more or less the old countries of the United Kingdom, Norway, Sweden, Denmark including Greenland, Holland, Belgium, Iceland and Ireland became this bloc, the United Kingdoms. Switzerland also joined, but only by transferring all the wealth and corporations because the actual real estate could not be defended. As citizens of the United Kingdoms you may still speak a historic language such as Norwegian, but everyone learns Anglic."

Bobby started to glaze over, then jerked awake as his sore back touched the seat. The Line Supervisor couldn't have seen that, but he did turn with a sour smile. "If I am boring anyone, please let me know. Am I boring you, Bobby B?"

"No sir."

"Good. As Timers you may occasionally hear of the neighbouring blocs, because you may be fighting them as a part of contract negotiations.

You may meet the MEEC, which I just mentioned, but your Supervisor will refer to them as the Krauts. Similarly, you may fight the Russ and the Frogs. Especially the Frogs, the FAC or Franco-African Corporation, as the UKs has a sensitive land border with them." He looked around the room. "Any questions?" By now nobody was stupid enough to ask anything, ever. "Then we will carry on tomorrow. Dismissed."

* * *

"Sarge, why do we have a Supervisor in charge? In the old black market vids there's leftenants and," Bells frowned, trying to remember.

"Lieutenants, Captains, Generals?" Sarge grinned. "They were inefficient. The army is run as a business, so we have Managers and Supervisors the same as any other company. If you ever meet a Director, kiss his or her shadow because you'll be shot if your lips sully their shoeshine." Sarge looked around the Timers. "Someone will bore you for three hours explaining that, but you only need to know that a Supervisor is the Ultimate CEO's personal representative in your miserable lives. If you piss him off, you'll probably take a Gaza Taxi ride."

"That's twice you've used that."

"That's a shock, Fenton, you can speak and you can count. That's a double first for you. I don't know why, but a suicide mission is known as a Gaza Taxi. It's an old thing and came down through the Squaddies or so I heard." Sarge smiled at them all and pulled an object out from under his desk. "For the triple, Fenton, what's this?"

Fenton leaned forward, inspecting the weapon. "A rifle Sarge."

"Hellfire Fenton, that's the most excited I've ever seen you. How many of you can use one of these?" Sarge looked around the room and nearly two score raised their hands. "Now we know who the bad lads are. This is not a rifle. A rifle is longer, as you will notice when a Squaddie finally deigns to wander past, and fires real bullets and not flechettes. This is a carbin."

"What's the difference Sarge?" Fenton's eyes were riveted on the weapon.

"This is cheaper, and much more fragile than a rifle. The carbin is prone to jamming if abused, so treat it better than you did your girlfriend." Sarge pulled a long blade from under his desk and clipped it to the firearm. "With this bayonet, the carbin will be your best friend for the next ten and possibly twenty years." He stood so everyone could see better. "This clip holds thirty flechettes, very sharp darts made of either plastic or steel. The selector allows single shot, triple burst or automatic. Please be careful about using automatic, because the Supervisor will take the cost out of your wages."

Sour smiles greeted that because they'd already been given the list of charges for their food, board, clothing, and equipment but ammunition seemed to be the only thing not on it. "Why is the ammo free?" Bells leaned forward. "Can we try one?"

"You will really wish you'd never said that, while you sit with a blindfold trying to strip this and fix a jam. The ammo is not free but is charged against the operation, not you personally. Use too much and your Super really will be upset."

Bells frowned. "Why plastic and steel, why not just steel? Won't that make it harder to kill the enemy?"

"Yes Bells. But the idea is to kill other Timers without damaging property, and plastic will go through your uniform or flesh but not doors. If there is property damage your Super will be held responsible and he'd better have a solid gain to show for it. Steel flechettes are issued on the front lines, but not always used." Sarge looked very serious for a moment. "One reason for plastic is that they will not go through a Super's jacket, so don't get creative. I suppose I'd better give this one to Fenton to play with since he's the biggest." While several were eyeing the big man up and debating having a go to get the carbin, the door opened and a Corporal brought in the rest.

*   *   *

"Bells, do you fancy a fight?"

Bells looked at the man, slightly taller than him but not as heavily muscled. "With you Beebi? Not particularly." He grinned. "But if you insist?"

"Not me you bledrin eedjit. A few of the others are pissed at Fenton for showing them up on the range. They're all blokes who were in the gangs and don't like a quiet type like that beating them. Snowman is

19

taking it personally."

"Why would I care?" Bells cracked his knuckles. "I don't mind the fight but I want something in it for me."

"How about someone who can shoot better than both of us together owing us a favour when the shite hits the fan?" Bobby shrugged. "I can't hit a wall from inside the room."

"All right, I'll risk it. I'm bored anyway." Bells cracked his knuckles again and followed Bobby along the beds until Bobby stopped and kicked one.

"Siflis. Do you fancy giving Snowman a smack, as payback?" Sarge had named Snowman after his waistline and very white skin, but the ginger-headed arse came from a gang and definitely wasn't fluffy.

"I'd love to but the other four will black my other eye at least." Siflis looked at Bells, and a little smile appeared. "Are you in, Bells?"

"Yeah, and they're picking on Fenton. He's not exactly tiny so if you can take one, we'll take the other four." Bells frowned at the little man. "Maybe we need another."

"No, not if you can keep the rest occupied. I've got just the thing for Snowman." Siflis fumbled under his bedding and put a rolled bundle in a pocket, then stood. "Let's go."

*   *   *

Fenton stood in the bogs, the toilets, his back against one wall and poised ready as the five men closed in cautiously. Three held lengths of wood while Snowman held a small piece of pointed, sharpened steel with a roughly made handle. Bobby pointed at two of them and raised an eyebrow at Bells, who remembered just in time not to crack his knuckles.

Fenton hadn't paid any attention to the three of them since anyone coming into the bogs carefully ignored the little tableau. Getting involved in someone else's strife wasn't always smart. Though as the three moved up closer the big man realised, possibly by the grin on Bells' face, and made sure he kept everyone's attention. "So what do you want, Snowman?" Fenton raised a big fist. "You can't shoot, you won't fight me and none of you want to speak, so why not just piss off?"

"I'm gonna cut you a little, just so your hand don't work so good and you can't shoot, smartarse." Snowman waved and two of those with wooden clubs moved in closer. Bells hit them from behind, grabbing the scruffs of their necks and pushing so both staggered forward towards the wall. Fenton sidestepped, lunged, grabbed the unarmed man by the shirt front and lifted him off his feet. A long step and Fenton straightened his arms, propelling the man backwards across the room to stagger into one of the stalls and trip over the toilet bowl. The other Timers who had now paused to watch the action scattered just in time.

Snowman opened his mouth to speak but Siflis crossed his wrists, then dropped something over his head. Siflis uncrossed his wrists, pulled, and put a knee up into the big man's back. The ex-poacher had to stretch to get his mouth near to Snowman's ear, then he spoke very quietly. "Wire noose, basted. If you move, I'll cut your head off." Snowman, his hand up trying to scrabble at the thin metal already partly buried in his neck, froze.

Bobby didn't try anything cute, he kneed his target between the legs. Even from behind that made the man bend and hunch his back in pain. Bobby clenched his fists together before hammering them down on the nape of the man's neck, driving him down onto his hands and knees. Bobby picked up the dropped club and smacked the arse upside the head, before moving on to help Bells.

Bells didn't really need help because he'd driven both men into the wall and got in a few licks before either recovered. Still, the men were noisy and nobody wanted the Corporals coming to look. One man crumpled when Bobby used the length of wood on him. "Let him fall over now, Bells." The last man couldn't fall because Bells had hold of his throat with one hand, alternating between kneeing him and bashing the man's head on the wall.

"Spoilsport." Bells let the man drop, looking round for another opponent. The one Fenton had thrown ran out of the bogs as Fenton headed for him, three men were out cold, and Snowman had now gone onto his knees. "Hey, that's neat Siflis. Just hold him steady so I can punch the basted a couple of times."

"Greedy. I'm keeping him for Fenton, in case Fenton thinks Snowman needs a little cut." The crude knife lay on the floor nearby. Bells eyed it up but Bobby put a foot on it.

"No, or the medics get involved. We can't make him unfit for duty." Bobby turned to Snowman and slapped the wood into his other palm. "But Fenton can beat the shite out of him." Bobby bent a bit to look Snowman in the eye. "If you give any of us trouble again Bells and Fenton will hold you down. Then I will beat your nuts to pulp before Siflis cuts off your head. If any of us gets hurt accidentally, Fenton can shoot you from a mile away or Siflis can sneak up and throttle you in your own bed. Understood?"

Siflis laughed. "I'd better ease off or nodding will cut his throat." Moments later Snowman nodded, but carefully because Siflis didn't ease off much.

"Do you want to cut him, Fenton?"

"No thanks Bells." Fenton looked at the kneeling man. "I'll let it ride this time just as long as there's no more trouble. Let him go, Siflis." The small man released the wire with one hand and flicked it to swing round the front and clear. Fenton punched the kneeling man in the face. "Sorry, couldn't resist. Now can I buy you three a beer?" They left without a backward glance as some of the other Timers started moving forward, towards the three prone men and the one clutching a broken nose.

"We should cripple him or he'll come after us." Bells glanced back, cracking his knuckles.

"No, he's just lost his backup because the one that ran won't be back and the rest won't want to fight us again. Snowman will have his hands full keeping others from getting a bit of payback now so he'll leave us be." Bobby smiled happily. "When a few of the others join together and kick Snowman shitless, Sarge won't be able to put it down to us." Bobby had seen it in the housing complex time and again. Once a man like that was injured, anyone with a grudge would move in.

"So how come you three came to help me?" Fenton looked at the others. "Not that I'm complaining."

Bobby slapped him on the back. "It crossed my mind that we can help each other to survive this shite, especially now I've seen Siflis with that wire."

During the next week Snowman spent at least half the time unfit for duty because quite a few people took the opportunity for a bit of payback.

Then he didn't come back from the infirmary, and nobody ever knew why. Sarge gave the entire Mob extra drill but didn't pick on anyone in particular. He did make a few comments about how the four of them always seemed to be together, asking if Bells had finally found a girlfriend or if Fenton had adopted Siflis as a mascot.

*   *   *

"Everyone wide awake?" The Line Supervisor found that funny and started every lecture the same way now. "Today I will explain why we actually need you enough to pardon your crimes." He turned to his screen and picked up the pointer. "Timers fight on the borders, assisting with contract negotiations. The best surviving Timers become Troopers, to keep order in the housing complexes. The best Troopers eventually become Squaddies, and are used for serious disagreements between the blocs. In theory, all disputes between the blocs are settled at boardroom level but experience shows that a level of physical pressure is usually necessary to ensure compliance."

Bobby groaned inwardly because the tone of voice meant more history. He palmed the sewing needle to jab himself when his eyelids started drooping. "The conglomerates within a bloc each hold shares, and will vote for or against any action to gain assets from another bloc. The first attempts at takeovers were similar to the old national wars, destructive and wasteful, so rules have been introduced." The screen altered to show a chart with symbols of planes and boats and men, mainly men.

"Firstly, air power is almost obsolete because that invariably destroys assets, though each block keeps a few planes and anti-aircraft defences in case of emergencies. Most pilots now fly Copters which are used for riot and rebellion suppression in the housing complexes. The ridiculous waste of money on the space race meant the corporations stopped that, though you will all be grateful to the old spacemen if you earn metal since the bio-metal interface came from their research. The intention was to create an interface allowing a spaceman to switch limbs depending on what he needed, so now we can clip a new leg on in minutes. The only delay is while the Kwikheal encourages the actual flesh part to knit to the steel."

"Recently there has been a small revival in space exploration." The Line Supervisor looked around the room at the increase in interest and smirked. "But you will never be Space Marines. Small probes are searching for asteroids with very high quality ores so they can be mined but that will not increase the number of pilots. All the work will be carried out by automated craft directed via light-beams from Earth. Since each bloc is keeping their results private, we have no idea if anyone has found a worthwhile target." The Line Supervisor sounded quite animated so maybe he hoped to be a Space Marine?

"The navy only retains sufficient ships to defend trade routes, or islands in the same bloc. Russ, the Chinas and Amazonia for instance have hardly any navy whereas SEPA, with all the South-Eastern Pacific islands, have as many sailors as soldiers." He swung round. "Why does the UKs have a navy, Bobby B?" The arse stressed the "B."

"Because we have islands, sir."

"Near enough, though we also have trade routes to the Americas and must defend the oil reserves under the North and Norwegian Seas. Most disputes are on land, along bloc borders. The UKs have two land assets that are particularly vulnerable, the refineries around Rotterdam and the mining in what used to be Sweden. Russ, Krauts and Frogs try to gain control from time to time by both negotiation and direct action. Timers are used in most combat because there is little or no investment in them so they are cheap." He swept his gaze across the room. "Please understand that you are much less valuable than the assets you are either capturing or defending. That is why you will use plastic flechettes in most cases, and are only allowed carbins."

He raised a hand. "Sergeant, if you will?" Sarge came forward and handed over a double-barrelled shotgun. "In combat the sergeant and your Supervisor will carry shotguns. Your Supervisor will also carry a grenade. These are weapons of last resort due to the property damage they can cause, and only a sergeant or Supervisor can be trusted to assess the situation properly. Any Timer found in possession of either will be executed immediately, using a firing squad from among his comrades to drive the lesson home." Sarge took his shotgun and went back to the rear of the room.

*   *   *

"Once we are Troopers, we'll have weapons and will be back in the housing complexes. We can go back to the gangs, but with serious

24

firepower." The Timer grinned.

"Don't be a prat Sands. They never send you home."

"They might, Google. At least some of us will end up in our home complex because we come from all over. We should all agree that the one who's local helps the rest to get a good place with a gang." Sands looked around the rest and a couple looked interested.

"You won't be home." Bobby didn't like the way this bledrin prat kept on about deserting. "If you walk into the same housing block you used to live in, everyone will run and hide or take a shot." He shrugged. "Chances are you'll be dead by then."

"But we should agree just in case."

"Not a chance." Bobby certainly wasn't shooting his mouth off about it, though he'd probably consider doing a runner if the chance came up. "I'm concentrating on staying alive."

"We'd get all the Divas, Beebi." Bells grinned. "Big rough heroes like us, they'd be lined up."

Bobby glared at the eedjit. "They'd stick a knife in you and steal everything down to your shorts. Now quit that shite before I shoot you myself."

Bells smirked. "No you won't, Beebi, you'd miss."

A new voice chipped in. "No point in waiting until then anyway. If you want to go over the wire, do it as soon as we get to Rotterdam."

"What, and start the revolution there, Preacher? Don't you ever get fed up of your own voice?" Bells, volatile as ever, didn't like Preacher so now he abandoned the whole idea of running.

"No, because they'd send Troopers or Squaddies and Copters to blow the shite out of us. But if we nip over the border with all our gear, the Frogs will welcome us. I've seen an old vid about it. They chopped their king's head off." Preacher spread his arms. "They won't give us back to the Kingdoms, will they? They've got equality."

"So where do their Timers come from? I swear, much more of this and I'm putting your name up for resident Homer." Fenton laughed. "Google reckons every Mob should have a Homer Simpson and if you say "Doh" now and then in among that shite, you'll be dead right." The discussion broke up in laughter as several others were put up for Homer.

*   *   *

After yet another live-fire exercise, Bobby gathered his friends together, glanced round and spoke quietly. "I hope you get this message, Bells."

"What message. Duck during live fire? We're supposed to do that anyway but those five didn't." Bells sneered. "Maybe Preacher really was our Homer."

"Beebi means it's sort of a coincidence that Preacher and Sands were careless just after all that shite they spouted, and those other three all looked interested in the idea of going over the wire. Even more of a coincidence they've all been shot neatly through the head." Siflis nodded slowly as Bells stared at him. The ex-poacher glanced round. "Though we can get through the wire if you really do want to check out the Divas in Rotterdam."

"Really?" Bells had already forgotten the five dead men. "I'm worried mine have shrivelled. I haven't seen a Diva since the basted Troopers arrested me."

"You won't see one yet, not until we've had one official weekend pass and have an idea of where to go." Bobby grinned. "Siflis can nip out and capture a sheep if you're desperate. That's if you really can get over the wire, Siflis?"

"Easy. Sort of through and under, you'll see."

Fenton frowned. "It's electrocuted, and there's alarms."

"Don't worry about it, so are the fences around the hunting preserves where the deer are. Worry about going to the bledrin front tomorrow. We're sixteen men down already after training." Siflis grimaced. "Now that really worries me."

"We've got reinforcements from the Timers we'll be replacing. Which is why we are lurking near the gates." Bobby pointed at a bus passing through the checkpoint into the camp. "According to Google they're coming this evening, so who do you think is on that bus? Let's go and welcome them, and get some idea of what happens up at the sharp end."

*   *   *

Fifteen minutes later the new men had been installed in their quarters. Bobby looked in the door and shook his head. "Shite, me and my big mouth. Why didn't I just agree with Bells and go into Rotterdam? Then at least dying would come as a surprise."

"Their mob didn't all die." Fenton didn't look reassured.

"No, but this lot all look scared of their own shadows, and every single one is wounded." Bells cracked his knuckles. "We could go under the wire right now?"

"Where to, you eedjit? Fenton, try to talk to the one curled up in the corner. You're the nearest to sympathetic we've got." Bobby looked at the rest. "Have you got the cards, Siflis? No cheating, Bells, because we're trying to make friends here."

"No point in playing if we don't cheat." Bells perked up a bit. "Maybe they scored a few Frog weapons I can win off them?"

"If you touch a Frog weapon you'll be shot. That might not worry you, but if I'm in the firing squad the result will be messy and painful because I'll miss the mark." Bobby followed Bells, shaking his head. They were all nervous about going on the front line, but Bells worried most about only having one carbin and bayonet.

"Are you blokes joining our Mob? We're just out of training so what's it like?" Siflis stopped in surprise as two men flinched and one burst into tears. This wasn't going to be good news. Twenty minutes of card playing later they'd found out just how bad it would be.

"I won, and without cheating!" Bells waved the creds, smiling happily as they left.

"Spend them quick, while you've got the chance." Bobby looked up as Fenton approached. "I'll bet you haven't any good news either."

"You'd win. That one had to attack a strongpoint head on with plastic flechettes because the building behind it held a telephone exchange that shouldn't be damaged. Thirty went in and four survived, thought they did kill the six Frogs defending the place so the Super told them that's a win." Fenton shook his head. "None of his Mob could shoot worth a shit but he says neither can the Frogs. They're as bad as us."

"Their Super liked that head-on shite, because he did it with these as well. There's fifteen in hospital, and these are the rest out of a hundred." Bobby felt a chill up his spine. "Sarge keeps saying he wants us all dead. Maybe that Super felt the same way?"

"Shite, shite, shite. I really do fancy going through that wire. Two of their Mob were shot for just picking up Frog weapons, which means all we've got is this shite carbin and the bayonet." Bells started with the knuckles again.

"That's enough because if we get into combat, we'll do it smart. We've got Siflis and his wire for anything sneaky, and Fenton's shooting to keep any Frog eating dirt if we have to attack. Once we're in among them, your head is a better weapon than a carbin, Bells." They all smiled because of how Bells laid out the Corporal giving hand to hand combat training, by nutting him. "I'll just spray flechettes and hope some Frog dives in front of one." The rest laughed because Bobby really wasn't accurate with a carbin, though possibly better than Bells.

*   *   *

Moving into the front line didn't seem too bad to start with. Unfortunately, three days later, the Frogs opened up at dawn on full auto. "Keep your head down." Fenton peeked around a window frame, aimed and fired before ducking back.

"I'm keeping my head down. If it went any further down, I'd be breathing worms. What are you doing anyway?" Siflis turned his head to look up at Fenton. "Trying to annoy them because if so it worked?"

"I've got a Sarge and a Corp so far. The Super is keeping his head down, and he's got a faceplate thing anyway." Fenton grinned. "If he lifts it for a fag break I'm going for it."

"You can't kill a Super!" Bells hissed that quietly and glanced around even though their Super would be in his sandbagged strongpoint. "Can we? Is it different with Frogs?"

"They're the enemy, Bells." Bobby took a quick look. "Since our Super can't see what we're doing, stay in hiding. Don't stick your head up when they stop or some Frog version of Fenton will shoot you."

"How will we know if they're coming?" Bells started cracking his knuckles.

"With this." The other three looked at the shaving mirror taped to a stick. Siflis put it up above the windowsill and angled the gadget so he could see. "Someone is waving his arms about over there." A shot cracked out. "Good shot Fenton."

"Only a Corp, that basted Super is keeping low."

"If they do come, stick the carbins up over the windowsill and empty them on auto. Keep the barrels down and we'll not need to look." Bobby smiled. "I might hit one that way." He looked round. "Since nobody is coming to help, when they get near run out of that door."

"The Super will shoot us. Desertion or cowardice or some such shite." Bells seemed torn between running anyway and diving through the window to attack the Frogs.

"No, because he won't see, and anyway we'll stop just through the doorway. Me and Fenton high, you pair low and we'll shoot them as they come through the window all bunched up." Bobby nudged Bells with a toe. "Unless you want to stay here in the room while they line up at the window and shoot at us?"

"Here they come."

*   *   *

About ninety out of three hundred or so Frogs made it across the open ground in the face of full auto fire from the Britz Timers. The ninety smashed through the windows into the houses Bobby and the rest were defending, and chaos descended. After the fighting died down Sarge came down the corridor to check on everyone, his shotgun still smoking. "Odd pattern of empty clips here, Beebi. All around the doorway like that, they look like an attempt to run away. Cowardice in the face of the enemy?"

"What enemy Sarge?"

The sergeant looked at the jumble of bodies just inside the window, then at the three further into the room. He glanced at Bells, sucking his knuckle. "Since none of you have a black eye, I suppose you must have made contact. Take a drink and keep an eye open. In a while there'll probably be a truce and then the Corporal will supervise while the Frogs collect the dead and wounded. Don't let them take weapons and ammo away."

"Wounded, Sarge?"

"Yes, wounded Bells. Though I suppose nobody actually mentioned prisoners to you." He looked at the still bodies, then at the bloody bayonet Bells still held in his other hand. "That was careless." He shook his head and carried on to the next room.

"Let's help those nice Frogs by heaping the bodies up by the window?"

Bells frowned. "Why Beebi? Sarge said have a drink and take a minute."

"But if there isn't a truce and the basteds have another go, helpfully heaping the bodies will block our window. That might persuade them to pick on someone else." Bobby climbed wearily to his feet and limped to the nearest dead Frog. The other three limped, winced and shuffled to help, favouring wrenches, bruises and flechette grazes from near misses. Training wasn't much preparation for the strain of actual combat.

"Does this mean we're Timers now?" Siflis frowned. "I don't feel different. Well I do, sore, bleeding and knackered, but you know what I mean."

"Hey, if we're Timers, we'll get leave. I've even got the creds we won at cards!" Bells carefully wiped the bayonet on a corpse. Bells might be a rough scruffy shite, but he always kept his weapons clean and sharp.

*   *   *

But when they went into Rotterdam, it didn't turn out anything like Bobby expected. The bus dropped them off outside a bar and all twenty of them went in. He nudged Bells. "These are Divas? They don't look much like Divas in the vids."

"They're women which is near enough, though three aren't many to go round. Shite, you're almost a baby aren't you, I forget. Have you ever?" Bells laughed as Bobby blushed and raised his voice. "Cherry here!"

Laughter spread around the bar and all three women headed for the new party. "It's a new Mob. Cherry picking time and I've got a cert right here." A tall skinny woman grabbed Bobby by the arm. "What's your name, Cherry?"

"Bobby B." Bobby looked around at the grinning faces; this definitely wasn't how he'd pictured his first time.

"I hope that B stands for Bigboy. C'mon sweetheart." She towed him towards the stairs, while the other two looked the rest over and tried to guess which were the virgins.

Bobby came down quite soon afterwards confused, sweatier and poorer than he went up. That might have been memorable, but not a cherished memory and the smell of the room might linger longest. Behind him the woman shouted across the bar. "One down, send up the next." Bobby drank his beer while a few men patted his back and the rest of his group went up the stairs one at a time. Bells looked pissed when he had to wait for all the cherries because the women were having some sort of competition, but eventually came down with a huge smile.

Though on the way back Fenton put it in perspective. "If I have to choose I might go for combat rather than that, but one thing's for certain. We've graduated now."

Timer

Bobby ducked as a Frog carbin fired down towards the United Kingdoms' line, but no scream meant the basted had missed. Unless the basted Frog had managed to kill a Timer outright. Too many Timers had died while they slowly turned from raw untrained troops into fighters. The lack of training, inadequate weaponry and no body armour ensured a high attrition rate. At least the corporations had a hard and fast contract to only use Timers against Timers, because trained troops would have slaughtered them all.

Since he'd lasted eight months, Bobby knew to keep low as he made his way through the row of houses that made up the new front line. He didn't know why he'd been asked to come to an observation post while off-duty, not that anyone cared how much Bobby knew and the order wasn't optional. He did know the Frogs wanted the refinery in Rotterdam, and his job was to stop them getting it. Personally he'd have given them the bledrin thing just to get away from here. Nobody below the Supervisor commanding this Mob of Timers really wanted to be here. Even their Sarge swore he had better things to do.

Now Sarge had called Bobby up here, and he knew for sure it would be to make him unhappy. Bobby opened the door and stepped inside, then he stopped and swallowed, or tried to because his mouth had gone very dry. Grenades weren't allowed except for Supers. Just touching one meant a firing squad or a Gaza Taxi, and Sarge had four of the bledrin things! Bobby glanced around but the other three Timers had the same sick look so this wasn't some sort of setup. Too late now to even report anyone, just being in the room without immediately shooting the rest meant he'd be found guilty.

"Shut the door Beebi and park it." Bobby did what he was told. "Listen up. You four like it up close, and can't shoot worth a shit." Bobby wouldn't have said that and Fenton didn't look happy either. The shooting bit might be true for Bobby but he didn't like it close up either. "So, to help with the shooting, when it's close up?" Sarge pulled four more shotguns out of a sack! Bobby looked properly and they weren't the same as Sarge's. Sodit, were they Frog shotguns? Bobby could almost see the line of his mates, sick as prats, aiming at the cloth pinned to his chest.

"Sarge."

"Might know you'd open it, Beebi. Still, you're already in the shite so go on."

"Sarge, why have you got Frog shotguns, and those grenades? Only Sergeants and Supervisors have a shotgun, and only Supervisors have grenades, so are we being fitted up for a Gaza Taxi Ride?" Bobby still didn't know why everyone called a suicide mission that, but he knew if you pooched it badly enough you might get that option instead of the firing squad. "What did we do?"

"Nothing. None of you pooched. Then again if you four did something I might not catch you, which is why it's you that's here. It's your chance to earn some metal." Sarge tapped his steel knee which wasn't reassuring. "You are the four sneakiest Timers in this Mob. Now if you peek through there, careful like, you'll see where you'll be sneaking."

Bobby knew already, because the only thing that way would be the flats the Frogs had just captured. The long block of flats that allowed the Frogs to shoot at workers this end of the refinery and disrupt production, the flats where the new Frog sniper lurked. Now Sarge expected him to crawl across the open ground towards the Frogs, bare-assed, with illegal weapons? If Bobby got wounded out there whoever found him would find the grenade, or the shotgun and they weren't allowed either. There again Sarge wasn't allowed to have Frog shotguns, or grenades at all. The four of them looked out, and at each other, and none of the others fancied it either.

Fenton sat staring at Sarge, and Bobby thought that they all probably had that bit of pleading in their eyes. Bobby intended staying right behind Fenton if they had to go since Fenton might be big enough to absorb the flechettes. Siflis, the sneaky, scrawny little shite, would make it if anyone could but he'd already started trembling with nerves. Though if he actually did sneak up on anyone Siflis was a dab hand with that wire.

They'd had a replacement Corp after one was killed, and he liked to prey on the young Timers. Bobby and Bells had thrown the body over the wire fence out of the camp, but without his head. They'd chucked his head in the pit with the other rubbish. Siflis said that it came off easier than a deer's. Bells stared down at his hands and started doing the knuckle cracking thing. He did that before going viral so maybe the eedjit might have a go at Sarge? Bobby kicked Bells's boot and grinned.

"I'm hiding behind Fenton, but I don't reckon you'll get much cover out of Siflis."

"You are a bledrin eejit, Beebi. We'll get killed out there!"

"Yeah, but with a grenade I'm gonna make somebody sit up first. If I get halfway I reckon I can reach the flats and blow the bledrin wall down. I hope the di.. Super has to pay for it himself." Bobby realised he meant it. If Sarge insisted, well the Frogs would bledrin well know they'd been kissed. The dick would have a heart attack at all the damage to corporate property.

"Good thinking, but then the dick'll have you shot." Fenton looked horrified. He must be to have called the Super a dick in front of Sarge, though they all did in private.

"I hope he comes to arrest me because if I'm getting a shotgun I'll save him a barrel." Or the grenade if I've still got it, Bobby thought.

"That's mutiny!" For a moment Bobby thought Fenton might pass out.

Bobby grinned. "Not unless I actually shoot the basted."

"Right, that's enough or I'll have to arrest you all, and shoot you while attempting to escape to keep your mouths shut." Sarge got all the attention. Bobby considered going for his carbin but if he hit metal, Sarge had all those shotguns.

"That's right, Beebi, you'll die if you try." Shite! "Now this is why you'll all live if you're as bledrin sneaky as I reckon, and have just a bit of luck." Sarge picked up a shotgun, broke it and slid two cartridges in. "This is a Frog shotgun. Once it's empty, chuck it away among the bodies. As long as it isn't clutched in your fat fist when that dick arrives, you're clean."

Bobby stared, astounded. Sarge must be bloody, red-eyed, fighting mad! He *always* called the dick by his rank!

"The same with these. You won't know but these are Frog grenades, taken from Frog Supers. First off you're wrong, Beebi, it won't blow the wall down but if you chuck it in through the window it'll frag everyone inside. Duck though because if you're peeking you'll lose your head."

"Peeking? I'll be nowhere near! We can't get up that close Sarge! Not with the bledrin lights!" Siflis started wringing his hands, probably to stop himself from going for Sarge, and Bells had started with the knuckles again.

"Don't get 'em twisted, Siflis. If you use that little wire of yours nobody will see you until you knock knock." Sarge made a knocking motion with the grenade. "That light will go out before you start, because not everyone is such a crap shot as Beebi. Now, for the top prize, what's this?"

"Telescope, a very small fat one?"

"No Fenton, it's a night sight. This is what a Squaddie puts on his rifle before he sticks it out of the window and blows yon sniper's head off. The trouble is there's no Squaddie or rifle to go with it because we can't bring up a Squaddie unless the Frogs use the Legion. In fact, this has to go back home tomorrow so you all forget you ever saw it." Nobody spoke but the question was in four pairs of eyes.

"The reason you saw it is so you believe the next bit. The sight is why I know where their lookouts are, but even better than that I can tell Siflis where the Frog forward post is." Siflis perked up. "Now all of you have a little peek through it, right at that mound there with the weeds and no grass." They all did and the mound jumped out and seemed to smack Bobby in the eye, though that did mean he could see the Frog helmet through the weeds. Sarge took the sight back and put it away.

"Why should we kill him? They'll put out a new spotter."

"To cover an attack, Beebi. You Timers won't realise but the last Super, the bledrin dick, screwed the pooch well and truly. Lining nearly all you Timers up in that open ground for a bledrin parade at nine every morning meant the Frogs knew when to attack and capture yon flats. Now this dick thinks he'll make a name for himself by taking them back." Bobby heard the sheer contempt in Sarge's voice, and remembered wondering how stupid the last Super had to be to blow himself up in the bogs with his own grenade. The grenade bouncing up and down in Sarge's hand gave a big hint.

Bells said what they all thought. "We'll get slaughtered running uphill over the open ground."

"The attack goes in at four, because somebody has been reading books that tell him it's the best time. The trouble is that the Frogs have the same book. Why do you think we stand to at oh three fifty?" Four heads nodded in understanding. "Well so do the Frogs. But because of the attack we'll all be in the trenches by oh three hundred, and the Frogs won't. All clear so far?"

They nodded because it was, but still suicide because of the lamps illuminating all that open ground, one from each front line. "Somebody suggested that if we borrowed a lamp from the refinery, one of the big ones, it would blind the Frogs during the charge. The same person didn't point out that the Frogs would open up on full auto and blow it away, along with whatever eedjit is charging over the open ground."

"Oh shite." Bobby shrugged when Sarge glared, how much worse could it get?

Then Sarge smiled, which might be nastier than his glare. "At oh three oh five some bledrin fool will trip over the switch and turn it on, just after the Frog light is shot out. The Frogs should all be looking this way to see why we shot their light. They'll get an eyeful of very bright lamp before they open up and blow it out. Go on Beebi, because you've got it."

Yes, Bobby could already see what that meant! "If our mob have their heads down they'll be safe, but the Frogs will have spots before the eyes. So if we sneak out there just then, we've got a chance to get to the forward post. Won't they send for different sentries? You know, because they can't see properly?"

"Would you wake up the Supervisor because they'd shot out our light and we'd shot out theirs, especially after the muzzle blasts show absolutely nobody with even their head up on our side? When nobody is even firing back? When you knew there was less than an hour before stand-to when he'd be up anyway?" All four Timers shook their heads, slowly. Not a chance, the basted dick would put you on the Gaza Taxi for a stunt like that. Sarge seemed sure the Frog Supers were the same and Bobby began to think he might live until morning.

But only for a few moments. Sarge started drawing in the dirt on the shed floor. "Look here, this is the block of flats along the hill." He stabbed a finger in two lower windows and two upper. "That's where the sentries are, and the quick response squads will be in there with them. That's so that the sentry can rouse them without us knowing, just the same way we do it." The Timers looked at each other. Four windows and four grenades.

"Why the shotguns Sarge? Why not chuck and run?"

"Good question Siflis, there's hope for you yet. You kill the sentries before tossing the grenades in so no smart basted chucks it back. The shooting will also help with awkward questions about grenades, like how come all the Frogs committed suicide for no reason. If there's shooting then it'll look like a bit of mutiny or panic, or near enough to keep you four safe."

"Safe?"

Sarge ignored Bells. "If there's no glass or the window is open, use flechettes to shoot the guard and save the shotguns for later. If there's glass it'll break close up but deflect the flechettes, so use the shotguns. I'll tell the Super the guards must have had grenades and dropped them when they were killed. He'll be so pleased that his attack worked he's not going to be really thinking anyway but for that to happen we have to take the flats."

"What? Four of us?" Bobby stared, gobsmacked. Up to now there'd been an outside chance of living, but now Sarge wanted four of them to capture a block of bledrin flats?

"No, you sodin Homer. As soon as the grenades go off, even if it's only one, I'm going to shout charge and so will the two Corporals and a few others. Since all the Timers will be wound up and ready, they'll go. They'll be told not to shoot, but that won't stop some of them. Your best chance of surviving is to go through a window, any window, and get to the back of the block."

"What about the rest of the Frogs in there." Bobby grinned. "They'll be upset so we'll need a few more grenades and more shotgun ammo."

"Nice try. There won't be many Frogs since you'll have killed the night guards and emergency squads. If you set up where you can see rest of the Frogs coming across the road from their barracks, you can use the shotguns to break them. They'll be all bunched up, running to reach their positions and coming in fat, stupid and half awake. Chuck the shotguns as soon as they're empty. Then use your flechettes to keep their heads down because our lads will be there as fast as I can chase them."

"So why? If we've got to take the flats anyway why are we risking the sneaking, why the grenades and stuff?"

Bobby looked at Bells in disbelief. "Because the other way at least half the mob will be shot crossing the gap, you eedjit. Sarge doesn't want..." Bobby realised what he'd been going to say, and remembered how many times Sarge said the sooner they were all dead the sooner he'd get back to real work. Then he remembered the Super ordering the parade to run forward into the flats and recapture them even though the Frogs were already inside and shooting, and Sarge ordering everyone to retreat to these houses. The Super had threatened Sarge with a firing squad for that, just before getting careless with a grenade.

"If you repeat that, you won't need a Gaza Taxi to get to hell because where there's four of these, there might be five. If one of you breathes a word about me caring how many Timers get shot, you'd better check real careful before you sit down anywhere." All four looked somewhere else, not at the metal ball bouncing in Sarge's hand. "Now here's your first lesson in how to avoid blowing your bledrin hand and head off."

*   *   *

Bobby looked at the lines of shadow and the hollows and stunted vegetation between him and the carefully hidden forward Frog lookout. He laid in their own forward lookout post, crowded with five in cover meant for one or two. A new lookout position because two sentries had been shot in the previous one by the Frog sniper, so that spot wasn't much of a secret.

The bodies had been a mess, or the heads were. The bullet must be huge but Sarge swore it wasn't from a rifle. A shotgun could shoot a bullet that big but Sarge reckoned nobody could shoot that straight with one. Well at least one Frog could. Bobby hoped the sniper stayed tucked up in his bunk fast asleep right now. He smiled. If not, hopefully the basted spent his nights in one of those four ready squad rooms.

A tap on his ankle told Bobby to put his face down to the ground and shut his eyes. Five minutes to go and time to make sure of his night vision. The dark glasses had helped but now their squad and no doubt a few other Timers needed to get used to real darkness. Bobby tried to count but his mind kept skittering off to the hard lump on his thigh and the wrapped bundle across his back. Even the sentry, especially the sentry, couldn't be allowed to see the shotguns or grenades.

Bobby really hoped none of his group were killed or badly wounded short of the flats, or the Super would know they'd all been carrying Frog gear. When Sarge left them for a while all four had made a promise. If they were hit bad, they'd chuck the shotgun and then the grenade, and hope the bomb went far enough not to kill the thrower. Sarge had been clear about the range of grenades and warned them not to use the bledrin thing in the open. Otherwise it would kill the eedjit who threw it which explained why they were used from trenches and houses.

Even with his eyes shut, Bobby could tell when the Frog light went out. The accountants would be stoked about that because the Frogs would break something in return, and a loss of equipment cost hard creds. Bobby put his eyes into his arm because there would be a brighter light any time now and it worked because he never saw the glow. He heard the storm of carbin fire from the Frogs and someone tapped Bobby's shoulder. Only the sentry, but he jumped a mile and heard a quiet snigger from someone.

As they slipped out of the sentry post Bobby realised how hard this would be if he hadn't sorted his eyes out. The Super had picked a moonless night, or probably Sarge had because the dick couldn't find his own with both hands. Bobby heard Bells curse quietly as a narrow beam of light came from one of the Frog flats and played over the open ground. A rattle of carbin fire came from the UKs lines while the four of them froze and hugged the ground, then the hand torch went out. Sarge had it covered. He'd found someone who could shoot a bit just as promised.

The crawl seemed to take forever but eventually they'd moved level with and then behind the slight hump covered in straggly weeds. The buzzer strapped to Bobby's leg only vibrated twice so in reality they'd only taken ten minutes. Three of them unwrapped their shotguns while Siflis unwound his wire, pulled his bayonet with a blackened blade in case there were two sentries, and slid away towards the Frog outpost. If anyone raised the alarm all of them were going to charge, because going back meant either a sentry or Sarge would shoot them. With a bit of luck, the shotguns would keep Frog heads down and they'd get near enough for the grenades.

Bobby lost him even if he knew where Siflis should be, the little sod had disappeared. Siflis reckoned he could do this because he used to sneak around in the dark with a wire though not after sentries. Siflis ended up in court and 'volunteered' to be here because the park owners weren't happy to find a scrawny Pleb strangling a deer, a deer kept for upper management to shoot when they fancied a break from pooching some Pleb workforce somewhere. Siflis reckoned he'd done it for years before they caught him. His Dad taught him, before Dad's luck ran out. Some Senior Group Manager or Director shot a deer one night and found it didn't have horns and Siflis reckoned the basted probably still had Dad's head mounted on a wall.

Thinking about that kept Bobby from chewing his nails down to his knuckles until the shadows by the Frog sentry post moved. A faint thud followed by what might have been a grunt disturbed the silence and two shadows merged. A faint scratching noise and a gurgling followed, though Bobby barely heard them even though he'd been listening. A light showed, just a glow, and without his night vision Bobby wasn't sure he'd have seen it even though the tiny bulb aimed right at him. This time Bobby saw Siflis coming because the ex-poacher only stayed out of sight of the Frog flats.

The third vibration on Bobby's leg came and went while that happened so there were less than ten minutes left because Sarge would launch the attack at half past anyway. He wanted the mob up and moving before the stand-to Frogs were awake and in position. That felt strange, having the whole attack explained upfront instead of being told to go here, shoot there, charge now, sleep now.

Siflis brought a sentry's helmet and now he put it on. The little sod smiled because they could see his teeth gleam, and he put his mouth to Bobby's ear. "Just in case someone sees us coming because this way I'll be challenged, not shot. Then I'll shoot the Frog and we go for it. It'll sound like he shot at me." His teeth gleamed again because Siflis also had both sentries' carbines and belts full of flechette clips!

It didn't really matter, Bobby realised. They could only be executed once for either the shotgun or the grenade anyway, so another weapon didn't matter but it still gave him a shock. The Frog weapons sounded enough different for even Timers to know, so Siflis made sense. Bobby took a carbin and belt, passed the idea to the others as Siflis headed off, then followed the ex-poacher.

One by one they followed, and now Siflis moved much faster. In the last decent hollow they paused while everyone checked their shotgun and carbin, and the grenade of course. Seven seconds, because the Frogs made their grenades a second less to catch out any Britz who captured one. All four knew which window to take and from here they could tell which had glass. Siflis would go last because his lay straight ahead and across clear, flat concrete, but without glass in the window and the little poacher smiled and patted the Frog carbin. The sneaky sod had been right to snatch the weapons.

Bells had an upstairs window with glass. He had started cracking his bledrin knuckles again. Bobby tapped the Timer's leg and Bells jumped, then settled. Bobby tapped one barrel of the shotgun, holding up one finger until Bells nodded and scowled. In this state Bells might let both go, and they might need the other barrel later. Fenton looked over and smiled, sticking up one finger in confirmation rather than an insult because he had the other upstairs window, and that also had glass.

Sarge had hammered that in; one barrel is enough to kill any one man, and Bobby believed him because he'd seen Sarge use his shotgun on a Frog attack. They all set off and Bobby made it to the wall of the block, then moved up next to his window. There he waited, because they had to all go together. For the fiftieth time he hoped these were the right four windows. Sarge had explained that the sentries stood back so they couldn't be seen, but even so this was a hell of a thing to take on trust. If only three were right, then there'd be eight or nine very alive and annoyed Frogs in the fourth.

The fourth vibrate had been a while back and sure enough the fifth didn't take long coming. Even as he swung round the side of the window frame with the Frog carbin up and snugged into his shoulder, Bobby heard a query in Frog lingo further down the row. Not Bobby's problem, his problem looked straight back into Bobby's eyes. The Frog's eyes widened and he put up a hand to stop the flechettes.

Fat chance, the sentry had moved forward and almost up to the window. Bobby didn't hesitate; he thrust hard instead of shooting. The Frog forward lookout might have blackened the blade to stop any reflections but that didn't affect the edge on the bayonet and the point slid into the sentry's throat. Bobby twisted hard and put out a hand to grab the sentry's shoulder and pull him forward.

The body slumped onto the windowsill with barely a sound except a rattle from the falling carbin. Not that noise mattered now. Some part of Bobby registered the sounds of a Frog carbin and two shotguns, and a query from inside this room. They'd all still be awake after the lights were shot out! That basted Sarge must have known that! Bobby knelt, put down his weapon and pulled out the grenade.

Pull, one, two, three, into the window, move back out of the window line, turn and cover his ears, shut his eyes. Even so the explosion came a shock, the sheer noise rattled Bobby's bones and there were echoes. When he turned and looked down the block, only two other windows were gushing smoke, shite! Then Bobby saw Siflis dropping with his hands on his ears and Bobby turned again and shut his eyes. Not as loud this time, but now four windows billowed clouds of smoke. Bobby leaned in through the window and put a quick burst from the Frog carbin into any movement, shooting one Frog staggering out of the bog with his pants down. Then he scooped up his own carbin and ran like hell towards Siflis.

All four went in the window together chased by a roar from the UKs' lines as the Timers surged up and out of their positions. A few flechettes whined past and smacked the wall. Shite, Sarge had promised no shooting! At least the wild shooting stopped quickly, though Bobby made a personal promise to kick some nuts later. All of them snatched up more Frog carbins and clips and went out of the door at the back of the room. That wasn't hard since the door only hung by one hinge. The Super would be stoked when he saw the redecorating bill in the room, because that would come out of the profit from the attack.

This block had the same layout as most Pleb housing blocks, each floor having a corridor down the middle with a row of flats either side. Bobby shot the Frog Timer at the bottom of the stairs, using the Frog carbin. "Keep using the Frog weapons so they don't know we're inside." The gleam of three sets of teeth smiling in the gloom answered Bobby so he beckoned to Fenton and they charged up the stairs, shotguns raised. Upstairs the Frog running out of the rear flat wearing a set of headphones flew down the corridor shedding blood and bits. Bobby spat in disgust because he'd wasted a shotgun shell. He switched back to carbin, the Frog one, to save the other barrel. Fenton still had one shell in his shotgun as well if a crowd turned up.

Inside the room they found a radio transmitter! That should please the Supervisor since it had to be worth as much as the redecorating so far. The pair looked into the two front flats with badly damaged doors and quickly put bursts into anyone moving. Both of them grabbed another Frog carbin and more clips, before heading towards the door at the end of the passage. That one led into the next block of flats, built at an angle away from the refinery so it didn't have to be captured right now. According to Sarge, the Frogs couldn't hold that one if the UKs forces took this block.

Or maybe they could since the door had a sheet of iron fastened to it. Bobby peeked through the small grill set in the metal. Shite! Frog Timers, still pulling on their belts and boots as they came, were running up the corridor straight at him led by a Supervisor. That basted had to be a Super with all the fancy braid and such and Bobby smiled. "You know how much I like Supers?"

"Ha! Yeah. So?" Fenton looked puzzled as Bobby put the shotgun up to the grill so the loaded barrel aimed through a gap, and let fly. Then he stuck the Frog carbin through the grill and emptied the clip.

"Just got one!" A loud boom from behind wiped the smile from his face and Fenton's, and they both jumped and then crouched. That had sounded like a shotgun, but behind them and upstairs! A few seconds later it boomed again.

Fenton leant over to whisper. "There's a live Frog in one of the flats! A bledrin Super or Sarge at least!" Fenton gripped his shotgun tighter and aimed it back along the corridor. The hidden weapon boomed again.

"Then one of us had better go back and kill him. Can you hold this door?" They both took a quick look through the grill. The glance showed no standing Frogs and the flapping doors said where some had gone. The jumble of bodies on the floor showed where the buckshot and the flechettes had ended up. Bobby quickly put bursts into some that still looked fairly lively, then ducked back as barrels came round several of the doorways.

A light hail of flechettes rattled on the other side of the door and some definitely came through the grill, but the plate held the rest. "So who does what?" Fenton obviously didn't fancy Frog hunting when the other basted had a shotgun.

"Give me the shotgun." Bobby held out his hand.

Fenton moved the weapon away. "Get pooched, you used yours up."

"No you eedjit, not for here. You keep sticking a carbin through the grill and spraying a clip down the corridor. We've got four Frog carbins and six ammo belts if I leave you mine so you'll have plenty. I'll take the shotgun and my own carbin and deal with whoever that is. He's shooting at the attack, so he'll not even hear me 'til it's too late." Bobby laughed quietly. "They'll know we're inside after hearing my carbin but I reckon they've noticed anyway."

"What about the noise out here? He'll know you're coming."

"It's all been Frog carbins and shotguns so far so he'll think those were defenders. Now give!" Fenton thought a moment and handed the shotgun over, then reached up one-handed and stuck a carbin barrel through the grill to let a clip go. Fenton rotated the stock as he did, to spread the happiness. "Smartarse." True, but sleek as well, there weren't three others in the Mob who could do that one-handed.

Fenton smirked. "Skill, now scat." Bobby headed towards the regular booms. The flat wasn't hard to find and Bobby wondered how much shotgun ammo the Frog had in there! More than enough to shoot any eedjit coming through the door. Bobby felt his nuts try and crawl up inside him because if he tried the handle of a locked door...? There had to be another way. The firing resumed after a pause and Bobby tried not to think of his mates coming forward into the buckshot. A burst of fire down below followed by a cheer meant the first of the Mob were in and shooting the dead sentries. Bobby made a decision and acted before he could double guess himself.

The walls in Pleb housing were made of thin plasterboard so Bobby moved away from it a bit and knelt, aiming the shotgun at the noise of shooting inside. As soon as the basted inside fired, so did Bobby, then dropped the shotgun and brought up his carbin to point through the hole. He put the full clip of thirty into the movement inside, though some would have gone wide when Bobby flinched from the boom and the chunk of plaster that blew out and covered him in dust. The flechettes must have done the job because the figure laid still as Bobby rammed in another clip with trembling hands. That came too close.

He tried the door and found it locked, so that had been a good call. With a big smile Bobby kicked it in, causing more damage for the Super to justify. Then he forgot the Super as he saw who he'd shot. This Frog had a different uniform to their Timers! It had patterns all over, and fitted properly where it wasn't tattered and red. A cold chill went up Bobby's back when he saw the flat-topped hat. Legion? There weren't supposed to be any Legion here, that wasn't allowed, not against Timers! Then Bobby really looked at the rifle, or single barrelled shotgun, or small cannon?

Bobby picked up the heavy weapon. It had a barrel a lot longer than a shotgun with a big fat clip underneath, and a box nearby held more clips. More firing echoed from the corridor so he slung his carbin before picking up the heavy box full of big square clips. Bobby hesitated then took the ration packs as well, because real soldiers got better rats according to the rumours. Carbins were hammering away downstairs, then a shotgun, and a grenade boomed as Bobby headed back towards Fenton.

There were eight empty clips on the floor and even as Bobby came up Fenton did his one-handed trick again. There wasn't a lot of reply but most of it came through the grill so the surviving Frogs were aiming now. Fenton turned and did a double-take. "Stone me, what's that?"

"Legion rifle. Look at the size of these." Fenton whistled at the length of the fat shiny rounds. Then he reached out his hand.

"Give me that."

"Why?"

"Because I gave you the shotgun?" Fenton grinned. "More to the point because I can shoot."

"How come you're here then?"

"Because I knock about with you three and according to Sarge that means I'm sneaky. Shite!" He spat. "That's it! I thought I saw Sarge the last time in Rotterdam, when we nipped through the wire for some unofficial R&R. He must have spotted us all." Fenton put his hand out again. "Come on Beebi, I can shoot straight through the walls the Frogs are using for cover with that." Bobby handed the weapon over. Put like that letting Fenton play sounded like a good idea.

Fenton checked the weapon over as if he knew what he was doing, and put it up to his eye twice. Then he took off the telescope thing. "I've not used one of those." He tried again. "Better." Fenton put the stock into his shoulder and the barrel just through one of the grill squares.

Fenton waited as several flechettes came through, harmlessly since the Timer still stood to the side. Then he stepped sideways, swinging the gun round, hesitated, and fired before stepping to the side again. Someone screamed as Fenton worked a lever at the side and a gleaming cylinder jumped out. Bobby realised where he'd seen something like that weapon, in those old war films!

A hail of flechettes hit the door but only some came through the grille so the basteds were rattled again. The two Timers grinned happily at each other. Not for long because the firing downstairs intensified and unless Siflis and Bells had found a bandolier of ammo, Sarge and his shotgun had arrived. What was taking so long because there shouldn't be anyone left down there to resist? Bobby listened and felt sure some of the firing came from outside, out the back. Meanwhile Fenton had repeated his step and boom, before ducking under the grill to the other side. "Got to spread the happiness."

"Yeah, well be careful because there might be another one of those through there. I'm going to see what the noise is at the back."

"Have fun, I will. Do you reckon I could keep this?" Bobby spun round to be met by a big smile. For a moment he'd thought the eedjit meant it. "Gotcha." Bobby snorted, hefted a Frog carbin and went into the first door leading to a back room.

Bobby found another small square room with a bedroom and shower room off to the side, typical of Pleb flats. He carefully peered around the window frame and the noise must have come from a Frog counter-attack. Bobby raised his carbin and then thought a moment, because from here he could see the whole lot. The attack had been beaten back looking at all the Frog bodies, but the Frogs were creeping forward again, massing for another assault. There were several Frogs further back, in a row of houses, shooting to keep heads down. Bobby could see them clearly, and there were more Supervisors. Three of the basteds! Though the Supers were too far for Bobby to hit even if the carbin would cause any damage through a Super's jacket. Bobby carefully moved back to the door and called through.

"Oy, Fenton, how good are you with that thing?"

"I can shoot the nuts off a bat with a carbin, so I can probably shoot the head off a Frog with this. Why?"

"How about blow the brains out of a Supervisor or two? Frog ones unfortunately, but you take what you can get." Dead silence followed for a few moments, then another boom.

"Are you serious, or is it payback? For the gotcha."

Bobby grinned. "Dead serious. There's three Supers and a dozen Frogs who think they can shoot, and I could probably hit some of them. I can certainly shoot the shite out of the Timers creeping up for the counterattack."

"What about this door?"

"We can leave it a couple of minutes and then I can do it, though I'll need two hands to do the twirly thing. Wait a minute and I'll get more clips for the Frog carbins." Bobby sniggered. "I bet the Frog Supers are really pissed off. We're using their ammo so not only are we killing Frogs, we're costing them to do it!" Laughter followed him up the corridor. A head showed at the top of the stairs and then ducked back.

"It's me!"

"No, I'm me. Come on up Bells. Are you done down there?"

"Not likely. Too many Frogs and the Super's had to send for more clips. I've come to see if you've got enough." Bells looked a bit wide-eyed but undamaged except for a bandaged hand.

"Plenty, we haven't been using ours." Bobby waved the Frog carbin.

"Shite, well start using them! The Super's already been asking how come the Frogs all shot themselves and Sarge is trying to cover! At least the Frogs are keeping the dick occupied." Bells looked down the corridor. "What the hell is Fenton using?"

"A Legion cannon. Tell Sarge we had a Legionnaire up here using that damn great thing. Now since the other half of the Frog army is through that door I'm going to get more Frog clips." He paused. "Tell Sarge about the Legion, and that a shitload of Frogs are massing to attack. We're going to interfere."

"Didn't you listen?"

"Just send Sarge up." Bobby ran off to get the clips. The big gun boomed another four times while he did, and Fenton had a line of red across one cheek when he got back.

"Nearly, they're getting smarter." Though Fenton still wore a happy grin as he said it.

"Not to worry since I'm not sticking my head up at all. Now come on, let's see just how good you are with that bledrin thing." Fenton smirked and picked up the ammo box. "How come you're slower than the Frog with it?"

"That'll get better in a minute, or until they start shooting back." Fenton followed Bobby into the room, peeked and whistled. "One of those might be a bit more than a Super going by the braid."

"So shoot him first, before they notice you. Then I'll empty both these carbins into the Timers and you shoot the other Supers." Bobby sighed. "You get all the luck." Fenton didn't answer, just sniggered and knelt by the window, and moments later the Legion weapon bellowed. Bobby stepped to the window, emptying both carbins as fast as possible into the Timers massing for the attack. Accuracy didn't matter aiming at a crowd like that. Then he ran back into the corridor and scooped up another Frog carbin from the floor. Bobby sent a clip through the grille, humming a tune softly to himself and grinning as he heard screams. Some Frog thought they'd got Fenton and started sneaking up. The big booms started up and Fenton definitely fired faster now, though not as fast as the Legionnaire had been shooting which seemed reasonable.

Bobby wondered how many years the Legion man had trained and had a little wobble as he realised. The Frogs used Timers, so they probably had the same training system. Up to ten years as a Timer, then up to ten years as a Trooper before becoming Legion, then however many years the Frog had survived after that. All those years and a lucky shite had stuffed the Frog full of flechettes as sure as if he'd been a Timer. Bobby had just repeated the twirling process with the carbin when a familiar voice came from behind. "What did I tell you bledrin idjeets about Frog weapons?"

Bobby turned and put on his innocent smile, the one that fooled nobody. "You said to chuck the grenades and empty shotguns so we did."

"Cheeky shite. What's this about Legion?"

"Hang on, there's half the Frog army behind here." Bobby put the carbin to the grill again and sent a clip to follow the rest. Sarge eyed the litter of empty clips.

"Having fun? Just how many is half an army?" Sarge moved up along the side of the corridor and took a quick peek through the grill. "That's not right. There's too many, and too many out the back. We're running out of flechettes."

"If you've got a couple more grenades we could clear that corridor. There's plenty of clips laid about out there." Bobby shrugged. "Frog clips but they seem to do the job."

Sarge laughed. "You'll die young, but it'll be memorable. Don't worry, there are plenty of clips on the way but we shouldn't have needed them. Now what's this about the Legion and what's that noise?"

"The noise is Fenton and he's pushing up the Supervisor score. All Frog ones, honest."

Sarge stared. "All? How many so far?"

"One through that door at least, and Fenton might get three if he's as good as he says. So four?"

"Five, you killed the radio Super. It's always a Super on the transmitter and that's wrong as well, that kit shouldn't be right on the front. You'll either get metal or an unmarked grave." Sarge laughed at Bobby's expression. "If you've killed enough Frog Timers as well it'll be the metal, but the brass don't like Timers who kill Supers instead of just Frogs. Now where's this Legionnaire Bells reckons you topped."

"I think he's Legion. He's got a flat hat." The scathing look he received for that shut Bobby up.

The low whistle when Sarge looked at the body made Bobby feel better. "D'you know what that is, Beebi?"

49

"Legion?" Though Bobby wasn't as certain now.

"That, Beebi, is a breach of contract. Flagrant. The Frogs have been caught with their panties round their ankles and it's poochy time. Not that you or me will be concerned because this'll be up to Director level so fast your head'll spin." Sarge looked around the room as he spoke, and peered at the hole Bobby had blown in the wall. "I knew you were the sneaky type, Beebi, and out-sneaking a Legionnaire proves it. Mind you, deliberate destruction of real estate?" Sarge laughed, "I reckon the Super will pay it out of his own salary if need be, considering the prize." Sarge bent nearer the corpse. "OK, hand them over."

"What?"

"The rats, eedjit. Word is that the Squaddies get better rats than the Supers, so the dick will want the Legion grub." Bobby sighed and handed the rations over, he should have eaten one straight away. "Nip into the radio room. The Frog Super's rats will still be there and our Super won't care." Bobby stared, Sarge had just told him to loot a Super's kit? He went off quickly, and came back with the rats tucked away out of sight but carrying a bandolier of shotgun shells.

"Since there's more shotguns about than Supers, shouldn't we sort of hide a few? Just in case there's trouble?" Bobby meant just in case the dick really did count them and wanted to cause trouble. He also fancied hanging onto a shotgun.

"You looking for promotion, Beebi? Of course we can't do that so you just throw the spares into that box there, along with the bandolier, before everyone starts adding up." Bobby stared at the metal box wondering what difference that would make? Sarge waved a padlock with a key in it. "Nobody will want to break property, because that's criminal." He put the padlock through the hasp and left it hanging open, then stuck the key in his pocket. Sarge flipped up the top of another metal box and handed Bobby a dozen more Frog flechette clips before tossing a few in with the shotgun ammo. "Just in case. Clip the padlock shut when everything adds up. Now let's go and check that door, then look at whatever Fenton's playing with."

All the way back down the corridor Bobby kept trying to remember, and yes, the rats by the Legionnaire were two short so Sarge had nicked them! Cheeky shite, but there again he'd let Bobby have the Super's and there were six of those. Did everyone loot? There'd been so many lectures and threats Bobby had thought nobody dared. Maybe it depended who did it or when? On top of that, what did Sarge mean about promotion? Timers like Bobby didn't have ranks so they didn't get promotions, or metal. The booming had died down to the occasional shot and the patter of flechettes on the wall inside the room explained why. Somebody had started shooting back. Sarge picked up a Frog carbine, stuck it through the grill and did the whirly thing as he let the clip go. One handed, the sleek basted.

Fenton looked round as Bobby came in. "Got all three, some Timers trying to shoot me and a couple of possibles who looked out of windows! Oh!" Sarge had followed Bobby in.

"Don't put it that way when anyone asks you. Beebi will explain." Sarge nodded towards Bobby and peeked out of the window. He took the Legion weapon and hefted it, then looked at the ammo. "Was there a sight with it, like I showed you?" Fenton fished it out of a pocket and handed it over wordlessly and Sarge went back to looking at the weapon and especially the ammo. Bobby quickly filled in Fenton about the rats and how many Supers they'd killed and why it might be a problem.

The boom of the weapon brought their attention back to Sarge. Sarge had refitted the sights, and apparently tried them out. "You seem to have nobbled our sniper." Sarge held up a round. "This end bit, the lead slug, is the same as a shotgun solid round. It drove me crackers trying to work out how the basted could be so good with a shotgun." He handed the long weapon back to Fenton. "Try it with the sight on. If the picture is blurry, rotate that, then put the crosshairs on the Frog's nose, eye, whatever. Splat." Fenton knelt at the side of the window and started playing with the sight. A few minutes later, while Bobby repeated the twirly thing through the grill in the corridor, the big rifle boomed again.

Harsh tones sounded right behind him. "Timer, that is an enemy weapon! Why are you touching enemy weapons?" The bledrin Super! "I should have known. Bobby B. Well I've got you this time."

Bobby braced, carefully well to one side of the grill, and dropped the offending weapon. "Short of ammunition sir." That wasn't going to work. The Super looked even sterner as his eyes swept over the scatter of empty

Frog clips on the floor then looked very pointedly at the pouches on Bobby's belt, nearly all still full of unused clips. "Er." The big gun boomed which saved Bobby for now, but then he realised that the bledrin rifle was a Frog weapon as well! Too late as the Super pushed the door open.

Bobby followed to find the Super with his shotgun pointed at Fenton, still knelt by the window. "Put down the weapon, Timer. Slowly."

"Sir?" Sarge tried to get attention while standing at attention, but it didn't work.

The Super looked at the empty brass scattered on the floor. "You and this other maniac are candidates for a Gaza Taxi, if I'm feeling generous. Just which part of don't touch enemy weapons didn't you understand? Shut up!" Fenton had opened his mouth to answer.

"Sir?" Sarge made a small gesture.

"And why didn't you arrest them both? You could be driving the Taxi if this was your idea. Well?" Bobby didn't think he would have spoken to Sarge like that even if he had been a Supervisor, not when Sarge had that look in his eye.

"Sir? Something more important. Something you must see before anyone else." Sarge had fixed his eyes on the wall over the Super's shoulder, and Bobby half expected it to start smoking. The last Super had been careless with a grenade but there were all these Frog carbins, and this had been a battle, so maybe this Super would get careless with flechettes?

Not yet, because the Super had finally listened. "You two, hold that door in the corridor and use your own bledrin weapons! Now this had better be important Sergeant, or stripes and metal won't mean a thing!" The Super glared at the Timers again before following Sarge out of the door. Bobby heaved a sigh of relief and so did Fenton.

Bobby glanced quickly out of the window and laughed. "Well you've got a nickname now." He eyed the big weapon on the floor. "Davy Crockett or Wild Bill Hickok?" A thick scatter of bodies showed where the Timers downstairs had beaten back the last attack. There were also an impressive number of people who had obviously been in cover, and each had a big red pool around their heads. "Come on, we'd better not let the Frogs through the door now." Fenton stayed silent as they went back and Bobby put a clip of officially sanctioned flechettes down the corridor.

"How deep is it, Beebi?"

Bobby shrugged. "Don't know but Sarge is on it so don't drop 'em and bend over yet."

"There's a lot of Frog flechettes still coming through here. They could hit anyone?" Fenton had been a bit slow, but he'd got there.

"I reckon Sarge will sort that out if necessary. Probably a messy toilet accident." Fenton's eyes widened. "Yeah, I saw his eyes when the Super started ranting. If Sarge looks at me like that I'm volunteering for a Taxi." Fenton looked relieved, even when a Corp with a dozen men came up and took over at the door. Bobby and Fenton headed for the radio room as instructed by the Corp and as they arrived Siflis and Bells came to the top of the stairs, heading the same way. There were voices inside the room.

"… was why the last Frog attack broke up, and there's been no more. We need to go higher with this sir. This will go right up to boardroom and it's your command so you get the credit." Sarge kept his voice steady and gentle, speaking quietly and persuasively, a bit like he did when one of the Timers started ranting about topping himself.

The dick didn't sound persuaded. "They've been using Frog weapons. Carbins, that big cannon, probably shotguns and grenades! That's dangerous!"

"What did you actually see sir? A burst from a carbin when they're outnumbered, and sniping to break up an attack. Against that they killed a real Legionnaire! On the front line shooting at Timers! A stone cold contract breach a mile wide. That sniper rifle has to be another contract breach since it's meant to look as if the shooter is using a shotgun. The radio is still working, with the codes, which is worth a serious bonus." They heard a rattle. "Look, the Super's grenade and shotgun are still here and the Legionnaire's got his grenade. If they were plotting trouble they'd have nicked a grenade at least."

The voices went down to a muttering, while Bobby cursed quietly. If he'd known about the grenade he would have cracked the door open and chucked it down that corridor. That would have screwed up the decorations and maybe cost the basted Super his basted bonus. The flechettes had messed up the paintwork but Bobby now wondered just what that cannon had done, and it had left a lot of evidence at the very least. Bobby had killed that bledrin radio Super with a shotgun! Shite! The four of them stood there at attention until the door finally opened.

All four had a strip ripped off them but quietly so the Super didn't want it advertised, or not yet at least. Then he put them on guard outside the Legionnaire's room and the radio room. The big rifle and ammo box along with the empty brass shells went back in with the Legionnaire and the dick left instructions that the four were to keep everyone out and answer no questions at all. As he followed the Super down the corridor Sarge dropped an eyelid and they all heaved a sigh of relief. Bobby threw two shotguns in the box and found that Sarge must have already done the same. There were four grenades in there as well which tempted Bobby briefly, but Sarge might not be amused if he came up one short. Where had they come from? The Legionnaire?

Bobby put four Frog carbins in the box as well, then he went and collected nearly all the remaining full clips from the nearby ready squad rooms. "What the bledrin hell are you doing? We're supposed to be guarding!" Siflis hissed it quietly but the poacher sounded close to panic.

"You're guarding. I'm getting rid of some inconvenient bits of evidence. Anyway, you never know when a Frog weapon might be handy to arrange an accident. Some careless dick gets into a fatal accident, a Frog flechette or shotgun type accident?" He looked longingly at the handgun in a holster on the Legionnaire's belt, but someone would definitely notice if that went missing. Bobby shut the lid and clicked the padlock. "Now forget you saw that." Bobby noticed that the Legionnaire's remaining rats were gone, so much for bledrin regulations.

"It's a wonder there's any clips left." Siflis grinned. "Frog ones, that is. We used a good few downstairs, but had to stop when our mob arrived." He looked down the corridor at the metal plated door. "The door downstairs isn't armoured and the Frog flechettes chopped it into flinders." He smirked. "We used a shotgun on the first bunch to come charging through. Sarge got it right. Fat, stupid and half awake and some weren't even dressed properly. We emptied a couple of carbins into them as they ran."

"Did you get the Super?"

"No Super in that lot. Did you get one?"

"Two, and Fenton got at least three, and it's a problem. Or maybe, though we killed a shitload of Timers so it might be all right." Bobby explained.

"We killed a shitload of Timers as well. I stuck my little mirror on a stick round the flat doorway to watch the corridor, then every time the basteds came past the corridor door one of us stuck a carbin round the corner and emptied it. They tried a big charge and that took my other shotgun barrel to stop, as well as a hell of a lot of bledrin flechettes." Siflis grinned. "Frog flechettes." His face sobered again. "Bledrin hell, Beebi, those shotguns are messy on a group!" Siflis sighed. "Bells had to nip back across to the entry room for more clips while they were running away after that."

"We did that as well, went to get more."

Siflis laughed. "I can see that from the heap of empty Frog clips. We probably used as many but we used ours bloody fast and they're scattered around a bit more." Siflis looked at the heap of clips and thought a bit. "Maybe we used more. When Bells came back over he looked out of the back window and saw the basteds crossing the street. He used the last shotgun barrel and emptied four Frog carbins one after the other, and the Frogs scattered." Siflis snorted. "We used up the Frog clips and were halfway through our own when Sarge came across the corridor. His shotgun kept them all a bit quieter while the rest of the Mob arrived."

"I heard a grenade as well."

"That was Sarge. The Super wouldn't use his and gave it to Sarge to throw. He's a sleek basted is Sarge, he rolled the thing down the corridor and got it dead right. It went off opposite the first pair of doors and the Frogs stopped shooting from there." Siflis spat. "The dick stayed across in the first room, the ready room we came through. He crawled over after Sarge got the Timers to build a wall across the corridor using the Frog bodies. The Frogs stopped trying to come down the corridor after that."

"Not across the street though."

"No, they tried again, with covering fire, and some got through the windows. That's where Bells bust his finger." Siflis laughed. "One thing, don't ever think Sarge is out of ammo. He must have shotgun shells stuck in every crevice and I'm not sure he used them all. Sleek basted probably kept a few back when he persuaded the dick to give up his own. The dick couldn't use them because he was over the corridor, securing the supply route for flechettes." They both curled their lips at that.

Siflis glanced down the corridor to where Fenton and Bells were talking. "The third attack might have done it because we were all getting short of flechettes. Then a bunch of the Frog Timers dropped, their covering fire stopped and someone started yelling from behind them. The rest broke and ran. By the time the basteds got organised again more clips had arrived so we stopped them easy, and after that we settled down to taking a shot now and then."

"I emptied two clips into them and Fenton shot the Frogs giving the covering fire. So what started the dick off? Sarge wasn't worried about us using Frog weapons."

"Yeah, well the dick spent most of the time in the entry room, the one we came in through. He started complaining about Frog weapons being removed, ammo missing, and Frogs killed by Frog weapons. Then he got onto the Frogs all committing suicide by grenade at the same time. I'm telling you Beebi, that worries me because Sarge thought he wouldn't care."

"We might still be all right." Bobby confirmed that the Legionnaire had been the sniper, and Siflis nipped inside to have a look at the rifle. They were both impressed with how bledrin well Fenton could shoot that rifle. Neither of them could understand about the breach of contract but Sarge had seemed pleased and it diverted the Super. They both hoped it made him happy enough to forget about Taxis. Siflis seemed happier when Bobby told him about the look in Sarge's eyes.

*   *   *

The four of them stood their guard duties and refused to answer a single question from anyone. Bobby did the same as the others probably did, he went over it time and again in his head. All four had been so unbelievably lucky. Siflis had a wrenched elbow, Bobby had a flechette gouge across the top of his shoulder, Fenton had the red line across his face and Bells had a broken finger, and the other fingers on that hand were swollen. Apart from bruises and scratches, that was it!

The basted Super left them on guard forever. Eventually a couple of

Timers turned up with water and hot soup with a Frog loaf. They waited while the four of them ate and tried to get answers or look in the rooms. The Timers were sent up by Sarge so he was still looking out for them. The four of them couldn't answer questions but nobody said they couldn't ask and here were four convenient targets.

A ceasefire had been declared, but since none of the squad was a bledrin Homer Simpson they'd worked that out themselves. After all the firing outside had stopped and the Timers up by the door weren't squirting clips through there. The Timers had even slung their carbins over their shoulders, which seemed a bit too casual for Bobby but the Corp seemed happy with it. Downstairs the Frogs had collected their dead but had to leave the weapons, which was normal. The corridor downstairs looked like a slaughterhouse and stank like one according to Siflis. Sarge had set seven Timers to cleaning up as penance, since they'd fired without orders at the start of the attack. There were lots of rumours about that no-fire order, including that the Squaddies had come in and cleared the way here, or that the Super had brought in a sniper to top all the Frog Supers.

Shouting started through the metal door and Corp answered, then opened it and went through! When he came back the Corporal had the Frog Super's shotgun and grenade. He put the grenade in a pocket and pointed the shotgun through the grille, and more voices sounded out there but no shooting. Bobby knew a Corp shouldn't have a shotgun and grenade, but he'd given up on what was allowed when the Super nicked the Legionnaire's rations.

Ten minutes later the Corp opened the door, and there were no Frog bodies. He kept the shotgun pointed down the corridor while the Timers went through and came back loaded with Frog carbins and clips. Losing that lot and the Super's grenade and shotgun must have burned the Frog Managers, let alone the Supervisors. Within minutes, unarmed Frog Timers came through the metal door in groups of four, bringing stretchers to take all the bodies except for the Legionnaire. Bobby remembered what Siflis said about his Dad and wondered if the Super wanted a Legion head for his wall?

By mid-afternoon two Supers with pressed uniforms and shiny brass arrived along with genuine, hard-faced Squaddies. The Squaddies carried real rifles with lead bullets, nasty looking weapons but still nothing like the size of that Legion cannon. They also carried half a dozen grenades each on their belts. Presumably so did Legionnaires, which explained the ones Sarge put in the metal box. The Squaddies left a pair of guards inside each of the two rooms but insisted that Bobby and the other three stayed on guard outside. The Squaddies seemed to be amused when their Supers weren't actually looking.

Then came a group with a lot more braid and shiny stuff or posh suits, and they went into both rooms as well. They were all smiling when the group came out, and the one in a suit nodded at Bobby when a Squaddie pointed. That worried him, but the Manager or whatever seemed happy enough. Another four Squaddies came up and stood at attention along the corridor so all four Timers smartened up sharpish.

Three Frogs came up the stairs and went in to see the Legionnaire. The first thing Bobby noticed was that they really did stink of garlic. Then Bobby realised one wore the same uniform he'd shot through the grill and must be a Frog Super. The other two had more braid and shiny shite, and from the way they avoided the blood on the floor they weren't used to being at the sharp end. All three looked very unhappy when they came back out of the Legionnaire's room and went downstairs, followed by the four Squaddies. Those were the first living Frogs Bobby had seen without shooting. The way the Frogs glared at Bobby and the rest, he hoped the next time their faces showed up was in Fenton's sights.

Then he had no time to think because the next Squaddie came to ask deadly serious questions and he wanted answers in a hurry. Bobby explained about the Legionnaire and the rifle, and confessed they'd used captured weapons. He had to, there was no other way of doing what they'd managed. He did skip the first entry and that the weapons weren't all captured right here. The other three all had a Squaddie interrogating them, and were relieved when nobody ended up arrested. The four Squaddies put their heads together, then the nearest nodded to Bobby. He said "You'll do," in a downright friendly way and then they marched off, stone-faced again.

A few minutes later more Squaddies arrived and took over guarding the outside of the two rooms. How many bledrin Squaddies were here? Bobby had never seen more than four at one time before. Being allowed to relax at last was welcome, but Sarge came with them and didn't look happy. He gestured, and the four of them followed him down and out through a front window back to the barracks without a word.

* * *

"In here and grab a brew. Nobody will be coming back for a while and when they do, you'll be gone." Sarge waved a hand towards the canteen counter.

All of them took full advantage and put extra sugar in the tea, as well as taking an extra doughnut apiece. They fixed Sarge a brew and two doughnuts as well. "I should have expected that." Sarge took a swig of tea. "Though an extra doughnut really won't matter now. The good news from your point of view is that the Super is squared away. The dick will get his promotion to Line Manager and that's good news for this Mob, and bad for where he's going."

"I thought he was going to push it? You know, about the Frog weapons and such." Bobby remembered the glare from the Super as they left. "Are you sure he's squared?"

"It's not down to him now because everything has gone to boardroom level. The Frogs are well and truly pooched and it will harm our lot's case if they put any blame on you four. There's rules as you know, contracts so the corporations don't lose too many assets while we're getting killed. One of them is about who fights who and putting the Legion in against Timers is a really big breach of contract. There'll be a high level board meeting, lots of lawyers, and assets or more probably the border will be adjusted. That part is above my pay grade." Sarge sighed. "It might not work out too well for you four, long term."

"Why not?" Bobby frowned. "Hang on, you said we won't be here when the Mob come back."

"Nothing wrong with your ears now, Beebi, though you forgot some of your bledrin instructions, didn't you?" Sarge raised a hand. "I know, it all went viral and you did what you had to, which turned out lucky because the Frogs were building up their numbers to launch an attack as well. They wanted to take these houses because from here they'd shut down the refinery. Buying them out would have cost Anglo-Dutch serious creds and assets." Sarge sighed again. "This is a very important sector, the nearest the Frogs have ever got to the refineries, and what you did means they've got to pull back. Well back, to pay for the contract breach. The trouble with that is what you did is above your pay grade. Timers don't pull that sort of stunt, so you can't be Timers any more."

Bobby stared. "What? But I've got another nine years to do. I'm not going down that bledrin mine!"

"The Chemworks will kill me! No way!" Siflis came to his feet, while behind him Bells started cracking his knuckles. Bobby frantically tried to find a way out because he meant it, he really wasn't going down that mine. Sodit, the judge gave him a choice!

"Calm down you silly shites. You stay in uniform, but it'll be a Trooper uniform." Sarge laughed, a bitter laugh, then sipped his tea while they all stopped panicking and stared instead. "You're supposed to stay as Timers until you learn how to stay alive or you die. During that time, you'd learn that the rules can be broken, providing it's deniable and you win." Sarge snorted. "You lot aren't too good with the deniable part, but you've got the rule breaking nearly perfect. Luckily you got the winning bit right as well."

All four looked at each other, baffled. Surely training for Trooper meant learning to fight? "But we aren't trained to be Troopers."

"No Beebi and that's why this might be bad for all of you, though the Directors don't really care about that. Because you are brave warriors who managed to survive the nasty cheating Frogs, you'll get metal and promotion. Timers can't be promoted, so you get to be Troopers even if you aren't ready." Sarge didn't seem real happy about that.

"Metal? How can we get metal? We didn't get hurt, not badly." Bells looked at his splinted finger. "Unless I get a metal finger?" He grinned. "I'd have a hell of a punch after that."

Sarge opened his uniform jacket and showed a patch of small metal squares fastened to the lining. They looked like steel and copper, maybe brass, and had writing stamped on them. Sarge closed his jacket and smoothed the Velcro. "That's metal." He rapped his kneecap. "It often costs this sort, but not always. You'll get one of those squares, and a few extra creds every month."

"That's it? That's metal? After all the bulsh about all the metal the real fighters have?" Fenton only said what they all felt because the Timers had heard about metal from day one. Metal arms, metal plates in skulls, metal legs, shite, they'd seen Sarge's metal knees.

"Well it's not much by itself, but there's extras and not just the creds. Why do the medics open everyone's jacket first, when they pick up the wounded?" Sarge wore a little smile and Bobby just knew he'd be wrong, but the official answer was...

"To check the heartbeat."

"To check for metal. Just one of these little squares mean you get the first treatment, and the best, and that's one reason they're sewn in that position. The other reason is that if a flechette is headed for your heart, if you're really lucky that bit of metal will stop it."

"So if I've got a lot, like you?"

"Yes, a heart shot probably won't work on me." Sarge looked at Bobby. "If Beebi had been accurate that the Legionnaire would have laughed and shot him while the flechettes were bouncing. Because Beebi is shite with a carbin, he put flechettes in the Frog's throat, an eye, his arm, other lung and even a couple in the gut, from under three metres away." Sarge shook his head. "That was on top of some buckshot in his back. I've never seen worse shooting or such a thorough job."

"He was pointing that bledrin cannon at me and I thought it would be loaded with buckshot!"

"Fair comment." Sarge grinned. "There's another benefit to having metal. When you four allegedly weren't in Rotterdam, you were turned away from some bars even though you were somehow dressed as Troopers. Turned away for no apparent reason?"

"Yeah. We were scanned and then refused but didn't get a reason. There were some truly sleek Divas in there as well." Bells sighed because he really fancied the Divas, the sleek types. Bells always complained that the Divas in the Timer bars were all spam, and were usually drunk, stoned, or bledrin ugly. In truth, on a bad day they'd be all three, fat and unwashed as well.

"Those bars have decent beer, no crowding, and enough of those Divas to go round. No spam allowed, only the sleekest, hot to trot and stone cold sober as you'll find out next time." Sarge grinned at Bells, and tapped his chest. "The scan only checked here, and if it shows metal you get in. Rest up first because those Divas love to pooch the metal, and you'll all be fresh meat." He'd started laughing now, and so did the rest at the look on Bells's face.

Bobby wanted to know more about the metal, not the bonus. "What are all the colours then, and why are they on the inside?"

"Well if they were outside they'd make a good aiming point for someone like Fenton, and on top of that the management don't want a lot of innocents reading that writing. After all, metal usually means someone broke a rule or two. It goes outside for official parades but they won't happen often. Otherwise you don't tell anyone you've got it and if they find out you never say why or where." Sarge looked at Bells. "Make up some heroic bulsh for the Divas. They know it's bulsh, but love it anyway. You already know why it's a good idea to wear it in a ruck."

"So what about the colours?"

"Gold, Silver and Bronze. No, not really you prats or your own mates would cut your throat in the night. It's what they're called and might even have been real back in the day." Sarge straightened. "Enough about the pretties. If you've finished scarfing all the doughnuts, I'll take you to your temporary home. Bring everything since none of you are coming back."

The four of them collected their kit and followed Sarge to an empty room in a small barracks for visiting Squaddies, further behind the lines. A room Sarge explained would be their new home until upper management sorted everything out and awarded the metal. Their Trooper kit would arrive before then. Then Sarge started explaining about the differences between Timer and Trooper and why he wanted to be a bledrin Trooper again instead of stuck with the Timer rules. Once he'd left they chewed it all to death before getting their heads down.

*   *   *

The Squaddies made it clear that Troopers were still well down the shite heap from real Squaddies, not as far as Timers but still a long way down. Over the next five weeks, the four of them ate regular, slept regular, and as advised by Sarge they all toughened up. All four used the gym as often as they could stand it and also ran with the Squaddies as instructed, which amused the Squaddies and nearly killed the four of them. Still, those were the orders, and by the end of the five weeks they were only knackered instead of dead on their feet at the end of a run.

The four of them were given time on the range. The Squaddies had more laughs at their shooting, though they reckoned Fenton had promise. Then the Squaddies offered to spar a bit. That nearly killed the four of them again but they all learned some really nasty shite. This time their trainers reckoned that Bells had promise. The Squaddies said it was a favour, a thank you, because if the Frogs had succeeded. The Squaddies would have had to retake those houses and then the flats. That would have got bloody because the Frogs would have put Legion in to hold the gains. Though they also reckoned part of it was they felt sorry for the four of them, that sending children to be Troopers without some training would be like drowning kittens. Worryingly, the Squaddies sounded serious about that.

The Squaddies were nearly friendly sometimes, and let slip bits like that. Timer Supers were jumped up little shites, apparently, and the Squaddies thought it bloody hilarious that the four of them killed so many Frog Supers yet missed their own. Every one of the Squaddies had started as Timers and then showed promise as a Trooper. When their ten years as a Trooper were up, or in two cases before, they got the offer. A couple eventually showed their metal, briefly, and nobody would get a flechette near their hearts or probably lung.

They asked Bobby about the B, everyone did, but Bobby didn't explain the B to anyone. He'd got in fights all his life over the B in Bobby B. His Mam told everyone the B meant he ran about like a busy Bee. A lot of kids at school said it meant basted, or bandit, and the last one meant a fight. He liked women, not boys. Basted didn't matter much because at least one in three didn't know their Da, and plenty of others knew their Da wasn't coming back. Bobby's Da stayed down the mine with about thirty of his mates, and his bones would stop there unless Britmine re-opened the collapsed shaft. The Squaddies asked why Bobby didn't drop it, and decided he kept the B because he was B-bloody-minded.

Fenton had a nickname now, Hood. Not for Robin Hood though that worked in a way. One of the Squaddies said they should all read the books about the Malazan Empire. Blacklisted books, but as Troopers they should get access if only when raiding Pleb black markets. In those, Hood was the God of Death. Fenton liked that and adopted Hood straight away, then the basted wouldn't answer to Fenton any more so it stuck. Everyone called Bobby B Beebi but he hung on to his real name as much as possible. Bloody-minded, though that wasn't the real reason for the B.

By the end of five weeks the Squaddies seemed to have sort of adopted the four of them, and before the ceremony had a chat. One of them, Ham, finally explained his comments about the four of them being a squad. "You four are a natural scouting and sniper squad. Siflis is a scout and he'll get you in, and out. Hood is your shooter, and Bells is close guard if it goes viral. Beebi, you keep your head and break rules, so you'll be squad leader." Ham grinned as he told them, probably knowing what they'd say.

"But will the Troopers care? We'll be new meat to them, and not even properly trained?" Bobby worried about them being broken up, since he could rely on the other three.

"The real record of this bledrin shambles will go with you. If your next Super has two brain cells he'll keep you together because you worked well as a squad. Not only that but he won't want a greenie getting any of his experienced Troopers shot while doing something stupid. You four are too young to be Troopers, nine years too young and he'll expect you to die young. If you all live long enough the squad will become settled and Supers are lazy." Ham shrugged. "They won't split up what works."

Ham stopped smiling and leant closer, dropping his voice. "Troopers are for security work. You'll be shooting Plebs, people just like you, in the company housing complexes. It's a shite job and it's at least partly meant to make sure you, and us Squaddies, are hated by the Plebs. That way we'll never retire and go back into the complexes where we might become a problem." The Squaddie frowned, and a trace of bitterness entered his voice. "Do not hesitate even if it's a woman because the Plebs will be shooting right back, and probably first. Or worse, the bitch with a pram will be pushing a bomb. You should have had years as a Timer to toughen you, break any ties to the Plebs, so it'll come hard at first." All four of them had a very sombre evening after that, but the next day they were on the move so didn't have time to brood.

The presentation of the metal turned out to be a long afternoon of bulsh. Very public, shiny bulsh and the speeches didn't really get specific about what they'd done. Though Bobby noticed that Sarge got it right, a couple of the brass were crowing about the border being pushed back two miles. Public meant people who were management or already had metal according to the shiny patches on the Troopers and Squaddies. No Timers. Bells nearly had a seizure when he saw the truly sleek Divas with some of the management. Fenton and Bobby B got a gold, Siflis got silver and Bells a bronze. They saw Sarge there, but Bobby, Siflis, Hood and Bells were driven there and back in an armoured truck and never managed to talk to anyone.

The leave afterwards came as a revelation and Bobby learned a lot more about what went on under a real Diva's clothes. They actually took them off instead of hoiking their skirts up! Some bledrin mind-blowing things followed and showed what an enthusiastic Diva could manage if she stayed sober. The other three reported similar experiences. It wasn't anything Bobby intended putting in his monthly letter to Ma, though he could mention he'd got metal against the Frogs without the censor giving him shite. Ma had been told officially and management sent a picture of the ceremony though she'd never get any details.

When their leave finished a truck picked them up and the four of them went home, or back to the UKs at least.

Trooper

Their first posting as Troopers came as another revelation, just as exciting but nothing like as pleasant as their first real Divas. The Super sneered as they came through the door, and waved a hand at four thin files. "I didn't believe this shite. Four children! I ask for reinforcements and I'm sent babies with the fuzz still on their chins." He sighed dramatically. "Well hard luck because I'm not putting an experienced Trooper with you, or you'll get him killed as well. You'll be dead in a week because these files say you barely know which end the bullet comes out of. Scout and sniper squad. Now piss off and try to die where we can get the weapons back." He waved an arm and a Corporal showed them out.

The same man showed them into an eight-man squad room in the barracks. "You live here. There'll be inspections but you'll get a warning. Don't get caught with notsi."

"What's notsi, Corp?" Bobby held the Trooper's eye, because they had to start learning, and fast.

The Corp rolled his eyes. "Bledrin greenies. Notsi. Not standard issue. Weapons or ammunition that you are not allowed to have."

"You mean like Frog carbins and shotguns and grenades?" Bobby frowned. "We were threatened with a firing squad for that."

"When you were Timers? What did you four do?" The Corp frowned, looking closer. "How old are you?"

Bobby cringed inwardly. "Sixteen."

"Shite. You are all dead men, regardless of how fast you learned." He sighed. "I suppose I ought to give you some sort of a chance. Every Trooper has notsi, but not grenades. Nobody has grenades, or double-barrelled shotguns, and hide anything else." He shook his head again. "The Plebs will slaughter you."

*　　*　　*

Ham had been right, which meant a lot of the time they didn't have an experienced Trooper to help them learn. Three of them really did have a hard time learning to shoot Plebs, but since the Plebs didn't seem to have any qualms about shooting first that didn't take too long to sort out.

Luckily Bells had no trouble shooting or knifing anyone, which gave the rest time to get their shite together. The other three learned fast and the lessons stuck, and eventually all four were accepted as a Trooper squad, not greenies.

The squad were moved a few times, to different housing complexes, but the general layout seemed more or less the same. Bare concrete housing blocks, a section of slums, workshops and warehouses, and several open spaces that held markets. Siflis became sneakier and talked less, Hood became more accurate and less concerned about shooting people with a rifle, Bells became twitchier, more prone to instant violence, and Bobby learned how to keep them all aimed in the same direction. Though he avoided being promoted to a Corp, because that might mean more men in the squad, or him being given a different squad. They'd made a pact, to cover each other, and that didn't include anyone else in the UKs.

Once they survived long enough to be useful, the four were moved to another unit and had to learn about a whole new housing complex and deal with a different Super and Sarge. They were moved twice more in the first three years but always as a squad. The four of them learned how to break rules and when, and how to deal with superiors. Better yet, as a tight group they weren't picked on despite their youth, or not twice in the same unit. Siflis really could be sneaky, while Bells could turn into a bledrin maniac at any time. Or any time Bobby told him to, because Bobby made sure Bells got his Divas and plenty of notsi weapons.

The last Super said he didn't want a bunch of wet behind the ears amateurs messing up his operations and had split them up. That had lasted for three months until the Super jumped off the top of a building. Bobby had been sat in full view when the Super tried to fly, so nobody could prove a thing. The replacement Super got the message and shipped all four out as a squad. The new Super stuck their chips in the reader, shook his head and said, "You four, who did I piss off?"

Then the Super said the four were a scout-sniper squad and threw them to a sergeant to sort out. The sergeant had asked to see the metal, which made a better spread now, then pointed out that he didn't mind the rule breaking but try to not let the bledrin management find out. The squad didn't care because they were together again. They'd settled back down into their old routine within weeks. That had been nearly two years ago and so far this Super either didn't know or didn't care what the squad did as long as the basted targets carked it on time. Not strictly true, he did flick Bobby about breaking rules but only trying to get a rise.

This unit of one hundred Troopers were called 3914 SSAB-Tata, and policed Residential Complex SSAB-Tata 17D. This particular complex seemed grubbier than most, with a worse drug problem than others they'd seen though it wasn't the worst. Unfortunately SSAB-Tata, the corporate owners, expected the Troopers to shoot agitators instead of addressing any problems. As a result, the Plebs here were more savage than in the other complexes Bobby's squad had served in. Now the four of them were sneaking through the darkened streets on yet another mission, though tonight's targets were drug growers and deserved killing in Bobby's opinion.

*　*　*

Siflis showed up in the gloom. He'd pulled up his balaclava so they could see the pale oval of his face. "Nobody else," he whispered, and pulled the face covering back down. Bobby saw the dark shadow melt back into the night and followed with the rest of the squad. He searched the still-warm corpse Siflis left behind and took the short-range radio and a snub nosed Pleb special. Bobby confirmed the revolver loads by touch, and found a dozen loose rounds in a pocket so the little revolver went in Bobby's boot. He'd look at it in daylight before deciding whether to turn it in.

Some Pleb weapons were good gear, and they all had several now. The chances were this would be good gear. The big drug growers always had creds for decent weapons because they took the least risk but set the price. The more dealers the Troopers caught, the more the growers could charge the starved market. Bobby thought it about time the Unit, the hundred Troopers under the Super, went after the growers. Raiding this complex of allegedly abandoned warehouses would lead to the burning of acres of illegal foliage.

Hood stayed right behind Bobby. The God of Death carried a real rifle these days. The weapon fired frangible rounds, which didn't break property because the bullets broke up straight after impact or if they hit brick. The rounds made a mess of Plebs, even ones with bits of captured or homemade armour since Hood didn't aim where there might be any of that. He fired a lot faster these days and loved the fancy telescopic sight on top of the long barrel.

Bells acted as rearguard because that way he wouldn't walk into a surprise. Bells still went viral when surprised, a real advantage for a rearguard, and probably carried more knives, small swords, brass knuckles and spare bayonets than the rest of them put together. Bobby always had an itch in his back while Bells held a carbin but that usually stayed strapped over Bells's back.

The dinky little automatic weapon with the long clip of plastic bullets that Bells had in one hand wouldn't go through a Trooper's jacket, or only enough to cause a flesh wound, a comforting thought. The weapon came in handy for close up work against unprotected Plebs since Bells didn't need to worry who got in the line of fire. Siflis reckoned the gun was Kraut, which meant very illegal and definitely not anything a Trooper should carry. Bells had traded an inlaid handgun and two long knives with inlaid blades for it and scored a box of the plastic ammo as well.

Siflis stopped moving as they came past the front of the drug growing complex. He started pointing out which guards were where, and Bobby sent it back to the Super on the tapper using Morse's code, whoever Morse was. The jumble of numbers made no sense unless you had the map marked with today's location codes. A series of gentle vibrations on his neck replied, telling Bobby they had ten minutes to close the back door. Bobby passed the news to Siflis and the squad crept on. They pulled back a little to go through the housing around the warehouses and approach from the back.

Another cooling corpse later they had the right place with a good view of the rear of the target and the two routes away, which would be why the corpse chose the spot. Corpse had another of the pistols and more loose rounds so Bobby passed that one to Siflis. The scout waved it away but Bells didn't. Bobby wondered how Bells found room in his boots for feet.

The tapper counted down the last ten seconds against their legs, directed from Unit command. Firing broke out followed by a bledrin great bang, all light and smoke as either the door went in or a booby trap blew at the other side of the buildings. It didn't stop the firing but although he kept to his own channel Bobby knew the raid had achieved initial success. The notsi weapons used by Plebs and gangsters were getting fewer while the Trooper carbins were firing short bursts, killing defenders instead of suppression. Any time now the survivors would try to get away. Sure enough a blank bit of wall slid forward and sideways, and a man with a rifle came out of the gap and looked both ways.

The two-way on the corpse buzzed. No message followed, so Bobby took a chance and buzzed back just once. The man peered up, undecided, so it probably should have been two. A grenade exploding around front of the weed farm made up the basted's mind and he beckoned. Another two men came out, both carrying rifles but Bobby put a hand on Hood. Not yet, because the Super wanted the boss.

Sure enough those two looked round and waved and a vehicle bonnet showed! That wasn't expected. Bobby thought about that for a moment and this had to be the money man because a working vehicle wasn't something everyone had. Plebs walked, so this had to be the boss's fast getaway and would have worked except for Hood's rifle. Bobby tapped Hood and the rifle spat. A muted clang followed but the vehicle kept coming, and the three men were looking this way! "Armoured!" Bobby hissed.

"Should I..."

"Yes, quick!" Hood fumbled for notsi ammo as the small van pulled carefully out of the narrow gap and started to turn away. Meanwhile the three men were looking towards their dead lookout and the radio crackled. Bobby ignored it, and as he heard the bolt go home on Hood's rifle spoke to his squad. "On two we open up on the riflemen with carbins. Put their heads down so they don't see the flash when Hood stops the van."

Mutters of complaint came back but Bobby saw Bells unsling his carbin. Bobby put a clip of solid rounds in his carbin instead of the legal flechettes because even if they were illegal so was the bledrin van. Anyway, ordinary flechettes might reach but wouldn't penetrate much.

"One, two." Three carbins went full auto and at least one solid round hit the van or other metal. The three men went for cover though one didn't make it. While they were still firing, Hood's big rifle cracked. They all heard the clang but the van kept going though still slowly turning. "Again, the other side, then move sharpish." It must have Frog steering, or maybe Yankee.

"You two, if they bail out shoot at their legs. They'll have armour." Siflis would know that but Bells needed it explained. He'd become their own personal Homer, even if he'd never actually said 'doh' or at least not yet. The rifleman who had dropped kept crawling, slowly, but he wasn't shooting so Bobby ignored him. Bells didn't and puffs rose over a wide area around him as more flechettes hit the road. The man stopped crawling.

Bobby put in a standard flechette clip and emptied his carbin at the two riflemen shooting back. The flechettes might come near enough to make them duck. From the dust coming up off the brickwork Siflis must still be using the heavier black market version. Management disapproved but they weren't being shot at with rifles using solid lead bullets. Even as the clang of the second hit echoed off the van Bobby realised the first one probably did the job. The vehicle hadn't straightened up and continued the slow turn into the wall.

The back doors burst open and Bells let fly with his little machine pistol. That didn't hit anyone at this range of course but the loud buzz of noise made the three men press back against the van for a moment. Siflis and Bobby opened up with carbins. Siflis must have switched back to lighter loads judging by all the puffs of dust. There were a hundred standard flechettes in a long clip and all Troopers used long clips instead of the short thirties given to Timers. The two hundred flechettes raised a cloud of dust around the three men as all three dropped, screaming.

Hood's rifle blew the head off one of the two riflemen and the other started to run. "Leave him." Hood sounded certain and sure enough the runner barely got past the van when he flew sideways and laid still. "Oops, forgot." Hood hadn't forgotten to switch back to frangible, he just preferred the solid bullets. He always said they were more accurate but the rest of them thought Hood liked the spatter.

"Switch back, there might be more. Not only that, but accidentally shooting our Super with the wrong ammo will get you into trouble." Brief laughter followed because so far this Super wasn't in danger of an accidental bullet. Then they all concentrated on the door and the rest of the wall just in case the back door had a side door.

"What about the others?" All three on the street behind the van started off screaming, though now one seemed to have fainted. The first rifleman had stopped twitching now and must be bleeding out from the growing stain around him. Hood probably asked just because he wanted the target practice.

"They'll bleed out, or management will ask them some questions." Bobby sniggered. "I doubt they'll get the option of metal." Bobby had some of the other sort of metal now, as plates in both legs because the toughened Trooper jackets didn't cover them. They all had enough protection inside their trousers now to stop flechettes except really close up. Nobody else showed even when the firing became muffled as the Troopers worked deep into the complex. Three or four minutes later there were muzzle flashes inside the darkened doorway, then a voice called out.

"Outlook, it's the Unit. Is it clear?" Bobby didn't recognise the voice, and it sure as hell wasn't the sergeant or the Super.

"Not for a question like that, you prat." Bobby replied on the channel, because he wasn't shouting so that some sneaky shite out in the dark got a free shot at the squad.

A different voice spoke up, on the radio this time. "Third squad requesting clearance. Bad Spliff. I repeat Bad Spliff." That had to be a Corporal.

"Backstop. All clear, come ahead Bad Spliff. Check the screamers for weapons."

"Wipe your own, Buttstop." The figure coming out raised a single finger in salute and headed for the screamers. Bobby and his squad stayed where they were, keeping an eye open all round while the Troopers took the belts from the trousers of the dead to tie off the legs on two screamers. Eventually the Super came out with his shotgun over his shoulder and Bobby's neck vibrated with the rally signal.

They came down while the Super wandered around the bodies. He looked up as they approached. "It looks as if the Plebs have been shooting each other again. After all we've got nothing that makes that sort of mess." The Super gestured at the splash where one rifleman's head had exploded across the road, and the pool spreading from the huddled corpse of the other. "What's in those clips if I check?"

"Don't know slur, they're all loaded at the factory. We're not allowed to mess about with them." Bobby smiled at the old exchange.

The Super snorted. He poked a finger through the two holes in the van. The door had been opened to show the two slumped figures still bleeding over the seats. "I see Beebi's Basteds are still the luckiest shites in the Unit. Else how would there be these dinky little holes in just the right places to shoot this pair through?"

"Pure luck, though it was good shooting to hit those holes. Maybe Hood should get metal for that, slur." Bobby could keep this shite running all day. He'd had practice because the Super seemed to enjoy flickin Bobby, trying to get to him, though he never really pushed. The Super stiffened, which had to be his personal coms, and moved off a bit to talk to higher about something. Something he seemed unhappy about from the body language. Then the Super came back, beckoning to the sergeant.

Though first he spoke to Bobby. "Well I hope your luck rubs off on all of us. Move out ahead of the rest and find us a way home. We'll torch this sharpish and follow." The Super sounded stone cold serious now.

"What, no search?"

"No time. Some sort of bledrin black newsletter has wound the Plebs up and it's going viral. If we don't get back soon, we won't get back at all." The Super waved a hand. "Get going. If in doubt, kill whoever it is and I don't care what you break." Bobby stared open-mouthed as the Super turned to the sergeant.

"Sarge, shoot all the prisoners. Then look over our wounded and use severe triage because if our men can't move by themselves, they can't come." Sarge opened his mouth to protest but the Super rode straight over whatever it was. "We move fast or we all cark it. Our badly wounded have an option, GV or a weapon and a good position until the Plebs get to them. Notsi hand weapons only because I'm not giving the Plebs a carbin." Sarge shut up.

"Super?"

"You still here? Sarge, if these four are in sight in ten seconds, shoot them."

"The truck is armoured, and will carry wounded." Bobby turned and trotted to the nearest corner because the sergeant would be counting.

"I could..."

"Not yet Bells." Bobby glanced back. "Too many witnesses."

"Later might be too late." Siflis gestured ahead as they came around the corner and out of sight of the Super. A glow showed among the buildings, directly between here and base.

"Find a way round. In case nobody got it, we kill anyone and break anything in the way."

"Yesss. About bledrin time!"

"In the way, Bells, not because it'll make a nice noise breaking. Hood, don't use up the solids until you have to. There might be more armour to punch through."

"Hellfire Beebi, there can't be another of those cars!"

"No, but some Pleb out there might stick a shed roof in front of a barricade, or some such shite. Save the solids." There might be another car as well but Bobby didn't want to tempt the Two-faced Bitch, Lady Luck.

"Shite. It really is bad then?" Hood changed clips as he spoke.

Siflis came back in time to hear the exchange. "I'll keep the heavy flechettes for later as well. The alley there is clear right now, but I can hear the Plebs in the flats nearby and that could alter. They're on about Aliens invading and Plebs storming the base to get weapons." He moved out in front again.

"Aliens?" Bells looked around wildly, waving his Kraut.

"Calm down Bells, they're Plebs so who knows what they're sniffing." Though Bobby thought Aliens seemed a bit more than the usual weird. "You lot move down the alley, and I'll tell the Super and warn him the road might close behind us." The four of them moved down the alley, avoiding the rubbish without any conscious thought after years of patrols. The tramp behind a skip laid very still so Siflis had taken the instructions to heart.

The answer from the Super was stark and simple. "Keep going and we'll try and follow. If we get cut off from you, get back to base and we'll either hole up or unleash hell. Luck, Beebi." Bobby flinched, because unleash hell wasn't a joke. It came from some old vid, but the reality meant calling down Copters and arty on your own position because you'd been overrun. That meant anything up to napalm if available and management authorised the cost in real estate.

"Luck, sir." The Super would know Bobby meant it since he didn't slur the 'sir' this time. A shout above and behind meant the luck hadn't lasted.

Bobby pulled out his long pistol with the fat barrel. "Where is he?"

"Last block we passed. Three up, four from left. Laser light in three." Bobby brought up the pistol, two-handed, and waited for Siflis to light it up. As soon as the dot of light appeared Bobby put three silenced rounds downrange and Siflis turned the laser light off. Screaming and shouting sounded from back there and lights came on in some rooms, but all confused.

"Move, move, move. He might only be wounded and tell someone. Come on Bells, rearguard from round the bledrin corner." They ran for the alley end and dodged round the corner. Behind them Bobby could see a glow as the Super torched the weed farm. With luck anyone coming that way would be stoned by the time they got through the smoke.

"Clear." The Squad moved towards the next corner, where Siflis crouched. "Beebi, one across and up, on the garage. There's another two down this side in a doorway. I don't think they're pooching so they might be waiting for us or dealers setting up a meet."

"Bells, as soon as I shoot get down the street and sort them. Silent if possible, but don't take a stupid chance." Bells suddenly had a long knife and a stubby revolver in his hands. "Hood, watch that garage roof. If I miss or he's got friends, don't piss about asking or worrying about noise." From the corner of his eye Bobby saw the long rifle barrel come up. "Light on him on two, Siflis." Bobby brought up the pistol. "One, two."

Bobby fired twice before flame lanced out from the rooftop, the second crack drowned out by Hood's rifle. A shadowy figure reared up, twisted and went down. Hood fired again. "Yours kept moving, Beebi." Bells had made it halfway to the doorway when two figures erupted. The stubby revolver let five go in a nearly continuous roar and as the men staggered and ducked Bells ran the rest of the way. Both hands lashed out as the pair went down and by the time the other three reached him the strangers were still.

"Dealers I reckon." Bells panted as he tossed a Saturday night special and two blades onto the pavement, but that would be excitement.

"Hood, take the blades and the special because it might get dirty tonight." Hood didn't carry much gear for close up and personal. Siflis cursed, quietly but continuously. "You OK Siflis?"

"Yes, maybe. Not sure. I can still use my arm but it's hit."

"Step into the doorway so we can stop the blood, we don't want a trail." Or Siflis bleeding out but showing concern openly wasn't what Troopers did. A quick look using a glo-light and the wound wouldn't kill the scout, though he wouldn't be using a knife in a serious fight with that arm.

"I can use a notsi pistol with that hand." Siflis knew the score. "Wait one and I'll check ahead."

"Not until we're off this street because the place is coming alive." Lights were coming on in the flats and voices were shouting questions as the four of them ran along close to the wall.

"There's bodies out there!"

"Who's shooting?"

"Is it the Aliens?"

"Look out!"

As they dodged round the corner someone shouted "It's the Bellamy's. Someone's topped them. All of them!" The noise behind grew. Ahead the glow showed clearly now and Bobby tried to work out how near the base the fire was. Too near he thought so he'd have to go around and come in from the back.

"Alley to the left." Bobby pointed and Siflis headed that way as the rest crept from shadow to shadow. There were more shouts in the night but a lot of them were aimless, just slogans, and none were about four Troopers. Behind them, well behind, an outbreak of gunfire sounded followed by the thud of grenades. Bobby took a moment to send the code for his position and that he'd been spotted. There were more shouts about Aliens which seemed weird.

Siflis gestured to the trio before darting across the road and into the alley. They followed without raising an alarm. Siflis signed quickly, to follow to the end then across the next street to the next alley. A shout went up as Bells reached the second alley, but no shooting. They ran like hell but the first shot chased them even as Siflis reached the end. "Keep going Siflis." Another shot whined off the wall. "You too Bells, there's no cover." The cursing from behind became more profane and louder.

"Trouble!" Siflis shouted back but kept running. He emptied a notsi pistol then aimed a second while pulling his carbin off his shoulder with his wounded arm. Shite!

"Keep going, blow through." They'd got no shelter in the alley at all, and the gunman behind couldn't keep missing. Bobby caught a glimpse of a dark opening nearly opposite. "Straight across and hole up." Hood came out of the alley as well, shooting to the side from the hip. The big rifle went onto his back before Hood emptied the Pleb special up the street in a continuous roar.

Plenty of fire came back raising dust from the brickwork, concrete and the road. As Bobby came round the corner he saw Hood stagger then limp onwards, reaching for his big rifle again. Bobby raised his carbin, spraying the clip into the chaos on top of a rough barricade. The squad had come out well behind it, their pistols and flechettes catching the defenders by surprise. Now some were still trying to scramble over, while others were scrambling back because they were being shot at from the other side. For a moment Bobby thought they could break through to whoever was over there.

Then more Plebs poured out of the doorways each side of the barrier and started shooting at Beebi's Basteds. "Get into that doorway opposite!" More of the survivors on the barricade were shooting back as the Basteds crossed the road, staggering from hits though mostly lightweight flechettes. The whines and sparks off the concrete road and buildings meant that the incoming included some heavier stuff. Bobby emptied another clip. Some of the Plebs fell, but others staggered and kept coming. "They've got jackets. Use notsi."

Siflis reached the doorway, kneeling to steady his carbin. The aimed bursts weren't as long but men crumpled as the heavier rounds punched through their protection. Not enough even when Hood's rifle boomed, throwing his targets backwards into those following. "Open the door Hood. Borrow Bells' Kraut." A wordless complaint followed but Bells threw the little automatic, before raising his carbin.

"Locked, Beebi."

"Break it." The Super said break anything necessary, and the squad had to get off this street.

Hood grunted, followed by a loud crack. "Lock's bust, but there's bolts. I'll have to kick it in." Bolts were illegal since the corporations had the right of entry to their housing blocks, and over-rides for the door locks.

The complaint from Bells this time would be because he enjoyed breaking things, and Hood had got the job. "Keep your mind on the problem up the street Bells." Between Siflis, Bells and Bobby, all firing solid rounds or heavyweight flechettes, the Plebs had slowed up. Now the mass still crept forward close to the buildings but with more care and none went out into the street, out where their comrades were still writhing and screaming. Some Plebs had captured Trooper jackets someplace, but hadn't taken the trousers.

The noise from the attackers outside muffled the crash as the door went in, followed by two sharp cracks and the ripping noise of the Kraut. Hood grunted and cursed. "You Oke Hood?"

"One in the thigh, but the jacket stopped the other. Shite, I've just killed a bledrin Granny!" Hood sounded really shocked. They'd all shot women, or sometimes stabbed them if the bitches got too close, but not usually a granny.

"She fired first. Can you clear the hall?"

"Yeah, hang on." The door scraped before Hood moved into the darkness beyond.

Bobby put in another clip. Shite, he only had four left and three were standard. "Slow up and take single shots, or triple bursts. No auto."

"There's hundreds of 'em coming out of the block opposite. We'll be proper pooched if they get close enough to rush."

"Just do it Bells. I've got something for that, and so has Siflis I reckon." Siflis glanced back, startled, then gave a guilty shrug and went back to shooting Plebs. Behind them the Kraut buzzed briefly. "Any time this year would be good, Hood. Especially right now."

"Last door." Clattering sounded over the gunfire. "Shite! Broom cupboard. We're clear but there's two corridors and if someone chucks burning crap down the stairs we'll fry."

"Everyone in. Hood, use that rifle on anyone showing a head up the stairs. Siflis, Bells, take a corridor each." Bobby headed for the broom cupboard. Disinfectant, bleach, ah, he sniffed the stench of rotgut booze coming through the industrial cleaners. As usual the caretaker had an illegal still or peddled someone else's rotgut. First though, Bobby took some mops and brooms over to the broken door to jam it shut.

"We're trapped, Beebi. They'll run all over us."

"Stop panicking Bells. We won't be here long. Just long enough to leave a surprise." Bobby went into the caretaker's office and the two flats opening off the hall. He collected every bottle or can that would burn fast or explode when hot and chucked them into the hall, including any in the broom cupboard. The lifts might still work but Hood dragged the granny and the caretaker across, using them to jam the doors open.

Hood fired once and Bells twice before Bobby finished. Behind the entrance door, braced with a broom handle for now, he could hear a crowd gathering. "Hood, give Bells the Kraut and keep watching the stairs. Right you pair, listen up. When I kick away the broom handle, the door will open because someone is pushing." Bobby waved his biggest notsi. "Put a fresh clip in the Kraut, and you put a full standard clip in your carbin, Siflis. Empty the lot into the crowd out there and they'll break."

"What if they don't." Sometimes it would be nice if Bells believed in things working out well.

"Then Siflis uses his little something, and then they will." Siflis nodded in agreement and waved the grenade at Bells before stowing it again. Bells nodded, then stared at Bobby.

"Sodin hell, Beebi, what's that?"

"Sawn-off single barrelled shotgun. Easier to hide than one like Sarge's." Finally, Bells' face broke into a happy smile. He believed in shotguns. "Ready?" They both nodded. "Three, two, one." Bobby kicked the broom handle sideways and it skittered away as he stepped back. The door flew open under the pressure and at least three men staggered in. Before they could recover the two automatics threw them back into the crowd before chewing into the packed figures. As the carbins fell silent, Bobby pulled the trigger.

The roar of the shotgun briefly drowned the screams and cries of panic and then the survivors were trying to scramble clear. The two automatics opened up again, chopping down even more. Bobby managed to get off a second round as the doorway emptied, of standing figures at least. Bells lunged forward with his blades raised to finish off anyone still moving. Siflis went straight in there with him until the screaming and moaning died out. Bobby watched with a big pistol in case a wounded someone had the smarts to use a weapon.

"Now what?" Bells had started panting again, but the action had cured his nerves.

"Grab any weapons and ammo, especially carbin clips, then chuck enough bodies out to shut the door."

"They'll be ready next time." Siflis took a peek round the corner of the doorway and let off a couple of triple bursts up the street. "They're already gathering again."

Bobby tossed his own grenade up and down. "We won't be here. Hood, make a Molotov with one of those bottles of rotgut, and toss it up the stairs. Throw a couple of jackets or something that burns up there first. You two, help me to shove the door shut again." The door scraped because the pushing from outside or Hood's kick had twisted the hinges.

Broom handles and mops were soon jammed against the floor and the door to keep it closed. It would be a better job this time, because Bells produced a small hatchet to make holes in the inner door and floor for the ends. Bobby and Siflis exchanged smiles because the amount of sharp steel Bells carried had become a standing joke, though handy sometimes. A crash and flickering light from behind signalled Hood's Molotov. "It won't catch, because the stairs are concrete and steel." Hood sounded disappointed.

"No, but it'll stop anyone getting nosy until after the door goes in."

Bobby looked at the heap of flammables and canisters. "We need more. Get the furniture from the flats and the caretaker's office."

Hood cursed, followed by a boom as he fired. "It won't stop the nosy basteds along the corridors."

"No, but we'll be gone soon. You can keep that lot in their rooms while we go the other way, if we leave a clear view for you to shoot through." The furniture started arriving and Bobby splashed rotgut on it, then some stain remover that smelled flammable. The caretaker's shoes provided laces for Bobby to tie his grenade to the door handle. He hung a plastic can of cleaner fluid up as well.

Bells threw a chair on the heap. "The grenade will only stop the first few."

"When the door comes in this should set something on fire as well as blowing the shite out of whoever is first. Eight seconds means they'll be well inside when it goes off." Bobby tied a lace to the pin, and then around the wrecked bolt loop on the doorpost. "When the burning fluid spatters the furniture will go up. With luck we'll break contact."

"Which way?"

"Towards the friendlies the other side of that barricade. We'll come out the other end of this block." Bobby waved to the corridor in question.

"What about the residents, the ones along this corridor? They'll come out behind us." Bells had gone back to his usual gloomy self.

Bobby grinned and waved a big plastic lump on a chain. "Caretaker's lockdown. I'll seal them in as we pass or shoot them with this if anyone comes out ahead of us." Bobby waved the silenced pistol. "We don't want anyone outside realising we've gone this way."

"I'd better stay this end then. If I shoot someone they'll hear it." Hood gestured at his rifle.

"Towards this end. About a third of the way up will be near enough. After all, you don't want too far to run once the grenade goes off." Bobby looked round. "All loaded? All set?"

*   *   *

The squad almost reached the other end of the block before they heard a savage roar as the attackers breached the doorway. Three or four seconds later Hood's rifle boomed, killing one of the leaders to keep the rest cautious and penned up in the entrance. Hood started running as soon as he fired so when the grenade went off he stayed clear of the burning debris. Even Bells looked happy at the resulting conflagration or possibly the screaming that went with it. By then Siflis reached the end of the corridor. He glanced both ways and signalled all clear.

Bobby passed the caretaker's override to Bells and went ahead. "Both doors are still bolted so they'll be locked. We can get clean away." Siflis looked left.

"No, we go that way, right. The plebs left on that barricade are still shooting at someone who's shooting back, so we join forces. Sodit, I forgot." Bobby had forgotten about the Super and the rest of the unit. He tapped the coms with a call-sign. The throat buzzer started soon afterwards, and went on for a while.

Bells must have read some of it from Bobby's face. "I hope that isn't orders to come back and get them."

"We couldn't anyway. The rest are in it, and deep enough to be blowing bubbles. Half the bledrin Plebs in the complex are on the streets and they've got real weapons, though we know that. The Super says the prats think we're here to disarm them all because they've been sold to Aliens." Bobby snorted. "No need to look at me like that, it's what the Super said."

Siflis laughed. "That's from the black news. The real reports say something has been found out in the asteroids, and it might be alien or advanced tech from the Age of Space. Everyone is supposed to work extra hard to help build the kit to look properly." Bells sneered and Siflis shrugged. "Don't look at me like that. When I was a nipper I read a story about finding an old space capsule, a true story. Now I play space games so I still notice this sort of shite. Anyway, the black news has got it all twisted as usual."

"They believe that, the black news? The official news is unbelievable enough, but that stuff is put out by glue sniffers and main-line shooters." Bells spat to make his opinion clear.

Bobby shrugged. "Well this lot believe it. The message from the Super is we're on our own, and I don't think four of us will be enough to survive.

We link up with whoever is over the barricade."

"OK Beebi, you're the brains. How do we do it?" Hood limped up and Bobby filled him in, quickly. Once Hood had finished cursing, Bobby gave them the plan, such as it was. "We go through that door and kill whoever is still on that barricade. Use triple bursts and aim, don't spray. The rest of the Plebs are trying to get past the fire because the stupid shites are still chasing us and all the downstairs windows have steel bars. We pick up all the ammo we can on the barricade and leg it over the top but Bells, remember to collect ammo."

"Yeah, I've only got one carbin clip left." Which was why Bobby had reminded him. Bells used as much ammo as the rest put together on most missions. Bells hunted through his pockets and pouches. "I've got the Kraut, four notsi pistols and ammo."

"Two notsi clips and most of one standard flechettes, one clip in a pistol and a spare, a couple of flares, and my grenade." Siflis didn't need to check, he always kept track of his ammo. "I've got a selection of notsi here from the bodies in the doorway." A quick check showed a spare carbin, five clips, five pistols and a fistful of assorted ammo.

"Five notsi and four frangible clips for the rifle, five standard for the carbin." Hood pulled out the revolver. "This is dry but I've got a semi with fifteen in it." Hood always used the least carbin ammo, preferring to stick to the rifle.

"Here, I've got ammo for that." Bells reloaded the revolver and stuck it in Hood's belt. "I've got lots of ammo for notsi pistols, and seven clips for the Kraut. Nearly eight." Bells looked defensive. "They're light and it uses a lot, so I carry a lot."

"Hood, give Bells three clips for his carbin, and use yours. When it's empty you can go back to the rifle." Hood pulled a face but reorganised. "Bells, take three of those extra clips from Siflis, and try to make them last." Bobby took an extra notsi pistol from the loot, loaded and sorted out a couple of clips. "Remember, triple bursts to save ammo. Let's do it." He tried not to smile as Bells stuffed the two pistols without ammo in his pack.

*　　*　　*

The twenty plus Pleb fighters on the barricade, concentrating on the enemy over the top of it, died in confusion. The squad rushed into their positions, quickly searching for carbin clips. Bobby stuffed some into Hood's pouches. "Use your rifle to slow that lot up." That lot meant the bloody great mob around the original doorway. They'd actually managed to rip out the bars on a window and people were being boosted in through there when a shout went up. Heads turned towards the squad, then a few weapons.

Unfortunately, there might be more angry Plebs heading towards the squad than flechettes to kill them. Bobby scrambled into a vacated firing position, looked over the barricade, and cursed as he saw the four vehicles in the square beyond. The basted Plebs must have either got hold of anti-armour rockets or a bledrin cannon. The heavy machine guns on the turrets of three armoured cars were only firing short bursts, which worried Bobby given the number of targets creeping closer.

Bobby looked at the state of the four vehicles. One laid on its back and the rest had lost tracks so the Plebs used mines. He glanced back. Shite! "Hood, get up here with your cannon. Siflis, Bells, go full auto for a bit and stop those basteds. There's a problem."

"What!" Bells screamed it, looking back and forth for a way out. "I knew it, I knew it! We're all gonna cark it!"

"I'll do it for you if you don't shut up. Hood's going to deal with the problem." Not really, but Bells going viral just now would pooch them all. Bobby lowered his voice. "Can you start killing the ambitious, the ones out front?" Hood stared at the scene.

"I haven't got enough rounds, Beebi."

"Target rich environment, Hood. Use the frangibles up first." At least that brought a small smile to the big man's face, briefly. "I want those Plebs to stop, maybe pull back a bit while they try to figure out what's happening. Then we get to link up."

"That doesn't look a good place to link up, Beebi."

"You like this better?" Hood scowled in reply. "Nor do I so we'll go for the armour because HQ will send help for them. I'll empty a clip or two into the crowd but we want the brave ones at the front going down." Hood nodded, settled down, and the rifle started firing. Bobby glanced back. Bells sat with the barrel resting on a body, shooting his carbin one-handed with the other hung straight down, while Siflis had knotted a strip of something round his leg. Both were using bodies for cover.

The Plebs in the street had fallen back but the ones with the weapons were spilling out of the doorway and window now, and the incoming started to increase. Bobby used up four of his newly acquired clips in long bursts into the square ahead. The crowds creeping towards the four vehicles stopped when Hood killed the leaders and four hundred flechettes tore into their flanks. Shouting and screaming spread, the heavy machine guns on the armour opened up in longer bursts, and the advance recoiled.

A light flicked from under one armoured car, a bit too fast but Bobby got the gist. They wanted covering fire. What for? Bobby wanted the bledrin covering fire, from those heavy weapons. Then he saw the figures gathering in the gap between one armoured car and the upturned one. No! They couldn't come this way! That would be suicide! Bobby fumbled for a flashlight to tell them but the three turret guns went onto full auto, walking the tracers across the attackers. The attackers hunted for cover behind bodies or bits of masonry.

Even as Bobby pulled out his light, the group sprang into action, racing across the gap towards him. Well over a score or so Troopers started out, carrying bags as well as packs and spare carbines. The turrets kept firing, as did a half dozen carbines from among the vehicles. "Covering fire, fast as you can at shooters." Bobby took Hood's carbine and rested it on the barricade before emptying that and his own in short bursts, alternating. He probably didn't hit much but it would look like two shooters and help to keep heads down.

The group of Troopers kept running though three had already dropped. Each time one went down someone else snatched up the bag or weapons and kept coming. Two more dropped and at least one only seemed wounded. Nobody slowed to rescue him. The Trooper started firing his carbine in triple bursts, bloody brave under the circumstance because he attracted plenty of replies. More of the group staggered but kept coming, all firing sideways from the hip as they did.

A line of flame shot along the floor from the barricade on the right of the square, heading for the running men. They tried to run faster, but the last three were still too close when it reached a buried charge. The last man in the survivors snatched the bags from two of the dead and ran for Bobby, then he stumbled. The Trooper swung the bags and let go, and did the same for his own before going down. Bobby ducked and waited for the explosion.

It didn't happen, the bags just landed with a clank. Moments later the first man over snatched one up as he came past. "Ammo," he called and tossed a bag to Bobby. A tug on the fastener and carbin clips spilled out! Bobby turned, tossing the bag towards Siflis.

"Ammo." Another bag went towards Bells, down to handguns again.

"Now to fix a few of those basteds." The men turned back once they were over the top and brought up their carbins.

"No. Kill these behind you first so we can escape." A pair of angry eyes stared back. "We can catch those basteds in the square when they break cover because we've scarpered." The eyes were still angry, but the man's lips curled up.

"Done." The Corp turned away. "Shoot this way first lads." None of the newcomers liked that idea.

Bobby pointed. "Aimed shots and clear our way home. Then that lot in the square will think you've gone and get careless, sitting ducks." The muttering turned into smiles without any humour at all. Bobby tapped Hood and pointed back down the street behind them. "Kill anyone with a decent weapon, anything that might go through a jacket. We open the back door first." Hood nodded and slid down a bit so the back of his head didn't make a target from the square.

Three minutes of aimed triple bursts and Hood's big rifle, and the mob in the street didn't want to pick up a weapon. They recoiled slowly, warily and still poised, but at least they pulled back past the burning doorway. That had caught properly now. The ceiling must be alight as flames were coming out of a window above the door.

"Corp?" The man turned to see what Bobby wanted. "What about the heavy weapons? We can't stop them taking the vehicles now."

"Those are nearly out of ammo anyway. The wounded who couldn't run are using up what they've got."

Bobby flinched. "Shite! We can't let the plebs have heavy weapons!"

The Corp's face set like stone as he held up a small plastic box. "This is why it's a bad idea to nick our wheels. Boom. I'll do it just before they get into the hatches."

Bobby looked at the plebs creeping across the square, getting even closer to the armour. The heavy weapons were back to firing short bursts again. "Can you get in touch?"

The Corp gestured to a man with a radio on his back. "Yeah."

"A bullet in their own head might be better, right at the end, and we can be away by then. We'll give it a while so there are plenty of the basteds climbing over all four vehicles and then click?"

"You don't want to see it? We do." The snarls on the fifteen faces were clear to see.

Bobby gestured to the crowd waiting for them, now slowly thinning as the word spread and more of them moved off sideways to find a way into the square. "If we do it this way the Plebs are distracted by all those goodies so we can punch clear and break contact. Siflis will find a way out for us once we're clear." Bobby didn't fancy a last stand just here, ta, and the boom wouldn't kill enough.

"Siflis?" Bobby pointed at him and the Corp smiled, a real one. "You must be Beebi." Bobby nodded. "Where's your Unit?"

"Super sent us ahead, then told me they're going down for the third time. We're supposed to get out how we can, if we can." Bobby gestured. "We've already picked up too many wounds. Four of us just isn't enough." He snorted. "We already had to resupply from the dead Plebs."

"But you've still got four. Sniper and scout squad, yes?"

"Yes."

"I've heard of Beebi's Basteds. This is your environment, and you haven't lost a man yet which is good enough for me. You're in charge. Now how do we get out of this?" Bobby stared for a moment, shook his head, and began to actually plan.

*   *   *

It didn't work all that well for either side, because Murphy stalked the streets in all his bloodstained glory tonight. The Plebs launched their first mass attack on the vehicles. Three heavy machine guns on the armour and the wounded Troopers with carbins, combined with a dozen Troopers with Bobby firing into the flanks on auto, slaughtered the basteds. The assault broke apart in blood and chaos. By then the trapped Troopers were firing even the heavy weapons in triple bursts so their ammo had about gone. Just as Bobby poised to break through the thinning crowd by the burning block, away from the square, another horde turned up and they brought plenty of weapons and ammo.

A storm of incoming meant there was no way to break through the reinforced mob in the street. Bobby took the enlarged squad back into the housing block through the already broken door. He left two of the new men dead on the barricade while others had picked up more wounds. "Jam that, and I mean jam it. Siflis, use your grenade." The remaining ten Troopers stared at Siflis as he produced the grenade, and Bobby used it to rig the door while others broke the lock to get out the other side of the block.

They ran straight across the next street exchanging fire with the score or so Plebs coming towards the firefight, before smashing straight into the next block. "Shite, no more grenades." Bobby hammered a knife into the gap between door and jamb to hold it closed.

"Here." The Corp from the armour passed another grenade and showed three more. "We've got throwers on the turrets, but the Sarge said the last eight wouldn't save the armour now. He thought four might help us escape, fair exchange since you were shooting the shit out of the Plebs attacking us."

"He's right. Rig that door. We keep doing this until we find an empty street, then Siflis finds us a deep, dark hole." Bobby went to the other door, already being broken, to check the next street.

The Corp spoke quietly. "We've got one here won't make it. He says he'll let them get in, then pull the pin, chuck it round the corner and start shooting." Bobby nodded, it was as good a way to go as any. As they left the block, the first grenade went off behind them. The Troopers cut down the nearest half dozen Plebs on this street and the rest ran, screaming about Troopers attacking the accommodation blocks.

Again they broke into and out of a block, and this time they might have killed the three Plebs and gone dark, but more appeared at the far end of the street before ducking back. Behind them a carbin ripped off a long burst before a grenade exploded. That should make the pursuers more cautious. The group heard the loud rattling of heavy machine guns followed by more grenades in the distance. The Plebs had reached the armour. In and out one more block, leaving another grenade and a Trooper who'd carked it, bled out, and the only two Plebs on the street died quickly. They were well clear of the square now and better yet, at the end of this street lay a warren of workshops, garages and warehouses.

"Break into the next block and out, but rig the door leading out yon side. Do it from this side and come back as fast as possible. They'll think we headed for the barracks or went to ground in that block and search it." A grenade exploded behind them. "Catch up quickly because we're going to disappear into that lot." Bobby pointed at the dilapidated buildings.

The corporal hesitated. "Base is the other way; we could try for it."

"Base will be up to their necks in bledrin maniacs and the Troopers will be trigger-happy basteds. One or the other will shoot us."

"Fair point." The Corp waved to one of his men and they ran across the street, while Bobby led the rest along the side of the accommodation block to the other end. Shortly after the Corp caught up, running into the narrow alley as Bells frantically beckoned, another grenade went off. Bobby heard the screams followed by the baying of the angry mob.

"Nobody shoot." Bobby held up his silenced pistol, while Bells held up a knife. Siflis unwound his wire to let it swing by one handle before moving ahead. Carbins were slung and bayonets and knives gleamed softly in the dim light. "Watch where you step, be as quiet as possible."

The Corp held out the small box, and then showed Bobby his wrist comp. "They're done." The terse message just said 'Luck.'

Bobby nodded. "Wait five minutes. The Plebs can't get the weapons dismounted by then, can they." The Corp shook his head, teeth bared in a silent snarl. Corp pressed his button five minutes later, long after the last of the booby-trap grenades had exploded far behind. The survivors were deep into the warren of alleys and narrow streets but still saw the result. The flash lit the sky five blocks away, followed by a long rumble, showing the totally excessive paranoia of SSAB-Tata when it came to theft prevention. According to Corp the charges would also send a signal to the Trooper Base asking for an air strike on their position.

Siflis felt his way through the night, while the twelve still alive followed him as silently as possible. One had to be gagged and more or less carried, and the chances of getting him to a medic in time were shrinking by the minute. Silently meant leaving a few probably innocent bodies but Siflis used his wire and Bobby his long barrelled pistol, and once a thrown knife from Bells, so nobody heard the unfortunates die. The bodies were quickly hidden under rubbish or inside sheds or skips, to leave no immediate trace. Before dawn the Troopers holed up in a derelict warehouse, using the water coming from the broken toilet cistern for washing and drinking. Corp, who now introduced himself as Sandman, sat with Bobby and gathered enough radio intel to finally get some idea of what had happened.

*   *   *

All four of the local SSAB-Tata Steel Corporation housing complexes had exploded in violence. No Copters had arrived as backup because the plebs shot two down with SAMs, surface-to-air missiles, so real warplanes had to be called up. Now the SAMs had been dealt with the Copters were concentrating relieving the Trooper bases and compounds, using shrapnel and napalm on the hordes laying siege to them. SSAB-Tata must be truly miffed since that had to be destroying whole housing blocks and costing a fortune. Corp managed to reach his own command on the radio and report his position.

"Corp Sandman with 659th Armoured, Tango squad, with eight Troopers and Beebi's Basteds."

The reply wasn't quite what Sandman expected. "Perfect. You say Beebi's Basteds are with you?"

"Yes sir. But they've been shot up. We all have." Sandman had a sinking feeling about this. The dick on the other end sounded too bledrin happy.

"How many of them?"

"Four."

Sandman could almost hear the smile. "That's all of them. Good. Their Supervisor needs extraction."

"With four men, sir? They're all wounded and there's thousands of armed Plebs out there. The Plebs have Trooper weapons and explosives. We're surrounded." The Corp could hear the pleading in his own voice, but pressed on. "Without Beebi's Basteds to find us a way home, I'll lose the rest of my men, sir."

Mock patience bled into the radio voice. "I know the Plebs have substantial weaponry. How many men do you have left, Corporal? Men fit to fight." Bobby sat next to the Corp, listening in after being urgently beckoned.

"Nine, including me, but that will be eight soon without extraction." The ninth man lay unconscious, bleeding from an ear and the corner of his mouth. There were at least two flechettes or bullets deep inside him.

"Well then, your best bet is to team up with Beebi. That will compensate for his wounded." The asshole safely tucked away behind concrete had done his sums. The lives of another dozen Troopers versus a chance to extract a Supervisor. No contest. The Corp stared at the radio, because anything he said right now would get him shot anyway.

Bobby beckoned, and the Corp passed the radio across. "Bobby B here slur. We'll need a sit-rep before we can try. Otherwise we'll run into trouble and might be too late for the Super." Bobby mimed sleeping and cutting a throat to the Corp, then mouthed "sod him" while listening to background muttering on the radio.

The muttering stopped. "You'd better get to him before that, or there's no point sending anyone to relieve you or you coming home. If you get to the Super and link him through, we'll send a relief column." Bobby covered the microphone and cursed quietly. Then he met Sandman's eyes and they both shrugged. May as well go for it.

"Perhaps you'd better give me the best sit-rep you can." Bobby paused. "Sluur."

"Smartarse. You know where the weed farm was?"

"We found it, sluur."

"Ah. Right. Well your Supervisor had to break east, to avoid the Plebs, but there were more coming. He made it to the tram station. File coming for the wrist map." Bobby listened to the rest of the sit-rep while looking at the small map on Sandman's wrist with the Plebs and Troopers marked in over the street plan.

The Super still hung on, holed up with maybe half the Unit, up to fifty Troopers. They'd got clear of the housing, right into the tram depot and the Troopers were in the station itself according to a Copter. The plebs in the tram housing and repair workshops and the trams themselves had them surrounded. SSAB-Tata wouldn't authorise napalm or even explosives there. Enough Troopers with carbins or machine guns could kill the Plebs, while the valuable real estate, trams and heavy equipment would survive flechettes and a few bullets. The dick on the radio didn't put it like that, just spouted economic use of weaponry and manpower.

Bobby had the job of getting through the surrounding Plebs and reaching the Super with a radio link. Once the Super confirmed he wasn't dying, an armoured relief column would be sent to extract him and the Troopers. "If he dies, the relief column comes home. I've heard all about you and your Supers, Beebi, and this one had better not have an accident."

"Yes sluur, of course sluur. Would never think of it sluur." The men nearby were stifling their mirth, because Bobby had turned the volume up a bit. There were rumours that some Supers were wary round Beebi's Basteds but this confirmed it for Sandman's Troopers. "Could I have your name please sluur, for my official report?"

"No need. Just do the job." Bobby clicked the radio off and the men nearby exploded into laughter.

Siflis stuck his head in. "Shut it you eedjits, or shall I just send up a flare and ask the bledrin Plebs to join the party?" The group shut up, but they were still smiling. "I'm stuck with a bunch of Homers." Siflis went back outside to keep an eye and ear open.

"We've got to do it, haven't we?" Sandman stopped smiling and looked decidedly unhappy, and now so did the rest as it sank in. "We can't even sit it out because that," he gestured at the radio, "tells them where we are. We, the Armoured, will do what we can but we're used to riding around in a tin box. You and your Basteds will have to supply the expertise and we'll supply extra firepower."

"The trick will be to avoid needing it. Here, look at this map." Bobby bumped wrists to pass the detailed map of the area around the weed farm and the sitrep map came back from Sandman's wrist comp. Hood, Siflis and Bells already had the first one because as a scout squad, all his men had to know the mission. Sandman sent two men up as lookout, so Siflis could come down and all the Basteds could help with the planning.

They agreed on a provisional route. While the rest were checking gear and putting an edge on favourite weapons, Bobby pulled Sandman aside. "What about him?" He indicated the dying man.

"Jasper is done. He'll cark it if we move him, he'll cark it if we leave him and there's no Copter coming." Sandman sighed. "I'll do it." He pulled his bayonet.

"Hang on. Hood?" Hood came over and Bobby kept his voice down. "Give me a GV." Bobby knew Hood always had a spare.

"Who needs a Goodnight Vienna? What if the Plebs catch me?" Hood glanced at the still figure and realisation hit. "Oke, but I've only got one more." He passed across the packet containing the hypodermic full of clear liquid. Nobody knew why the lethal doses were known as Goodnight Vienna, but the name had stuck. Bobby passed it to Sandman. "Unless you want me to?"

"No. He's one of mine." Sandman glanced at Hood. "If we make it, I owe you." Hood grunted and moved off while Sandman went over to Jasper. A few moments later he started removing weapons, ammunition and body armour. The rest noticed and a couple of men went over to help before burying the body in debris.

Dawn had broken, but the amount of sun filtering through the low cloud barely classed as daylight. The dim light revealed deserted streets so the rioting Plebs were either at the remaining firefights or sleeping it off. The rest seemed to be keeping their heads down, probably wisely since there were Pleb bodies here and there that had never been near a Trooper let alone been killed by one. Some old scores had been paid off in the dark, along with a bit of opportunistic mugging. Siflis led the twelve survivors down windowless alleys or through empty shops and sweatshops where possible. Where they weren't deserted, the silenced pistol, garrotte and knives kept anyone raising the alarm. For two slow hours the dozen heavily armed men crept on, or waited patiently for the right moment to cross a street or alley.

* * *

"We are totally pooched." Bells might be right this time. Bobby looked at the hundreds of Plebs crouched behind every possible bit of cover, and all looking at or aiming a weapon towards the ornate tram station. Ornate and badly chewed by flechettes and a few heavier weapons, but the windows still spat out flechettes now and then. Bodies littered the approaches to the station, with a thick swathe between the trams themselves and the beleaguered Troopers. The bodies were mostly Plebs, but there were too many Troopers mixed with them for Bobby's liking.

"They'll run out of ammo in the end if the management don't send help." Sandman might be right, but the only way to get help involved going right through that horde.

"We can't break in through that lot." Siflis snorted. "Even at night I couldn't get through there. They're thicker'n fleas on Frog spam."

"My wrist comp can't raise anyone in there so something happened to their coms. We need a diversion." Bobby looked up at the Copter high above, circling without actually doing anything. "Pity they can't provide one."

Sandman chuckled. "We'd need more than that. We'll stick out like a bledrin Line Manager in a spam-house."

"We can cure that part." Bobby nodded to the Pleb bodies laid in the room, presumable killed while driving the Troopers into their present position. "Our weapons won't look out of place." Too many of the Plebs besieging the tram station had carbins and there were even Trooper sergeant shotguns out there. Bobby marked the positions of the Plebs on his wrist map.

"Dressed like that our own lot will shoot us and they'll shoot straighter than the Plebs. We need some sort of cover." Sandman had a point about the Troopers. They would be trigger-happy.

Bobby fixed Siflis with a glare. "How many flares have you got? The real number."

Siflis looked a bit shifty and then confessed. "Three red, one white and two green." He shifted uncomfortably. "But I've only got two pistols for them." Behind him Bells sniggered because Siflis hoarded gear and hated even admitting he'd got it.

"I've got a flare pistol, but we used up the flares trying to get help." Sandman spat on the floor. "For all the good that did."

Bobby looked back out of the window and reassessed, because that was better than expected. "You haven't got a shotgun or another grenade or two as well?" Sandman shook his head ruefully. "Right, we've got a plan. I just hope HQ really do send the column, because we'll never get out again on our own."

"You heard the dick. They won't abandon a Supervisor." Sandman didn't sound totally confident.

"I'm more worried about him carking it once we're in there. The last update the dick got before base lost the signal was that the Super had caught one. He's still alive, but if it was a bad one?" Bobby shrugged.

Sandman's brow furrowed in thought. "They know he's alive, so there must be some contact."

"Yeah, that's odd. Why do they need your radio in there before sending relief?" Bobby shook his head. "It doesn't matter. We go in there, or die out here eventually."

"So what's the plan?" Sandman smiled. "Yours must be better than mine, because I can't think of any that don't finish with me face down out there."

"Can you talk to the Copter? If not, it will have to go through the dick back in Control and the flyboy might not get the message through all the dohs. It'll take forever to get that bledrin Homer to understand, and then he's too full of his own to just pass it on."

Sandman adopted the monotone used to deliver official announcements. "Troopers are not allowed to contact Copters in case we divert them from essential missions." The rest sounded a lot more caustic. "Like taking fresh bog paper to the management."

"Typical. Well here's how it will go if the basted will pass the messages." The four heads bent in to listen and then spread out to pass the word. The men started stripping clothes from the right sized bodies, and conducting a thorough search for weapons and ammo. Bobby sighed, and contacted the Homer in Control. "If you want to get us in there to put the Supervisor on the radio, this is what we need. Sluur."

∗   ∗   ∗

Bobby watched the Copter as it moved away a bit before settling into a straight run. The twelve of them were now in a different building, one that gave them a better run at the tram station. The bodies in here had now been searched, and everyone's pockets and packs were crammed with various types of ammo and notsi weapons, the better ones. Some of the rejected weaponry might be as dangerous to the user as anyone else. "Let's go, nice and casual like, and slouch. We're Plebs, remember."

"Speak for yourself, I'm management slumming it." That brought a few nervous laughs but Bobby ignored Bells.

"You've got it straight?" Sandman, next to Bells, nodded. Siflis unravelled his wire and let it hang from one hand, then took position just behind Bobby.

The group wandered out of the doors and towards the rear of the Pleb lines. A few glanced back so Bobby waved. One of them gestured and Bobby spoke quietly. "Crouch a bit lads. The nice Pleb doesn't want us catching a flechette." All of them bent over and continued forward. Bobby moved over towards one of the two who appeared to be in some sort of command on this side. The man carried a shotgun and had two plebs just in front of him, presumably guards, while he sat behind the rest to direct them. Sandman moved towards the other possible commander, who also had a shotgun but only one guard.

Bobby stuck a hand in his pocket, casual-like, and eased his silenced pistol out a little. The man looked back and smiled. "We've gottem trapped like rats. There's a Super in there and I want the basted alive."

"Me too." Bobby smiled back and kept coming to pass nearby.

"That's a different shotgun. Where did you get it?" Bobby had the single barrelled in his other hand and he waved it. "Off a body of course." A couple of men glanced back and then looked forward again.

"Shite, what's that for!" The man looked forward where the Copter had just dropped three napalm kegs at the opposite side of the tram station. "Are they breaking out?" The rattle of weaponry rose as Plebs on the other side and a few here tried to shoot the Copter. As he came past the distracted commander Bobby brought out the silenced pistol to shoot both the guards in the back of the head. Then he knelt, quickly pulling them down below the heap of boxes. Bobby laid a carbin over the boxes as if he had taken over guard before glancing across.

Sandman sat holding the shotgun, with the dead Pleb out of sight at his feet. He'd even put on the dead man's safety helmet so that from a distance nothing had changed. Bells had settled in to replace the guard, holding some sort of oddball automatic. His wounded hand held the Kraut so Bells must still have some ammo. Bobby didn't look back because he knew the Pleb commander would still be sat behind him. Siflis would be holding the Pleb upright, though the wire round the dead man's throat would be impossible to see with his head tilted forward a bit.

The rest of Bobby's men came past, but then it started to unravel a bit. "Hey, you're not..." At least someone threw a knife instead of shooting the Pleb but more heads started to turn.

"Fire!" Three arms came up and three red flares shot off towards the tram station. One fell a bit short but all three started burning, emitting clouds of evil smelling smoke. The next two, the green ones, filled out the short line beyond the Pleb forward positions in no-man's land. Bobby raised his voice and pointed. "Smokescreen! Come on, let's get the Doggies." The Plebs often called the Troopers the management's guard dogs, or Doggies.

All twelve of Bobby's men started running through the startled Plebs, aiming for the front line. "Come on, quick, while we've got cover." Cries of agreement rose, and some of the Plebs lurched to their feet.

Behind him more shouts of "kill the Doggies" started up. Bobby hoped he could stop the Plebs now the basteds were started. The Plebs behind the piles of boxes and bodies forming the forward positions turned, startled, as a growing crowd pounded towards them. Bobby didn't give them a chance to decide on joining the twelve out in front or not.

"Now, Troopers!" All twelve opened up from the hip and the fifteen or so Plebs died in a hail of flechettes and buckshot. The twelve Troopers jumped up onto the forward positions then down the other side, running as if the CEO himself was after them. As he came over, Hood put his arm straight up and fired the white flare, before stumbling as his wounded leg buckled.

Bobby made a dozen paces before flechettes came whining past from behind and a few came through the smoke and flame ahead, from the Troopers. The smoke stank worse than the usual because the flares were burning into the thick carpet of bodies, so he daren't get nearer. "Drop! Get rid of the jackets!" Other voices took it up as Bobby pulled hard at his own Pleb jacket. The deliberately loosened fastening at the back split, and it came off and hit the floor. He turned and dropped behind a pair of bodies laid partly on each other, forming a small breastwork.

The ripping sound of Bells' Kraut cut through the air, and the hail of plastic catching the forward Plebs as they came over the barricade. Moments later more and more carbins joined in on full auto. The front ranks following Bobby died while the Plebs still coming over the bodies and boxes wavered as their comrades went down. Bobby got another round into the shotgun and let fly. The roar echoed a louder one from Sandman, letting go with both barrels of his capture. The combined buckshot tore holes in the crowd hesitating on the forward barricade. Then Siflis gave them both barrels of his new shotgun.

Someone in the tram station must have decided the sudden burst of firing meant trouble and a hail of flechettes came through the smoke and flame. "Heads down, heads down!" A Trooper flechette through the back of the head would be just as fatal as a Pleb fired bullet. Bobby put his carbin over the top of his protection and let a full clip go. There were only Plebs out there now so he swept it across to catch them about waist high. He peeked over, just in time for the finale.

The Copter arrived a bit late but if he'd needed the time to be that accurate, Bobby wouldn't complain. A long line of flame gushed skywards just behind the Pleb barricade, followed by screams and then thick smoke. The flame still burned inside the smoke as the screams reached a crescendo, then started to taper off. Bobby wasn't paying attention any more. "Crawl back, get away from the fire." Even as he spoke, Bobby carried on shooting any Plebs still this side of the wall of flame, as did most of his men. Shouting from behind caught his attention and Bobby rolled onto his back.

The smoke from the flares had thinned. He stuck the nearly white vest he'd taken from a body before they started onto the end of his carbin and lifted it, waving. "It's Beebi. Don't shoot, it's Beebi." He screamed it as loud as possible and four or five other voices took up the refrain, it's Beebi, until a bullhorn sounded from the tram station.

"Beebi? Why are you here you stupid basted?" The voice paused. "Ah, right. Do you want us to stop shooting?"

"Yes, you bledrin Homer. I've got a dozen out here, and we're part dressed as Plebs." Back in the tram station Bobby could hear the calls to cease fire. "I'm going to stand up. If you shoot me, I'll set Siflis and Bells on you!" Bobby went up onto his knees, calling out to his group. "You lot watch the Plebs. Two men give cover at each side so I'm not shot while I sort this." Short bursts started up on both flanks.

The bullhorn blared out. "We see you. Oke, come on in."

"Not until we get some more ammo or have you got plenty?" Bobby still had clips from the bags Sandman brought, but the bodies around him carried a lot more.

"Shite, no!" Another silence followed. "Yes, of course we have, but the Super says do what you usually do." Bobby smiled because his squad were always in trouble over stripping corpses for weapons and ammo.

"Right lads, sound off. Who made it?" Nine answered and two of the voices came from much too near the Plebs. One of those came from Hood and he didn't sound good. Bobby scuttled over.

"You bledrin eejit, you've got yourself shot." Hood's left leg looked a mess. "Hang on, I'll stick a bandage on."

"Thought I'd sprained it. That's three times tonight, all the same leg." Hood face had gone sheet white, and his grimace didn't come close to a smile.

"Lucky you, it's a metal job so there'll be no scars." Hood passed out when Bobby straightened his leg which stopped him twitching and probably screaming while Bobby tightened the tourniquets and lashed a carbin to the leg as a splint. He put on two tourniquets since the leg had to be a lost cause and they'd stop the rest of Hood from bleeding out. "Hey, give me a hand." The Trooper nearby stopped searching bodies to hook a hand under Hood's armpit, and they dragged him to the tram station. A Corporal stood just inside the door, hastily unbarred as they approached.

"Give me a dozen men to strip out ammo and weapons, sharpish. That smoke will die down soon."

The Corp glared at Bobby. "First, the Super said not. Second, I'm a Corp three and you're..."

"In charge. Do it." The Super might be through a door and didn't sound good, but his ears and voice worked. At least the Corp didn't argue so Bobby headed back out and sure enough a dozen Troopers came out after him.

"Every weapon, every round, even if it's notsi. Come on, sharpish." The flames from the napalm were dying back though the smoke still made a solid wall, a lot better than Bobby's impromptu version. Siflis came past, clutching his wounded arm and cursing but he'd got at least a dozen carbines slung round his neck and a pack full of something. Another five minutes and Bobby pulled everyone back inside. The volume of fire from the flanks increased as the Plebs recovered and moved people round the smokescreen.

Bobby came back inside last. He looked around properly, and everyone seemed to be wounded but mobile. A medic moved towards Hood with a hypodermic but Bobby caught hold of the man's arm. "No GV for Hood."

"I know, I saw the metal. This will stop the leg hurting as much." The medic scowled. "Reserved for you metal basteds."

"Who have just broken through that bledrin horde and into this hole to get you out." Bobby held the man's eyes until his gaze dropped and he nodded acknowledgement. Then Bobby beckoned Sandman and went to find the Super.

The Super looked a mess, his own personal abattoir. The splint and blood-soaked bandages on his leg looked bad enough, but the sodden mess of dressings on his gut told the real story. "Why are you back here, Beebi? I thought you had orders. From me?"

"Well some, er, Supervisor in Control changed them, sir. They want to talk to you before they'll send a relief column." Sandman offered the radio.

The Super's face hardened. "Yes, they would. Give me a minute Beebi, and then we'll have a chat." Bobby turned to go. "Ah, before you go, you'll need these." Bobby stared. Triple stripes!

"Er, not really sir. I'm no good at command. Anyway, the Corp out there is senior, and Sandman might be?"

"He is, they are, or rather they were. Battlefield promotion. I told you I'd get you one day, Beebi." The Super's smile showed some blood, a lot of pain, and some real humour as well. "Payback for all the times I've checked my bog before sitting."

"I though you meant to give me a Gaza Taxi sir, not stripes. I'll swap?"

"You're already in the Taxi, you bledrin Homer. I'll explain in a bit. Cut off two stars, because it's only to Sergeant One. Cover them when we break out, because that lot are targeting anyone with stripes." The Super coughed and swore. "At least you can carry a bledrin shotgun legally. Now sod off until I call. Sort that lot out." As Bobby exited the Super's voice followed. "Put the stripes on now, Beebi."

Sergeant

Bobby showed the stripes, then borrowed a couple of safety pins from a medic to hold them on temporarily. After a long look the Corp accepted the promotion and did what Bobby asked. Bobby went round the station to made sure the ammo and weapons were distributed, and all the notsi ammo went to someone with a weapon that could use it. That and the flechettes from Sandman sorted the ammo situation, but Bobby stressed that everyone had to stick to aimed triple shots. If the Plebs thought the Troopers were short of ammo and charged, then they'd be pooched. A lot of the men cheered up at that. Bobby didn't understand that when all he brought were nine men and most of them were wounded? He thought they all must have got too much smoke when the weed factory burned.

Sandman just laughed about the stripes. "You've been giving me orders all day, it's about time you made it official." Bobby worried because a Sarge had to have more men, at least a dozen, and he didn't want to look after more than Bells, Hood and Siflis. Then he cheered up when he realised they'd probably all be dead by tonight so it didn't matter. Bells produced a thin knife to cut the stitches on the surplus stars, and also a sewing kit. A sewing kit? For fixing new sheaths and pockets Bells claimed, but the needle and thread also fastened on stripes well enough.

When he called Bobby back to talk, the Super looked worse. "Sit, Beebi. You pair, go and work on someone who'll make it." The two medics left. "I'd offer you a drink, but I'm not allowed one so you can suffer as well." Bobby grimaced; that meant really gut-shot not a hole in the belly.

"I don't drink anyway."

"Shut it and listen. First off, you get the stripes because you might get the men out and Corporal Ellis won't. He'll make a competent defence, and die bravely, but he won't pull some crazy stunt and give them a chance." The Super raised a hand to stop Bobby replying while he took three very careful breaths. "Your squad are all nutcases, but the good sort and it's why I've left you alone." The Super took another couple of breaths. "Now the dick in Control has pooched you well and truly."

"Er..."

The Super gave a short laugh and winced. "Yes, we know what you call us though he really is a dick. He put you on the Gaza Taxi to cover his ass. You are supposed to die trying to get in, and then he doesn't have to send an expensive armoured column into that shitefest out there." The Super did the short laugh and wince thing again. "But you pooched the little toad, because you got here."

Bobby smirked. "I always obey orders sir."

The Super smiled and actually seemed happy. "You get it done, which isn't the same. Now I've pooched the basted in return. I've told him I'm fine, and to get the bledrin armour rolling, soonest." That sunny smile shouldn't be on a man who was so obviously dying. "Bump wrist maps and I'll give you the route the armour will use."

"But..."

"But I won't make it. But you can't break out." The Super wagged a finger at Bobby. "But I can make it happen. I will, just so you know that a Super can be a bledrin maniac as well." His face sobered. "They'll stop the armour once I die but if you've broken clear, keep going and get as many men out as possible. The armour might wait, and if not they'll have blown a hole through the Plebs because they're rolling now."

"Can't we dig in and wait if they're coming?"

"No, because I won't last. Then when I cark it the armour will stop, and you'll all die because hell will be unleashed."

Bobby stared, shocked. "You'd do that to us?"

"No. Control will. You know all the stories about last defences, and the Super unleashing hell as the basteds closed in?" Bobby nodded. There were never any survivors from those. "The Supers didn't do it. The Supers died." He tapped his chest. "If I die this signal stops, and another goes off. It's an aiming point. Since they know I'm in trouble there'll be at least two real warplanes way up high just in case. The Plebs have never had a Super's body as a trophy, and never will."

Bobby stared, stunned. "But what about the men?"

"Do you think the upper management actually care about them, compared to the embarrassment of a Supervisor's head on someone's wall?" The Super shook his head. "Not this time, Beebi. This time there will be survivors."

"How? Why?"

"Why is because I've been a Supervisor too long. I like my Troopers so I don't fit and don't get promoted. You assholes do a shite job, and do it well." The Super took a few more careful breaths. "Now I'll explain how we'll manage that. When you break out, I'll stay. The plebs will storm the place because you'll leave me a couple of carbins. I'll bet you've got plenty of spares." The Super looked quizzically at Bobby but he didn't answer.

"Yes you have, you always have. The Plebs will charge in here, and as they come through the door I'm going to eat a bullet. You understand eat a bullet?" Bobby nodded. "It's a Supervisor or Manager thing, if we really pooch it. In this case it will send the signal." He smiled. "Then hundreds of the Plebs chasing you will disappear in a cloud of smoke and body parts. Once you break contact, my creds are on you keeping the men going and getting them out."

"They'll shoot me. The management." Bobby knew that as soon as management realised Acting-Sergeant Bobby B had left the Super, they'd be picking a firing squad.

The Super waved a little disc in a plastic sleeve. "You'll have Sandman's radio to contact your own Control, because I've given them the right frequency now. When we're ready to go I'll transmit your orders. Orders, Beebi, and they're also on this disc. In return I want a favour."

"A favour sir?" Now Bobby had really lost track. How did a temporary Sergeant One do favours for a dying Super?

The Super pulled out a small package with writing on the front, encased in plastic. "Post this for me. It's postage paid and won't be opened by anyone because of who it's going to. This contains a last message to my family and it is important, Beebi."

"No problem sir. I'll tell Bells and Siflis about it, in case." Bobby shouldn't post anything without giving it to the office, but thought that more than fair exchange to get anyone out of here. Shite! A Super with balls! And brains! It was a bledrin pity he was going to cark it.

"Right, good idea. Get the Troopers sorted, Beebi, and I'll get the hole opened."

"Where, sir?"

"Shite. I'm starting to lose it so we'd better hurry. When you're ready a Copter will drop HE on a concentration of Plebs. He's got plenty to choose from but it'll be between here and the engine sheds. The second drop will hang and land just outside the end of this building and on top of the nearest Plebs. Oops." The Super gave a short laugh and winced again. "I must stop that. Anyway, the Plebs won't expect property destruction, and while they're recovering you'll take the men straight through the wreckage. The two HE drops will have badly disrupted the cordon just there and you'll only have a short dash to the engine sheds. The doors should be blown in by the HE and there's lots of big iron to hide behind in there. The rest of the Plebs will storm this place before they follow and then, boom."

Bobby thought it through. There were a lot of problems after that, but none that would be worrying the Super. "Thank you, sir. For the men. I'll be ready as soon as possible." Bobby did what he'd always sworn not to do; he gave a Super his very best attempt at a parade ground salute.

"That was still a crap salute, Beebi. Now sod off before I start crying or you try to kiss me goodbye." Bobby did as he was told, because he'd got something in his bledrin eye that needed rubbing. It didn't take long to get organised. Most of that came down to persuading everyone the Super would do it. Even a Homer could understand this battle plan, charge as soon as the explosions stopped and kill anything in the way. Bobby took two carbins and an extra clip for each to the Super.

"Time already?"

"Whenever you like, sir."

"Give me a hand over to the window, Beebi, so I can shoot lumps off the trams."

Bobby did his best to smile. "That's deliberate destruction of corporate property sir."

"I won't tell if you don't. Ghhnhu."

"Sorry sir." Bobby surprised himself by meaning that.

The Super tried for a smile, though it didn't have much humour in it. "It's all right. A spare clip for each? Long clips? Will I have time?"

"Fire triple shots at the paintwork. When they charge, go full auto. You'll get them off all right." Bobby tucked a notsi revolver into the Super's jacket front. "In case none of them can shoot."

"A notsi? It might jam."

"It might misfire, but just pull again. Revolvers don't jam. Certainly not that one because it came from Bells." A real smile tugged at Bobby's lips.

A real smile came through the pain to answer him. "Ha. Got you! I'll report it when we get back."

"See you at the hearing sir." Bobby waited while the Super called the Copter, then collected the radio.

*   *   *

The Super's plan worked and there really were warplanes lurking on high. Unleash hell went well past spectacular, and Bobby could see why there were usually no survivors. By the time the debris and body parts stopped flying about the surviving Troopers were already a good distance from the other side of the engine sheds, opening a gap. Under forty of them now because although only five died in the actual breakout, another four were hit too hard to move far. They volunteered to stay and slow up any pursuit as long as they could. The men promised it would be long enough to bunch the basteds up right around where the Super's body was.

Hood should have been left with them, but Bells and Siflis put a shoulder under each of his arms and more or less carried him. That medic shot to sort the pain worked like magic because he didn't scream once. In fact, when they paused in the sheds, Hood started using his rifle. It wobbled a bit so maybe Hood wasn't hitting much but probably kept heads down. Then he passed out again as the whole group moved as fast as possible away from the fire and the fury.

Hood didn't slow the group up because another three were being held upright, others were limping and at least five were working one-handed. Bells had Hood's arm lashed around his neck and one arm bound up but could still use a hand to shoot. He now had seven notsi pistols as well as the Kraut. Initially the whole group just went straight forward, away from the tram station, then cut sharply towards the armoured column if the basteds were still there. During the first pause Bobby called HQ to let them know there were survivors.

Bobby didn't answer the radio questions after confirming that some Troopers were still alive and heading to meet the armour. He didn't want to argue just now, especially if he got the wrong dick on the radio because then when Bobby got back they'd need two firing squads and a Taxi, just for him. The route ahead seemed clear without a single armed Pleb, and at first they all thought that was blind luck. Then the group ran over a dozen armed Plebs heading away from them.

That cost another Trooper dead and two collected extra wounds but the Plebs were more surprised or training counted because all twelve died. The prisoner answered the questions first time, quickly, without holding them up or needing severe persuasion so Sandman cut his throat nice and clean as a thank you. According to the man, every Pleb with a weapon had been told to get to the armour. Some Pleb had cracked the radio codes so mines were waiting for the vehicles. Everyone had been asked to bring petrol bombs, for when the armour had been stopped.

"Beebi to Armour. Beebi to Armour." He hadn't any call signs but the radio had picked up what had to be the armour on this channel.

"Call signs, dickhead."

"Not got any, tindick."

"Yeah, that's you. Why are you calling us?"

"You're supposed to be heading to the tram station to pick us up." Bobby had everything crossed, but that superstition was obviously bulsh because…

"Not you. Our passenger cancelled so we're heading home again."

"According to our prisoner, you should mind where you step. Might be an idea not to park under anything tall as well." Bobby didn't bother crossing anything this time.

"What?"

"Mines and Molotovs. We saw a homemade mine at work and it flipped an armoured car." Bobby smiled to himself. "Here, I've got one of the passengers." He passed the radio to Sandman.

"Corporal Sandman, 659th Armoured."

"Shite! I thought you were dead." The radio shut up, and then a few moments later a different voice came on. "Who is this?"

"Corporal Sandman of the 659th with Sergeant One Bobby B and the remains of the unit trapped in the tram station, 3914 SSAB-Tata. Sir." Sandman shrugged at Bobby, the radio sounded like a sir.

"Yes, we heard about Beebi." The voice didn't like what it had heard. "We thought you all died when the Super unleashed hell. Why did you get out?"

"The Super sent us out first because he'd been hit. He said it would give us a chance to get clear and gave Beebi his map. Where are you?"

"Heading home. What?" The "what" wasn't aimed at Sandman and faint muttering followed before the radio went dead. Beebi's enlarged Basteds kept going while waiting for a reply and Bobby passed the word that he wanted another prisoner.

"Put Beebi on."

"Beebi. Er, Sergeant Bobby B."

The voice didn't care about rank. "Whatever. What's this about mines?"

"We've been having a good run, with no real opposition. A prisoner said that's because they've dug in mines to catch you lot. Every Pleb is heading your way with a bottle of petrol and a bad attitude." Bobby didn't need to cross anything because this voice was already interested enough to wait to talk.

"Shite! Where are the mines?"

"He didn't know." Nobody had asked since right then it didn't matter. "We're looking for someone to ask. Don't go into any narrow places."

"Bledrin comedian. We're in a big square right now, reorganising to go home, and the Plebs are shooting from every window. Not that it's having any effect on armour." A note of alarm crept in. "Unless they've mined the square?"

"Not unless it's already gone boom. Mining a square didn't work so well last time and cost them hundreds at the least. I reckon they'll have covered the roads forward and back at least." Bobby didn't want the armour to move so he laid it on a bit. "Those mines are big, and even a near miss will blow tracks at least."

"Beebi. Search party coming this way. Fifty or sixty and forward scouts say they're searching the buildings." Bobby didn't even know the man but that didn't alter the news.

He glanced at those nearest, leaving the radio mic off. "That last group of Plebs we chopped must have got off a message or someone heard the fight. We'll break sideways once I look at the map." Bobby didn't want contact with the enemy, not yet and not in those numbers. He keyed the radio to talk to the armour.

"We've got a big group coming this way, and one of them has to know more if we can snag a prisoner. We can't just kill them all because there are too many and they'll have time to call for help. We'd be buried in Plebs, so I'm going quiet for a bit." Bobby waited for a reply, though he intended doing it anyway.

"Right sergeant. We'll wait to hear from you before moving." At least the use of sergeant sounded genuine this time.

*   *   *

Bobby looked at his map, at the state of the men, and pointed to an accommodation block before raising his voice. "In there lads."

"Again? We'll never get out."

Siflis laughed. "We got out last time Bells. Someone try that door and break it if it's locked."

A voice raised in automatic protest, "We can't do that! They'll take it out of our pay."

"The Super told me to kill anyone and break anything necessary. He didn't confine it to Plebs." Bobby glared and the Corp subsided. "What's your name anyway?"

"Corporal Ellis." Someone said 'Elli the Funt' just loud enough to be heard and the Corp whirled.

"Ellis." He looked back at Bobby. "Break that bledrin door, and the next time you argue will be the last." Ellis looked around at the glowering faces and the pistol in Bells's hand and headed for the door.

Within moments the door swung open. "Inside you lot, and keep quiet." Sandman produced a pistol and waved it at Bobby. "This won't be as loud as a burst of carbin if someone's waiting."

"This is quieter." Bobby waved the silenced one. "You take the rear with Bells. Someone else help Hood." He looked round to make sure it happened. "Can you still throw, Bells?"

"Yeah but slower with the second knife because I can't hold it ready." The notsi pistol disappeared and a knife appeared instead.

"Sandman, let Bells take his throw first if someone comes, to keep it quiet. Use the gun if he misses." Bobby looked round the group. "We're going to go down the corridor in here and we'll pick a room on the opposite side to where we came in. With some luck we'll go out of the window after they've gone past outside, and while they're still going room to room in here."

"If not?" A mystery voice, but fair enough.

"We kill this lot and head for the armour as fast as possible." A ripple of laughter followed that, gallows humour because the shooting would attract more Plebs.

"I'll hold them up." Hood had a stubborn set to his jaw, and Bobby knew the sniper had it right. Hood couldn't move quickly so he should be left as a sacrificial rearguard. He'd even volunteered to make it easy for Bobby.

"If that's what happens, Bells will leave you the Kraut." Bells didn't complain, a bad sign. The group moved down the corridor and several men tried doors.

"They're all locked!"

"Lockdown. This lot are on lockdown."

"Break one in."

"No!" Everyone went quiet while Bobby explained. "They'll see the broken door and know it's us, or at least they'll check. We need an open door. Head for the stairway and if need be we'll try the next floor." The group headed on down the corridor and from well ahead came shouting and thumping.

"They're at the door at the other end, so they'll be trying the one by the stairs soon. What about the broken one behind? They'll come straight in and then we'll be caught between them." Corporal Ellis hesitated, torn between going on and defending behind.

"Calm down, don't be a Funt, Elli." Siflis smiled innocently as the Corp turned towards him. "I kicked a knife under the door and drove one in at the top as wedges. It's solid."

*   *   *

Bobby almost shot her. Two doors ahead a tousled head came out of a doorway, looking towards the stairway and the banging beyond. Instead he accelerated and even as she turned towards him, Bobby had her! She went back into the room with a hand round her throat and two more men came through the door with blades ready, but the apartment seemed empty. A quick check of the shower room and bedroom and one of the men gestured to her with a knife.

"No. Because our friend here is going to relock her door for us." Bobby looked into the shocked brown eyes. "Without screaming. Aren't you?" Her head tried to nod so Bobby let it. "Shhh. No noise." He turned to the men. "Everyone in here, as fast as possible but silent. I want Ellis."

Ellis came round the door and his eyes widened. Bobby didn't wait for a comment. "Six men, three doors down. Break the lock, kill anyone in there, ransack the room, pull out the bars and unfasten the windows. Do not open them. If you're quick, you'll get back before this door's locked." Ellis's mouth opened.

"Four doors down." Everyone looked at the woman. "Empty. Quieter." She probably didn't want her neighbours killed but still had a good point.

Bobby looked back at Ellis, "Four doors down. Move or die!" The corporal moved, collecting men. The rest crammed into the flat and tried to spread out but there wasn't space. "Absolute silence. They'll break an outside door soon since nobody's answering." Bobby looked back at the woman and put the pistol away. "You can override the lockdown?"

"A boyfriend did it, a long time ago. So we could, well." She looked away.

"If you want to live, when the last man's in, you lock the door. Then when the searchers have gone, unlock it and we'll leave."

Her answer wasn't defiant, just resigned. "You'll kill me anyway."

"We'll tie you up, and gag you so it takes about an hour to chew through. By then it won't matter." Though killing her would be a lot simpler. Right now Bobby worried more about Ellis. If the Funt took too long Bobby would lock the door and let the seven men fight and die in the corridor, but he didn't want to lose seven men.

Splintering noises sounded from the main door down the corridor as the last Trooper almost shut the broken door four down and legged it to join the rest. "Done, Sarge."

"Now lock this place down." The young woman produced a keycard from her dressing gown pocket and drew it across the inside of the lock. Not through the reader, but the lock buzzed and the red light came on. Bobby turned the room light off and they all waited in the faint glow of one remaining street lamp outside.

Shouting echoed out in the corridor now, and fists thumping on doors. A voice down the corridor spoke up. "They're not in here, it's all locked down."

"Check the doors."

A minute or so later. "This door's broken!" Muffled shouting and crashing followed and soon afterwards voices outside were denying having missed anything. Fists banged on other doors now and questions were being shouted.

"Check the other doors. Ask who's in there."

Bobby pulled his bayonet, putting it close to the woman's neck. "Answer, and make it good. If you don't, you'll die first." He moved the blade away a little until she nodded, jerkily. Moments later a fist banged on the door.

"Open up."

"It's locked down." She sounded frightened, but that wouldn't raise any alarms under the circumstances.

"Who else is in there?"

"Nobody."

"Did you hear anything?"

"Some people came past going towards the stairs and there was some banging. What's happening?" Bobby smiled reassuringly, then hoped he looked reassuring when she flinched.

"Some Doggies running for their lives. We'll find them." The voices moved away and the commanding one sounded again.

"You three, check up the stairs but I reckon they've gone. With luck they'll reach the armour, then when they go home we'll get the lot." General laughter followed that, then died away. Voices and footsteps moved down the corridor and silence fell.

*   *   *

Bobby put a finger to his lips as several started to speak. He pointed to the radio, then to the shower and toilet cubicle and to himself. Bobby crammed himself in there and shut the sliding door, not easy with his Trooper gear on. He used the radio to contact the armour. "Bobby B."

"About time. Did you get one? A prisoner?" Typical dick, didn't care about how many might have been lost.

Bobby took a deep breath and kept it polite. He needed the transport. "Don't head straight home. That's definite. Ten minutes and we may have a better source."

"Ten minutes? Why so long?" A short pause followed. "And sergeant still means you call me sir."

"Yes sluur." Bobby smiled to himself. "The main group have missed us but three were left to check around. In about ten minutes they'll walk right into our hands and then we'll have a chat. The ones outside were shouting about catching us and the armour on your way back."

"Well done sergeant. They tried to rush us here, but that didn't work and you were at least partly right. There were plebs throwing petrol bombs from the buildings but we're too far away." The voice chuckled. "Lights them up nicely though." He paused, then sighed. "We'll wait here for one hour as fair return for the info on the mines. Then we will break out because I don't want to give the Plebs too long to think."

"Thank you sir." That deserved a real sir. "If we don't make it by then, it won't matter. Must go. Noises." Bobby turned the radio off. Someone had started arguing inside the flat and those were Hood's deep tones. Bobby took out his silenced pistol before carefully easing the door open a little.

Ellis had the woman backed up against the wall with her dressing gown open at the top, and had hold of her breast. He wasn't doing any more because Hood had jammed his big rifle into Ellis's spine. Hood still looked sheet white but the rifle stayed rock steady. Hood spoke again. "No."

"Why not? The sarge will." Ellis drew a thumb across his throat while two other men started to move behind Hood. "Seems a waste."

"He said no." One of the moving men stopped suddenly as Siflis spoke from right behind him. Another man stirred, but a stage cough caught everyone's attention. Then everyone stood very still. Bells had used the Kraut in the breakout so they all knew what it was and these men also thought Bells crazy enough to pull the trigger. They didn't know if the ammo would go through a Trooper jacket at this range. It would, just, and might cause flesh wounds, but Bells would aim at their faces anyway.

Ellis still wasn't backing down so Bobby coughed as well. He crooked a finger at Ellis. The Corporal came over, pale-faced because Bobby kept the pistol on him all the way. When he came near enough for whispering, Bobby spoke. "Why shouldn't I kill you, Ellis?"

"But she's only a Pleb."

"A Pleb who saved our lives." Bobby made a snap decision, probably because he didn't like Ellis. "She lives. Now you pass a message to your crew, or Siflis will pass it." Ellis glanced at Siflis and flinched from the evil smile. "If any of them breath hard on the woman, or in the direction of my squad, you all bleed." Bobby smiled and he got this expression right because Ellis flinched again. "What happens?"

"We all bleed."

"Now piss off and tell them." Bobby kept half an eye on the Corp as he headed over towards Hood. The first couple the Corp spoke to gave Siflis a startled glance so the message went home.

"Cover up." The woman pulled her clothes together. Bobby looked at Hood. "You look rough. Go in there and lie on the bed." He looked back at the woman. "You go as well." She shrank into herself a bit. "No, eedjit, not to get in the bed with him. He's the one that stopped them and anyway pooching is the last thing on Hood's mind. Get him a drink and see if you can do anything with his leg? Pad it or something so he doesn't bang it about as much." She nodded. "What's your name?"

"Margaret."

"We'll be here for a little while Margaret, then we'll sod off and leave you." This time he meant it.

Margaret seemed to believe Bobby this time. "Take me with you."

"What?"

"I told them a lie, those others. If only one person hears you go they'll find out and come for me. They'll kill me but not straight away." Her eyes were wide and really frightened of that thought, not Bobby, which surprised Bobby. Troopers were usually the worst thing that could happen to a Pleb.

Bobby glanced at Hood, weighing up his size and hers. He smiled because this would really piss off Ellis, and more importantly it might save Hood. "You have to help. No passengers. Are you strong enough to help him to walk?"

"Yes. Anything as long as you take me."

"Right, get him comfortable, and get yourself dressed. Trousers if you've got them." Bobby went around to make sure everyone drank, and used the bog while there was a chance, and to tell them hands off the woman or else. Those who needed to do so dealt with wounds or changed dressings on older ones. He gave the searchers upstairs seven minutes before going to get Margaret.

"Time to go." Bobby looked her over. She'd muffled up in a coat with a hood and baggy trousers. "Do you need to do something special, or can I open the door while you get Hood up and ready to move?"

"Put the back of the card to the lock and go across it the usual way. The same to lock it from outside." Margaret handed the card over and Bobby squeezed through everyone as they finished settling weapons and burdens into place. He put a finger to his lips, unlocked the door, and cracked it open as quietly as possible. Siflis slid his little mirror out to look both ways.

"Clear."

"Everyone keep very, very quiet." Bobby eased out of the door and listened. There were voices upstairs so his timing must be about right. Bobby put his head back inside. "I need five men with working legs and arms. I want two of these men dead and one alive, but silently. Better dead than noisy." Five men detached themselves from the rest, creeping through the door and after him. Three crossed to the other side of the foyer, then the six of them waited.

It had to be worth a try but in the end, silent meant dead. Bobby himself cut the third one's throat as he opened his mouth. That's the trouble with stunning someone; not hard enough and they yelled, too hard and they died. Bobby beckoned to the flat down the corridor. Moments later the whole group were on the move, as quietly as possible. Margaret walked under Hood's armpit, taking as much weight off his leg as possible. Her eyes widened as they passed the three bodies, now being thoroughly looted.

Partway down the outside of the next block, Margaret repaid them for her life. As voices approached she pointed to a pair of low doors. The padlock quickly yielded but instead of finding a storage cupboard they all slid down a coal chute. The small group of Plebs passing by never even glanced at the doors, or not enough to notice the missing padlock. The boiler room exited near the other end of the block, up a set of stairs, and the small force crept on.

In the end, coming out of the last block to join up, they had to make a noise. "Bobby B to Armour. I can see you from a stairwell, two floors up, but we'll have to shoot our way in and then it's a long way over open ground. It's the only way to get through the Plebs behind the barricade."

"Where. Plain-speak because they've broken the codes."

The armoured Troop Carriers had turned in different directions to point their frontal armour at the nearest barricade or accommodation block. "Barricade directly ahead of your third vehicle. We can kill these I reckon but the rest will shoot us crossing the open ground."

"Double click when you're set, and come ahead when they break. Be quick because they'll hear this radio message." This Super had brains as well. The armour fired up their engines, and when Bobby clicked the seven vehicles lunged for the exit towards Bobby. Their heavy weapons lashed the low barricade and the defenders scattered because the Plebs wanted the armour down that road, any road. The armour stopped short of the barricade and any mines. "Come on then, quick."

Beebi's reinforced Basteds poured out of the building, killing the Plebs hiding in the doorway and the one opposite. The armour swivelled, as did the turrets, to lash the nearest buildings and barricades while the rear doors of the troop carriers opened. All of Bobby's group made it because the fallen were brought with the Troopers, but some were dead when the heavy doors slammed shut. Bobby glanced at Margaret before taking the tags off the slightly built Trooper lying on the floor by his feet. Just in time.

"Strip them and dump them." Those were standing orders with the dead so a couple of the Troopers stripped the body near Bobby. Those stripping the other body in this carrier proffered the snapped tags, signifying the man had carked it, for Bobby to add to the pocket full he already had. The Super kept advancing between the sitting Troopers until he reached Bobby. "Sodit Beebi, you really are a Sergeant. You've even got the bledrin stripes on so now I know we really are in the shite."

"All legal slur. Though you could take them away for not saluting?" Bobby smiled. "Or carrying a notsi?" He waved his shotgun.

"Still a cheeky basted. Anyway, you're allowed a shotgun now." Sandman passed Bobby a standard double barrelled one with a bandolier half full of shells. The Super shook his head. "Not in my chain of command, all praise the ultimate CEO and his blessed minions. Now make me happy and give me a clear run out."

"We tried, but the basteds all carked it."

"Shite. I hope you've got your fireproof underwear on. Pick East or West since you've got to be Lady Luck's favourite boy tonight."

"South-East." Bobby smiled.

"Smartarsed basted. There's a sodin building in the way."

Bobby grinned. "How strong is the front of this thing?" The Super looked at Bobby, puzzled. "I've been thinking about it after seeing your transport. If you go through an accommodation block anywhere but where the stairs and lifts or the concrete firebreak cross-walls are, it's all plasterboard. Even a bledrin flechette goes through them close up, so if you can ram through the outside walls?"

The Super grinned back at him. "We don't have to ram them. The light cannon on two of these babies will go through a brick wall like Epsom's. We'll loosen them up then yes, the armour on the front will do the rest." He turned to go, then turned back. "Though the bill for the property damage will probably mean eating a bullet, or at least a lot of shite."

Bobby beckoned and played back the recording from when the Super first told him to get clear. "Break anything and anyone. Those are still my orders. Do you want me to aim the weapon?"

"No sergeant, but I want that recording for when I'm sued." Bobby copied it to the Super's wristcomp. "How far to get clear of the mines?"

"I don't know but three streets seems a good bet."

"Good enough. I want the same lottery numbers as you this week, if we make it." The Super tapped his head for luck and went.

The armoured troop carriers had pulled back after picking up the survivors but now they lurched into motion again. The whole vehicle shuddered as the cannon struck up with five rounds rapid. It fell silent while the carrier clattered forward until the nose rose, followed by a solid impact on the front. The carrier hesitated and then ground on, up, and over an obstacle before rumbling onwards. Behind it the others would be lashing the front of the block with heavy flechettes to stop any petrol bombs.

A muted cheer echoed through the steel shell, despite the continual small impacts on the exterior. The vehicle stopped and the shuddering started up again as the gun chewed holes out of the opposite exterior wall. Then the carrier went down and presumably outside again. The same procedure happened twice more before the vehicle slowed before picking up speed. The rescued Troopers echoed the muffled cheer from the fighting and driving compartments forward.

A medic came through into the rear to work on the wounded. He just shook his head at Hood's leg. "Metal." He moved on to Margaret, huddled inside her coat and hood. "Let me look at you."

"Not that one." Bobby kept his voice down.

The medic looked annoyed but also inquisitive. "Not down to a sergeant. The Super says I'm to check everyone. Still, why not this one?"

Bobby leaned in closer and kept his voice low. "Spook."

"Still got to check him."

"This one was in deep cover, and broke it to get us out. Do you want to identify one of The Horseman's deep agents?" Bobby chuckled. "He'd shoot you to keep the identity secret."

The medic moved back as if Margaret was infectious. "That's bulsh." He glanced at Bobby, then Margaret. "Above my pay grade so I'll leave it to the Super."

"Good enough." The medic checked Bobby over before resetting the splint on his forearm. The basted wasn't overly gentle either. Once the medic moved on to the rest and got busy with bandages, Bobby moved up closer to Margaret.

"Don't speak or keep your voice as deep and quiet as possible. Here." Bobby passed over the tags. "That's who you are for now. Wear them and show them if you really have to. Claim to be a deep cover spy for The Horseman. Put these gloves on because your hands are too small." Margaret took the studded leather gloves and her hands disappeared inside them. The tags went inside her hood.

"The Horseman?"

"That's what we all call the Spook-master since nobody seems to know his name. It's supposed to be because he's the Headless Horseman, or one of the Horsemen of the Apocalypse, or all of them. He's in charge of all the spies and cameras, the ones you don't see, and some deep and dirty shite. Just keep saying deep cover, and The Horseman won't want it broken."

"Deep cover." Her voice deepened a bit. "The Horseman wants it kept deep."

"Good enough."

Bobby sat back and tried to work out what to do about the young woman. He'd brought her to keep Hood alive and flick Ellis, expecting to leave her behind at the end. Then Margaret had come with them, helping Bobby to support Hood during the last dash. If any Super knew Bobby had brought in a Pleb woman, he'd shoot her or Margaret would end up in the spam house. She'd be cleaning Trooper's quarters in the day and servicing Troopers at night which wasn't much of a thanks for saving Hood. He owed her for that. That basted Ellis would turn Margaret in just so he could give her a good pooching in the spam house and rub it in Bobby's face. She'd have to disappear before that arse opened his flap though the Corp wouldn't dare do that until he'd got safely away from Siflis.

At least trying to work out where to hide a young woman in a Trooper base kept Bobby occupied. The Super showed up before they got back, to speak very quietly to Bobby. "I'm told that's a spook."

"Yes. Deep cover. Broke it to get us out so I feel responsible, and a bit nervous about The Horseman." Bobby smiled. "Might be best if none of us noticed him being here?"

The Super looked long and hard at Bobby, then glanced at Margaret. "You want to say anything?" Margaret shook her head, firmly. "All right, Beebi. On your head." The Super left and Bobby heaved a sigh of relief.

*　　*　　*

Thirty minutes later the carriers were unloading and he started sweating again. Bobby caught hold of Siflis and Bells. "Get Margaret and Hood into the bog. Tell Hood he needs to go. Tell her she needs to help him. Now and quickly. Then clear the bogs of Troopers."

It wasn't that simple because Sandman followed, he'd turned out to be too bledrin smart by half. Bobby turned stop the Corp. "I'm going to do something that will put you in a Gaza Taxi if you're involved."

"Again? Tell you what, I'll help but I want that notsi shotgun. You don't need it now you're a Sarge." Sandman grinned, the stupid basted.

Bobby shrugged. "I need the bog clear for five minutes."

Sandman glanced at Margaret helping Hood through the door. "All of you in five minutes? She'll never manage it."

"No, you bledrin eejit. She's going to disappear, else where will they put her?"

The Corp looked at the door thoughtfully. "Yeah. She saved my ass so

I'm in. Ellis will open his flap."

Bobby smirked. "In five he'll never find her."

"This I've got to see." Sandman waved over one of his surviving men. "This is Attica. He's sound, my word on it." He turned to the approaching Trooper. "Hey, Attic, we need the bogs to ourselves for a few minutes. A meeting of the unruly, but we need a blind man on the door."

"Oke." The Trooper put on an innocent expression. "Never saw nobody go in or out, sir. Bogs were out of order. Terrible mess it was, sir."

Three confused Troopers came out doing up their flies as Bobby went in. The Basteds and Margaret were stood in the middle of the floor, looking puzzled. Bobby gestured to one of the stalls. "Get in there Margaret, and get undressed." Her hood went back and she looked warily from one to the other. "Then put this uniform on." Bobby proffered some of the gear stripped from the dead men. "You are whoever it says on those tags and these are your Trooper uniform. Come on, sharpish."

Margaret looked at the stalls and back. Ah, Bobby had got used to not having a door on them. "Sandman, you're a big lad. Stand in front will you?" Everyone looked at the stalls, Margaret, and Sandman, and realised. Though Bells surprised Bobby when even he turned away.

Four minutes later a slightly built Trooper with his face covered in camo paint helped Hood out of the bogs and over to the ambulances. Then Trooper Nathaniel Wright came back to meet Sergeant Bobby B as he exited the bogs, limping to disguise her walk. Bobby, Bells and Siflis took her into their quarters where Bobby explained. "You live in here. There's supposed to be eight in here but we aren't very welcoming so there's just us four. Five now. Long term we'll work it out, but for now we'll bring you food and keep you out of sight."

"Why? There are women out there." Margaret looked at the beds apprehensively.

"Those women clean the quarters in the day, and they work in the spam palace at night. If any Super sees you, that's where they'll put you. That or shoot you." Bobby really didn't want to be more specific, and everyone knew what a spam palace was.

No they didn't. "What is a spam palace? What sort of work is it?"

"It's a place for women. For the men. For the Troopers who want to meet a woman." The snigger from Bells didn't help but meant that Margaret got it. They all knew because she suddenly looked anywhere but the three of them and blushed. After that Margaret became very keen to stay out of sight until Bobby worked something out, not even objecting when Bells gave her a Trooper haircut with a knife.

*   *   *

The debrief turned out to be simple. Bobby handed over the little disc, and the orders on his buzzer and recorded on the radio were copied. He had his forearm re-bandaged and the base medic reckoned the bone had only been cracked. Bells would get metal in his arm, Hood would get most of a metal leg, and Siflis would get away with losing a toe. The rest of their wounds were just meat. The injections of Kwikheal could deal with that and any infection after the bullets or fragments were dug out. Everyone had gained even more interesting scars but that came with the job. The survivors were placed on leave though they were kept in the base.

Meanwhile fresh Trooper Units came in from outside the area and swept through the housing complexes. The new Troopers worked by the rules, only using flechettes, but the sheer number of casualties over the last two days seemed to have taken the fire out of the Plebs. Eventually the rebels or rioters were broken with the minimum of additional damage to buildings and plant. The surviving Plebs, the ones who could prove they weren't involved, went back to work. Any who couldn't prove their innocence went to work camps though the Troopers assumed that some of them would end up in the new crop of Timers. The bulldozers moved in and rebuilding started.

Bells only needed a plate in his arm, to keep the forearm bones in place and replace some of them. Within a week he could use his arm but wasn't allowed to put a lot of strain on the repair for another few weeks until the Kwikheal finished the job. He made a few hints about having a woman handy in the quarters, but Bobby put it to him straight. Margaret saved Hood, which made her off-limits unless she actually offered.

Bobby knew the real problem. Bells didn't rate the Trooper Divas and every week or two the squad made time on a patrol to let him visit one of the sleeker Pleb Divas. Now he couldn't get a bit of variety, even with a woman three beds down. Bells backed off though he still eyed her up when Margaret couldn't see him.

Though Bells didn't do that as much after Hood arrived back in the barracks because she took up nursing duties again. Hood exercised as much as possible with a leg missing and while pumped full of painkillers and Kwikheal. He had to clip his new leg onto the bio-metal interface plate four times a day to let the nerves and wiring mesh, but while laid down so he didn't strain the healing join. Margaret usually clipped and unclipped his leg because it was easier if someone else lined it up. The rest of the time Hood hopped around one-legged.

* * *

Bobby and Siflis were bored after a couple of weeks, just hanging about healing and eating and the healing didn't take long with Kwikheal. Neither of them neglected exercise or keeping their fighting skills honed either sparring or on the ranges, and probably overdid it to keep occupied. Then Margaret learnt enough to really train, which certainly relieved some of the boredom. Siflis treated her like a sister. He even let drop his own sister used to beat the crap out of him three out of four. Now he wanted Magpie up to that sort of standard.

Margaret now answered to Magpie, a good nickname for a Trooper that wouldn't attract attention if overheard. She said most people called her Maggie so she'd respond to Magpie without thought. Siflis came up with Magpie, meaning the Trooper might be 'one for sorrow' in the rhyme so bledrin dangerous, or a thieving shite, but either worked. Every day Bobby and Siflis taught Magpie how the Trooper unit worked and how to act like one of the men. Most of the talking happened as she sweated, using weights or exercises to toughen her up. She practiced hand to hand with and without knives or knuckles in the quarters, as well as having a crash course in how other weapons worked.

Then Margaret spent some time on the ranges as Magpie. The nickname meant never having to use her adopted name which would stop anyone who knew Nathaniel Wright from realising he'd had a face transplant. Margaret's face caused problems but luckily she hadn't been petite or pretty, and a faint application of camo looked as if she almost needed a shave. A few men looked effeminate anyway but those men were usually good with knives or fists because of the shite they got from other Troopers. Hopefully others would assume the same about Magpie, until the squad could actually make her dangerous. Sergeant Bobby B added Trooper Nathaniel Wright to his squad, officially. A sergeant should have more men, and Trooper Wright's old Corporal died on the way to the tram station, so the paperwork went through without making waves.

So far nobody had given Bobby the extra four squads to match his rank, which suited Bobby just fine right up until he found out why. The banging on the door startled them all. Magpie went and laid on her bed with her back to the room while Bobby opened up. The Sergeant had a dozen Troopers with him, all tooled up, and a grim look on his face. All of them were strangers, not from 3914 SSAB-Tata. "Are you the alleged Sergeant One Bobby B, aka Beebi?"

"You know I am, and there's no alleged about it." Bobby put a hand behind him and waved it to stop Bells starting anything. "What's the problem?"

"You are under arrest."

That caught Bobby out. "What for?"

"I don't know and don't care though the word is you dumped a Super, left him to die." His voice confirmed the Sarge didn't care, but he'd got orders so that didn't help.

Bobby's mind raced, trying to make sense of it all. "Bulsh. I had orders and handed them in."

"You are to bring your recorder, as evidence."

Bobby opened his mouth to point out it everything on it had been copied into the record, but the sergeant had his orders. "What else do I need?"

"These men will empty your locker. Please open it or we are authorised to break the lock." A little gleam showed in the Sergeant's eye at that.

"I'll open it." The basteds would make a real mess of the job on purpose and if the locker ended up trashed, Bobby would end up with the bill. Two Troopers gathered everything into sacks, including what lay on top. They checked under the mattress and pillows, and checked the empty beds.

"Notsi? Naughty boy." They'd found non-standard knives, ammo, and several firearms which was why the Supers usually leaked news of an inspection, otherwise all their Troopers would be locked up. The Troopers only took Bobby's notsi so he shrugged. The sergeant gestured to the door.

"Beebi?" Bells came up on his toes, ready to go.

"No, let me find out what it's all about." More to the point the dozen Troopers were fully armed and primed to go, and Bells, Siflis and Hood weren't. "It'll be some mix-up with the paperwork." Though Bobby didn't think so, not with three squads of Troopers from a different unit sent to arrest him. Not that there were many left of the old unit, because another of the wounded had carked it and three were crippled past anything metal could fix. Twenty-four out of a hundred and forty if the rest of the wounded made it, the whole unit including Sandman's six men only made a Sergeant's file now.

*　*　*

Unexpectedly, Bobby wasn't roughed up in the stockade, even when he stripped to be scanned. He put on the orange suit as instructed, before being put in a cell on his own without any more information on charges. There he stayed, listening to the drunks moan and puke, until the following day. His defence lawyer arrived mid-morning, a full Manager, not even an assistant Manager which raised a few alarms in Bobby's head. A Super usually acted for Troopers, or sometimes just a clerk.

"You are in a lot of trouble, Acting-Sergeant."

"What for sir?" Bobby kept it very polite. It wouldn't be smart to start flickin the man who would hopefully clear this up.

"You are charged with deserting a wounded Super, leaving him for the enemy, and it's a good thing for you that he died. If the Plebs had taken him alive and paraded a Super through the complex you'd be dead already."

"I didn't desert him, sir. I had clear orders, sir. They were transmitted, and on a disc, and on my own recorder." Bobby didn't understand. Had the Super screwed him after all? "They couldn't have taken him alive, because I left him a pistol and two carbins."

"What!" The Manager looked up from the file, jerked out of his studiously bored pose.

Bobby shrugged. "He asked for something so he could eat a bullet when the Plebs came through the door. So that his signal would stop and you'd call down hell on his position."

The Manager looked worried, which didn't help Bobby's peace of mind. "You shouldn't know about the signal. How do you know?"

"The Super told me, to explain about calling down hell to cover our escape. He wanted survivors." The Manager didn't look convinced. "He said he'd been a Super too long and didn't see why we had to die. The orders are on all the records."

"No they aren't." Bobby stared open-mouthed as the Manager carried on. "The only orders that could be recovered were the original ones telling you to go it alone, you and your squad. Those were superseded by HQ when you were sent back." The Manager tapped the file in front of him. "There are charges here for destruction of property since those orders were no longer in force. I hadn't mentioned them since they are negligible in comparison."

"What about the radio message, the orders to the Copter, the disc…" Bobby ran down as the Manager shook his head.

"According to HQ, the Copter attack went in for you to break out with the Supervisor, not to leave him behind. Their recording equipment malfunctioned after that so there's nothing on disc. Your disc, the one you brought out, has been damaged beyond recovery as has the record on your personal equipment. Apparently you came close to a massive electrical discharge and some heavy magnetic influences somewhere, or you lied and tried to cover your tracks."

"My buzzer recorder and wrist comp worked fine right up to when I got arrested. The radio messages to HQ?" Bobby didn't need the Manager to shake his head because Bobby realised he'd been well and truly stitched. Not by the Super, so it had to be the dick at HQ who'd sent the squad back in.

"There's no record on their gear. The Super at HQ is adamant that the orders were to get your Super out, and that was the whole plan and the only one. The Supervisor in the armour is being charged with endangering his equipment by waiting once he knew the Super wasn't coming." The Manager gave a little smile. "He is quoting the orders you played back to him as a defence over claims for property damage. Swears you aimed the cannon."

"I did." Bobby reckoned that even if he went down over this, the Super had pulled out a score of Troopers by waiting.

"If you could get the spook to testify, that might help."

"The spook disappeared when we unloaded." Bobby smiled, just a little one. "You could ask The Horseman's lot?"

A real smile answered him. "That lot won't confirm they actually belong to their own unit." The smile disappeared again. "There is also a woman, a Pleb? There is a suggestion that she's a spy for the Plebs and used you to penetrate the base."

"She was a random meeting that got us out of trouble. Elli, Corporal Ellis will be the one who'll know where she went since he was sniffing her skirt." Bobby thought that's who had opened his trap, so may as well throw some shite that way. "She wasn't in the troop carrier I got into, so I've no idea if she even made it that far."

"I'll mention that."

"Corporal Ellis was also near enough to know what the Super planned, and that he was alive and conscious when we left." Bobby knew he was grasping at straws, but tried anyway. "If we were running out don't you think the Super might have used the two carbins and ammo I gave him. On us?"

"Corporal Ellis?" The Manager opened the file and read something. "He claims that you excluded him from all discussions with the Super, who was probably unconscious by the time you left." The Manager read some more. "According to this you threatened to kill Ellis and his men if he didn't obey you."

"I threatened to kill him and three of the men if they raped the woman who was getting us out of there." Bobby sighed. "Though if I'm locked up and those four are loose, I bet none of the rest are answering questions."

"You Troopers never do, not about other Troopers. Corporal Ellis and three men have one story, you and your four Troopers have another." The Manager rubbed at his chin and read some more while Bobby absorbed the news that Magpie had given evidence. "This is a mess. I don't like the idea of so much evidence going missing. It's a good thing for you that the charges involve the death of a Super, and that you have been involved in the deaths of others."

"No I haven't." Bobby answered automatically, though he didn't think it mattered any more.

"There's a question mark over the fate of your previous Supervisors, especially the last one. Questions about why he went up on the roof, and why he then seems to have jumped?" That came with absolutely no smile.

"I was in the canteen when it happened, in plain view of at least thirty people including several sergeants and a Super." Bobby thought that would be old history now.

"Then there seem to be a lot of dead Supers involved before that. Being close to you isn't healthy for your superiors."

Bobby looked shocked, he'd practiced. "The only Supers I killed were Frog Supers and I only killed two. I got my first metal for that."

"So it says here. Regardless of that, no Super or Line Supervisor in the Justice Department will attempt to defend you which is why I've been dragged out of my office." The Manager glared at Bobby. "Which I don't appreciate but it might be a good thing for you." Bobby decided against pointing out that he hadn't dragged anyone anywhere. "Because now I'm wondering if someone has been trying a bit too hard to make this case open and shut."

"Why? I was given orders. We killed a shitload of Plebs, saved the armour and brought a score of Troopers home. Why does anyone want me charged?" Bobby shut up because he could hear a bit of a whine creeping into his voice.

"At least you are consistent; no plea for leniency or excuses and you haven't varied an inch so far. Either you're a good actor or a good liar, or Control have been..." The Manager stopped. "The Supervisor who sent you back in should have rolled the armour once he knew the Plebs had the Supervisor trapped, especially considering the man's family connections."

Bobby kept quiet because the man wasn't talking to a Trooper. He was thinking out loud but it would be on the tape that recorded the meeting and anything might help. Then the Manager came back from wherever his mind had been and looked straight at Bobby. "His defence is that if you hadn't deserted the Super, the plan would have worked. It's hard to dispute that since over a score of Troopers got out. The medics are saying they last saw the Supervisor gut-shot and dying, but none of them will commit to a real opinion on how fast."

Bobby jumped a mile when the Manager slapped the file closed. "I need to look at all the evidence again, personally. Even if you are guilty, there's a few others who should be answering questions." He stood up and Bobby heard the door locks open.

"What about me, sir?"

"You are in the stockade on charges, and that means you sit in a cell until the court martial." The Manager left and then the guards unclipped Bobby's shackles so he could stand and shuffle back to the cell.

*   *   *

Ten days later Bobby still sat in his cell though the drunks had left. A new neighbour arrived but Corporal Ellis wouldn't be supplying any conversation. The black eye and swollen nose were intriguing, but Ellis didn't want to discuss the injuries. One of the guards curled a lip and looked at Ellis and then Bobby. "I don't know what sort of unit your old Super ran. We've a Sergeant on charges for getting a Super killed, and a Corporal on charges for attempted rape of a Pleb woman. The rest are on lockdown because of the fighting."

"Fighting?"

"No discipline. Fighting each other and won't say why. In my opinion 3914 SSAB-Tata should be split up and transferred out, then the whole unit can be rebuilt from scratch."

"Fourteen ST are veterans and if they're fighting each other, someone should find out why."

"Who? You're the only sergeant left, one Corporal is in here, and there's only two other Corporals. One was in the fighting and isn't even in your Unit, and the other is away getting new feet." The guard shook his head and walked away.

Bobby had a good idea what the fighting would be about if Ellis had

129

been beaten up, especially if the attempted rape back in the flat had come up. Unless Ellis had found out about Magpie and tried again though Bobby thought Siflis or Bells would have knifed the Corporal in that case. Bells had stopped hinting about pooching and become more protective as Magpie learned to fight, treating her more like a trainee man. That Corporal from another unit could be Sandman, which meant the rescued Troopers from the 659th Armoured were still being kept with the survivors of 14-ST. Someone had kept this all contained in the barracks until…. A chill went up Bobby's back. Until a certain acting-Sergeant had been safely dropped into an unmarked grave. Actually Troopers shot by firing squad went into the furnaces, but it worked out the same.

Ellis refused to talk to either Bobby or the guards. The following day the Corp went off with a Super wearing justice office's unit markings, who had to be Ellis's lawyer. When the Corporal came back he gave Bobby a grin full of malice and as soon as the Super had gone he had to spill it. "It's you or me, smartarse. Guess who it'll be once I give my evidence, and then I walk."

Bobby sneered. "Perjury, especially to stitch up another Trooper, will get you a Gaza Taxi. Don't do it, Elli."

"Don't need to make anything up, just confirm that I didn't hear what you and the Super said and you were the last to see him. They've got you anyway even if I say nothing." Ellis smirked. "Then my charges will be dropped. There'll be no witnesses since I'll be the senior Corporal left and I'll get those stripes."

Bells or Siflis would make sure that didn't last but Bobby said nothing because the cells would be bugged, electronic versions as well as the little biting basteds in the bedding. He'd tried to get Ellis to say something incriminating, but it wasn't happening and the Corporal had it right. Without the records of his orders, Bobby would be thoroughly pooched anyway.

The first hearing three days later confirmed that. The opening speech took all of about five minutes and four of them were the Area Manager judge spouting his bit about impartial justice. The prosecutor submitted a sheaf of paper and discs of statements about who had said what, making it clear the whole trial would be a formality. Bobby's defence council submitted nothing but asked for the trial to be put off for another three weeks. The judge didn't want that since it all looked open and shut, and for the first time Bobby really began to be pleased he'd got a Manager in his corner.

The judge quite obviously didn't want to be rude to someone of Manager rank, even one inferior to his, and eventually allowed the delay. Though reluctantly, which meant that discussion took longer than the rest of the proceedings. Bobby started getting curious about his Super, the dead one. The Manager finally persuaded the judge by referring to family connections and their expectations, or bullied the judge from the tone of the exchange. The Manager went on about how the relatives would be determined to get all the details, and it would be best if their wishes were honoured. From the glare he received from the judge, Bobby wouldn't expect much mercy in the sentencing.

*　　*　　*

The three weeks were incredibly boring. The guards allowed Bobby to work out in the small gym attached to the stockade for the purpose, and he went through combat exercises in the cell. Bobby even raised a smile from one by asking if he could use the firing ranges. At least Bobby knew his squad were all intact and now had confirmation that the remnants of 659th Armoured involved in the rescue were still here. One of the women who came in to clean the cells left a message under his pillow, not signed and very short but in the squad code. Bobby read it surreptitiously before eating the slip of paper.

Four days later he had another message. Ellis's three friends were in the hospital. No details but despite the lockdown and the cameras in the corridors, somebody must have got into their quarters. The rest of the message told him Magpie kept training and Hood could walk better. Very sparse but the contact cheered up Bobby. He'd been worried that his squad had been moved away or split up, possibly even locked up elsewhere as accomplices or some such shite.

*　　*　　*

This time the morning of his trial meant a lot of cleaning and polishing in the cell block. After their shave and shower both Bobby and Ellis were given haircuts and clean uniforms instead of prison onesies. The guards wore their best uniforms, parade style with everything polished which seemed a bit over the top because most of them didn't go into the courtroom. Their Supervisor turned up, the first time Bobby had seen the man, looking very smart but harassed. After a thorough inspection and some ass-kicking over flecks of dust, the Super left. Ten minutes later he came back and waited, obviously expecting visitors.

The Manager, Bobby's defence, came through the door and he received a salute of course. A feeble excuse of a salute compared to the ramrod straight, quivering attention and salute for the next person in. A someone without any uniform or rank markings, and who definitely wasn't a member of the Army. A woman for starters, one who had been a truly sleek Diva in her day as far as Bobby could judge. Her smile still stunned at twenty paces.

A smile aimed straight at Bobby who wasn't stupid and regardless of the lack of uniform he threw her his best salute. From her lip twitch his salute hadn't got any better, especially compared to those from the guards. Bobby tried really hard to work out what she might be. Not Royalty, because she didn't wear any diamonds on her head, but her clothes made Bobby think of Royalty. Long, flowing and silky, and the cost would probably pay the entire Unit's bar bill for a year. A black armband struck the only jarring note.

"You are the last man to see my son alive?" Bobby blinked and tried to work out who she meant and the frantic mouthings from the Manager weren't helping. Luckily the woman seemed to realise, and took mercy on him. "Supervisor Lord Alaine Bertram Curen of the Fourteen ST Troopers?"

Lord? Alaine? Bertram? Bobby had only ever heard Curen three times but that meant the Super all right. This was his mother? Bobby rallied. "Yes. Er. Ma'am?"

"Excellent. Would you mind telling me about it?" Bobby cast his eyes desperately at the Manager and the guard Super. She expected him to talk about it here? He'd been warned not to discuss the case with anyone. His frantic looks were noticed. "Oh, not here of course." The woman looked over at the Super. "I'm sure you can find us somewhere private and comfortable." Bobby didn't think she'd consider the interrogation room comfortable but the Super started nodding.

"Of course Duchess. One moment please." The Super almost strained something exiting at speed while trying to stay at attention. Bobby tried to remember where Duchess fitted into the hierarchy, not something he usually paid attention to. The top people in each major corporate body had titles. Duchess wasn't Royal but she probably had a beer with them or whatever they did to socialise.

"Perhaps you could take the young man out of his cell, so we aren't delayed?" The guards were there in an instant, keys in hand. They started to fasten the manacles and chains to Bobby's wrists, waist and ankles, passing them through the bars before opening the door. "Are all those necessary?"

"But he is a suspected murderer, ma'am." Bobby knew how the guard felt as those eyes zeroed in. Those eyes didn't expect a "but" from anyone, let alone a Trooper.

Then she relaxed a little. "Oh yes, of course. Perhaps just the wrist ones?" Bobby wanted to smile at that, because splitting the chains from the wrist manacles would be a bitch of a job and there wasn't a snowball's chance of the guards refusing. A guard ruined his fun by heading for the desk and bringing back a pair of handcuffs. By the time Bobby had been handcuffed and let out of the cage the Super arrived back.

✳   ✳   ✳

As Bobby shuffled down the corridor his defence Manager brushed past near enough to murmur "Belinda, Duchess of Ironhills. Behave."

Bobby stared after him, because Ironhills had to mean her family owned huge iron ore deposits somewhere in the United Kingdoms, or maybe all the iron deposits. He didn't have long to wonder. The room the Super escorted them to had to be his own, for relaxation, not his office because there were comfortable chairs. The Duchess took the big luxurious swing chair while the Manager took a smaller armchair, probably dragged in here sharpish because the colours clashed even to Bobby. The Super headed for a straight backed chair with a padded seat but stopped at a raised Duchess finger.

"This is a private discussion between a bereaved mother and the last person to see her son. I don't believe we need witnesses. Manager Bryant will be here to defend my frail bones if necessary, as he is a friend of the family." That seemed news to the Manager from his expression. "Since this will take some time, please remove the sergeant's handcuffs and arrange some refreshments."

The Super tried. Bobby could see the man gather himself to object at least three times and abandon the idea in the face of those implacable eyes. "Yes Duchess. Of course. Do you have a preference?" Snapped fingers brought the guard with keys while the other scarpered to round up the preferences. Bobby couldn't even identity some of the food, though the smell that arrived included caff. Strong caff without that sharp tang from the usual cheap shite Troopers could get. Bobby only knew the difference because he'd looted some real beans from a drug dealer.

"Please sit, sergeant." Bobby sat in the only remaining chair and managed to keep his face straight despite the expression on the Super's face. A hint of a curve on the Duchess's lips showed again, was she flickin the Super deliberately? Bobby knew he'd be the one to suffer once she'd gone but just now he didn't care. "That will be all." The casual wave of a hand to include the Super and the guards left no room for manoeuvre, though the Super made one last attempt to keep some sort of control.

"The judge will be starting in five minutes, Duchess. The case? To try alleged Trooper Sergeant One Bobby B?"

"Well you had better go and tell him to wait." So casual and yet the Super would be slow-roasted for delivering the message, mainly because even an Area Manager couldn't roast a Duchess. At least Bobby assumed that from her casual, dismissive tone and the Duchess hadn't mentioned asking the judge. Bobby sympathised with Manager Bryant's attempt to keep a straight face, because he wanted to laugh as well. Usually Bobby really hated the bledrin nobility on the odd occasion he thought of them, because after all they owned the world. The same world that regularly dropped shite on Bobby and his ilk from a great height, ably assisted by the Managers and Supervisors. Right now this Pleb wanted to wave flags and cheer for the Ironhills, because he'd never had any personal grief from a Duchess but plenty from Managers and Supers.

"Caff, tea or wine?" The Duchess looked at Bobby with her hand over the tray of drinks.

Bobby had never tasted wine, the usual tea tasted of dust, but that caff smelled rich and pure. "Caff please. Duchess?"

"Belinda when we are alone. Manager Bryant will not mind using Jakkob for this occasion, and if you don't mind I prefer to call you Bobby. Though I am curious about the B after Bobby. What does that stand for?"

Bobby tried looking away and shuffled a bit, but her eyes stayed looking at him. Calmly, with no impatience at all, though they held a total certainty that he'd tell her. Then she smiled slightly. "Ah." The Duchess looked up and around the room, and raised her voice a little. "Should even one word of this private conversation be recorded or passed on by any other means, I will be *very* annoyed. That applies even if someone listens and then says something in their sleep. Please consider that I not only know who The Horseman is, but I also know where he lives." The Duchess turned her eyes back onto Bobby. "Now, you were going to tell me what B stood for."

Bobby sighed. "Baby," he whispered. Then cleared his throat. "Baby, because I was Ma's first, and last. She shortened it to B when I got older and it stuck." Bobby tensed, ready to punch Jakkob if he laughed, but the Manager looked elsewhere.

"So why did you keep it when you joined the army?" Bobby tried to find an answer he could tell her but she saved him after a few moments. "Ah, not really a question to ask a man, especially a Trooper. From your record I would not have expected that." The Duchess actually seemed lost for words for a moment. Not for long. "Now, Bobby B, I would like you to tell me about my son. Lord Alaine Bertram Curen, or Super to you, or possibly dick."

"Not dick, or at least not often. The Super was hit bad when we arrived."

"No. Not yet. First I want to hear about his life." The Duchess tapped her handbag. "He wrote about his men and their missions so I know something of you, and of Hood, Siflis and Bells. I know the names of many of his unit, and what he thought of them. Now tell me what he seemed like to his men."

Over thirty minutes and two cups of caff later Bobby came back to that final meeting with the Super. He talked through it all, the promotion and the breakout right up until the armour rolled into the barracks, though he did miss out Margaret turning into Magpie. Finally her questions stopped, followed by a short silence. "What you have said matches what Alaine told me about you and his men. I will speak to the judge now." The Duchess tapped her wrist and spoke to it. "We are ready now."

*   *   *

The three men who came in the doorway were definitely not Troopers. All three had the look of Squaddies but dressed in suits without any hint of rank, though the cut and cloth should have meant Manager at least. "This sergeant is apparently a dangerous desperado, so don't lose him on the way." Her tone sounded amused, but the look the men gave Bobby wasn't. He raised both hands a little to let them know he wasn't going to cause trouble and one rewarded him with a small nod.

The walk to the courtroom didn't take long without the shackles, but it wasn't long enough for Bobby. He kept trying to work out if he was deeper in the shite or not. The judge had been angry enough about the delay in trying the case, and now he'd been kept waiting in his own court. Bobby fervently hoped that the Duchess intended speaking up on his behalf, some sort of character reference, because that should have some weight and possible lighten the sentence. Against that the bledrin judge couldn't get at the Duchess, but he would be fixing the punishment for all charges and shite flowed downhill.

His squad, sitting outside the court along with Corporals Ellis and Sandman and a dozen other Troopers, came as a hell of a surprise. Bobby started worrying about Magpie being here, because he didn't think she could pass for a Trooper on the stand. Though with all this lot to work through Magpie wouldn't be on the stand for long. Bobby hoped that caff had been as strong as it tasted because this would be a long trial and falling asleep would look bad.

Suits packed out the court itself this time. There were a lot of Supers, through Line Supervisors up to various levels of Managers, many of them military with a lot of braid and brass. Some weren't showing ranks so maybe The Horseman or some of his people were here. One look at the Judge, Area Manager Svend Billings according to the nameplate on his desk, and Bobby feared the worse. The judge's blood pressure had already reached dangerous levels and he aimed a definite scowl straight at the prisoner. The Duchess headed for a seat at the front and the Manager there moved away sharpish when one of Bobby's mystery guards spoke to him. The guards chained Bobby in the dock while Manager Bryant sat down at his desk nearby and shuffled paper.

The judge brought the court to order, then spent the same four minutes running through the same preamble. He finished by looking straight at Manager Bryant. "Since you asked for the delay, do you have any objections to the case being tried this time? No sudden desire for another week or two?" He had no problem with being rude to a Manager this time, laying on the sarcasm thick enough to make several of the spectators wince in sympathy.

Though it seemed to bounce off Manager Bryant. "None at all, Judge Billings. We have only one new item in defence of the sergeant."

"Alleged sergeant."

"As you say. Belinda, Duchess of Ironhills and mother of Supervisor Lord Alaine Bertram Curen wishes to address the court." The Manager indicated the Duchess which seemed a bit superfluous.

"I will listen to any statements with regard to the sentence once the evidence has been heard and a conclusion reached." The judge turned to the prosecutor. "Perhaps we could have the first witness?"

A cleared throat stopped the prosecutor from answering. Manager Bryant held up a hand. "My apologies but the Duchess has brought additional evidence, in a case where much of said evidence seems to have been mislaid." Bobby heard a definite edge in there, the sort that could bring blood. "Evidence which might shorten the case considerably and save you some time." Bryant shrugged. "If you still wish to hear the witnesses afterwards than that option is still open."

Bobby glanced over and the Duchess wore her little smile again, the one that meant shite for someone. Evidence? What the hell sort of evidence would a Duchess have? The Judge looked at her, and at the prosecutor. Billings really wanted to keep going, but curiosity had started eating at him and probably everyone else as well. His eyes went back to the Duchess. "Duchess? I would be obliged if you stepped up to be sworn in."

"No need, Judge. I wish to place a portion of this information on record." The Duchess pulled a data disc box from her handbag. "Since only one directory is relevant one of my men will supervise the copying."

Judge Billings frowned, probably unhappy to even hint that the Duchess might be pulling a fast one. "The court will require some confirmation that this evidence is legal. Someone must swear to the information being correct."

"Judge?" Manager Bryant waited a moment until he had the Judge's attention. "I believe that the deathbed evidence of a man who knows he is dying is considered to be under oath?" Most of the eyes in the room went to the disc box. "This evidence was dictated by Lord Alaine Bertram Curen just before he died, and I am told it is clear from the evidence that Lord Curen knew he had been fatally wounded."

"How long before he died?" The judge moderated his tone and attitude as if a magic wand had been waved.

The Duchess stood up and answered. "Minutes. This was dictated after the orders were given to Sergeant Bobby B, and after the Supervisor had concluded his communications with HQ. The information includes all his orders to everyone concerned." She swept her eyes around the court. "My son asked the Sergeant to save as many as possible, and would be content with the result."

At least three Supers and a Line Supervisor were already moving towards the door, a door that crashed open to reveal a Sergeant and a score of Troopers with weapons ready. "Secure the court, Sergeant. Nobody will leave until I have read this evidence." Judge Billings brought his hand out from where he'd presumably pressed the panic button, and swept the court with his glare. "If anyone tries to leave or make a call, shoot them through the legs." Armed Troopers moved out around the perimeter as the Sergeant saluted. "Duchess. Given the personal nature of this information, would you prefer to retire to my chambers while the disc is copied?"

"Certainly, though I must insist only the indicated directory is copied. The rest is family business, his last will and some private messages." The Duchess rose, still wearing that little smile.

"Of course. The accused will seat himself with the defence until I return." A guard unlocked him allowing Bobby to move out of the dock sit down. He really wanted to know what the hell was on that disc and

Manager Bryant should know.

The judge made a muttered request to a clerk, and the man spoke to his wrist. The judge and Duchess had disappeared into judge's chambers with one of the dangerous looking men by the time a tech arrived with the copying kit. The clerk took him through as well. Five minutes later the tech came out with his equipment and the Troopers allowed him to leave. Then everyone sat and waited.

*   *   *

Manager Bryant leaned over. "What will that disc say?"

"You're asking me?" Bobby stared at the Manager. "I thought you knew."

The Manager looked back, equally puzzled. "Only that it was the last thing he sent her and would help you. Not that it was the last will and after all the other recordings. Now what the hell will it say?"

Bobby had no idea, but knew what it should say. "What I told you. Unless the Super decided to pooch me anyway."

Manager Bryant smirked. "Doubtful or mummy wouldn't have been having social chats with you."

Bobby smiled because that meant a lot of awkward questions for the dick who'd stitched him, at the very least. Then he thought he'd ask while he had the chance. "What is a Duchess anyway? How high up the tree of whatever?"

"Gods ask permission before getting in her way." Manager Bryant smiled at Bobby's expression. "If she decided to use Fourteen ST as a personal guard for a trip down the river or as waiters for a dinner party, everyone would salute and say yes ma'am. I suppose she'd have to square it afterwards with SSAB-Tata, or their Baron or whatever, unless she already owns enough shares." The Manager leant back and fanned himself with the evidence file. Then he looked at it and smiled.

A very hungry smile, shark type hungry. "Comparing what that disc says happened with the evidence taken so far could be interesting. Perhaps those who decided to drag me out of my office will wish they hadn't bothered? Nobody anticipated there being another record and some people's memories were a little erratic."

Though that prompted another question for Bobby. "How did she, the Duchess, get involved? You know, if Gods don't usually bother her." He couldn't see someone tapping her on the shoulder with a casual query.

"A matter of courtesy. I sent a letter explaining that we were looking into the circumstances of his death and would get to the bottom of it." The Manager frowned. "Though I sent that to the widow." He looked at the door to the judge's chambers. "I'd love to know how she got that disc."

Bobby suddenly realised the only way anyone outside the army could have a record of the Super's last few minutes. "I posted it."

"What! When?" Several people looked over and the Manager lowered his voice. "When did you post it?"

"As soon as we got back though I didn't know what it was. The Super asked me to, as a last request." Bobby smiled. "Seemed a fair swap for a score of Troopers."

"Well that answers questions of trust if the Super gave you his last will." Manager Bryant shook his head and then glanced back and across at the seats full of spectators. "I'll bet Line Supervisor Peter Varney wishes he hadn't come to gloat. Though I don't think he'd have time to cover his tracks even if he wasn't locked in here."

Bobby repeated the name silently a few times to drive it into his head. That had to be the basted dick at HQ who'd pooched him, several times.

"Forget him. You'll never get near him and anyway if you've been telling the truth and the disc confirms it he'll eat a bullet. Or he will if he's fast enough since otherwise upper management might have him skinned alive on vid as an object lesson to the rest. Though not a public lesson, the management will probably want to keep this quiet." Bobby glanced across, startled. "How did I guess? You have a reputation. I think it might be fifty-fifty he tried to get out here to escape from you or the judge." The Manager reconsidered. "Not fifty-fifty because you wouldn't kill him here with witnesses."

Bobby ignored the none too subtle hints about topping Supers. "But it's still his word against a disc."

"Fair enough if the rumours had been true, if Supervisor Curen stayed a Supervisor because he had fallen out with mummy and the family kept him there. From mummy's reaction I'd say there's been no rift, so anyone daring to suggest her little boy lied had better find a deep, dark hole then concrete a lid over it. Ah, good."

The clerk had reappeared to beckon both Manager Bryant and the prosecution Super into the judge's rooms. They went in, the clerk came out, and everyone settled down again. The next half hour must have been boring for most of those present. Bobby kept busy churning over what had happened in the last minutes in that train station, and wondering exactly what the Super had put on the disc.

After all, even if the Super's last orders stood and cleared Bobby of running out, there'd still be all that collateral. They'd wrecked three accommodation blocks when the armour punched through but there'd been a fair bit here and there before that. That fire would have been a hell of a mess, and he'd left grenades behind six doors. Bobby also wondered what would happen to Ellis. Would his unknown benefactors throw the Corporal to the wolves over the attempted rape charge, or get him out to keep his trap shut? If they pulled off any surveillance and let the Basteds know, Bobby could sort out that little problem for them.

Even if Bobby got off and stayed a sergeant, life promised to be a bit difficult afterwards because Bobby and his squad were marked men now. There would be a new Super, who would look at that record and either see all the dead Supers or the successful missions. Either way a lot of Supers out there had already made up their minds. Manager Bryant made that clear, when he said that no Super in the justice office would defend Bobby.

Bobby sighed in relief when the door opened and the five people came out. The Duchess had that serene look about her with just a tiny hint of her smile, so she still expected to dish out some shite. Both Manager Bryant and the prosecutor were keeping their faces absolutely blank, but judge Billings looked red-faced and bug-eyed furious. Everyone stood, and then sat after the Duchess and judge.

"Case dismissed."

"What about the damage claims?" The assistant to the prosecutor spoke before his boss could answer and both quailed under a magnificent glare.

"Case. Dismissed. Clear?" Judge Billings looked at the sergeant guarding the door. "The Duchess and her party are free to leave, of course. So is Sergeant One Bobby B and Manager Bryant. Everyone else remains here until I have looked through all this evidence. I will expect adequate answers to all the discrepancies." At least a half dozen objections died half-formed as they met the judge's glare.

The Duchess stood, still with her half-smile. "I wish to place on record my thanks to Judge Billings for his patience and devotion to the cause of justice in waiting until all the evidence could be gathered, and to Manager Bryant for his diligence. It would seem that Sergeant One Bobby B has upheld the best traditions of the Troopers, and I will follow his career with interest." Bobby stared as he saw the flinches and then glares from several Supers and Managers and realised that she had just made sure he was marked. He received another of those blinding smiles and the Duchess left. Bobby saluted the judge as required before marching out, followed by the Manager.

Outside the door the corridor had emptied. No witnesses or guards remained so Bobby collapsed into a chair. "She's killed me."

"How?"

"I'm already marked by my record. Now everyone in there knows who to blame for the shite they're getting from the judge, and if I ever come up before him again." Bobby shuddered.

The Manager laughed. "Judge Billings will be very happy once he's worked off his temper on all those convenient victims. After all, he's just got a commendation from one of the ultimate CEO's handmaidens. So have I, and that will do no harm to my record or promotion prospects. On top of that you have just been given a steel umbrella, from a Duchess no less. Anyone shovelling anything your way will assess how interested the Duchess is in your career so unless they catch you with your hand in the creds or holding a smoking gun, you are clean."

Bobby stared and reassessed. That lot daren't pull anything? Not a chance, they'd just be a lot sneakier about it. Manager Bryant put a hand on his shoulder. "Though no Super will want you and your squads of Troopers in his unit. Definitely your squads because those stripes will be permanent as soon as the paperwork can be processed."

"He said it. The Super said he'd get me. He knew I'd been dodging any chance of promotion. Basted." Though Bobby couldn't get any heat into it. "What happens now?"

"Go and see your squad, get drunk, visit the palaces and find a Diva? Sew those stripes on properly? No doubt some poor basted will arrive to take charge of you eventually." The Manager turned to go. "Goodbye, Beebi. Forgive me if I hope to never see you again?"

"No problem." Bobby sat there for a few minutes and then walked out of the building, past guards who never said a word, and headed for the barracks.

The squad got drunk together, though Hood took Magpie back before she had enough ale to make a mistake. They took a couple of bottles and both were fast asleep when the other three finally rolled in, but in their own beds which meant that Bells lost the bet. Apparently Hood had been sort of running the squad and definitely protecting Magpie, and Bells reckoned Hood had a thing for her. The big man reckoned he owed her because he wouldn't have made it without her, and had expected to die as a rearguard.

Bigger Basteds

For nearly two more weeks nothing much happened. Rumours circulated of a taxi ride after Corporal Ellis disappeared from the unit roll along with his three sidekicks. One of the rescued men, Corporal Sidden, called Sudden of course, learned to walk with two steel feet and helped with discipline. Corporal Sandman kept his men under control and helped with the rest, but nobody wanted trouble. They were all waiting for the other sodin great steel toe-capped boot to drop.

Magpie opened up a bit, and learned to relax just a little. She relaxed most around Hood, still helping him with his metal leg now and then, but despite what Bells kept saying nothing actually happened between them. She dressed and undressed behind her screen, and as far as the rest knew only had Trooper clothes. She took the screen down in the day, in case of inspections, and the rest made sure she had a full set of kit if that happened. After the bledrin shambles the stores didn't query requests for new boots and a helmet, so she ended up with gear that fitted.

Magpie padded her shirt and jacket to hide the curves, adding a bit more muscle to her appearance. Nobody wanted to know if she strapped her chest down or just wasn't that big, because when Bells mentioned it Hood back-handed him onto his arse. Bells kept eyeing her up now and then but also pitched in to make her as good as possible with a knife and at hand-to-hand. He also managed to keep his hands to himself in hand-to-hand, because the rest swore they'd gang up and geld him if he didn't. That or hold him down for Magpie to practice her knife work. Bells seemed torn, fascinated at having a woman in the squad but sort of proud as she learned to be a real Trooper.

Magpie worried about her first real action, about if she could shoot Plebs because she'd been one just weeks ago. So did Bobby. "Are you sure you can do it? If some woman comes out of an alley with a knife or a bomb, you've got to shoot. If we sneak up on a target and someone pops up in front of you the knife has to go in quick and sure. Otherwise you'll kill us all."

"How do you do that? All of you, all the Troopers, don't give a shite about who you kill. I've gone over it and over it, and I'm sure I can hit what I aim at, near enough, and stick a knife in the right place. I'm just not so sure about doing it to a live person." Magpie kept her voice down because this talk had to be really quiet. Neither of them wanted the rest of the squad worried.

"We had a lot of trouble with the same thing, this squad did. We were too young." Magpie looked puzzled so Bobby sighed and explained. "You might have noticed we're a bit young for Troopers."

"Yes, but the rest leave you alone, and they respect you." A little smile flitted over her face. "Some are just scared."

"The rest did ten years on the front lines, as Timers. They spent those years being sent on suicide attacks and being told every day their lives were worth less than a broken window." Magpie paled. "I mean it. The first Mob of Timers we relieved had lost seventy out of a hundred in two attacks. If we hadn't had a sergeant who told us to run when the Super said attack we'd most likely be dead. They train Supers that way, because dead Timers are cheap."

"But the news tells us you are our brave protectors, fighting to defend the borders."

"Timers are untrained, barely armed, and mostly scared shiteless and the enemy ones are the same. I doubt one in ten survives to be a Trooper. By that time all that matters is staying alive." Bobby knew he sounded bitter, but he'd never put it in words before. "Their friends are all dead, they've killed more strangers than they can count, and they've not seen home or a friendly face outside of a spam palace since leaving home."

"But surely, when they come back home to the housing complexes, meet the Plebs again?" Magpie barely whispered that, then looked up in sudden understanding. "You never meet us, the Plebs."

"Not properly because you avoid us, curse or spit behind us, or outright try to kill us. A Pleb, an ordinary peaceful citizen, becomes no different to a Frog Timer or a Kraut Timer. They're just someone we might have to kill so we can go back to barracks alive and get a beer and a woman." Bobby sighed. "The only reason I didn't kill you at first was to flick Ellis, because he tried to rape you. Then you helped Hood, so I owed you, we owed you. Now we've got to know you." Bobby's chuckle and smile had no humour at all. "You are the first woman I've known since my sixteenth birthday, apart from visits to a Divas."

"I thought you four were friends, you know, from a long time ago?"

"We've been together from our first days at Timers, which makes us freaks. Right from the first days we stuck together and we've all four survived which is why it meant something, you helping Hood." Bobby explained the whole thing, from that first fight with Snowman down to a Pleb women helping Hood home instead of him dying as rearguard. "We are closer than brothers now even if Bells reckons he'd cut our throats if we touch his notsi, and Siflis won't talk half the time, and Hood would rather sleep with a rifle than a woman."

Magpie sighed, a long, sad sound. "Now you have a sister. My parents are dead, my own sister won't face me, and if any of my neighbours knew what I did, I'd be a long time dying." She sat quietly for a while, thinking about it. "I'm Oke with shooting a drug dealer, anyone to do with drugs." Her smile looked almost whimsical, with just a bit of steel in it. "I might like that. I might even enjoy knifing one. If someone shoots at me, I suppose I'll shoot back. If not, shoot me clean so I don't end up in the spam palace, all right?" Bobby nodded, too shocked to answer. "I really don't know if I can shoot a woman coming out of an alley with what might be a bomb, but I will shout?"

"Fair enough, all of us except Bells had trouble with that. Even after five years Hood had a shock on this last trip because he killed a granny, one who'd shot him in the leg first. We, the squad, will cover you the first time out and give you a bit of space after your first kills. If you can't handle it, we'll steal some women's clothes and you can slip back in among the Plebs." Bobby shrugged "We owe you that."

"Thanks for the option but I'd rather not go back. You've no idea what it's like for a single woman without family, just trying to make a living. Some arse always thinks he should be her protector." Magpie sounded bitter now. "Even if they start off nice, eventually they think they own you, like that ex who fixed my locks. That was the only good thing he ever did, and then it turned out he just wanted a bit of, well, you know, on the side. Here I get good food and clothing, nobody gives me shite, and you're making sure if I ever meet some oik of a Pleb he'll be in trouble not me. Even while Bells flicks me he teaches me to fight, really fight." Magpie laughed, and meant it. "If I ever went back after this training some youth in a gang would grab my arse and I'd break his arm and cut his throat. That might take a bit of explaining!"

That made Bobby smile. "As long as you're sure?"

Magpie's answering smile was bitter-sweet. "Hard luck. Did you ever have a little sister, Beebi?"

"No, nor a brother. I'm an only one." Bobby looked up the room to where the rest were keeping well out of this. "Though now I suppose I've got both. We're a bit screwed up but welcome to the family, Magpie."

"Don't worry, I won't let you down." After that talk Magpie seemed more determined and spent more time on the ranges and practicing dry-shooting or loading notsi in the barracks. Hood swore she'd be all right. Both Siflis and Bobby agreed the sniper had got a bit of a thing for her, though Magpie didn't seem interested in men at all. Attic and Sandman knew about Magpie of course, but kept quiet. They thought the whole thing a huge joke and were waiting to see if the squad could turn her into a real Beebi's Basted, and what would happen when she actually went out on patrol.

All the survivors were wondering what would happen to them, and when they'd be back in action. They had just been given over six weeks leave, a rare occurrence. Few Troopers ever got more than a three-day pass. Pay kept coming in so they could drink and visit the Divas, but no resupply of ammunition. The last of the wounded came back making them up to twenty-two again, and some started to call themselves BIB, Beebi's Invisible Basteds.

*   *   *

Then nine new Troopers arrived with a request for Sergeant Bobby B's recommendations, because his file of Troopers should have four more Corporals. That didn't add up either, a sergeant had a four or five squad file of twenty men, not thirty with six corporals. Though as usual with orders, nobody wanted to discuss them. Bobby hadn't a clue how to sort the new men out, so he treated this order the same as any other orders. He discussed the whole thing with his squad. They looked at the files on the new men and so did Sandman. Bells grinned. "They'll fit right in."

Siflis sniggered while Bobby privately had to admit that Bells could be right. Every one of the men had a string of suspected transgressions but nothing proved that would warrant more than a few stripes with the strap. Better still, every man had earned plenty of metal so they could fight. Magpie laughed when she finished reading. "These look a lot like your record, or how you described it."

"Not really, Magpie. I'm sure mine has a lot more hints about dead Supers though yes, all those insubordinations and notsi violations look familiar." Bobby glanced round. "I would bet we've all got files like mine."

"Nothing about Supers on mine." Sandman grinned. "I stayed innocent until I ran into bad company."

"There'll be no Supers on mine. Not yet?" Magpie grinned. She could relax a bit because everyone present knew about her. "Maybe you could arrange for me to get one, the one who stitched you, Beebi? Just so Nathaniel fits in?" She frowned. "I reckon I could do that, top a Trooper Supervisor, because that's a Pleb dream."

"Why would our records have anything about Supers? We only lost three before this mess, four if you count the one when we were Timers, and then this last one but that obviously had nothing to do with us." Bells looked round at them all. "What? I've not said we did anything. Beebi had lots of witnesses for the jumper. And the first one, everyone knows that had to be a loose pin on his grenade."

Bobby waved a finger around the walls. He'd become more paranoid about electronic bugs since that Duchess really seemed to think a Super's private room had been wired for sound. "You'd better stop sniffing the stuff the Divas use, Bells. Either that or I'm taking all your weapons away until the fantasies stop."

"If they let us see our files we wouldn't make stuff up." Bells retired into a sulk, pulling out a short, fat blade and a small stone to sharpen it.

"What about these, and who gets to be a Corporal? We've only got Sandman and Sudden now Elli has been Funted." Siflis pulled one record across. "Oy, Hood, we've got another shooter." He sniggered. "One who varies between deadly accurate and very nearly killing a Super a couple of times."

Bobby looked at the record. "Very, very nearly but he didn't, so accurate and smart. Have we got another scout, someone like Siflis?"

"Doubtful, but we might have a decent scout." Hood ducked as Siflis slapped his head and they settled down to get the job done.

Attic made Corporal both because they all trusted him after he helped cover for Maggie. Hood didn't much like being made Corporal but as the others put it, he'd been bossing them about anyway. Two of the new men were put into Sudden's squad and then the files revealed that one of the new Troopers had already been a Corporal and been busted. For insubordination, almost a qualification in this company, so when they'd finished laughing Corporal Beddard got his stripes back. Reaper, the new sniper, ended up the Corporal for another scout and sniper squad.

The recommendations were accepted and resupply authorised in a sudden outbreak of efficiency, more worrying than the usual apathy or obstruction. The survivors, now Sergeant One Bobby B's new file, were being kitted out for something but there seemed to be no attempt to bring the 3914 ST back up to strength. More than that, Sandman and the rest of the armoured had been amalgamated, not sent back to their unit. Bobby tried asking and written orders told him to make sure the men were fully equipped and sharp so he did. The orders were sodin frustrating, because he couldn't ask a written message any questions.

The Troopers complained but soon buckled down to hard exercise and training with their weapons, because that made sense to any Trooper. Magpie had found an aptitude for knives and pistols and became a lot faster, though the exercise made her wiry rather than build her up to look more masculine as hoped. The squad pitched in to add more padding here and there to disguise her with even Bells volunteering his sewing skills. She dropped into a role as close support for Hood to free up the other two so Bells could stay rearguard with Siflis out front. Magpie still weighed in a bit light for hand to hand but good enough since Bells should be there by the time anyone closed. Being average with a carbin made her better with it than Bells, so they complemented each other.

Not knowing what would be happening to them made everyone nervous, so they tried to prepare for anything. Everyone shared around the notsi, to let the new men have a few bits of this and that. Bobby worried that if the whole lot were shipped off somewhere else entirely the Supers would search the baggage to stop any booze or drugs being smuggled, and the notsi would be impounded. Bells became almost paranoid about finding a way to keep his Kraut automatic even if he'd only got two clips left. Tension rose as the time dragged on. The Troopers were honed, toned and fighting fit, but nobody would give them somebody to work it off on.

*   *   *

A call to report to the HQ building came more as a relief than a surprise to Bobby though being asked to bring the Corporals seemed unusual. The seven of them dumped their weaponry because that wasn't allowed in HQ, smartened up and headed over at the double, then sat and waited. The room they were finally shown into contained a fully armed squad of Troopers and an Area Manager.

They all saluted. The Area Manager returned the salute, and his might possibly be as bad as Bobby's. "Sit down, all of you." The officer scowled at them all. "You are a problem." Bobby opened his mouth but the look didn't want a reply. "The 3914 SSAB-Tata has been reformed using mostly Troopers fresh from Timer training, and a few veterans from elsewhere to get them started. That means you have no unit."

Sandman moved in his seat and opened his mouth but the scowl pinned him. "The 659th Armoured have been brought up to strength. Nobody wants you." The scowl moved across them all. "Thirty-one veteran Troopers who have enough metal between them to give a troop carrier a hernia, and not a single Super wants to take you on." Just for a moment Bobby thought the Manager would spit. "Wimps and pussies. I've looked at the records and there's not a single solid fact to say any of you killed a Super. Not one of ours anyway."

One of the Troopers came forward and handed out files. The manager waved at him. "No, he isn't armed because you scare me. He's here because some pussy higher up insists that whoever gives you the news is protected."

"Gaza Taxi." Bobby said it without any thought.

The Manager laughed. "Not a chance, Beebi. All of you just went for a spin in one and came back laughing, with a new paint job and souvenirs. Nothing so simple this time though you'll need everything you ever learned to stay alive. If you open those files you will find the new organisational structure and purpose of the Trooper Rapid Reaction Force. Or maybe I should call it Beebi's even Bigger Basteds. I am Area

Manager Gunnar Erikson and I have the dubious honour of being your officer."

Nobody opened the file because every one of them wondered why thirty-one Troopers had an Area Manager in charge. "Don't stare. I'm not getting my hands dirty in the field but I will decide if you are the right people for the job and arrange your missions. Read the files and then I'll answer questions. Make sure you read the files all the way through because they stay right here, and you never tell anyone outside this room what they say. Just to get that through your heads, these men will leave before the questions so I don't have to shoot them to preserve security." The startled Troopers stared at him while seven pairs of eyes got busy reading.

They read and paid real attention because the first part turned out to be a copy of their own records, and Bobby found out his steel umbrella from the Duchess had gone on there. There wasn't a mention of her, just warnings about possibly consequences for anyone making unwarranted accusations, and that his demise would attract attention from outside the army. An armour plated umbrella though it didn't stop anyone putting him in harm's way as part of the job. There were also plenty of statements that said he hadn't killed various Supers, phrased to say he might have, so no wonder Supers were edgy round the squad. Bobby did feel a bit pissed he'd got the blame for the first one because he felt sure Sarge did that.

The next part seemed to be a bit vague about the actual job, but made it clear that Sergeant One Bobby B answered only to the Area Manager. Bobby had no idea who the Area Manager answered to, but the TRRF weren't in any recognised Army organisation. They were in the Army, though that didn't become clear until Bobby asked, as his first question. The armed Troopers really were sent away as soon as he opened his mouth. The next hour turned out to be livelier and more entertaining than expected, not least because Gunnar answered the questions without any bulsh. He set the tone by telling them he should be called Guns, and he'd kick the shit out the first one to say sluur.

*   *   *

The following day two buses carrying the TRRF or BBB, Beebi's Bigger Basteds, stopped in the middle of their new home or at least Bobby's wrist map said so. Two buses for thirty-one men because all their gear including notsi and the ammo came along without even a casual search, despite part of the trip being by plane. The Troopers disembarked and Bells put his hands on his hips and his nose in the air. "I ordered seven-star, and room service."

"First find a room with a roof." Sandman had a good point. Stretching away in each direction the derelict industrial buildings didn't seem to have a single intact roof, let alone accommodation. At least half the construction consisted of massive concrete walls, while rusting steel or weathered brick made up the rest.

"Big nasty basteds like you should be right at home sleeping rough." Area Manager Gunnar Eriksson walked out of a huge doorway in a concrete wall and ran his eyes over them.

"Speak for yourself." Magpie barely breathed it but Siflis sniggered.

"Don't bother standing to attention or getting in ranks." The Area Manager paused and smiled. "Though since you haven't even tried, that was a waste of breath. In that case the speech is short and sweet. I am Guns from now on. Don't salute because I won't reply, since mine is possibly worse than Beebi's." A ripple of laughter ran around the Troopers. "You are going to sweat like pigs running around in here training for your new job, while I have a beer and take the piss. I will keep you fed and clothed, and there'll be a few Divas if you do well. I'll replace your ammo including notsi because this will be live-fire, but if you take a pot at me I'll shoot back."

"Is there someplace weatherproof, Guns?" Bobby figured he'd see if their new officer meant the informal bit before someone got chopped down for it. He'd been informal in private, but out in public? "For the ammo, because it's not used to roughing it."

"Through here behind this thick concrete and safely away from prying eyes is a dinky little barracks, with all mod cons. By that I mean canteen, food, beds and showers. There are no cooks, and minor transgressions will lead to laundry duty. I'm confident someone will misbehave before your shorts turn green and rot off. You do not exist, or more to the point, nobody knows where you went." Bobby turned to look at the buses and Guns continued. "The buses will not be collected and you'll need them. Supplies will be dumped at random points near here. You will treat collecting them as a combat mission. Anyone watching the drop dies, though you can bring one back for a chat first."

The Troopers weren't smiling now and even if they weren't at attention, they weren't relaxed any more. "Anybody?"

Guns grinned at Bobby. "If you find a nosy Super, this one will be sanctioned. Is that clear enough?"

A ripple went through the Troopers, and some smiles and murmurs. "Shut it, this is serious." Bobby scowled at them. "These buildings are derelict so we can shoot the shite out of them, and I'm guessing the Corporals can tell you all what the new job is now." He waved his hands around. "We'll be practicing targeted strikes on guarded Pleb criminal organisations, infiltration, assassination, and hostage rescue. One-off dirty jobs that the local Troopers haven't got someone either hard enough or sneaky enough to get done."

"How do we practice infiltration?" A Trooper looked around, baffled. "Who do we infiltrate?"

"More like sneak through and steal their favourite notsi, squad against squad. The losers will be cooks and laundry assistants unless they really pooch it and then I'll get creative." Bobby glared. "You will be watching over my fragile body when we do this for real in some steelworks or housing complex, so you will be trained or dead." Bobby watched that sink in. This lot weren't worried about the threats, they were interested in the new job. "Split up into your squads and find quarters in there. The one with gold taps and wall-to-wall Divas is mine. There's cold food, sandwiches and sausage rolls, in the canteen. We'll meet in there at fourteen hundred by which time your Corp will have explained everything properly. Now unload the buses and piss off."

"That's supposed to be parade dismissed, Beebi."

"They don't understand that, sir, and you really don't want us to practice drill."

"No I don't, and I meant it about dropping the sir. I wouldn't want anyone to realise an Area Manager is slumming here." Guns nodded towards the Troopers. "Eventually you'll have to find people among that lot for real infiltration, getting among the Plebs to get local news. You'll get the spook reports but sometimes you'll want a Trooper's take on it all."

"I've got just the right person. Innocent, innocuous, you'd never figure who it was if they served your caff." Bobby kept the smile from his face at the sceptical look from Guns.

* * *

Guns still looked unsure when the first mission came in. "You'd better be right." Guns muttered that quietly as he stood with Bobby watching the Troopers load their gear.

"We've been training for three months. If you don't let us kill someone soon, they'll start on each other or maybe look for targets." Bobby frowned. "I don't think any of us have scored an Area Manager, and I really don't fancy the shite if we do."

Guns ignored the implied threat to his own health. "I'll look out for one. This mission should warm them up nicely but remember to stay invisible until the job's done."

"If the spooks are right, no problem." Bobby smiled happily. "I don't like the basteds who produce drugs anyway, so I'm really going to enjoy this." Guns smiled as he watched them go. He knew most of the Troopers hated drug growers and drugs labs so he'd put this one on top of the heap.

* * *

Approaching the weed farm had a nasty touch of déjà vu, but only a touch. Bobby and Hood's squad were covering the front this time, because Reaper and his rifle covered the back. Bobby stayed with Hood's squad during the approach to cover any nerves from Magpie, and in case she let slip her sex. She seemed torn between the opportunity to shoot some basted drug grower and letting the squad down by going over the top. Bobby nudged Hood in the ribs. "Remember, check for the black cross before shooting anyone." All the Troopers had dressed in civvies over body armour with a small black cross taped to their backs, chests and each arm.

"For the twenty-third time, I got it." Hood glanced over at Bells, knowing exactly who the reminder had been really aimed at. "Though it feels weird, not being in uniform and not using Trooper weapons."

"The weapons won't make any difference to Bells, he never uses

Trooper gear anyway." At least Magpie had stayed loose enough to flick Bells about his notsi.

"Piss off Magpie. Since we're in civvies, you could have worn a skirt and livened the place up a bit?" Bells grinned, because he knew what came next.

Sure enough, Hood butted in. "Magpie can't, because the rest of the Basteds don't need to know. Not yet."

"Maybe, but I bet you'd like her to wear one." Hood didn't answer and Bells sniggered. Magpie glanced at Hood with a little smile before straightening her face and turning towards the target, all business again. The rest concentrated on the job, because Bobby had just activated the ten second count on their tappers. On ten the shooting and explosions started, but because all the weapons were notsi Bobby couldn't tell how the Troopers were getting on.

"Sandman here. One man down, main door open, two squads in." Bobby, no longer smiling, tapped an acknowledgement and kept moving forward. He'd practiced this, controlling an attack, but this would be his first real operation. He now had a bit more respect for the Supers, the few who actually planned operations instead of throwing the Troopers in. He also had a lot more idea of why sergeants tended to be a bit short-tempered when Troopers went off the plan.

"Stopper here. Movement." Bobby acknowledged and replied with a quick reminder to Reaper he should seal the way out. Bobby really needed the top men or one of them trapped and alive so this time Reaper would kill the first man out of the emergency exit, a tunnel to the other side of the street. From the burst of firing that way the target really wanted to get through there and didn't mind using up a few men.

Though it didn't last long since the men died as fast as they came out. Instead the firing inside intensified, before finally dying away. "Attic here, Plan B, we've got steel doors." Bobby grinned, this drug boss thought another gang had attacked so he'd forted up and would be calling for backup.

"Sandman, use the door-knocker. Try not to kill them all." Though if the spook had been right the boss, known as Smoke, wouldn't be near the steel door. Bobby headed through the building followed by his old squad. He felt relieved because Magpie had broken her cherry without hesitation, though emptying the revolver into the man was a bit over the top. She might calm down now. Though she'd not used a knife yet and that caused some people real trouble the first time.

"I always wanted one of those."

"Button it, Bells." Bobby grinned because he sympathised. They'd all love to have a go with the armour piercing rifle, the door-knocker. Sandman got to use it because he'd used the cannon in an armoured car and calling the weapon a rifle really stretched the description. The boom and sharp explosion from deeper in the building underlined the difference. Another boom and crack followed.

"Sandman here. Hinges gone one side. Doors still up so I'll take out the other hinges."

"Wait, Sandman, I'm nearly there." Bobby paused on his way through a room full of tall, luxuriant greenery. Genetically altered Hemp, super-strong and viciously addictive and the drug of choice for Plebs who couldn't take the reality of life any more. At the far end a dozen men and women dressed only in their underwear sat with their hands on their heads. "Who are they?"

"Plebs. They work like this so they can't steal product. Do we top them?" Sudden frowned. "They weren't armed."

"Keep them for now. Keep any gang prisoners separate, and don't top them yet." Bobby grinned. "Just in case their bosses cark it before we can chat."

"Oke."

Bobby came up behind Sandman and inspected the steel double doors. The hinges on one side were twisted metal but although the door sagged, it stayed upright. Bobby raised his voice. "Just remember, you bledrin Homers, aimed shots. Don't shoot the boss and stop after the first volley." He paused. "That means you Bells." A ripple of laughter answered but Bells kept quiet. Bobby continued in a quieter voice. "Take the hinges Sandman, and be ready if there's anyone cute waiting behind a steel plate when it drops. Do it now."

The door dropped with a crash as the last hinge gave way, and a short firefight killed the five armed men waiting behind it. One had steel protection but Sandman blew a hole clean through the metal, and him. "Can we keep this?" Sandman patted the weapon hopefully.

"We'll see." Bobby used his bullhorn, an odd name for the tiny electronic amplifier, to contact whoever still hid behind that door. "Give it up, Smoke. We're moving in and it can be over more bodies if you want." He paused. "We'll have jobs for men who know the contacts and the business."

A defiant voice answered. "Not for the boss though."

"You can have a job, but not as boss. Your choice. You've tried your radio and landline and they're down, and your rathole is blocked." Bobby laughed into the speaker. "If you'd rather cark it I'll bet one of yours will do the job for me, just to live."

"Wait!" Smoke must think that likely. "Give me a couple of minutes to talk to my partners."

"Two, that's all. If you burn product or records, you'll die slow and nasty." The Basteds settled in, weapons ready. Behind a second door, not armoured because there were already several holes in the timber, voices were raised in argument. Three shots rang out in a quick tattoo. "Hold it!" Bobby got it out in time and several Troopers lowered their weapons, looking a bit sheepish.

The defiance had gone when the voice spoke again. "We're coming out. You won't kill us, right?"

"I won't touch you if you're helpful. Open up." The door creaked open and two men came out, followed by two more who wore some body armour but carried no weapons. "Strip down and kneel." As they did Attic's squad went past them and into the room, weapons ready.

Moments later, while the men were still stripping, Attic used the tapper to report. "One dead, no damage." Bobby didn't reply. He gestured for Bells to pull the boss away from the others once he'd got down to skivvies.

*   *   *

"Who are you, what gang?" The man who claimed to be Smoke frowned. "Your accents are wrong. If you've come in from outside, you've made a big mistake."

That seemed a curious response, since most of this gang were either dead or captives. "My name is Beebi, and these are my Basteds. Now why is this a mistake? I've got the growing sheds, and enough of your men already started giving up contacts and prices to get the business rolling again." Bobby grinned. "Well?"

"There's five of us, five gangs and we work together. The fix is in which means we've got the Plebs and the Troopers stitched. You need me or the rest won't accept a new player." Smoke looked around all the men present. "Without me the others will come down on you and wipe your Basteds out."

Bobby thought about that for a few moments, then chuckled, "Luck with that. So who are the other four?"

"No chance. They'll skin me if I give them up." Smoke looked back towards the body in his hideout. "He belongs to one of them and didn't want to surrender. The rest won't even talk to you unless I introduce you."

"Which is why you killed him. Never mind, just give me the names, locations, gang numbers, anything you know about their operation." Bobby chuckled again. "All the good stuff."

"Aren't you listening? You need me to introduce you, or it won't work." Smoke stared from one to the other.

Bobby sighed and glanced at the disguised Troopers. "Who wants to start cutting?"

"That's the boss isn't it?"

Bobby turned, startled both by the voice and the sheer venom in it. "Yes."

Venom that showed on Magpie's face. "Then I'll do it."

"Are you sure?" Bobby daren't say more because most of the Troopers thought Magpie had been a Timer or Trooper for at least ten years.

Magpie glared at Smoke, a knife already in her hand. "A bunch of shites hopped up on chemicals robbed my sister. They didn't rape her, but they beat her half to death. She couldn't work, so she lost her medical benefits, and in the end some arse gave her weed to kill the pain and memories." Magpie spat towards Smoke. "She ended up on the street to pay for the habit, and that killed my parents. I dreamed of getting someone like this on his own, and now I've even learned how to use a knife properly."

Bobby looked over at Sandman. "Bring in any prisoners who might know something we need. By the time he bleeds out, they'll want to tell us their granny's birthmarks." Bobby nodded to Magpie, still wondering if she'd really do it. "Start cutting, but he's got to be able to speak." As she started forward Hood and Bells grabbed Smoke's arms and pinned him. Bobby smiled at him. "Start talking."

"You said you wouldn't touch me!"

Bobby's smile never faltered. "I won't, he will. Talk."

"You'll kill me anyway." The words were defiant, the tone sounded like begging for a way out.

"Yes, but nice and clean."

Magpie's grin wasn't a pretty sight. "You'll want me to cut your throat after. Otherwise you'll beg someone to sell you a lot of weed. For the pain and memories."

Pure shock stopped Smoke from replying, then he screamed as Magpie made her first cut. That settled any doubt about Magpie and blood because she stuck the knife deep in his bicep and twisted. "Stop him! What do you want to know?"

"I don't know. Tell me everything I might want to hear. Who the fixer is would be good, but anything else." Bobby paused while Smoke screamed again. "He'll stop cutting once I'm satisfied." Behind Sandman five men were dragged in and forced to kneel and watch. Every time they tried to look away a Trooper slapped their faces forward again. Only one actually lost his lunch, but they all grew paler as Smoke eventually babbled everything he knew.

*   *   *

"Cut his throat, Magpie. He's not making sense any more." Bobby gestured towards the five kneeling men and the three who'd come out of the hideout with Smoke. "Do you want another, or are you done?"

Magpie's voice came out as barely a whisper. "Enough thanks." She cut Smoke's throat. "Let someone else have a go."

"Wash up and have a drink." Bobby looked at Hood and jerked his head, and the sniper followed Magpie. She looked rough, probably just coming out of rage and realising what she'd done. Bobby looked over the eight gangsters. "Smoke told me a lot but you'll all know a bit more. Tell me, every tiny thing, or you end up like Smoke. Sandman, I need another cutter."

"I'll do it." Siflis grinned, and he really did look an evil little basted when he wanted to. "I reckon I can improve on what Magpie did." The eight men all began talking at once. Fifteen minutes later they were all laid on the floor with their throats cut nice and clean because none seemed to hold back.

"Why did you need all that info, Beebi? The spooks will have a lot of it, and none had the name of the fixer, the contact in the local Troopers." Sandman frowned. "The mission is to shut down the drug producer. Even if you give all the info about the others to the local Troopers, someone will warn the gangs or that sort of evidence won't hold up in court."

"How much do you like drug producers, Sandman? Not the dealers, the producers. Smoke told me this is only a fifth of the organisation, loosely speaking, and Guns said shut off the production from this gang. It crossed my mind our orders could be taken as meaning shut the rest down as well." Bobby sighed. "It'll likely mean losing men, but this place cost one and training cost us two. Well?" Sandman, Siflis, Bells, and Attic began to smile, as did the five Troopers who'd brought in the captives.

Attic answered for them. "We all grew up in Pleb housing, and we all know a story something like Magpie's. I'd rather cark it busting a drug grower than training."

"Pick a couple of wounded men to hold the Pleb workers here, and then top all the gang members. Let the workers loot the place but don't let them go until I pass the word. Tell the men to burn the place before leaving, and to make sure the ultimate CEO himself can't put it out." Bobby headed for the door. "Get the other Corps, we've got a bit more planning to do."

* * *

Nearly six hours later dusk had started to lengthen the shadows as Bobby stuffed the contents of the fifth safe into a bag. "Send the message to the other four locations. Let the Plebs go, torch the place, then head for the rendezvous."

"Sarge? We've got radio traffic. Sounds like Troopers and they're coming here in a hurry." Attic waved an arm around at the Troopers, still dressed in civvies. "They'll open up on us."

"There must have been another panic button. That or someone reported the firefight." Bobby raised his voice. "Hood, Reaper, get your squads out to let us know when their scouts arrive. Don't kill them, just report. Get into uniform once you're out of sight but save the Pleb gear to wear again later."

"On it." The two squads left at the run. Bobby noted with relief that Magpie looked a lot better now. She'd been rocky for an hour or so and according to Hood had barfed, but where nobody saw her. Two more men had barfed during the cutting in the other drug factories, because several of the Troopers had issues with drug suppliers and were enthusiastic with their carving.

Bobby turned to the rest. "Everyone but those guarding Plebs get into uniform and get set at the front. Do not shoot when the Troopers arrive unless it goes viral then kill them all, quick. Sandman, bring that bledrin cannon." Bobby headed for the remains of the front entrance, peeling off the civvie gear as he went. Attic threw him a pack with his Trooper jacket and a Trooper sergeant's shotgun. Other Troopers were pulling flechette carbins from the small electric van they'd found in the second target and commandeered, though they all kept their notsi as well.

A few minutes later Bobby's buzzer vibrated. "One armoured troop carrier. Heavy machine gun." Crusty, the other scout, kept it short but that's all Bobby needed to know.

He raised his voice to let the men know as well. "Sandman, we've got an armoured troop carrier with a machine gun turret so find a good spot for that cannon. The rest of you, it's only a score of Troopers. Even if a Super has roused his ass, do not shoot him." Silence fell and they could all hear engines, then those stopped.

Siflis reported in. "Armour stopped. Sergeant in charge. Sniper and scout squad moving out."

"Tell me where they settle in. Hood, put your sights on the sniper but don't kill him." Silence fell again for several minutes.

"Crusty. Eleven-ten from you, two floors up."

"Oke. Hood?"

"Reaper. I've got the sniper. Holding for your word."

"Hood, watching the armour in case they send another squad out."

"Oke." Bobby stepped out into the open, his Trooper sergeant's stripes in clear view and his shotgun swinging from the sling. He opened his arms wide and faced the right direction, but even knowing where the incoming squad were he couldn't spot them. "Which window?"

"Left, from your direction."

Bobby brought one open hand round to point at the window. "Attic, tell them."

The bullhorn blared. "Trooper scout squad, we see you. Send your sergeant to talk. Do not make any aggressive move." Voices murmured behind Bobby, and then Attic's voice, kept low.

"Radio says they're reporting back." The radio definitely came under notsi equipment. Guns had produced it with a strict warning that nobody could be allowed to capture the receiver intact. Trooper radios only worked on pre-set frequencies and needed a Super's codes to change over. Beebi's Basteds had one that received all Trooper channels. It lit up to tell them when someone nearby sent a message to anyone, and allowed the radioman to listen in.

Bobby frowned. "Is there a dick or is Sarge in charge of that armour?"

"Wait one." More muttering followed. "A sergeant in charge with a dick riding his shoulder over the radio. Sarge is bringing up the rest of the Troopers and the armour." Attic paused for more murmuring from the radio man. "They're coming in ready for a ruck because he isn't sure you are a Trooper. He's reported to his dick and is waiting for a reply."

Bobby held out his hand. "Bullhorn please, Attic. Sandman be ready in case their dick sends back the wrong answer." He lifted the tiny speaker and his voice boomed out. "Unidentified scout squad. Tell your sergeant this is a black operation and I'll show him my ID, but only to the sergeant." Moments later Attic confirmed the message had been passed.

The sergeant did what Bobby probably would have in the same position. He parked the armour where the turret could cover the whole front of the building with the smoke leaking out of the broken windows and the bodies scattered in the entrance. For long minutes Bobby stood looking at the armour while the sergeant reported in, and Attic told Bobby what he'd reported. "He's been told to bring us in."

Attic had barely finished when the turret swivelled to cover Bobby and the loudspeaker on the troop carrier spoke up. "Lay down your weapons and step forward to be identified."

Bobby spoke quietly. "Attic. What is his Super called? Not dick, his real name."

"Supervisor Karlsson."

Bobby raised his bullhorn. "Black operation, above Supervisor Karlsson's pay grade. Come forward and I'll show you my ID. Just you, and all you ever verify is that it's Trooper ID."

Attic reported that the dick wasn't accepting that. The loudspeaker on the armour spoke again. "No. Come here or we open fire and identify the bodies."

"It won't work like that. Fair warning, if your sniper tries to shoot I've got two rifles on him." Bobby paused. "If your turret moves, you lose it. Corp, show them your answer to armour."

Bobby heard a muffled yell from inside the armour when someone spotted Sandman, then the sarge spoke up again. "What is that? A one-man cannon?"

"Near enough, and it'll definitely go through your armour so don't move the turret to target him. You can still bottle us up, we both lose men, it goes up higher to get more Troopers involved and then it hits the fan. When it gets to the right pay grade you'll all be told to back off and go home, and I'll pick up my dead and leave. Your Super will get shite, and will heap it onto you." Bobby sighed, into the bullhorn so the sergeant could hear it. "I've already lost three men and I've got wounded from sorting out your shite. That's enough for today."

Attic kept quiet, reporting once Bobby had his finger off the bullhorn button. "Beebi, spotter at the rear reports a smoke plume from the direction of target three."

Bobby called out to the sergeant again. "There'll be reports of fires in a few moments, big ones. Do you know what this place is?"

"I've been told this is a gang fight over drugs."

"Come and look." A long silence followed. Bobby knew the sergeant would be weighing it up. If a fight kicked off he'd lose the armour and some men, and if Bobby really had snipers behind him it would be a lot of men. Then if higher really did know all about this the Super wouldn't take the rap, the sergeant would.

A hatch opened, while another voice spoke on the loudspeaker. "The sarge is coming out. If anyone kills him, I'll open up and sod that cannon." A sergeant came out and stood for a moment, looking left and right. Then he started walking, steadily, and Bobby smiled slightly because he'd also got his shotgun on its sling, ready.

Bobby waited until the sergeant stopped a couple of paces away. "I'm going for my ID. Tell trigger-happy to behave."

"He's not trigger-happy."

"Nor are my men, but accidents happen all the same." Bobby reached into his pocket nice and steady, taking out the slip of plastic. He took a pace forward to pass it over, and the sergeant ran it through the reader all ranks from sergeant up carried as part of their kit. His head came up, startled. "Hush Sarge. No names. I didn't expect you to recognise me."

"Ha. Maybe not officially but rumours say you've got a sponsor, high enough to give me nosebleeds." The sergeant relaxed, putting out a hand to make a complicated gesture. "They won't stand down but the fingers are off the triggers."

Bobby spoke to the side. "Pass that along." Then he faced the sergeant. "Don't confirm my name, but there will be rumours. You do know this complex has a drug problem, a big one?"

"Yes, but we always hit the wrong place." He looked up at the building behind Bobby. "This the right one?"

"One of them. You can have a really quick tour but then it burns. Don't be downwind."

The sergeant stiffened so his tapper or buzzer were talking to him.

"How many did you hit?"

"Five, all the big ones, and the rest are burning right now. They had protection to keep you away. Are you coming in or can we piss off?"

The sergeant looked wary. "The message from my Super is to keep you here. I told him what you said and he doesn't care, he wants you taken in or pinned down. There's backup on the way."

"No there isn't, or not yet. I don't want to kill Troopers, Sarge, but my orders come from higher than a Super and I'm not to surrender to local forces." Guns had never said that, but there were too many Supers out there who'd love Beebi the Basted to be the victim of mistaken identity and a burst of flechettes.

"That thing really will kill the armour?"

Bobby laughed. "Come and look at the door in here. You know the big drug bosses always armour a safe room?"

"Yeah. That's why we know we've never found the right place. Lead on." He sighed. "The Super will still insist I arrest you."

"Just come and look." Bobby led him to the small armoured room, showing him the twisted steel where Sandman opened the door. He led the Sarge to a corner. Bobby took off his wrist com, indicating for the sarge do the same before moving away. "This room is a dead spot so nobody can snoop on the gang boss, all the safe rooms were the same. Nobody can monitor so they won't know you've taken that off and can't record what we say. How do we get both of us out of this mess?"

Sarge sighed. "I can't let you drive away. The dick would put us all up against a wall."

Bobby smiled. "You can't seal us in. You've only got twenty men and the armour."

"I'll have to try." A smile hovered on the sergeant's lips. "Did you really top a Super?"

"It's nearly a qualification for this lot. We've got an official name but our boss calls us Beebi's Bigger Basteds and he really is way above a Super." Bobby thought about that little smile. "How hard will you try to pen us in?"

The sergeant thought hard. "I can only seal the front properly in case that cannon takes out the armour?"

"Sarge." Attic put his head round the door. "His dick is talking to the armour and reckons half the complex is in flames. Says the sergeant is off-air and to get ready to break in."

"Shite! You can listen to our radio?" Bobby nodded and the sergeant shrugged. "I'm convinced, this is a black op and official. If I watch the front very carefully?"

"Don't come in when it starts burning because we really will torch it." Bobby smiled. "There really are only four other fires but they are big ones. Those were my orders, to make sure nobody can set them up again. Now get your gear back on before the armour gets chewed up."

Sarge did exactly what he'd said, set up a defence line to seal off the front of the building. Bobby threw a coat over his uniform before going to see the score of prisoners. "You've got three minutes to loot the place, then its gonna burn and Troopers will be crawling all over it. Just head home nice and steady and nobody will be looking for you."

"Where do we get a fix now?" The man looked terrified, but addiction overcame the threat of death.

"You don't because the big producers have all closed so you won't be able to afford what bit of shite is still available. Take enough to get yourself clean over the next couple of weeks. If you don't get clean, tough." Bobby looked at the rest. "Now get dressed, load up and run like hell."

"Ain't you taking over? Who are you?"

"Beebi's Basteds. Just pass the word around. Any shite who thinks they can't be touched might get a visit." Bobby grinned. "We don't care if it's a Pleb, gang boss or a Manager."

"You'll get us on that bledrin Taxi, Beebi." Sudden, the Corp with metal feet, kept his voice low and looked really uneasy.

Bobby turned to answer just as quietly. "No I won't, because I've done some serious thinking about what management really wants. They will want everyone to know what we are, Troopers, so the Plebs don't think we're revolutionary heroes. A lot of us are suspected of topping Supers so they'll use us to keep their own in order as well, and I'm all for making the management nervous. Now let's get finished and head home. Guns will bust a blood vessel when he hears about it." That cheered everyone up as the news spread. Guns could be spectacular if he'd been flicked hard enough.

Three minutes later the first squad of Bobby's men went out through the emergency exit, disguised as civvies again. Five minutes after that, three minutes after the dick at Trooper HQ sent out more Troopers and armour, Bobby left as smoke began to spread through the labs. He glanced up as a Copter swept over the area before sauntering casually away to join the rest at the rendezvous. Bobby did worry about their pass to get out, but the authority on it must have been greater than the one sealing the exits. The guards on the exit might have looked happier if they'd known that being over-ruled saved their lives.

*   *   *

Beebi's Basteds were late back to the airstrip for their lift home, very late, but the plane had waited. When the plane landed at the other end the guards on the buses, caught in the glare of the landing lights, didn't look very happy. Guns had left a terse message to not take any sightseeing tours on the way home. The Super filed onto the plane with his men and left without even knowing who he'd guarded the buses for.

Guns had questions, but in private. "Did you not understand your orders?"

Bobby kept his voice level, and no hint of expression on his face. "Yes, close down a drug producer in that complex."

"One target, not five. The riots have already started, because the addicts know they'll not get a fix tomorrow or maybe the week after." The Area Manager looked more worried than angry.

"It'll do them good. A few might even stay off the shite."

Guns glared. "Is that why you ignored your orders?"

"I didn't. I carried them out, to the full. The spooks didn't give us the full story because that target was only a part of the organisation, sort of." Bobby bit back his smile. "I've got tape and paper evidence, and discs which will have more."

"It had better be good."

Bobby started emptying the first bag onto the desk while Guns took

167

out a disc player.

* * *

Nearly an hour later Guns's first question wasn't about the evidence. "Why did they scream, some of them?"

"I needed answers quickly. We didn't have truth drugs so we used knives."

Guns flinched. "Who did that?"

"Several men, all volunteers. I asked them to, and watched so nobody got out of control." Not too far out of control, Bobby amended mentally. Magpie hadn't been the only one with issues.

Guns sighed. "I've had everyone up to a Viscount screaming at me about the property damage and the dead Plebs. Now you tell me it's just five buildings, all weed farms and labs, and nearly all the dead are gangsters." Guns shrugged, and a little smile broke on his face. "Actually they haven't been screaming at me, but the one person who can find me has nearly burned out the wires. I'll tell him it's a learning curve."

"A learning curve?"

"Yes. Nobody has ever let a crew like yours loose to solve these sorts of problems. Today I learned that if your orders give you a centimetre, you'll take the whole bledrin motorway." Guns shook his head. "The management have learned that if they want a wolf pack, there might be a bit more blood than expected and you won't sit and play fetch. The spooks have learned to tell the truth, and to get their men out ahead of you if they didn't already do that. But as a plus the problem is fixed, and the local Troopers can arrest a shitload of dealers and general bad boys."

He gestured at the paper and discs. "Even if none of this is clean evidence, the spooks now know who any other contacts are. The Horseman will catch the basteds when they try to contact the new men, those who move into the gap in the market. There will be a cost to the owners, lost production due to riots, with some of the lower management losing bonuses." He paused and looked at Bobby.

"We did the job. That cost us three men and others will need metal, but we reckon the result is worth it so I'm not going to cry over some dick's bonus. It'll teach them to keep their house in order." Bobby let his smile come. "Once the place calms down, production will go up without so many drugs available to the workforce."

"I'll pass that message." Guns leant back and stretched. "I could kill a drink, but I've got to stamp on all the fires you just started. Piss off and join the party." He finally smiled properly, and then laughed. "If anybody tries to give me too much shite, I'll offer to send you bledrin maniacs to explain."

The party didn't last long because they were all knackered. Magpie had already left when Bobby joined the rest, with Siflis to keep an eye on her because a couple of Troopers had commented about Hood going off with what they thought was another man. When the party broke up and the rest of the squad went to their room, Siflis whispered that he thought Magpie had cried herself to sleep. In the morning she seemed fine, and the subject never came up again. Though the cutting settled one thing. Magpie had no problem with blood or a straight knifing after that.

*　*　*

After the first mission, the TRRF went on a mission about once a fortnight for six months. They varied from a straight snatch of a crime boss and the killing of another to other strikes similar to the first one. This time they'd only been back three days so their injured were still with the medics and the replacement for their dead man hadn't arrived. Bobby read the thin file. "This info is real, and we can kill a couple of Supers?"

"Not officially, though if a few turn up as collateral but you save the generators, controls and most of the Supers and Managers, nobody will make waves." Guns sighed. "Don't let your men go on a hunt, all right? If they do kill a few you'll have to give a reason that will fly, to me at least."

"I've got it. What about the buses? Do we travel in them this time?" The location wasn't all that far away.

"No, you'll drive to an airstrip and leave by air so you'll come in from another direction." Guns pointed at the door. "Get your people organised because this is urgent."

Urgent was right, the Troopers who weren't too badly injured were ready to roll inside the hour. "This is short notice so I hope everyone knows who we are, that nobody comes over all official and takes our notsi?"

"The guards for the buses will come with the plane as usual, and you won't be searched or any crap like that." Guns glowered. "We've gone over that every time you go out, so why do you want to hear it again?"

Bobby sniggered. "Because you're a bag of nerves before we leave and I'm stopping you from wiping all their noses and kissing them goodbye."

"Piss off Beebi."

"We're gone, Guns."

* * *

The Area Manager watched them go down the road and yes, his nerves were jumping. He'd bitched about a force like this for years, but every Unit hung onto their best men. Then over two score of hard basteds turned up and no Super wanted them in his Unit. Gunnar smiled. The Supers weren't all pussies, but a bunch like this would screw up most Units because out there in that housing complex they'd bonded. Keeping them all locked up together, then Beebi walking away from the court case clean, had finished the job. They all thought Beebi the Basted could shite fire and walk on water, and that Supers were just targets once they strayed into the wrong place.

They'd certainly shat fire, and bullets, in a good few places now but today would be different. This time, instead of the usual blunt object, they had to be a precision instrument. Guns laughed quietly to himself at the idea of Beebi and his men as a precision instrument, then hoped they kept the Super count down to a reasonable number. Though if they did this job, Guns knew the apprenticeship would be over. He already had four files that needed a bit more finesse, ones he daren't give the TRRF until he knew Beebi could restrain them if necessary.

* * *

Bobby explained the job on the way, then they all waited in a car park at the target location while the local management gave his version of the job. "Do not damage anything. I want those filthy basted Plebs out of there without a scratch on the paintwork." The Manager glared at Bobby. "I expect you to save the management, all of them."

"Paintwork or Supers, sluur?"

"What!"

170

"If it's a choice between a dead Super or a bullet hole in the equipment, which do you prefer? If a Super carks it, there'll be splatter of course, but that will wipe off the hardware." Bobby indicated the Troopers with his hand. "I need to let the others know before we go in. Sluur."

The Manager or possibly Director, hard to tell because they all wore expensive suits, stared at the Troopers slouching nearby. The slouching had become a sort of trademark now. So had the plethora of notsi, blatantly displayed, and the bandoliers and clips of illegal ammunition that festooned every Trooper. He flinched from some of the looks, then looked back at Bobby and flinched again at something about Bobby's face. "I know about you. You're not to kill Supervisors." He hesitated. "Unless it is unavoidable. Do not damage the generators or controls."

"Thank you sluur. Now if we can talk to your people and get eyes on the building?" The man waved at a group of five before leaving, walking rapidly. Bobby smiled, just a little, as four suits and the Super in charge of security approached. They looked like deer being driven to the same watering hole as a pack of wolves.

*   *   *

After listening to all five, and getting eyes-on the problem, Bobby held a meeting with most of his old squad and the Corps. Eventually he sat back and smiled. "Yes, all right, I agree. We'll have to top two Supers."

"Didn't think you'd fight that hard over it Beebi." Bells grinned. "Are you going soft on Supers or worried about shite from that Director?"

"Neither, but I've got to justify it to Guns. He won't care how many Supers cark it but we're not to top them just for the hell of it." Bobby frowned. "We might have just found our sort of officer."

"So why isn't he here, because the basted proved he can shoot?" Guns had provided live fire for some exercises, getting close enough on a regular basis to prove he did it deliberately.

"I asked and that's not allowed. He's supposed to be low profile." Bobby grinned. "Maybe nobody wants him either. Now just to be an arse, we run through it again. The Plebs, rebels, filthy upstarts or general scumbags have the computer controls for the generators, the actual control panels and switching gear, and allegedly enough explosives to turn it all to scrap and rubble."

"What do they want, you never did say?"

"Because they won't get it, Attic. They want a shitload of prisoners released, strikers and rioters from the housing complex." Bobby shrugged. "Even if that happens, the men in there aren't getting out alive."

"They've got enough weaponry to stop the guards on the plant, and enough explosive for seven necklaces." Sandman frowned. "We all agree if they'd really got a shitload of explosives they'd let someone see them to prove it. Instead they've put a Super or Manager in the middle of each door or window with explosives round their neck. If anyone breathes hard on the wires over the openings, the Super loses his head."

"Clever, because management won't authorise killing their own." Hood glanced at Bobby. "Though you say this Director type just did."

Bobby laughed. "No he didn't, he just set a priority and clearly told me to take the place without damaging the gear or killing management, if possible. The two-faced shite just passed it to me."

"Oops, that's a mistake." Sandman looked at the schematic. "It would be easier to go in five places at once? Seven?"

"Don't get greedy. Just because this will be your first Super."

"Mine as well." Magpie grinned. "This is a Pleb dream. Can I top one of them?" She really had loosened up now, enough to occasionally flick Bells about underwear. She reckoned the reason he asked about hers was because Bells wanted to borrow some.

Bobby shook his head in mock despair. "No, but you two cherries can put a clip of solid rounds through the window and door and trip the wires. I suppose the rounds will hit the Supers, but then those nasty rebel bombs will blow their heads off so nobody will look too close." Bobby raised his head as a Copter went by overhead and another lined up to do the same. "At least those are doing their job. Hood, you and Reaper get set up. Three-click when ready, I'll say eight when its time." The radio had been spouting random numbers now and then for an hour, but among the unused ones was eight. Just so anyone listening to radios didn't realise when the code message was passed.

"Get set?" Hood sniggered. "I thought you'd got to run this past management again?"

"I will, I'm just going to ignore what they say and go in the door and this window. Unless they say go home, we'll deal with it?" Bobby rolled up the schematic. "Sandman, Magpie, count two after the snipers shoot, then open up." As Bobby left another random shot rang out, aimed at the open sky.

*   *   *

Just over five minutes later, Bobby's tapper three-clicked. Bobby brought his hand down and the motors behind him whined into life. A Copter cruised in, aiming to pass just clear of the target. "Eight." Two flat cracks sounded as one. Bobby watched one of the lookouts on the roof flip backwards as a heavy bullet blew through his head. The other sniper would have killed the second lookout but anyone in the building would assume more of those random shots. Then Bobby lurched as the jeep surged forward, though he still tried to watch the Copters.

As soon as he'd said eight, two spare Copters hovering nearby had accelerated straight for the target. The one nearby went past as usual, blanketing the area with sound. The two spares, the noise of their approach drowned out, headed towards the big square brick building and ropes unfurled. Two seconds later automatics stuttered from nearby, followed by two explosions.

Bobby saw the explosions as his jeep burst through the flimsy hoardings put up so the besieged Plebs couldn't see to shoot at anyone moving about. He propped his shotgun on the sandbag sat on the bonnet in front of him, bracing as the jeep raced straight for the shattered ground floor window. Lines of smoke flew past as first the flash-bangs and then the smoke preceded him into the building. "Fire." Flechettes erupted from the two other passengers, both aiming carbines.

At the very last second Bobby fired both barrels of his shotgun, loaded with plastic instead of lead buckshot so he wanted to be close. He hung on as the jeep hit the low brick below the window, lurching as the metal plate on the front smashed straight through. The jeep bounced and crashed back down, the driver immediately turning the wheel while braking as hard as possible. Bobby grabbed his shotgun, bouncing around on its sling, and crammed in two more rounds.

Flechettes whined, then heavier weapons sounded. His goggles picked up the heat from a real firearm. Bobby gave the man both barrels, because that weapon might go through body armour. The high-pitched burr of the Kraut meant the second jeep through the window had arrived with Bells aboard, and turned left or it would be buried in the back of this one. Up on the floor above flash-bangs exploded, followed by shots but not many and quickly stilled. Siflis would be up there because the most agile Troopers went in through the skylights.

Bobby charged forward into the offices at the rear of the room, ramming in two more rounds but using one immediately on a man with a grenade. He grabbed the dead man and flipped him onto the grenade, then dropped on top. Behind him the two Troopers dived back out the door. Four seconds later a giant kicked the dead Pleb into the air, flipping Bobby off into the wall. He glanced round, relieved to see no real damage to the equipment apart from scratched paint and spatter, then staggered out to find the fighting had finished.

∗   ∗   ∗

Sudden limped over. "We lost one man, but the other two should make it if the medic gets here sharpish. There's no explosives on the equipment though a couple of the corpses had grenades."

"Grab the grenades and sort out any good quality notsi or ammo." Bobby looked round and waved two Troopers over. "Nerd, Sparkler, check those necklaces. If you can't make them safe, tell the Managers and Supers to sit very still until someone who can gets here." Bobby opened a channel to the plant security. "Come in but don't point things because my Troopers are twitchy. Don't go near the wired openings."

"Aren't they safe yet?"

"My people are looking very carefully. Do you want to come over and stick your fat fingers into the wiring, save us the job?"

"No! Did you capture any of the rebels?"

Bobby sighed. "Of course. We asked them really nicely to put down their weapons and they said yes and put on the kettle to brew the caff."

A different voice came on. "Comedian. I wanted to know."

"These men knew they weren't getting out alive so no prisoners. Sluur." Bobby smiled, unseen by the Super on the radio. "We captured some management, most of them alive?" He held the earpiece away until the Super finished venting.

Though Bobby kept the smile off his face when he came out to find the Director waiting. "I said no damage!"

"A window and a low brick wall, non-load bearing, one set of entrance doors, some cleaning and decorating, a few desks and chairs and maybe a comp screen or two in there. Two skylights on the roof, and there's some broken dials and spatter on the machinery and controls. In return you got the place back still operational with two Managers and three Supers still alive."

"But I said no damage and no deaths."

"You refused permission to blow holes in the brickwork, so we had to go in the windows or doors." Bobby shrugged. "Two entry points is the minimum." He tapped his wrist comp. "I've got your exact wording, sluur."

Bobby listened patiently while the Director screamed a bit. He didn't care because he could see Magpie and Sandman celebrating in the background, toasting each other with a beer. Once the Director wound down Bobby collected his wounded, all but two who left in a Copter for serious attention and more metal. The notsi body armour Guns had found someplace made a big difference. Bobby frowned, he suspected this had been a test of some sort and wondered what sort of missions they'd get now?

Payback

The first supposedly precision operation must have been precise enough, because the TRRF were given more jobs that didn't involve killing everyone. Fourteen months later, after a succession of missions from straight hits to hostage rescue missions, Guns brought them their first really black op. "We want you to find a bomber, one who doesn't care about collateral. He's killing a lot of Plebs as well as Troopers and causing property damage. A couple of hints led to booby-traps, because there's a leak or a sympathiser so the bombers knew before the Troopers made a raid." Guns grimaced. "Worse, the spooks think the bombers know when any Trooper operation is actually planned, and they can't find electronics or how the information is passed."

"So what's our job?"

"You go into the complex without the local Trooper Unit knowing." Guns sighed. "Without the local management knowing, right up to Director." He looked Bobby straight in the eye. "You will be repaying a debt. This is for the Ironhills so I reckon you'll be dealing with an embarrassing problem for your patron."

"I don't mind, she did right by me. What sort of problem?"

Guns put the thin file on the desk. "That goes in the shredder once you've read it. On the face of it there's a mystery leak in lower management or the Troopers, and some Pleb revolutionaries. Reading between the lines, especially bearing in mind upper management won't know about you, someone high up is playing silly basteds. It boils down to political stuff to get promotion or smear a rival. There's always this sort of shite, but this arse is using bombs. They're costing the Ironhills serious creds to make a rival or superior look bad, but I'd guess the person is too smart or too high up to be fingered." Guns looked downright hungry for a moment. "The basted is getting people killed in a power game, but if you unpick the bottom layer of the communications I reckon The Horseman will follow the trail upwards. Then what happens depends on how well the Duchess knows The Horseman."

Bobby smirked. "She knows his name, what he looks like and where he lives; she said so when she thought spooks were listening to us."

Guns sniggered. "Then it'll be a mysterious disappearance, or a botched mugging or robbery." Bobby stared and Guns smiled at him. "Management really do police themselves, at least sometimes, and I'm far enough up to know how it works."

"Good to know." Bobby frowned at the file. "Are we being used to top another Super?"

"Nobody that insignificant. This is best if nobody ever knows you were there, not officially. Unofficially I'd guess it'll be leaked to make sure a few people get their house in order." Guns looked quite sad for a moment. "Neither of us will ever retire quietly, Beebi. We've rattled the wrong cages." A brief smile flitted over his face. "Not unless the Iron Duchess finds you a quiet country cottage."

"I'd die of boredom, unless everyone else comes with me? You could teach me manners." Bobby opened the file, because talk of the Duchess always made him a bit uneasy. Though he really did owe her so payback seemed fair. Especially since this basted killed job lots of Plebs just to get a promotion.

* * *

Getting into the complex and buying a small cheap place to stay wasn't a problem, but the next bit could take time because the TRRF didn't do subtle. Sandman frowned, looking out of the bedroom window at the locals in the street. "What are we supposed to do exactly, if we can't break heads or at least raid someone? For that matter, why are we here because these Plebs look happy enough. Not exactly laughing, but not ready to riot or revolt."

"I told you, the problem is in upper management. Some super-dick looking for promotion. He's using bombs and blaming the Plebs to stir the shite." Bobby looked out of the window at the Plebs streaming past, coming home from their shift in the Potash Mines. "The housing here is decent for Pleb blocks, and there's no starvation, but there'll be plenty of youths looking for thrills or an easy cred." The group exchanged glances, being young and looking for thrills or creds had been how most of them ended up 'volunteering' for the army. "Someone is using young idjeets to set off the bombs, and because the bombs kill Plebs it'll stir up shite eventually. Then the arse will solve the problem, catch the bomber, and get his promotion."

"We'll not find upper management here. The basteds won't come slumming to a black market electrical workshop." Sparkler smiled brightly. "Though mending kettles and toasters is a bit of a holiday for me."

Bells cracked his knuckles. "I don't fancy working in the Potash mine, but we've got to find a way to fit in somehow."

"I'm not going into a mine." Siflis had started twitching. "I joined up rather than go to the Chemworks."

"I joined up rather than go into a mine so I'm with you there, but we have to find a way to blend in. It'll just take a couple of us, to find a few of the local likely lads." Bobby grinned. "Then we can take over a low-profile black operation and nobody will wonder why a group of fit men aren't down the mine." His smile faltered. "The first bit, getting information on the locals, is the problem. Everyone here knows all about mining Potash and we don't so we'll stand out."

"I'll do it, find you the local bad boys. I did some waitress jobs at caff houses, and sold a bit of home knitting and embroidery for the family on the market before sis had her problem." Magpie shrugged, embarrassed. "If I'm the shy type and don't talk much, I'll get away with the accent. Someone will come along to shake down the owner or pick up the weekly payoff. That or some smartarse will brag a bit or show off a few more creds than he should." She blushed just a little. "I'll have to encourage them to talk, so we'll need someone to be on over-watch in case some randy shite gets heavy. You know, follows me after work." Her smile became a little bit more feral. "Knifing the scroat might spoil my cover." Bobby's first reaction was no, but Magpie had always insisted on being one of the team. Then she gave him a reason he couldn't argue with. "You'd let any of the rest do it but they'd never fill out a skirt and blouse the same."

The thought made him smile. "I never thought of that, you can dress like a woman."

"I am a woman, sort of, which means nobody will ever guess I'm a Trooper, will they? Oy, quit that." Magpie ducked away as Siflis rubbed her Trooper cut.

"You'll need a wig." Bobby sniggered. "That'll blow Guns's mind, one of us in a woman's wig. Maybe I'd better buy one local." He nodded at Magpie. "You're on. You'll have a squad watching from here and there, especially when you walk home. Practice the accent so you get near to local, though I can hear a mix out there."

"You'll never get the local Yorkshire right, so stick to a mild version and swear your Ma came from someplace else." Hood frowned. "No, your Dad, because there's no reason for a woman to change complexes but a man can be brought in for expertise. I'll keep a rifle covering you. If it goes wrong, just run and we'll drop whoever follows."

"Work on what you need. Ah, have you got any clothes left? You know, dresses or anything?" Bobby hesitated. "You'll have to give one of us sizes. Otherwise you might look like a bloke buying dresses for yourself."

"Just for a dress, then with a wig I'll buy the rest." Magpie's blush deepened when Bells muttered sexy knickers. "I haven't got to live in a bledrin accommodation block and all that, have I?" She curled her lip in a sneer. "Some block caretaker will want a favour to get me a flat at short notice, or the local protection will want paying off and maybe not in creds. I've lived in those places, remember, and only Divas usually swap blocks."

Bobby hadn't thought of that. "We can't pay someone off or they'll be nosy about how you got the creds. We'd need more than one person there anyway, because we won't leave one of ours hanging out there without cover. What about a private place, a flat or a room not in a block?"

"It would have to be cheap so as not to attract attention but even then I'd need an income to afford it." Magpie frowned. "Though at least nobody bothers to shake down some Pleb renting out a room."

"You need freedom of movement and a reason you can afford it so your cover will be you've got a bloke, and he's got a decent job in the mine. You earn a few creds at the market which means the pair of you can afford to rent a private flat." Hood hesitated. "The bloke will have to visit, and often enough to look as if he lives there. It would be better if he actually lived there." Beebi managed not to flick a glance at either Bells or Hood.

"Not a chance. I'm sleeping in the shed or whatever with the rest of the Troopers." Magpie glowered. "I'm not shacking up with one of you randy basteds just for cover."

"You can stay here." Sparkler waved a hand round the bedroom. "There's two bedrooms and I'm supposed to be a local bodge-it, scrabbling to get by, so I'll rent one out." He shrugged. "Pick a Trooper to act the boyfriend and he'll be here anyway if anyone gets nosy, but he lives in the other room or the storeroom with the rest of us. We'll squeeze up to leave an empty room." Magpie nodded and the group started to work out exactly what they had to do. This should be spook work, but the spooks had failed. Now Beebi's Basteds had the job, and none of them liked failure because that might mean being put back in some Trooper Unit. They wouldn't take well to scrabbling about some complex busting heads and taking shite from a Super.

*　　*　　*

Within days the Troopers were stir crazy from living in the storeroom and one bedroom of the scruffy little repair shop without letting the neighbours know. Beebi let a few go out to visit the local Diva palaces and see if they could pick up gossip. He sent the men who got a bit antsy without a regular ration of pooching, which meant Bells for one. For the rest their only relief came when they stood over-watch on Magpie. Only half of them could take a turn at doing that since the rest didn't know her sex. They knew Magpie had gone undercover, but not how, and as the days stretched past a week Bobby seriously considered extracting some men until later.

The first real break came as Magpie walked home after work. She'd just started through an alley when a voice called from behind her. "Eyup love, wait fer me."

Magpie slowed just a little, her eyes searching the shadows, and slid a thin knife into her hand. She glanced back. "What do yer want?"

"That's not friendly. I just wanted to walk yer home." The youth came closer, smiling, and tried to put an arm round her. "It's not safe wandering around the streets all alone when it's getting dark."

Magpie avoided the arm, and gave a small head-shake to the shadow down low by a rubbish skip at the alley entrance. No point in killing the shite for this. "I'm not alone. My boyfriend is coming to meet me." She sniggered. "He's a big bloke. You don't want yer arm round me when he gets here."

"I ain't afraid of no bloke on the complex. If he gives me shite I'll get the rest of the lads to call round, see how big he is then." The youth smirked. "No need for that if yer a little bit more friendly?" Magpie avoided his arm again, and wondered if she really would have to kill the stupid shite.

"Oy, nark it. That's my bird." Hood's deep voice echoed in the alley and Magpie smiled, though she still had the knife ready. This youth might just pull a notsi.

The youth did start towards his pocket, but hesitated and unknown to him that kept him alive a little longer. Siflis had Beebi's silenced pistol, Hood wore brass on the hand in his pocket, Magpie had her blade, and Bells would be just outside the alley behind them acting as backstop. The youth glanced around and must have decided shooting might attract attention. "Yer might be making a mistake. Do you know who I am?"

"The basted trying it on with Susanne, that's all I need. Just back off. Come on Susanne." Hood put out an arm, wrapping it around Magpie when she moved down the alley to join him.

"Watch yer back, big boy. Next time I might not be on my own." The youth looked at Magpie and smirked. "I know where to find yer tomorrow. See yer then."

Hood twitched but Magpie put an arm round him. "It's all right. The boss won't allow any shite from the likes of him." She glanced back. "Sod off before he loses his rag." The youth retreated, muttering, while Magpie and Hood stood watching him go. She elbowed Hood. "You can let go now."

"Sorry." Hood grinned. "When you put your arm round me I thought you'd got comfy tucked in there."

"Piss off." Magpie sniggered. "Boyfriend? When did you get the job?" She'd avoided picking anyone to stand in as boyfriend despite or maybe because of a lot of flickin from Bells.

"When you said your boyfriend was a big bloke. I'm the biggest bloke who happened to be nearby." Hood frowned after the youth. "He seemed to think I should know him."

"Overinflated ego. There's six of them trying to break into the protection racket at the market but so far the other two gangs are keeping them out. They haven't enough muscle." She squeezed Hood's bicep. "Hmm, maybe we'd better talk to Beebi. Now let go of me. I want to get home and back into proper clothes."

"Oops, I forgot." Hood grunted at the elbow in his ribs and Magpie scowled at the chuckle from the shadows by the skip. "How come he followed you?"

"I might have smiled at him a couple of times, just to get him to brag a bit. Typical youth, they can't see past the skirt and blouse." Hood made a non-committal noise so Magpie elbowed him again. "You can keep your eyes ahead as well."

"Hey, I'm a boyfriend, I'm supposed to notice what you wear."

"Ha, boyfriends tend to wonder more about what they can't see, and you can forget that. It's illegal to get into another Trooper's underwear."

"Underwear?" Hood moved to try and avoid her elbow, but not far enough. Behind them Siflis wore a rare smile because he thought if anyone else had said and done what Hood just had, Magpie might have used a knife instead of an elbow.

* * *

Bobby really liked the idea of a small gang of chancers who were trying to muscle in. He let a couple of Sandman's squad out to cruise the market nearby, just in case this arse got heavy in public, and asked Magpie to find out more. With Magpie's other information on the local gangs demanding protection in the market, Bobby finally had a way into the local underworld. The Troopers who were getting stir crazy spent several nights out and about, working off their surplus energy and frustration while thinning out the local heavies.

This time the youth didn't wait for Magpie to leave work. "Hello gorgeous. Have yer weakened yet?"

Magpie rolled her eyes. "What, in the head? Do you really want to be stomped?"

"Ha, we've just taken another three stalls." The youth looked over at the stallholder. "Another week and we'll be making an offer to yer boss.

Maybe we'll give him a special rate if you're a bit more friendly." He picked up an apple from the display and bit into it, staring a challenge at the stallholder. The man frowned but looked away. His current 'insurers' had lost three of their five enforcers in a week. One fell from an accommodation block and two were found in a skip with their throats cut. Worse, a lot of the potential replacements around here had been having accidents as well.

"I keep warning yer, the answer is no and he really will stomp you." Magpie kept a little smile on her face. "Now let me work. You're scaring off customers and then my boss won't be able to pay." The youth swaggered off and Magpie sighed loudly, but her boss kept his face turned away. That confirmed it, the stallholder expected a takeover soon. She hoped so, because Beebi wanted her to say no and hint yes to the would-be gangster, while more and more she was tempted to knife the slimy little toad.

*   *   *

Magpie didn't have to wait long, just two days. "Now yer might want to be more friendly." The youth waved the creds at Susanne and put them in his back pocket. "I'll bet yer boss would up yer wages if he got a discount." She looked down, avoiding his eyes. "Just a little delay on the way home for a bit of fun, and I can get his insurance halved." Susanne looked over at her boss and he turned away. "Or I can arrange for three or four of us to meet yer boyfriend in a dark alley, and he can have a nasty accident."

"No." Susanne barely whispered, still refusing to meet his eyes. "Don't hurt him."

The youth leaned closer. "Well then you can start by calling me Slash." He leaned a little closer. "Well?"

Susanne sighed, and gave him a shy smile. "All right, Slash."

"That's better. When do yer get off?"

"Five, but I mustn't be very late or he'll come looking." She tried to look nervous and just a bit excited.

"Don't worry, just a little taster this time." He chuckled. "Maybe yer boss will let you off early?"

"Not this time. People will notice." Slash went to put an arm around her. "No, not here. People will see. They'll talk."

"Don't worry. In a few more weeks none of them will dare. Then maybe I'll tell yer bloke to piss off." Slash laughed. "We'll have a few more heavies then, so he'd best listen."

"No, don't. I'll do what yer say but don't do that to Fenn." Hood had suggested calling her Susanne, so Magpie had made up his name.

"All right, for now anyway. See yer in the same alley, and don't give me no crap. Is he coming to meet you again?"

"No Slash. Not tonight, but I can't be very late." Another little smile hinted she might be looking forward to this, just a bit.

"Oke, see yer later, gorgeous. Or more of yer later." Slash swaggered away as Susanne kept her eyes down to hide her anticipation.

Susanne worked the rest of the day without smiling or even speaking to her boss, showing her annoyance because he hadn't helped and shame at what she had agreed to. Avoiding him wasn't hard, he didn't want to meet her eyes even when she bid him goodbye. She dragged her feet a little on the way, and even more when she saw Slash lounging in a doorway.

Slash leered. "Come on, anyone would think yer didn't fancy this. This room is empty so we can get cosy."

"Not in a room." Susanne wasn't going into a damn room with the shite. Anybody could be waiting. "In the alley, just a quick taster yer said." Slash laughed at the hint of fear in her voice.

"C'mere then. Just in the doorway."

Susanne hung back. "No, you'll pull me in there, then Fenn will come to find me." Her voice dropped. "You'll shoot him in there, in private."

"Only if we aren't done by then."

"Hey, I told yer about that sort of thing." Susanne knew the shock showed on her face as the large figure blocked the end of the alley, because she'd practiced the expression.

Slash turned with a snarl on his face. "What are yer doing here?"

"Luckily, I decided to come and meet my bird." The man paused. "Though I was coming to see you and yer mates later."

"Why?" Slash tensed, hand in his pocket on a weapon and ignoring

Susanne entirely.

Fenn shrugged. "I heard you needed muscle, and the two of us wondered what the pay is?"

"Two?"

The reply came from behind. "We work as a team." Slash whirled, glaring at the shorter but definitely muscular figure now blocking the other end of the alley.

He turned back as the first man spoke. "But I'm in charge. My name is Fenn." He smiled but the result looked more of a threat. "My woman isn't in the package, all right?" He beckoned. "Susanne?" She ran up the alley and he put an arm round her. "So can we do business?"

"Maybe. Not here." Slash reassessed. This Fenn looked a real brawler, and the other man had that look as well. The Cutters were looking for more muscle because there seemed to be a shortage. That Susanne looked a bit scrawny anyway, not exactly Diva material so no real loss. He'd only pushed because she seemed a bit frightened and possibly interested. He'd thought she'd give it up under pressure. Slash pointed at the room behind him. "I've emptied this place and he won't be back until morning so if yer come back in two hours, after dark?"

Fenn nodded, his arm tightening slightly around Susanne. The little shite had intended a lot more than a taste. He smiled slightly at her wriggle and wordless protest, letting the smile broaden for Slash. "We'll be here. No fancy stuff or it'll be bloody."

"Straight business, though if yer want to bring her?" Slash intended flickin the basted a bit, but for a moment thought he'd made a mistake.

Fenn turned the snarl back into a smile and relaxed again. Susanne looked up at him. "I don't want to Fenn, but if yer want me to come and it's just business?"

The gangster smiled. "Two hours." Slash turned, hesitating because the end of the alley had cleared with no sign of where the second man might be. He shrugged before heading off to collect the rest of the Cutters, all six and the two new heavies. If the meeting didn't work out, he might still get his fun with the girl. Behind him, Susanne elbowed Fenn twice before he let her go, though she smiled just a little when he couldn't see.

*   *   *

The blonde Diva coming towards Scar wore a big smile and a short skirt. He shook his head. "Sorry darlin' but I don't pay."

She kept coming. "It's been a slack night, how about a freebie?"

The young man shook his head, regretfully. "Not now, I've got to stay here. Though maybe later?" Scar started to turn at a slight scuffing but arms came around his face, cutting off sight, his air, and most his hearing. That all became irrelevant as a sharp pain under his ribs drove higher, until all pain went away. Hood bent to lower the body, then unwrapped his arms from around the man's head.

Magpie wiped her blade on the corpse's jacket front, nodding towards the shadow watching from a nearby yard. She slid the cleaned knife into the sheath hung down her back under the blouse before taking off the blonde wig. Magpie replaced it with the black Susanne wig from Hood's pocket, waiting impatiently as he adjusted it. "Are you putting him in the skip in the alley?"

"Not yet, Siflis says there's a heavy outside the door with Slash. Whether we clean up depends on how the meeting goes." Hood looked at her skirt. "That's a new one, a bit shorter than usual."

"Stop it!" She blushed a little. "I made a mistake when I bought it. It was supposed to show a bit of leg, not make me look like a Diva!"

"It'll make leading that little shite to the slaughter a lot easier." Hood scowled. "That's if we get an agreement." As they headed down the alley Snook slipped out of the shadows in the yard, leaving Scar's hidden backup in a crumpled heap. He pulled Scar's body into the yard and stood in Scar's place.

Slash stood in the doorway glancing both ways as Bells appeared at the other end of the alley. Any questions about what the sentries said died as he saw Magpie's skirt. "Yer never wore that to the market, girly. Yer a real Diva?"

"Behave. Did your partners get here yet?" Hood nodded over towards Bells. "We've talked it over and Susanne told us how much of the market you've got. You need us."

"We'll see. I'm supposed to search yer." He leered at Magpie. "Really carefully."

"No you aren't unless I get to search you first, and all your partners. We're all armed to the teeth, so any pooching goes both ways, right?" Hood glared and Slash shrugged.

"Worth a try. If you come to work for us, do we get to share?" Hood stared until Slash turned away and rapped on the door. "If you start it, remember there's others out here as well as this one on the door. The heavy scowled and Hood sneered at him. "You'll never get away." Slash opened the door and raised his voice. "They're here, and the bird. Diva I reckon." Hood, Magpie and Bells followed him in.

Five cautious minutes later the three Cutters agreed to employ two extra heavies. For the third time Slash suggested Susanne should be part of the deal and this time Hood shrugged. "Just you and just once to seal the deal."

"Fenn! No!" Magpie clung to him, horrified.

Hood ignored her. "Where's the bedroom?"

"Through there is the kitchen, with the bedroom up the stairs. You mean it?" Hood nodded and Slash grinned, then leered. "Don't take long gorgeous."

"No Fenn, I won't. Not with him!"

"Go on Slash, I'll have a word and she'll be up." The youth left and as the door closed behind him Hood turned to Magpie. "You've got to understand, sometimes we have to change the rules."

"But I don't want to." She looked at the door. "He's a creep."

"Oke, we'll change the rules." Both grinned as they finished the charade, letting Slash get out of hearing. Hood turned to the remaining two Cutters. "Slash is a liability. He keeps his brains in his pants and has a loose mouth."

Carver and Cutter, the two leaders, stared for a moment, baffled. Then Cutter laughed. "If you were flickin him, Slash won't take that. Remember you work for us so tell the Diva to get her ass up there and we can finish up and go home."

"Wrong." Hood moved aside. The pair stared into the muzzle of the Kraut automatic, held by a grinning Bells. "You work for me." Hood pulled out a pistol. "Dump all the hardware and sit on your hands. Before you get cute, the sentries and their backups have all carked it. Any time now someone will shoot the one on the doorstep with a silenced pistol so you're the last two." A soft thump outside the door signalled the demise of the guard.

Carver hesitated. "Three, and you'll kill us anyway if we disarm."

"Two because Slash won't be walking back down the stairs, but we need you. Though we can manage without?" The two young men disarmed and sat on their hands. As they did Bells passed the Kraut for Hood to hold in his left hand, pulled a knife and went through the door into the kitchen. A short while later a voice upstairs rose in a sharp query before cutting off abruptly.

Bells came back down, wiping the knife on a piece of Slash's shirt. "Sorted. Have you explained?"

"Not yet. You pair are still the Cutters, and you've just hired some new heavies." The two men looked at each other, baffled. "We want to keep our heads down, because after the last bomb we made it out just ahead of the Troopers."

"It was you!"

"No, you bledrin Homer. We had a nice bit of business, so why would we want to stir up all that shite? I'd like to know who it was?" The two would-be gangsters looked at each other and shrugged. "I didn't think so. Nobody knows but they ruined our business which is why Susanne ended up working on a stall. Now we need time to get set up again, and a bit of income. About half that market will do it." Hood grinned. "We've got the muscle. You two can be our public face in case anyone got a vid of us, but only if you don't piss us about."

"What do we get?"

"A tenth of the take. We'll back down the other market gangs far enough to give the Cutters a half, but that's enough."

Cutter frowned. "Why not take it all?"

"The spooks will pay attention, and then the Troopers will bust us. Half a market won't make waves." Hood scowled. "You keep your traps shut about us, especially round the Divas. That Slash would have caused you trouble in the end, messing with women who aren't willing. Make your minds up."

The two muttered together and agreed, pointing out they could get Divas anyway, willing ones. Then they sat shocked and silent as four grim looking men came in to collect Slash before escorting them to the skip to see the other five bodies and four more grim, competent looking men. Hood let the two remaining Cutters pick up their weapons but neither had any intention of flickin these men let alone trying anything serious.

'Susanne' left her job the next day, allegedly because her boyfriend didn't want Slash round her. Magpie really did feel aggrieved, but only because Bobby wouldn't let her top Slash. He didn't want the Cutters to talk about a woman in the markets who could use a knife. Over the following ten days thirty Troopers made sure both the other gangs lost enough of their heavy muscle for Cutter and Carver to extend their control. When the Cutters had half of the market, they called a meeting with the other gangs and agreed a treaty. Bobby didn't really want a piece of a market but now nobody wondered about hard looking men without visible means of support. Better yet, he took over a bigger house as his gang headquarters which gave the Troopers some breathing space.

Magpie retired the short skirt but to her disgust had to stay in women's clothing, and undercover. There were three large markets on the complex dealing in home-made or black market products, and one had been near the scene of two bombs. Bobby thought it unlikely the bombers would blow up their own neighbourhood so she found a job on the third market, on a stall buying and selling second-hand clothing. Life settled down, once more becoming almost boring. Her 'boyfriend' escorted 'Marge' to work, because Bobby didn't want any trouble this time.

*　　*　　*

Trouble came anyway but to the local Plebs, not Bobby. Another bomb exploded, with massive loss of life. Although the bomb seemed to be aimed at the Troopers, most of the casualties were Plebs. Bobby reported over the radio. "Not a whisper before now, no hint of an organisation or warning this might be coming. With luck this bomb will shake some information loose."

"No hint? That's tight security, yet the bombers the Troopers shot at the last one were average locals with no record. There must be a network." Guns sounded frustrated.

"It's early yet. We've got ears in a few places, and a safe base. Sooner or later something will slip. You were right about there being no revolutionary movement. Most of these Plebs just want the bombs to stop." Bobby hoped something happened soon. The inaction had started to get to the Troopers again, enough so he'd let a few get into a scrap with members of another gang just to take off the edge. Only fists but it kept the other gangs wary, and reminded them the Cutters had some hard men. The Troopers had quietened down a bit but it wouldn't last. "Are we being pushed?" Bobby meant the Duchess.

"No, not by the one who knows you're there. That one seems more pissed about the deaths."

"The cost, real estate and lost production?" The bomb had targeted a Trooper patrol outside a THULL company store but two work buses were caught in the blast as well as the Plebs in the store.

"No. Well yes, but the actual deaths." Guns sounded harassed. "Really pissed. Get our friend a name." Guns avoided any names in these contacts, as usual.

"We might now. Luck."

"Make your own. Out." Bobby sat for a while afterwards, thinking, but he couldn't move without some hint. One name, one house.

*   *   *

Six days later after several false alarms, Bobby might have a name. "I've got a possible. He's not been to work since the bomb." Magpie gave Bobby the address where the man lived. "His new girlfriend hasn't been seen around either. There's half a dozen people who know him on the market, and they're worried. Not that he had anything to do with the bomb, they're worried he's lost the plot over his new live-in. She's a real sleek Diva, according to everyone who saw her."

It all seemed a bit thin to Bobby, not exactly a lead unless Magpie had picked up more. "Is there any connection with the bomb at all, or any sign the Troopers or the spooks are looking?"

"Nobody is looking for him at home or in the market, or nobody has spotted anyone, and someone saw him alive just after the bomb. Street rumour reckons all the bombers were shot or died in the blast when the store guard spotted them." Magpie shrugged. "This man drove into the right places to bring explosives out, but since he's only a driver so did a lot of others. Someone else had to be involved in the actual theft, and that's if the explosives were stolen. It's an outside chance but all I've got."

"If we weren't desperate I'd probably ignore it. How are the Plebs taking the bombing? Is there any hint of this Worker's Equality Movement?" The whole complex had been fly-posted with stickers claiming WEM responsibility.

"Not a hint, and not even any real sympathy. Most people are pissed off about the new restrictions and searches to get into any company store or work. It puts an hour a day on their shifts, an unpaid hour." Magpie frowned. "It doesn't make sense because a bomb like that would have taken out a Trooper armoured carrier, so why blow up the store to get six Troopers on foot?"

"Because killing the workers in the buses messes up production, closing the store makes life difficult for the local Plebs, and the restrictions make the workforce less cooperative. I told, you, its politics." The looks around the table varied from disgusted to murderous. "Snook, you and Siflis are doing nothing useful so you're on shifts for two days until we know there's nobody watching the apartment. Then we go and visit our mystery man." Bobby smiled. "I'll be so very pissed if he's lying exhausted in bed with his Diva."

*　*　*

The man wasn't in bed. His body had been diced, sliced and put in the freezer. From the state of the bathroom he'd been jointed in there, though the worst had been cleared up which explained the lack of stink to alert neighbours. "But no Diva." Bobby frowned. "No prints or DNA either I'll bet."

"There's a few women's clothes, but second handers." Sandman scowled. "Second handers? Maybe Magpie will recognise them?" He raised his eyes. "I'd pray but the ultimate CEO and his minions aren't accepting my calls."

"Strip the place of clothes, and every scrap of paper or any item that might have been bought in the last year. The Diva, whoever she is, didn't do this for profit or she'd have taken the vid player and everything else not nailed down." Bobby looked at the mess in the bathroom. "This looks like more than a lover's tiff."

* * *

To Bobby's surprise Sandman's call must have got through, and a minion angel or demon answered his plea in a roundabout way. Magpie showed them the marks that told the purchaser if the clothing had already been sold as used. Every second hand dealer used them, so they could tell how many times the clothes changed hands and reduce the price they offered. Magpie went on a very careful shopping spree for clothing, to find where the marks belonged.

Having half one market paying insurance helped because Troopers posing as Cutter heavies went around those stalls and asked which mark they used. The rest took ten days, and gave them two stalls where all the Diva's clothes had been stocked at some time. Finding her only took another three days, because although she'd changed her hair this one turned out to be a truly sleek Diva and liked shopping. That might not be conclusive because she could be making her creds by high-class pooching.

Siflis sat back and sighed. "She's at it again. We followed her and she's moved in with another driver. The same setup which is careless or she's getting overconfident."

Bobby frowned, still not totally convinced this had to do with bombs but it was all they had. "Are you sure she's not just hot for drivers, or for carving drivers up?"

"Hah, yeah, right. You haven't seen her. More than that, she spends too many creds on clothes, second hand but nearly new. Looks a million creds in them, and probably out of them considering the state of the driver though he's still going to work. Work that takes him into the Trooper barracks." Siflis looked over at Magpie. "If you weren't so skinny you could steal all her gear afterwards."

"Slim, not skinny." Everyone including Magpie stared at Hood. "Just saying, right?" He shrugged. "That Slash liked Magpie well enough in a short skirt."

"Maybe I should cut your tongue out?" Magpie glared. "Or you could just shut up about that skirt?" Hood held up both hands in apology.

"If we've dealt with Magpie's love life, here we go again. Close surveillance, and at least we got lucky with the stalls because they're on the same market so she doesn't stray far. Siflis has vid of the Diva so all look at it, her face not the skirts." Bobby sighed. "Then we hope she really is connected to the bombs, and someone contacts her in a way we can spot."

*　　*　　*

Instead she contacted someone, by dead-letter placed in a ventilation grill in an alley. Maybe she'd got a little careless over time because Snook spotted the drop. Observing the grill wasn't popular because the only way to keep a permanent watch meant crouching in a skip peering through a hole drilled in the side. Eventually a man picked up the letter and the Basteds had the next link. This one wasn't high enough up to be the target, just a clerk in a company store. Finding his contact took more time as he also passed notes by dead-letter but in the changing rooms of a local baths. The third contact moved about all over the housing complex, some of them where a Trooper stood out even in civvies. Magpie left her job in the market to vary the type of watcher. This man picked up from at least two other drops but the followers couldn't find out how he passed information on. After a month, Sparkler and Nerd fitted up a little bug, Magpie bumped and put it on him after a dead-letter pickup, and the next contact dropped into place.

He used a message board, posting a note. The message read like a secret boyfriend confirming he'd left a voicemail on a netcaff comp and giving a filename. Sparkler spent the creds to use the comp, and tried to hack the message while doing so. He couldn't, not without being obvious because the coded file was protected by a voice password. Several Troopers became customers in the netcaff, sitting near enough to identify who used the comp. When the comp accepted the voice code and released the file, the bug left by Sparkler let them know.

The Basteds followed this contact, a woman, to the offices at the mine entrance. She worked there, rather than actually inside, but anyone passing through could take the message further. Since she wasn't a dead-letter drop Bobby wondered if he'd got far enough up the tree. He hoped so because even Magpie couldn't get into the offices or the mine without real ID that either the target or spooks could trace.

Bobby wondered if he should tell Guns they'd hit a dead end, or try to pick up another trail, but the bomber didn't wait. "She's on the move, the Diva!" Attic stopped, panting. "She just left with two suitcases and the driver is still in there. No sound of an argument, which makes no sense."

Bobby had already started to move, calling for Sandman and Sudden. "Who's following?"

"Snook, and the rest of Reaper's squad. She's moving fast." Attic paled. "Can we stop the bomb?"

Bobby flinched. "We've no idea where it is."

"General alert?" Magpie had barely said it when her face set. "The trail will go cold. A couple of convenient deaths up the chain and the trail is gone. We're pooched."

"But it'll be the last. She's running for her safe house." Bobby tapped his wrist com to send the codes to all the followers. The travelling man would suddenly feel ill because his tail would stick a dart in him. He'd wake up someplace where they'd have checked him for poisons, bombs and tell-tales, and eventually he'd spill everything he knew. While the Troopers raced for their positions, Bobby contacted Guns.

"Have you got something?" Guns sounded harassed.

"It's on. Another something."

"Any idea what?" Guns' tension sounded through the radio link

"No, but we've got movement and we'll snatch a link. A voice-com link into the offices." Bobby daren't even say mine or bomb. "He'll also arrive with three names and addresses, suppliers, enough to be a trail. Where do you want him?"

Guns sent the coded location. "Extraction?"

"Will be clean, with no trace of us by name." Bobby smiled. "Two culprits if you need a red herring later?"

"Please."

"Out." Bobby headed for the door. "Sparkler, I want a door open."

* * *

The Diva hadn't put the driver in a freezer this time. He lay in the bed, eyes bulging and face black so nobody would be sampling the caff nearby. What Sparkler did instead, as soon as he got in the place, was disconnect a thin wire from the clock next to the bed. The bared ends of the wire rested in the pool by a spilled bottle of hooch. Nearly pure alcohol from the smell, and the five other bottles nearby would make sure this apartment burned well enough to melt the copper and destroy any evidence. Sparkler waved the wires at Bobby. "If she hadn't given herself plenty of time to get clear, we would have been too late."

"Can you make that look as if the fuse just failed, fastened badly or something like that?" Bobby smiled. "Or at least make sure you don't leave prints. I reckon The Horseman will love this place since the second cup has lippy on it so the Diva didn't wipe this place down."

The Trooper frowned. "I thought we were giving her safe house to the spooks, once Reaper has followed her home?"

"Her controller might get to her first, or get her out. Once the spooks have DNA she'll never hide, and somebody pays for her lifestyle so between the two the spooks have another trail." Bobby waved to the two Troopers in civvies. "No boot prints please. We are gone." He grinned. "Let's go and disband the Cutters."

By the time Cutter and Carver were laid wide-eyed, bound and gagged in the back of a van, none of Beebi's Basteds were grinning or even smiling. "The basted, the basted, the basted." Nobody minded Magpie's chant or the way she hit the van seat every time. Not now they knew the next atrocity.

Six Trooper carbins on full automatic had opened up on a Trooper patrol squad at point blank range as they marched past the market. Six hundred heavy flechettes had slaughtered the four Troopers and torn a swathe out of the stalls and the packed crowds shopping among them. This time the slaughter did spark a protest from the Plebs, and the local Troopers were in no mood to be gentle. The attackers had allegedly suicided when Troopers moved in to take them, blowing up a quarter of an accommodation block with the residents and some attacking Troopers.

"There's a lockdown, nobody in or out of the complex." The Trooper listening to the radio looked round, pale-faced.

"Pull up." Bobby opened his pack, throwing a bundle to Magpie. "New unit patches, be quick." He ran back to the other three vans to pass them the new patches, tell them to bloody some bandages, and give new orders before running back to his van. "Drive for the nearest exit. Tell the gate guard we've got wounded and have snatched two suspects, live ones for The Horseman." Bobby sighed. "If that doesn't work, use blades and silenced weapons."

Shocked faces looked back. "Kill the Troopers?"

"We are a black op, and someone in the Troopers will be dirty. Do you want the top basted to get away?" The faces hardened.

*   *   *

The faces were still hard fifteen miles down the road when the four vans pulled up at the rendezvous. Cutter, Carver and the snatched contact, still fast asleep, went into yet another unmarked van. Bobby looked around his van and called Guns. "Parcel delivered. Do you have a straight smash and grab, or better still smash and kill?"

"Why?"

"There are fourteen hundred dead or wounded Plebs behind us and the number is still rising. Stress relief. We had to let it happen." Bobby couldn't tell Guns the rest, that Beebi's Basteds had been living in the complex too long. Some of them had remembered who they were, that they'd lived in places just like that. Then they'd had to drive away and let the Plebs, some of them probably people they'd met, be slaughtered.

Though maybe Guns understood. "Wait ten."

Beebi's Basteds arrived back a day late with six men missing and a dozen carrying minor wounds, but they'd lost their savage edge. Four of the missing men would come back with metal, and somehow the two dead were a blood payment for the casualties in THULL residential complex 83B. For once Beebi's Basteds held no party.

Bobby talked to his squad, privately, and it didn't sit right with any of them. They'd got closer than most to the Plebs in THULL 83B, with Magpie working right in among them. Magpie, Hood and Bobby were probably affected worse, though Siflis tended to bottle stuff up so it was hard to tell. While Bells wasn't usually bothered about anyone outside the squad being hurt, this time even he was pissed off. Not exactly sorry for the dead, but he did wish they'd nabbed the basted who organised it and maybe sat him on a bomb with a long fuse and no way out. Magpie wanted to nail the basted to the floor so she could improve on her drug dealer carving.

*   *   *

For eight days the Basteds trained with a ferocity that sent them to their bunks knackered every night, and two off to hospital. There were also a good few minor injuries because of how hard they pushed, so Bobby wasn't surprised by the summons. "Sir?"

"Guns. Never mind, all your Basteds are in the same mood." Guns sighed wearily. "This might help." He slid a news print across the desk and tapped the headline. The highlights told the story.

"*TERRORIST ATROCITY. Earl and family savagely attacked and murdered. Attackers linked to THULL 83B terrorists. Notorious Cutter gang finally cornered and slain.*"

The pictures showed three burned-out cars with guards and figures in civvies scattered near them, then the faces of Cutter and Carver staring with sightless eyes.

Guns tapped the pictures again. "I'm told The Horseman went up and down the links you supplied in two days flat while the arse sat smirking and patting himself on the back. That's him, his family and their personal guards, who must all have had at least had a hint. Or maybe not, but this is a message and not for the Plebs." Guns pushed the print further. "Put it on the board in the canteen." He smiled tiredly. "Your patron has expressed public satisfaction with how the investigation has been completed, and her shock and horror at the loss of life in complex THULL 83B. She regrets the death of a trusted colleague. Herself declared a disaster in THULL 83B within hours and moved teams in to deal with the casualties and damage, but now nobody will be interfering with them."

Bobby put the print up and within an hour the party started. Hood took Magpie back to the squad quarters after a few drinks when she became decidedly tearful. There were still men who didn't know she wasn't a hard as nails male Trooper.

*   *   *

"Yesss." Bells grinned and rubbed finger and thumb together. "Pay up."

Bobby eyed the screen of sheets across the end of the quarters, hiding the last bed of the eight. The short skirt laid on the floor at the end of the bed showed that Magpie might not have been all that upset, or had recovered enough to get changed out of her Trooper uniform into a skirt she allegedly hated. A skirt she'd allegedly thrown away. Bobby grinned as Hood's sleepy voice rose from behind the screen, followed by Magpie's. "Not a chance Bells. You last made that bet over a year ago, not about tonight."

Bells flicked the pair a bit, while Bobby and Siflis shrugged and let them get on with it. Hood and Magpie shared a bed permanently after that. Hood still kept his gear in his own locker of course, in case of inspections, and the pair kept the noise down if any of the others were in the room. Hood's close protection became a little closer, and definitely keener out on missions. Bobby worried about someone else spotting a change but even those who knew about Magpie's sex never noticed.

Though all the Basteds noticed how the missions altered after THULL 83B. There were more where the Basteds ended up doing their own infiltration, or at least some of it, and gradually more and more Basteds learned how Beebi managed that. Men often did some of the investigating, but a quiet woman who took menial jobs and never asked questions brought the best results. Since they had already fought alongside Magpie and a good few Basteds knew about her knife work on the drug boss, she didn't get any grief. In their own way the Basteds who knew were proud of her, a woman tough enough to be not just a Trooper but a Basted.

*   *   *

Over two years after THULL 83B, Hood's squad had become Magpie's primary protection squad whenever she went undercover. She still acted as Hood's close support on sniping and scouting missions, but not on this one. Magpie, dressed in a skirt and blouse, stepped out of the shadows and into her squad who closed quickly around her. She sagged against Hood, briefly, and then straightened and faced Bobby. "Got him, or them. That's all three of the leaders on vid and tomorrow night there will be a meeting with one actually there."

Anticipation showed in Bobby's voice. "The bomber?"

"Yes, he's shown at last. He only makes them and never takes part in planning, and that's why we can't catch him." Magpie yawned. She'd been working extra shifts after one of the staff had been conveniently mugged. Shifts wearing the little bug that recorded whispers across a crowded room, and the tiny vid recorder in a blouse button.

"That and the suicide switches." Bobby spat in disgust. Twice they'd caught a bomber placing the charge and both times he or she had detonated the device. That had cost Bobby three men, two dead and one retired, crippled.

"Maybe not. There's a few rumours that the suicide switch isn't exactly voluntary. The last one, the woman, wasn't the type according to friends. Now, can I get out of this bledrin women's gear?" She huffed in annoyance at a faint ripple of laughter.

"You are a bledrin woman." Bells sniggered. "Though we've never seen the underwear to prove it."

"I'm a Trooper. My tags say so, and it's illegal to be interested in another Trooper's underwear." The squad moved around Magpie, turned their backs on her, and a few minutes later the group had one more Trooper and one less woman. One Trooper stuffed a bundle of clothes into his pack.

"Our secret weapon." Magpie grinned at Bobby in reply. She had become invaluable because the one thing every Pleb knew was that all Troopers were men. With a skirt and a tight blouse Magpie obviously wasn't a man, and her collection of wigs hid her Trooper cut. Magpie didn't infiltrate, because that was what The Horseman's lot were supposed to do. She just served drinks in a caff house or worked on a market stall and put her finger gently on the local pulse without anyone, even the spooks, knowing she existed. Then at the first hint of a suspect she wore the listening bug, or the tiny vidcam.

Right now Magpie had been working in a caff house. Not the real pure caff but enough above the usual to have a steady client base. The spooks had put the caff house on a list of possible meeting places. Magpie had just spent three months working down that list including three weeks in this particular caff house because she'd struck gold. Meanwhile the rest of Beebi's Basteds rattled cages all over the complex, smashing the local crime infrastructure. Not to catch the main rebels because they were too smart, but to make sure that the usual underworld stopped operations. That way the rebels stood out better and any strike against them wouldn't run into opposition from local gangs.

After four and a half years, Beebi's Bigger Basteds were honed. Not the same men after all the casualties, because the Trooper Rapid Reaction Force were brought in for the difficult jobs. Right now Area Manager Eriksson, Guns, had given them the job of breaking a small rebel group. A rebel group with eyes inside the Troopers, or electronic bugs at least. Smart rebels who demanded better working conditions and were building support while slowly bleeding the local Troopers and their employers, CyberBlast-Sage computing conglomerate.

Troopers had been ambushed in the housing complex, transport links had been periodically severed, and there had even been explosions in the plant itself. Most of the damage had been caused using bombs without exposing the main players. The bombs were sophisticated devices which incorporated CB-S electronics as an additional slap at the local employer.

Snook, the other scout, came out of the shadows. "All clear. Nobody followed her and there's seven pairs out covering all the ways for target one to get clear. They'll watch for any other target as well."

"Good. Another couple of nights and we'll know where at least one of them actually goes at night." The three main suspects had a net of Pleb eyes out around them so nobody could try and follow or snatch them. Once tentatively identified by Magpie, however, suspects were put on a list and pairs of watchers installed on routes they might take. Then the next night the watchers moved to another possible spot until the right route or routes were slowly filled in and the destination identified. The same method quickly weeded out the innocents since they went straight home every night.

The rest of Reaper's squad came up to collect Snook and the two squads headed to the barracks. At least this time the local Troopers knew that Beebi's Basteds were here. The TRRF often used that name for two reasons. It backed off nosy Supers, and stopped the locals from realising they were anything but a blunt instrument. On other occasions the locals never even knew the Basteds were in the area until people started dying but that complicated logistics.

"Caught them yet?" The gate guards sneered, a normal response because despite all the raids the bombers were still active.

Hood just raised a finger and kept going as it never went past a sneer. A figure with plenty of polished brass moved to intercept and Bobby sighed. "Go on in. His lordship wants a word."

* * *

The Area Manager responsible for the local Troopers and the safety of the CyberBlast-Sage housing complex and manufacturing facilities really was a Lord, a Baron, which Bobby now knew meant well down the nobility pecking order. Though still a long way above a Trooper, even a Sergeant three, far enough above to be really ticked that Bobby didn't come under his authority. "Any progress Sergeant?"

"Slow but sure slur."

"Lose any more men?" The basted had decided on flickin Bobby about his losses. Again.

"None of yours either, since they knew where the last two were planted, slur. The rebels are sticking to breaking material now after losing a few members themselves." The last broken ambush cost the rebels half a dozen operatives, and really had knocked them back.

The Baron kept pushing. "When will you actually catch anybody important? Have you identified them yet? Just give me the word and I'll drop a hundred men and armour on their doorstep."

But they'd be gone when the hundred arrived. Bobby knew that and so did Lord Ellis-Brante if he thought about it. "I'll let you know as soon as we have a target." Bobby couldn't even blame the man. The Baron no doubt got grief from his employer, and then some semi-secret trouble shooters had been foisted on him to solve his problems. Not a recipe for promotion, even for nobility. "If you don't mind, slur, I've been on patrol and need to sort out the debriefs and clean up."

Lord Ellis-Brante returned the salute and stamped off, straight to complain no doubt since Bobby's coms bleeped before he could get to a shower. Three words. "Sit-rep. How long?"

Bobby sent an even shorter reply. "Two weeks." Then he headed to his quarters and worked through the reports from various watchers and squads, so that if asked he could be more specific. Finally finished, Bobby went for his shower and cursed to find Hood leant against the shower room door.

"She won't be long."

Bobby smiled. "You're not scrubbing her back?"

Hood smiled in reply. The big, previously serious man smiled a lot more these days, ever since the evening the rest had come back to find that screen hung up between the end bed and the rest of the room. "No, but if you want yours done?"

"You volunteering? Or does Magpie want company?"

"No. But there's a couple of Troopers who were fighting over sod all and there's no latrines to dig here."

"I'll think of something disgusting." Bobby leant against the wall and waited. He could only blame himself because he knew Magpie always came late for her shower. That way it wasn't too obvious that Hood's squad let her shower alone though only the reinforcements didn't know about Magpie being a woman. Their woman, a Trooper, a proper Beebi's Basted who pulled her weight and did her own killing. They'd only recently arranged a fatal training accident for a new man who seemed a bit too nosy, Horseman sort of nosy, about who went undercover. The spooks had to be trying to figure out how the Basteds worked because not even Guns knew.

Hood broke the short silence. "Sarge, I've got a problem."

"You must have, to call me Sarge."

"Yeah, well, it's a sort of official problem. I want to make this official, somehow. Me and Magpie. You know?" Hood wriggled, embarrassed.

"Do you want to marry her or just make her a dependent so she gets the blood money?" A sudden thought hit Bobby. "You haven't gone and... Well you have but is she pregnant?"

"No! I'd like to marry Maggie, but even if she said yes she'd be discharged and I'd never see her except on leave." Hood shuffled a bit more. "She'll not get pregnant because Magpie is careful. She's got some of the tablets the Divas use. It's just that one day, maybe? But in the meantime if I cark it?"

There was one way, Bobby thought, without letting Guns know. "Sometimes a Trooper will make a squad mate his heir if he's got no family. That way someone gets the blood money, the death payments, so you could do that." Bobby blew out a long breath. "But not more if you want to keep her here. Even Guns would probably chuck Magpie out if he knew about her being female."

"It's a wonder he hasn't guessed."

"Maybe it's like the notsi. Guns does know but as long as we do the job Area Manager Gunnar Eriksson won't ask." Bobby didn't think so. A big difference yawned between a notsi or two and having a woman in the squad. "Do you want to risk asking him?"

"No, forget it. Well not entirely, can you sort out the blood money thing?" Hood still sounded almost embarrassed and kept his voice down.

Which puzzled Bobby. "Doesn't Magpie know? That you feel like this, that you're asking?"

"No." That came out almost a whisper. "She keeps saying that she's been lucky and that's enough for her."

"Talk to her. At least let the lass know how you feel." Bobby felt like the big Trooper's Da about now, rather than four years younger. "Do it before making arrangements. Magpie might want to do the same."

"You think?" Hood sounded startled.

Bobby rolled his eyes, unseen by the sniper. The woman had a choice of at least a score of fit, dangerous men if she just liked the type. Instead Magpie stuck very strictly to Hood and never even flirted with anyone else. She flicked a few, but they all knew it was that, just flickin. If the situation had been a bit different Bobby thought they'd be married and waiting for the first kid by now, though then she wouldn't see Hood more than a couple of weeks a year. Being a Trooper didn't encourage home life.

Magpie came out fully dressed, of course. Even in the barracks she kept fully clothed in her padded gear except when in their own quarters, and mostly then. "About time. I give you the clean jobs and you still take longer than anyone else." Magpie grinned, giving Bobby the finger as Hood moved to meet her. They walked off side by side. No hugs, no holding hands, and even looks had to be neutral outside the barracks room. At least they could sit with each other in their quarters and relax a bit even if Bells teased them. Away from their home barracks the pair never relaxed properly.

Bobby dismissed Hood and Magpie from his thoughts, concentrating on the mission as he showered. They had narrowed the blocks where the other two leaders lived but hadn't actually nailed the apartments down. In the end Bobby decided to risk losing them temporarily, because now he'd got vid of their faces and could find them again. The bomb maker would die tomorrow night and the Basteds would raid the caff house. He'd arrest everyone there including Magpie, shut the place down, and squeeze any small players. Done like that the other two rebels wouldn't realise they'd been made as well, but there'd be no more sophisticated bombs.

Bobby wasn't sure if the talk with Hood had pushed the decision, because this way Magpie would be publicly arrested and couldn't be used for any more undercover work on this job. The woman had been undercover a long time in this one complex even if she changed her hair and clothes styles between jobs. It only needed someone to remember seeing her in another place that had been raided and she'd be dead, if she got lucky. The young woman who had been more frightened of Pleb rioters than Bobby and the Troopers had come a long way from then, but she still faced the same fate if it went wrong.

He also wondered if he'd been doing this type of job too long, getting too close to the Plebs. A bit of him wanted at least one of these rebels to get away. With one of them still out there CyberBlast-Sage might have to treat their Plebs a bit better to stop the movement growing again. This group actually had quite reasonable demands and a bit of Bobby couldn't see why the Company couldn't have a least met them partway before it came to bombs. He sighed. That was way above his pay grade. Troopers were trained for one purpose. They really were the Company Guard Dogs, the Doggies.

*   *   *

Hood sat in the back of the troop carrier, holding Magpie and cursing in a steady monotone. Bells stood by the door into the front of the vehicle so nobody else could come in, because the crew weren't Basteds and Magpie still wore her skirt and blouse. "It's just a knock on the head, Hood, she'll be fine."

"But that could be bad, really bad. She might have brain damage. Even if they save her, it'll mean a proper hospital, and they'll know." Hood looked up, and Bobby was pleased he'd made sure only their squad and a few very trusted others came in this carrier. The big man's feelings were written all over his face. Even they weren't, the way he cradled Magpie's unconscious body in his arms would have made it clear she wasn't just a comrade. "I'll lose her anyway. Though as long as she lives I can manage that."

Bobby wasn't sure Hood or Magpie could manage separation, not after living together for so long. He had to cut back on Magpie's undercover crap because tonight one of the rebels had made her. Luckily the squad covering her were alert and reacted fast enough. Bobby snorted to himself, Hood was always on edge when Magpie went undercover but this time it worked out. A rebel had come to meet the bomb maker, looked at the waitress, and did a double-take. He shouted, "She's a spy!" and grabbed Magpie.

Magpie stuck a knife in him and made a break for it, but one of the other men got her with a chair. By then Hood had already shot the two who produced guns. Even as Magpie dropped, Bells and Siflis came in through the door with knives and pistols and went viral. There wasn't anyone left to interrogate. Reaper nailed the bomber when he slipped out the back to get clear. "You'll have to put her in a Trooper uniform, Hood. Before we get back, or everyone will know."

Hood looked worried, but for once Bells put him at ease. "We won't look you eedjit, and even I'm not stupid enough to offer to help. She'd cut my nuts off even if you didn't." He grinned. "I bet she's not wearing the sexy stuff anyway, not on a job."

By the time Bells and Hood carried her in to see the medic, the Basted's medic so he'd keep his trap shut, Bobby had made a decision. Any more undercover jobs for Magpie had to be short ones. One or two jobs in a complex, no more even if the job took longer and maybe wasn't as neat. Then he spent five hours helping Siflis and Bells to keep Hood penned in their quarters, until the medic told them her skull was intact and Kwikheal would deal with any other damage. Hood couldn't be allowed near Magpie or the medic would guess about their relationship, then so would the rest of the Basteds. Most of them thought Magpie didn't fancy blokes, but if they found out she pooched Hood? Bobby didn't trust some of them to carry on ignoring her sex. They'd want to try their luck.

Guns and the Baron were both curious about why everyone in the café died, but Bobby just kept saying it went viral and the bomber was dead. Twenty hours later the medic let Magpie come back to her quarters. Bobby, Siflis and Bells went to the range to practice with carbins for a couple of hours and left her with Hood. When they came back even Bells didn't flick them about the cuddling, though he did flick Magpie about whether or not he'd seen her underwear.

Even without knowing the real reasons for Bobby's reluctance, the other Corporals agreed that Magpie couldn't be used again on this job. The Basteds settled down to finding out exactly where the other two rebel leaders slept.

*   *   *

Three days later Bobby had an unscheduled call from Guns, Area Manager Gunnar Eriksson. "You've killed the bomber so wrap it up."

"I'd planned on catching at least one leader alive, so that we can roll the lot up properly." This call really worried Bobby because Guns usually left him to it. "Is there pressure?"

Guns hesitated, which rang a few alarm bells in Bobby's head. "Yes and no. Not local, or about this job. Can you kill the other two?"

"That might take a while because they have to drop at the same time. Any warning and we'll spend months finding the second again. Don't you want the rest of them?" Usually the task included a clean sweep of every possible minor player. Bobby might have qualms about his job, but he did it properly. After all, only this job and his steel umbrella kept the squad alive.

"Kill one and give His Lordship what you've got once he's dead. Let him break down doors and suchlike, and with the vid he'll probably get the other. It will make him much happier and impress CyberBlast-Sage which can't be bad." Gunnar sighed. "Can you extract whoever the hell you've got embedded?"

"Yes. Everyone's already out and safe." Bobby smiled at the "whoever the hell" because Guns regularly tried to find out. Occasionally Bobby let him know which one of the men had been undercover, but Guns wasn't fooled.

Though this time Guns didn't follow it up, so the reason for urgency must be serious. "Let me know as soon as it's all done. Remember, give His Lordship as much help as possible since you can't do the job properly this time."

"Yes sir."

"Piss off. Out."

Bobby smiled. Guns knew that Beebi had been flickin him with the, "Yes sir," and the officer didn't care. In fact, Guns insisted on no names or ranks when they spoke like this, over a radio. Then Bobby frowned. There had been jobs with a deadline but Guns had never nudged to get a job finished faster, or left one part-finished. In the end he couldn't come up with an answer, so Bobby went to collect his Corporals.

*   *   *

The meeting didn't take long. They could get a sniper near enough to both leaders to drop one, then everyone would pull out. Before sending out the squads, Bobby did as he'd been told and gave the Baron a shot at glory. "This file is all the locals we have identified including vid of the important ones. It's time-locked so please don't try to open it." Bobby handed the disc to the Baron.

"Don't you trust me?"

"You slur? Yes, of course, but there is a leak of some sort out of the barracks. One of these names might give you it." Bobby shrugged. "We'll be finished by then."

"Finished? How, if these people need collecting?" The Baron frowned, puzzled. No doubt he'd been told the culprits would be dead or handed over gift-wrapped.

"We will have broken the centre, killed two out of three ringleaders, and you can roll the rest up while they're trying to reorganise. There's vid of the third man in there. I can't say more and please don't even hint that a breakthrough is close. Don't make any sort of move until the file opens." The Baron grinned and agreed, he would get to drop all those men and that armour on someone's doorstep after all.

*   *   *

Bobby replayed that conversation in his head when he knocked on the Baron's office door just after midnight. Engines roared in the background as troop carriers set off for a dozen addresses. "Enter." Bobby stepped inside.

He tried to be polite about it. "You were very quick, your Lordship, considering when the file opened."

"We were on alert because of that bloodbath. At least a score dead and injured and they can't all be rebels. There were women caught in the crossfire." The Baron looked truly shocked and rightly so, it had been a shambles.

"You were on alert before that. The reason you are so efficient and the reason for the bloodbath are the same. You told someone." The Baron opened his mouth to deny it but Bobby didn't want to catch nobility lying and got in first. "Someone warned the targets just before either sniper pulled the trigger, a very trusted someone because they both ran without checking. I'd told my men to kill one at least, and stressed they weren't to let both escape. The first pair of Troopers in our cordon with a shot opened up with carbins or did you want both the ringleaders to escape, considering what they've done here?"

"No of course not, but I..." The Baron stopped, braced himself and owned up. "I did tell three people, trusted people. Not details because I didn't have any, and only ten minutes before the file opened. They were told to get their sergeants rounded up and keep them in a room, ready to go, to save finding them all."

Bobby grinned. "Simple then. The first target had a warning at 23:52 and fifteen seconds, the second one ten seconds later. You have names and a time frame, or just squeeze all three and their sergeants. Maybe this is for the best if the leak is so high."

The Baron frowned. "Don't you want them? Don't your superiors want a traitor?"

"No slur. Take him out the back and shoot the basted for all I care.

We've got an urgent job so I will need your bus, the one for collecting reinforcements from the station. I'll leave it at the airport." Bobby got out because whoever the spy turned out to be, the Baron was already in shock over how high he'd got. That would probably turn to rage fairly soon so Bobby wanted to be gone rather than be a convenient target. Though if Guns needed the Basteds so badly, whatever he'd got waiting wouldn't be a picnic.

Heavy Metal

Dawn had just staggered over the horizon when the plane landed at the nearest airstrip to what Beebi's Basteds called home, their barracks. Bobby immediately started really worrying because Area Manager Eriksson waited on the tarmac, and he looked grim. Guns never showed up at the airstrip. He had the usual buses waiting, and the usual score of Troopers guarding them, but this time the Troopers helped to shift the gear and stow it in the bus instead of getting on the plane. "I hear you even got the spy, or the Baron did."

Bobby shrugged. "The Baron must have worked it out, because I left that to him. It was pure luck we got a straight lead." Bobby was more concerned about Magpie, though after three days of Kwikheal her dizzy spells had stopped. She still had headaches, but reckoned she could use a knife if necessary. Bobby just hoped this wasn't another rush job and Magpie would have time to recover properly. He'd already reminded Hood not to carry her gear.

Guns grimaced. "Yeah, well your luck ran out. Management want a word and they've descended into our own personal shite-heap to meet you. Upper management, way above my pay grade, far enough above that I'm not invited to this meeting."

"What?" That must be seriously high up the corporate tree. Bobby couldn't remember talking to anyone above an Area Manager apart from the Duchess, except on a job. Upper management, boardroom level, didn't usually get their soles grimy down here among the Troopers, and especially near the Basteds.

"Your lot aren't exactly inconspicuous are you? Maybe you've finally stamped on the wrong set of toes?" The Area Manager shrugged. "Though in that case they should be after my head as well. Nobody told me anything but if you've finally pooched it, so have a couple of your old friends." He smiled. "The barracks is that way. No sightseeing on the way, don't call us, and have a nice day." His laughter followed them up the road as the buses headed towards the barracks.

"How bad is it?" Bells started worrying straight away, of course.

"You heard, the sooner we get there, the sooner we know." Bobby had his own worries to deal with. Upper management were too upper for Troopers to chat to.

"Do we ditch the notsi?" Bobby could hear pleading in his voice, because Bells hated even the parades when he'd been awarded more metal because he had to wear purely standard weaponry. He felt naked without his notsi, not standard issue. Considering the amount of notsi on the buses, the heap on the road would be conspicuous.

Bobby sighed. "No, if they asked for us, they know what we are and a couple of spares won't matter." Unless some super-dick in upper management needed an example, Bobby thought but definitely didn't say. Though why go through this bulsh first?

*   *   *

Fifty armed Troopers were waiting. Nearly all the men were told to go straight to their quarters and stay there though they kept their weapons. Two Troopers separated Bobby and Hood's squad from the rest and relieved them of all weapons before they were let into the canteen. The strange Troopers increased Bobby's worries because strangers weren't allowed here. The Troopers promised to guard the weaponry, which might have been bulsh but as soon as he stepped through the door Bobby knew this wasn't a total stitch-up.

Sarge sat at one of the tables, the original Sarge from his Timer days, now a Trooper Sergeant-Major with three stars and the crown on his stripes. Then Bobby felt unsure again when he saw the Line Supervisor behind him. He recognised the same dick who'd been in charge of him as a Timer. Bobby saluted. The dick looked as if he'd swallowed a Jiff, not just sucked it, which seemed a bit of an overreaction.

"At ease. I've read your chips to catch up and I truly have no idea why you or the Sergeant-Major got this job. I've got it because of you and the complete shambles you left behind." Bobby stared, baffled because he'd been given metal and promoted after that fight. The dick, the Super, had been promoted to Line Supervisor so he should have been happy. Though he'd stayed a bottom level Line Supervisor for nine years, so maybe that hadn't gone well.

"Slur?"

The dick glared at the slurring. "The Sergeant-Major will explain. After all, no point in having a dog and doing the barking." Bobby could see the look in Sarge's eyes, the look that made Bobby think of carelessness on toilets, boom in the bog. Bobby had his own spare grenades now in case he wanted someone to be careless, and he knew Siflis had one. A few of the others probably had something nasty tucked away if Sarge had lost his.

"Yes, slur." Bobby looked at Sarge who sighed, then smiled.

"You've just won the lottery, and a long, all expenses paid holiday. You'll be going to exotic places, meeting new people…. And hopefully not having to shoot any of them. Come on, let's get a warm drink." Sarge paused. "They told me it'd be your squad, your old one." He looked curiously at Magpie.

"Magpie is part of the squad." Sarge shrugged. They went to get a hot drink, and two doughnuts which brought another smile from Sarge. The dick paced the floor the other end of the canteen, scowling about something. When Bobby and the squad were all sat around a corner table in the canteen with a hot caff, Sarge started with a strange question.

"How are you with world news? Not who's pooched who, or who started the latest politically inspired food riot, I mean the news about the other blocs and space?" He looked at the four blank and one hesitant faces and sighed. "Some time before you volunteered for this unit," all of them snorted, "there was some news, about a discovery?"

"Some alien wreckage, or something from the Age of Space?" The other three looked at Siflis. "Hey, I noticed because I play space games on the pad. I told you, I always liked the space stuff. Though that all disappeared from the news a bit back so I suppose it was a false alarm."

"There was all that crap about selling Plebs to Aliens, back when…." Hood glanced at Magpie and shut up.

Sarge cut in. "Someone found a chunk of Alien space junk. What wasn't advertised is on here." He gave them five pads with a second glance at Magpie. "Read now, and swallow before letting anyone else see them. Then give them back to me because I'll be right here in sight of you." Sarge looked round. "It'll take a while. What sort of quarters did your lot score?"

"Usual. Eight-man squad block." Sarge kept looking, and Bobby gave up. "All right, nobody else wants to bunk with us so it's private." Actually Bobby was in charge so he just told the rest the room was off limits to give him some peace and quiet. More to the point Hood and Magpie could relax and hold hands. Bells had imposed strict limits on the amount of kissing because he'd get frustrated, but Magpie could wear a skirt twice a week.

"Let's go." Ten minutes later the five of them were stowing their returned gear and then they all started reading. Sarge prowling round the room peering at this and that distracted some of them, especially his inspection of the privacy screen in front of the last bed. Then the content really grabbed their attention, all of them.

* * *

The pad information started five years ago with a fluke, a tiny turn of fate on which might depend the very survival of their whole civilisation. As that long-ago lecturer told the Timers, automated probes had been sent out sampling asteroids for metals. When the probes tested an asteroid they also took pictures of the surrounding area and attached them to the file. A small team looked at all the pictures just in case anything of interest showed up and it did. An operation left over from the discovery of a complete craft from the Age of Space. The astronaut had died long ago of course, but the craft had been a valuable find.

In this case the pictures caught something else, in the background. A bored operator flicking through the reports noticed the anomaly, a picture of a perfectly straight line and flat, smooth surface where none should be, right out in space, in the asteroid belt. He enlarged the picture, looked again, reassessed and his first impression was right. The surface couldn't be natural.

He flagged this latest file and sent it to the head of shift. A few minutes later the woman turned up at his desk, wanting an off the record opinion. "Why did you flag this?"

"That surface is too smooth, and the edge is too clean and straight." The operator shrugged. "In my opinion."

"How sure are you? Off the record." She sounded as if she already had an opinion, she wanted confirmation.

The operator knew better, but the excitement of the moment got to him. "Either another bloc has a different sort of probe up or the object isn't from now, it came from the Age of Space." He pointed at the picture to demonstrate. "Anything that's been there for a long time, even a completely natural fluke, would have been worn. There's all sorts of junk from asteroids down to dust hitting every object, but this is pristine." He refused to mention the third possibility, because she'd just take the piss.

Though the pause meant she might have thought the same. "I'll send it up the line." She bumped the file up the line with the frames flagged for attention. "Let's hope the Supervisor arrived in a good mood tonight." They both grimaced.

The Supervisor must have opened the file straight away because they both stood on his carpet in ten minutes flat and he wasn't scowling. Both confirmed the first two ideas. "Forget about another probe. There are eight corporations currently in the asteroids and we all plot exactly where each other's probes are." The Super hesitated. "I doubt it's from the Age of Space. Nothing on record is that big, and right out there. How sure are you this isn't natural?"

The Supervisor pushed hard, but both were certain that the shadow couldn't be natural, not even a natural freak which might be important in any case. "You'd better be right, because I'm asking the boss to send the probe back to have a closer look. That will shorten its working life. If this is nothing, you pair are taking the blame." A little smile flitted across his face. "If it's what none of us want to say, you'll get a hell of a bonus."

The file went up to the Line Supervisor with all three analyses and his recommendation. The next step took an hour but only because the Line Supervisor called a couple of colleagues to get their opinions. The decision making progressed so quickly because processing probe pictures bored everyone; very, very little of note ever happened.

Nothing of this sort had *ever* happened. The Line Supervisor bumped the notifications up to the Unit Manager. A long dormant snoop bug noted the speed of the notifications and consultations and their upward progress. It alerted a small burst transmitter gathering dust in a hollow under a window sill. As the pictures, attachments and increasingly urgent tags went up through the organisation, electronic and human observers took note. Several units tasked with just this sort of investigation bent their human and electronic will to finding out what.

"I don't like spy vids much anyway Sarge, and this one hasn't got a Diva in skin-tight sod all. Can't we skip to the end?" Bobby waved his pad and Bells nodded.

"Read it. All of it." Sarge went back to look at Magpie's privacy screen again.

*　*　*

Out in the asteroid belt the probe went back to the site of the anomaly. The other blocs with space capabilities, all eleven of them, took note and three sent probes to investigate. The spies redoubled their efforts. As the first probe came to rest and began to transmit more pictures, the original picture was finally acquired by four space-prospecting blocs. For once true excitement ruffled the ennui of absolute power in the boardrooms at the very top of the World's true governments. Other organisations found out in their own ways, and at third, four, sixth hand the picture spread across the globe.

The results went up through the echelons of SEPA (South-East Pacific Alliance) bloc, the original discoverers, with almost the speed of the supplementary probe as it clawed its way out of the gravity well. The new pictures showed a piece of debris from a spacecraft, not from nature! A plate of metal just over two metres thick and averaging just over one hundred and thirty metres wide by almost three hundred meters long travelled among the asteroids in a long path around the sun. Quick calculations that the object weighed over six hundred thousand imperial tons meant it had never been lifted into space from Earth.

The object had definitely been manufactured, so it must be an alien artefact. More, it was a piece of a larger object since the edges showed ripples and bubbling. This was alien space wreckage! Even as the probe's masters salivated over the possibilities further pictures showed small objects, cosmic gravel and dust, being repelled before contact. Something in the wreckage remained functional!

Some very hard hearted, unimaginative businessmen had a shiver of what came close to religious awe at that. The calculations that followed had only one conclusion. The discovery couldn't be hidden and the other blocs couldn't be kept from it, so SEPA traded all the pictures and analyses in return for cooperation. By the time the fifth, the Chinas bloc, agreed, the rest clearly understood they daren't refuse. A war to stop the six allied blocs gaining control of the force field technology would be ruinous.

The other probes that arrived made their own inspections but the original had already died, burned out when it tried to touch the fragment. The MEEC, the Mid-European Economic Consortium consisting of a swathe of old countries from Germany to Greece, contributed a partially constructed spacecraft designed to exploit an iron-nickel asteroid their probes had pinpointed. The Franco-African Corporation Space Agency admitted the secret project in their African base did involve a similar mining craft. Both blocs received funding and technology to hasten completion, with an emphasis on probing and sampling rather than mining.

Negotiating teams sparred over who would construct a craft to take man back to the deep cold and dark for the first time in well over a century. Bobby smirked when he reached this bit, because that old instructor would have a seizure at the idea. He had time to smirk because the five pads were synched and didn't move on until everyone had read theirs. The next part started to look familiar.

*　*　*

Several blocs released the news to their Plebs, their workforces, as a way of diverting them from their miserable lives. Some managers and directors used the interest to encourage the Plebs to work harder and longer. The black news and rumours claimed that an alien warship had crashed on its way to either colonise, sterilise, or ally with Earth. Others claimed that it had come in peace, and that one or another bloc had destroyed it so now Earth waited for retribution. In some housing complexes riots erupted over stories that Plebs were to be sold to aliens as food or slaves.

"Complex SSAB-Tata 17D." Bobby blinked and looked up as Hood broke his concentration. He'd come to exactly the same conclusion but kept his trap shut.

"Where?" Sarge broke off his pacing.

Bobby sighed. "We heard the rumour during riots in a housing complex. That rumour killed a lot of good men." He shrugged. "One of them a Super."

"Your famous steel umbrella?"

"Famous?"

Sarge snorted. "Infamous, though even my rank doesn't tell me more than that. Now finish reading before I start a locker inspection and cite you all for notsi violations." He eyed up the blatantly illegal weaponry hung on the walls or laid on the spare beds.

They all snorted at that, then bent to reading again though now the pads switched to pictures and vid and voice. Pitch blackness filled the screens, broken by tiny bright points of light. At least three gasps marked the first sight of the fragment, a genuine alien space object.

"Attempts have been made to touch the surface, and any unpowered objects have been rejected." Onscreen a succession of objects were launched to impact gently on the plate. All were rejected without touching. *"Powered probes on wires were employed."* Two more dead probes floated in the void. The cameras zoomed in on the melted ends of the wires coiling and looping lazily as the hulks spun gently. *"Eventually a probe fired a ball-bearing at the plate to break what appeared to be a relatively weak repulsion field."*

A probe spat out the small steel ball, and almost instantaneously a flash of intense light emanated from an innocuous dimple on the fragment. Once again some squad members gasped. The ball-bearing flashed into oblivion as a thin beam, only visible as it burned through the vapour, continued deep into the probe itself until the fuel supply exploded. *"No further attempts were made until the adapted mining vessels arrived."*

Onscreen the two mining craft were bigger than a probe. The front section of one detached and approached the fragment, dwarfed by the expanse of steel. At the established limit of the repulsion field, the probe attempted to contact whatever still lived in there. *"This probe is using a laser beam to maintain contact with the mother craft, to prevent the alien artefact from reaching the larger computers and the information and instructions they carry."*

"Shite!" Siflis spoke but Bobby couldn't have put it better. A fine net of wires snagged the sacrificial probe, and the close-up showed them punching through the casing and burrowing deep inside. Moments later a hatch opened in smooth steel plate, launching a small pointed missile trailing a wire. The missile struck the mother probe, punching through the outer plating.

"*The mother craft computer was programmed to self-destruct to avoid capture or interrogation, but the alien artefact has already overridden that.*" A second tiny missile neatly skewered the other converted mining probe and that didn't have chance to self-destruct either. "*On investigation the Franco-African Space Agency, FASE, admitted burying a special instruction deep into their core programming. If the computers were invaded, all probes would be instructed to launch a kamikaze attack on the alien artefact.*"

The close-ups disappeared. A long-range camera showed probe after probe starting their engines, then falling cold and silent. A flickering blur of lights on the artefact heralded probes exploding in rapid succession. The explosions, short sharp flashes without the flame and smoke so beloved of vid makers, died away leaving the two specialist craft still firmly snared. "*Nothing further happened for just over one minute, during which time it has been assumed the artefact ransacked the electronics aboard the two craft for information.*"

Onscreen the fragment sprouted ports and hatches to become a very strangely shaped spacecraft, before slowly but smoothly turning to align one flat side at ninety degrees to Earth. "*Nineteen hours and fifty-seven minutes later, the screens on Earth that fell silent when the probes were attacked came back to life.*" The screen showed a schematic of the solar system highlighting Earth, the Alien craft, and a point well out into space beyond the last planet, Neptune.

"*Within an hour observatories reported a strong signal that seems to emanate from the third point, which is located in the Kuiper Belt approximately seventy-three AU from Earth. The signal will have taken almost ten hours to reach Earth, and we assume the alien craft contacted another craft or facility.*"

"Shite Sarge, Beebi, how am I supposed to follow this?" Bells looked round and threw up his hands in despair. "Can't someone just tell me what to do? Are we being invaded or what?"

"Everyone else feel the same?" Three other heads nodded with varying expressions of relief.

Siflis didn't. "Not yet. I understand it so far. The mining probes found a bit of alien spaceship, and it's still working and talking to us. The blocs are combining to deal with it instead of killing each other." He looked at his pad. "I want to see what they found and what that other signal is."

Bobby scowled. "You might, but we'd rather someone told us in small words so hard luck Siflis." He looked at Sarge and waved the tablet. "This is way above our pay grade Sarge. If something isn't in range of something I can hit it with, why do I care?" He glanced back at the pad in alarm. "Are they invading, or does some bledrin maniac want us to attack them?"

Sarge laughed. "I asked more or less the same question." He looked at the screens. "At about the same time. Hit escape, then confirm you watched up to the interrupt point." He looked around the room. "Take what you need from here, because you won't come back."

"That sounds much too familiar, and the last time meant a bledrin rough year or two. Is this one a real Gaza Taxi?" Bobby glanced at the pad. "Gaza spaceship?"

"No Beebi, you've got a thing about Gaza Taxis. By not come back I mean the same as last time. You'll go someplace else but in theory you're supposed to survive. Get your kit." He looked at the privacy screen. "Who's bashful?"

"Me, I wear frilly underwear." Magpie got her voice as deep as possible but Sarge still stared suspiciously.

"Didn't take you long to get their sense of humour, did it? Just a hint, flickin me isn't smart." He smiled happily. "Bring the underwear, it'll liven up the trip." Sarge didn't watch to see what underwear everyone packed, though he did frown at the sheer volume of notsi and ammo they all tried to stash away about themselves. "I've heard nasty rumours about you, Beebi. I reckon some might be true, especially after seeing this little barracks tucked away in the middle of no-place just for you and yours. What's the Super count now?"

"He got a Lord, but we share the Supers and Managers around." Sarge blinked, the first time Bobby had ever seen him thrown off-balance, and stared suspiciously towards the screen and Magpie's voice.

"I warned you about flickin me." Then he caught the grins from the rest and annoyance turned to curiosity. "Later, and you will tell me." He waved them out through the door. "Take me to your leader. Area Manager Gunnar Eriksson I'm told, or his office at least."

*   *   *

Bobby hesitated at the door into Guns' office, because the room already seemed to be full enough. Inside were Area Manager Eriksson, looking a cross between worried and pissed off, Bobby's old Line Supervisor, the lawyer Area Manager Jakkob Bryant, two of those mystery men who followed the Duchess about, and a man in a suit who looked to be in charge.

The suit spoke up. "Just the two sergeants. They can tell the rest of the squad." Bells tensed but Bobby shook his head just a little. "If you give your squad your weaponry, Sergeant Bobby B, that will make it much easier to fit in here." Bobby didn't know the man in the suit, but the little smile looked pure Duchess so he passed his weapons to Hood and Bells. "I suggest your men stay in the corridor, and make themselves comfortable." The voice wasn't asking.

A half hour later Bobby came out in some sort of daze, and Sergeant Major Bjorn Kelsey didn't look much better. Line Supervisor Steven McKay looked sick and terrified, and very reluctant to be alone with the rest. Bobby collected his weaponry while Sarge picked up another heap, then waved towards the door at the end. "Straight out and into the bus. Do not talk to anyone you see. The Line Supervisor will drive the bus, and we'll talk." The rest looked startled. Line Supervisors didn't usually act as taxi drivers. Though as soon as they climbed aboard this Line Supervisor started driving, while Hood's squad started asking questions.

The simple answer, that Beebi's almost original Basteds with the dick in charge were going into space, only brought more questions. Though even the detail didn't help much. The six of them would be trained in low-grav and working under heavy acceleration, and in using spacesuits as well as specialist weapons. By then there would be a destination, though somewhere in space seemed to be a given. Bobby laughed. "I hope that basted lecturer finds out Timer Bobby B is a Space Marine, and bursts a blood vessel." Hood explained to Magpie while the rest laughed, even Sarge.

"Can the Army do that, move us to the Kingdoms Air Force, or Space Marines?" Bells frowned. "I chose Army. I don't fancy flying in planes, and those space things don't look safe." True enough, Bells hated the planes that took them all on missions.

"The Army might not be able to, but we've all agreed to become private contractors working for THULL or some space prospecting subsidiary of theirs." Bobby grinned. "The pay and bonuses are better than even Squaddies, and any time on this job counts towards our promotions and pensions." They all laughed at the joke, because only cripples ever drew pensions and any promotion seemed to have got lost in the paperwork.

Siflis sobered. "When did I agree?" He grinned. "Though I will. Real Space Marines!"

"In a minute. You really don't want to say no." Bobby pulled out the contracts and activated the electronic versions on his pad. "We were asked for, very specifically."

"The Ironhills?" Hood hesitated and glanced from the Sergeant-Major to the dick.

"They know now. We are here because the Ironhills believe we can be trusted." Bobby smiled. "Do you want to say no thanks?"

"Not a chance." Bells grinned. "Nobody ever trusted me before." He looked at the document and his grin widened. "Nobody ever paid me like that before." The rest agreed once they'd looked, then four thumbprints on Bobby's pad settled the contract signing.

Or maybe not. "Sarge?" Hood frowned as two heads turned. "The first one. Sergeant-Major is a mouthful."

The original with the steel knees, now a Sergeant-Major, smiled. "Smaj works. What's the problem now?"

"What if a thumbprint doesn't match the original on record?" Smaj didn't have a problem working out whose, because the rest looked at Magpie and she blushed.

His face hardened. "What happened to the original Trooper Nathaniel Wright?"

Bobby shrugged. "Killed in action. I gave Trooper Magpie the tags at the same time as we threw the stripped body out of the back. You know what happens to our dead."

A scowl answered that. "What will the thumbprint come up as?"

"Nobody. I'm not on the records." Magpie kept her voice low. "I really do belong in the squad, I earned my place."

"Even topped a Super to qualify." Bobby grinned when that diverted Smaj, as intended. "We let the cherries have one as soon as possible." He lowered his voice and leaned closer. "How much dirt do you want to have to keep secret?"

The Sergeant-Major thought hard. "I want to know, but I don't need to. Judging by that meeting either the Ironhills know or won't care. I'll add a note saying the original thumbprint might not be right because someone in the office was flickin Trooper Nathaniel Wright, but I've witnessed this thumbprint." He grinned. "I'll bet the original matches by the time they're compared, and the Army will never see the note because you don't work for them."

Bobby shook his head. "No bet." Even Bells refused that bet, though Bobby had to explain what happened in the meeting to him twice more. By then they'd arrived at the airstrip. Another of the suited bodyguard types, already waiting there, took the contracts and a copy of the electronic ones from Bobby. Sarge passed him the electronic note.

"A Line Supervisor with only five Troopers? Will there be more men?" Hood looked at the small plane waiting nearby. "Not in that."

The dick scowled. "I'm a Supervisor again, one with only five men instead of a hundred. The basteds demoted me to lead you lunatics, before giving me the same bulsh non-Army contract as you. They reckon I'll keep the seniority and pension and get the rank back, but demotion is on my record."

Bobby stared. "When did that happen?" The officer still had Line Supervisor badges on his uniform.

"As soon as you assholes put your thumbs on the contract. Thanks a lot." The Super spun on his heel and climbed onto the small private plane. The rest followed him inside, sank into the luxury seats, and disappeared from Army records.

*   *   *

The Army might have lost them, but Army training stayed right with the Basteds. For three weeks they all worked harder than they ever had before at old and some entirely new skills. "But why can't I kick off a wall?" Magpie glared at the trainer.

"Because there are no walls in space. You train in here because we can't train you up there. Now, use the jets to move and take his knife." He indicated Bells.

"Fat chance, with or without jets." Bells laughed. "Won't we be using lasers? If we're fighting in space?" At the moment the squad were in a room on a jet plane that stayed more or less weightless for short periods.

"You learn about lasers in a while. Right now you'd start tumbling, pull the trigger, and cut all your squad mates and your life pod in half." The trainer sighed. "As I tell you every time you ask. I can see the signs and you've had enough today. Finish this exercise and when the weight comes back we'll land and revert to theory."

"No, no, anything but theory." Siflis rolled his eyes. "I'd rather go for stress acclimatisation." Both Bobby and Bells got to him despite being virtually weightless, pinning Siflis against the wall. Stress acclimatisation meant being pummelled by a machine that crushed them with up to five times normal gravity but expected them to carry out set tasks.

"He doesn't mean that." Bobby glared and Siflis kept quiet.

"See, that went better. You pinned him perfectly even weightless. Now why don't you do it the rest of the time?" The instructor sounded almost plaintive.

"Because it isn't real, it's a bledrin exercise." Magpie flicked a knife down the room and nailed a floating dummy. "I can do that all day, because the dumb thing just floats."

Bells punched the wall, rebounding in a slow cartwheel. "We need opponents."

"More opponents you mean?" The instructor sounded downright savage now. "You crippled two instructors and the rest won't spar full-out any more. Even your own Super won't spar with you."

Bells grinned. "Not twice he won't."

Though Bobby frowned. "So how do we learn?"

"You want real practice? I'll arrange some, and see how you like that!" As the weight started to come back on the instructor spoke into a sleeve mic. "Take us back. They're bored."

"Me too." The instructor glared in the direction of the cockpit while Beebi's Basteds sniggered.

*   *   *

The trainer delivered a tirade along with the squad, finally leaving them with Smaj. He shook his head. "Don't flick the trainers. You need to learn."

"So how come you don't?" Bobby waited for the scowl at his usual flick but Smaj sighed.

"I'm not coming. I'm to watch the training and take part in some, but then wave you goodbye. Then I get to train the rest of your TRRF." Smaj beckoned. "Come on, we've got a mission profile at last." Six big smiles followed him into the briefing room.

Six glum faces and a smiling Siflis came out. The Super left immediately without speaking. Bells spoke first. "Six months? We have to lie in a coffin for six months?"

Smaj shrugged. "You'll be asleep most of it. You'll wake up for a bit to do intensive exercises while the rocket sticks on another one gee, then it'll cut again while you sleep."

"How come the trip takes six months if they've got an Alien Rocket? I understand the rocket bit. The nice Alien Wreckage that isn't wrecked gave the boffins the plans." Bells glared. "I know that Geek explained but can I have it without numbers and things?"

"You'll feel five times the weight until we get into space and on course, then you'll be weightless. The rocket will accelerate at one gee so you feel your proper weight for an hour of exercise each time you wake up." Siflis waited for Bells to nod understanding. "Eventually the one gee will be slowing us, but you'll still feel the same weight because we'll be going backwards. Then we exercise like maniacs for eighteen hours at the end until the rocket stops. If the fuel holds out."

They all stared at Siflis because that came close to waxing lyrical for him, or babbling. Then Magpie elbowed him in the ribs. "I understood that and felt better until the last bit. How come it makes sense to you?"

"I told you, space games." Siflis grinned. "This is sort of a dream come true, or a gamer obsession anyway."

"Can't we go faster and get there sooner?" Bells snarled at Magpie when she went to elbow him.

"Grouchy." Magpie dodged a half-hearted swipe from Bells. "Even I understood that bit. If we go a lot faster, we get squished because the rocket can't stand the strains of dodging any bits of rock at higher speeds. We can only go this fast because of the lovely Alien Space Rocket."

"Not a whole rocket, an Alien motor that uses less hydrogen or reuses or something. I got that. I don't fancy the rest of the rocket. If five blocs are building it, it'll be a bledrin disaster waiting to happen. It'll break down and then we're some impossible number of miles from home and completely pooched." Bobby mimed firing a pistol. "We can't even shoot something to feel better."

"We'll have plenty to shoot at the other end. Squads of Troopers from eight other blocs? I know it's a joint exercise but we'll end up fighting." Hood grinned. "Do they really expect us to play nice together?"

"We'll know soon, when the other squads arrive. Maybe that's what sour-puss meant by finding us someone to spar with?" Bobby sniggered. "If they let us all fight before leaving it'll cut down on weight in the rocket. Half the squads won't be going."

"I'm sort of curious about all the others. It's not like Troopers ever get to meet, is it? Timers fight Timers, Squaddies fight Legion or Spetnaz or Sturmtroopers or whatever the hell bulsh name they're called, but Troopers all stay at home." Bells frowned. "I still don't see why the blocs don't send those, the Squaddies and the like."

"Maybe because they fight each other all the time and wouldn't be able to resist. Maybe they reckon we are all friendly types." Everyone laughed. "We'll know soon, because the others will be here tomorrow." Bobby sighed. "Then we get the lecture again. Maybe today's was because we'll be too busy fighting at the next one to pay attention?"

*　*　*

Though finding out more about the other squads came as a bit of a shock. "I want to spar with the Frogs. Please?"

"You and nearly every other Trooper here, Bells. Did the instructions get lost in translation and they sent Divas?" Bobby looked at the five pretty women in short skirts with a Frog Super in charge, a man. He recognised that uniform.

"Bang bang." Hood grinned. "Last time I saw that uniform was through sights."

"One of that other squad is a woman I reckon, the Confeds, and maybe one of the SEPA though they're dressed the same as the rest." Siflis frowned. "Maybe SEPA, there's four squads that are sort of deep tan."

"Could be Indies, Chinas, Amazons or Mexes. Maybe Sheiks, I don't know the difference by sight, or what some of their corporations are." Line Manager McKay must be in shock to join in the discussion, let alone admit ignorance. "Those aren't Confeds, they're from the north, the Yankees." He laughed, the first time Bobby's squad had ever heard him do so. "They'll probably try to kill the Confeds."

"Are you sure none are the equivalent of Squaddies? There are some hard men there." Bells eyed the other groups.

The Supervisor laughed again, maybe it was hysteria? "Have you looked at yourselves lately? You scare me more than they do." He suddenly seemed to get a grip. "What am I doing even talking to you assholes? Smarten up. You're on parade."

Bobby didn't even straighten up. "They aren't, and their salutes are worse than mine. When do we meet?"

The Super scowled, then abandoned trying to take control and answered. "As soon as all their weaponry is stowed. That'll take a while." The heaps growing on the tarmac in front of each squad compared favourably with what Beebi's Basteds brought. "Nobody is allowed to take a weapon into the meeting."

"Those Frog Divas are bringing weapons, at least a pair each. Oomph!" Magpie smiled happily as Bells doubled up around her elbow.

Bobby tutted. "Maybe that's why they're dangerous, Bells? You get looking at those weapons and forget the rest. Come on, let's get the good seats."

*　　*　　*

There wasn't a fight because the canteen had one wall lined with Squaddies carrying real rifles, not flechette carbins. Beebi's Basteds got the good seats, near the entrance to see everyone as they came in. The rest spread out to the other tables, one table per squad. The two North American squads sat at opposite sides of the canteen and glared at each other.

All attention soon moved to the screen set up on a wall, showing pictures and then schematics of their transport. Though first the suit out front congratulated them all. The nine squads had been chosen by their blocs to take part in the greatest combined operation in mankind's history. They would go to space, out to the far reaches of the solar system. The nine squads would investigate the source of the mystery alien signal and secure the transmitter for the good of all mankind.

The suit turned to the drawings and pictures and explained how they'd get there, ignoring the sceptical glances or the glares between squads. When the survival and delivery system had been explained the squads were allowed to talk among themselves, though Bells still had trouble concentrating. "I'm telling you, those Frogs are Divas. That one with the red streak in her hair just put her leg up so her stocking top showed, then winked at me."

"Which means you'll be looking at her leg when she cuts your stupid throat." Magpie rolled her eyes. "Hood will have to watch your back, instead of the other way round."

"Forget that. No backs need watching until we get to the target and then their legs will be in a spacesuit." Bobby sighed. "The Director reckoned all our squads are allied, but the Confeds and Yankees are already a breath away from a fight. We consider the Krauts and Frogs natural enemies because we fight them as Timers and the rest must have the same problem." Bobby thought quickly. He'd have to be polite to the dick and get him working in the team because some of those other officers looked hard nuts. "Sir, are you sure you can't get extra weaponry stowed on the ship?"

The Super stared for a moment, probably startled by the sir instead of the usual sluur. "I don't know. We can only take a limited number of weapons and only plastic flechettes or plastic buckshot, the Directors out front all seem certain on that. There's a weight limit and lead ammo is heavy, and so are extra weapons so there's a list. Every bloc gets to inspect and supervise the others loading their capsules so I don't see how we can get extras aboard."

"What about on the way?" Siflis smirked. "Every capsule is launched individually, then clamped to the rocket part in orbit. Can't we have a few extras lurking up there with a sodin great magnet to tack them onto the side?"

"With crews made up of a dozen blocs operating the docking gear?" The Super looked suddenly thoughtful. "I'm more interested in ways to make sure we're connected properly, because our air and food must be in that rocket. I don't like the idea someone might thin out the opposition by not connecting something up quite right." Bobby noted that the Super hadn't swallowed this alliance bulsh either.

"The food? Nutritious liquid diet. I might consider it a mercy if that's cut off." Bells squirmed. "I don't fancy the other part, the waste disposal."

"I'm not keen on having my tackle clamped in a tube for six months, but the tube up my ass worries me more." Bobby grinned at Bells. "That'll give you some idea of how the Divas feel, Bells." Then he frowned. "Didn't anyone else think the drawings and pictures of the capsules looked different to the cutaways. Shorter, and a bit fatter maybe."

The Super frowned. "Can't see why they should be. I don't like the plan for the other end."

"You mean the mad scramble to board whatever it is? If we're all allied, there should be a planned approach and I didn't hear even a hint. They're even keeping each squad in a separate capsule. The rocket releases all the capsules well short of the target, then each capsule approaches the whatever and spits out the Troopers with their packs." Bobby looked around the table. "Even if everyone plays nice, has it occurred to you that all our food and air is on that rocket, or in the capsule?"

"Incentive scheme." Super McKay looked sick. "We've got what's in our suit tanks. If we haven't got into the target, I doubt the rocket will let us resupply."

"It'll know if we succeed, because that's where all the coms are sent through." Magpie paled. "If we've got in and sent all the information, will there be enough food or air for all the squads? What did Smaj say, he'd be training the rest of TRRF? It'll take six months for them to get there once we've reported on what's waiting." The rest looked at each other and paled as well.

"We might have to ally, unless management knows something we don't. How do we know the whatever will be empty when we get there?" Siflis looked at faces showing expressions ranging from alarm to almost panic from Bells.

"Aliens! Blood-sucking giant aliens with tentacles and disintegrator beams. Oh shite. No wonder the pay is so good, we'll never get to spend it." Bells looked from one to another, wild-eyed.

"Bells!" Bells jerked at Bobby's sharp tone and calmed a bit. "There's no mention of aliens."

"Look on the bright side Bells, if they've got disintegrator rays you'll have no left blood to be sucked." Magpie smiled sweetly as Bells glared.

Super McKay's face twisted into a snarl. "So either a bloodbath, starvation or aliens. You finally did it, got me on a bledrin Gaza Taxi. Pooched, well and truly pooched." He swallowed hard. "Now I know why you got me. We're all expendable. Nobody wants us."

Bobby wanted to say no, that the Duchess wouldn't do that, but this would be economics. Beebi's Basteds made a small but reliable force, because she'd assume the dick would cark it in the first two minutes. Then she must think if anyone could get the job done, this squad would. Sometimes Bobby wished he'd been a crap Timer, and a crap Trooper, and never met Supervisor Curen. Though life would have been a lot more boring. Then he realised that there would be supplies, for one very simple reason.

"There'll be air and the rest because whoever secures the assets has to survive, though all of us are expendable and I mean all of the other squads are as well. We've got to remember that. We're being sent out without a blind idea of what's waiting, one way scouts. There'll be a bit of extra food and water in each pack and capsule to make sure we get there and into the transmitter, and for any fight. Then with what's on the rocket there'll be enough to keep at least some of us going, to hold the objective until support arrives." He locked eyes with each one in turn. "The alliance business might be complete bulsh, in which case there might only be enough for one squad. Our squad." Bobby's eyes stopped on Super McKay. "That means we need you lean, mean, and a fighting member, Mickey."

The Super bridled. "Don't start that, it's Supervisor McKay you cheeky basted."

Bobby pointed at each member in the squad. "Siflis, Bells, Magpie, Hood and I'm Beebi. Squad names." He grinned. "Your squad name is Mickey and you are a basted, a Beebi's Basted."

The Super hesitated, thought about it, then straightened. "In that case we should be Mickey's Basteds."

"They'd call us Mickey's Monkeys or some such and won't give us any respect. We need that respect so they hesitate before attacking, set themselves properly, because then we get a bit of warning. I'll bet their Managers have files about Beebi's Basteds. You'll get a file on each of the other squads, and it'll show they've all got a name and a nasty rep back home." Bobby shrugged. "If I'm wrong on that then we're Mickey's whatevers. Deal?"

The hesitation went on longer this time, but in the end. "Deal."

"Welcome to the squad Mickey. Don't make plans for your spare time, you won't have any." Bobby wasn't sure if he could make the dick useful in the time left, but if he could make Mickey dangerous enough to attract some of the incoming that would help.

* * *

Though there seemed to be no time at all, because the following day every member of every squad had to report for a full medical. Though not Smaj, he bid them goodbye because he had to go and start training the rest up. Magpie hung back, staring at the medical centre. "Beebi, they'll find out I'm a woman." The Basteds' own medic had been squared with threats and persuasion, but not the medics here.

"So are a lot of the others Magpie. These are UKs' medics, so tell them you're undercover to catch the rest by surprise." Bobby forced a grin. "Explain you'll show your underwear at a strategic moment."

Magpie didn't smile. "What if they throw me out?"

"And replace you with who? You're trained." Bobby nodded towards the Super. "I'll tell him. He won't want to admit you've fooled him."

"Mickey? Shite, he's an officer, he'll expect me to bend over whenever he gets an itch." Magpie looked a bit wild-eyed now and her sleeve knife slid into her hand.

"No he won't. I'll tell him if he wants to pooch anyone, he should remember who'll be teaching him knife fighting, and how much better than him our Magpie is." Bobby sniggered. "He'd be safer going to the Frog Divas." The files had been delivered to Mickey just as Bobby predicted. The Frog squad were called Les Putes which meant Divas. They weren't really Divas because the squad had a reputation for killing Supers, usually enemy ones.

At least that brought a smile to Magpie's face. "If I have to fess up to them, we could compare Super scores." She headed for the queue outside the medical centre.

"Mickey."

"Sir out here, you bledrin eejit."

"That's the least of your problems. You need a bit of background about Magpie."

When Bobby finished, the Super stared towards the medical block. "Too late now, she's in there. So how long has your squad kept your own personal Diva?"

"Not a Diva, Mickey. She'll teach you how to use a knife, and can slice and dice you in her sleep." Bobby smirked. "Anyone trying to pooch that one might find he's missing the tackle to complete the job. All I'm asking is you keep quiet. If anyone official asks, you confirm she's undercover."

"But she's not."

"Yes she is. How do you think we got the jobs done, all those on the record? Most of the TRRF know, but nobody who's been with us less than a year." Bobby laughed. "Guns doesn't know, though he might think she's a bandit."

"That's illegal, two Troopers. He should have investigated."

Bobby laughed again. "Which bit of our files said legal?" Then he leaned a bit closer and lowered his voice. "She really has killed Supers, so if one gets a bit nosy?"

The Super blanched so he got the real message. Then a calculating look came over his face. "True. If we survive this, I might just find her a name to add to her score. If a Diva visits him and he carks it, they'd never look at me or for a Trooper. Deal?"

Bobby blinked, then reassessed the Super a bit. Well, what was another Super more or less? Magpie wouldn't mind. She had enough Pleb left to hate all Supers, and enough Trooper to do the job. "Deal. Let me have the name." Bobby would have smiled at the next thought, that the Super probably wouldn't live to collect, but it wasn't funny because neither would Magpie.

Thirty minutes later Bobby went in for his medical. "What sort of an examination is this? Where are the others?"

"You'll see them soon, Sarge. On the table please." The medic grinned. "No pleasant surprises?"

"No and just remember, she's undercover and The Horseman follows her work. Personally." That must be true in a way if the Duchess really did know the spook-master's name and identity.

The medic paled. "She didn't say The Horseman. Just a moment." He went into the corner with his com and although he couldn't hear, Bobby caught "Horseman" and "don't touch" stressed in a slightly panicky voice. Shite, he hadn't thought of the medics getting Magpie on her own, stripped and unarmed! She'd probably cripple a couple but enough could pin her down without her weapons. The medic came back.

Bobby looked him in the eye. "One fingerprint, and she'll come after all of you with a knife and even officers will look the other way."

"We're medics! You can't touch medics."

"We're Beebi's Basteds. We touch Supers and Managers but no, she hasn't topped a medic yet." Bobby made his smile as nasty as possible, nasty enough judging by the flinch. "We won't have to help her. Ask our Super who teaches knife work."

"I've got it, all right? I'll repeat the warnings to the rest. Hellfire, the sooner you go to sleep the safer."

"Sleep!" Bobby really felt relieved he'd frightened the little shite, because a sleeping Magpie wouldn't even cripple a couple.

The medic held his hands up defensively. "Implants, metal, all authorised. Your Super gets the same." He held up the little gun and Bobby laid back and held out his arm.

*   *   *

When he woke up Bobby wished he'd asked more questions. Magpie looked across from her bed. "Maybe it would have been better if they'd called in the instructors for a pooching party while I was out, and maybe half the nearest Trooper barracks. I'd heal from that." She looked down the bed at the cover over her legs. "I'm not likely to heal from this!" Just below her hips the bed covers dipped, and then laid flat right to the end of the bed because there were no legs to hold them up. No wonder she sounded bitter.

"I'd no idea." Bobby shook his head in disbelief. "Are the brass looking for a bloodbath because I can't see the other women being any happier, and I'm not overjoyed." His legs ended in the same place now, a long way short of where he should have knees. Bobby held up his hand, displaying the remaining two middle fingers and thumb. "I reckon I can still use a knife and a gun with these."

"We're not likely to be running around causing trouble, are we?" Siflis's eyes widened. "Shite, what did you say? The capsules in the pictures were shorter than the drawings?" He looked at his stumps. "Now we know how much shorter."

"This should be easy for you, Hood. You've already got used to one metal leg." Magpie tried for a smile.

"I can help you?" Hood grinned, "It'll be easier if you wear a short skirt?"

Magpie looked stricken. "I packed it and now you won't like it any more, not with metal legs sticking out."

"Put stockings on." Bells leered. "I'll look."

"Shite, I'd just thought that the Frog Divas wouldn't distract you but it won't make any difference." Bobby rolled his eyes. "Maybe the medics should have cut a bit higher on you."

"Ooh, can I get a metal one? With hydraulics?" The medic who came in probably wondered why a group of involuntary amputees were laughing and throwing pillows at each other. Though he retreated sharpish when they switched to throwing bedpans and anything solid they could find at him. Maybe he'd have to increase the meds even more.

*   *   *

Once they'd had more meds and stopped throwing things, a Manager came to see the squad. He insisted that supplying metal to allow them to carry out their duties came under their terms of enlistment and their contracts. Not that anyone had much of an option now. They could learn to live with the metal and go to space, or be in breach of contract and be given a dishonourable discharge. Discharge meant being dumped in a Pleb complex without either legs or the metal replacements. Beebi's Basteds assumed that was what happened to the SEPA and Amazon Troopers who had to be replaced when their interfaces were rejected. Mickey re-joined them and wasn't any happier about unexpectedly losing his legs, admitting that if he was discharged, his family weren't wealthy enough to buy him new legs.

During the first acclimatisation exercises one of the techs actually told them the reason for taking everyone's legs and two fingers from each hand. Extremities would chill quicker on the trip and keeping enough blood flowing to their legs during six months of inaction would be difficult. Arms could be kept tucked close to the body to conserve heat, but fingers might still freeze and need amputating. If that happened, the two metal fingers would be enough to grip because the metal little finger swivelled and became opposable, a thumb. The planners' assessments concluded that taking everyone's legs off would be more efficient than trying to avoid frostbitten feet and gangrene. Though the Basteds thought it more likely amputation worked out cheaper for some reason, or some arse had decided the Troopers wouldn't need legs in space anyway.

For the next nine weeks the squads were pumped full of painkillers and Kwikheal while the bio-metal interface plates healed properly. The second week their metal legs and fingers arrived so their nerves could mesh with the electrics. At least Bells could concentrate since Les Putes wore loose trousers, but nobody flicked them about it because they also looked murderous. All the squads looked in a vicious mood, so none of them were volunteers for that amount of metal.

At least the limbs didn't cause as much trouble while they were weightless though a good part of that training took place without their legs at all. Learning to handle the legs and fingers turned lethal fighters into stumbling amateurs in some respects. That didn't last long, since every single member of every squad seemed determined to get on top of the new metal as soon as possible. Some of their enthusiasm might be so they could work off the anger off on the instructors. The trainers started off with smiles because all these hard Troopers were floundering around like Timers, but within a fortnight two instructors left on stretchers.

The injuries were nothing to do with Beebi's Basteds, but they took note that the culprits didn't seem to be punished. So did the trainers, and backed off the flickin or deliberately making the amputees look incompetent. The squads trained with savage intensity both with and without their new metal, learning to utilise any extra advantages of having metal legs and two metal fingers on each hand.

At least a short lecture addressed the issue of Aliens. "Some squads have expressed concern about possibly finding Alien lifeforms at the destination." From the looks on the other squads all of them had been wondering. "The Alien artefact transmitted this picture." The screen showed a lot of stars. "Then this one." Another picture of stars came up. "It sent the pair three times. When the pictures are compared, there are discrepancies." Two of the pictures slid together and some of the stars had moved. "Astronomers have calculated that, comparing the starfields, the artefact took the first picture approximately one million years ago and took the last one when making contact."

"Are they sure?" The speaker glanced at the guards along the wall. "Sir."

"No, but the margin of error isn't enough to matter. The shortest time lapse between the pictures, about eight hundred thousand years, answers one question. There will be no Aliens waiting to greet you. Now you can all concentrate on training for exploration and possibly breaking and entering." The lecturer turned off his screen, packed up and left without further explanation though to be honest the squads had all understood the bit that mattered. No Aliens so they'd only got each other to deal with.

*   *   *

Adapting to metal legs turned out to be easier than dealing with metal fingers. The theory about using just the two new fingers sounded great, right up until the practical exercises. Magpie's pistol drifted away from her and she made a lunge to grab it, then wafted her hand to stop her slow spin. "I can't do this. I am so knackered I'm likely to doze off right here."

"You can't be knackered because you haven't got any. Us blokes are definitely knackered so we're relying on you to beat off Les Putes." Bobby could sympathise in truth, because working with two fingers and a thumb taped down should be possible. Actually getting the metal fingers to bend in the right way to compensate turned out to be a lot harder than the theory. Bobby knew that at least part of the trouble had to be learning to use his index finger to hold the pistol, and his little finger to pull the trigger. Lack of sleep made up the rest of the problem because none of them could rest properly with the healing flesh and new metal, not yet.

"Why didn't the basteds make the little finger longer? Ah, yes!" A line of light sprang out from Hood's pistol and completely missed the floating target. "I hope space is easier to aim in than water." The six of them in their spacesuits were immersed in water to be weightless, as were the targets. To the left, Les Putes hit their second target. Bobby curled his little finger, just a bit more, and yes! He clipped the floating figure and it glowed green.

"Sleek basted." Bells shook his pistol. "I could throw it better." Then he turned slowly upside down because shaking the pistol set him rotating, and his other arm had been strapped down for this exercise. Worse, they had to do this legless so he couldn't use them to steady himself. A ripple of laughter from the rest came over the coms but stopped as a third Frog target lit up.

"Sodit." Magpie jammed the pistol between the stumps of her thighs and flipped backwards, a slow-mo flip in the water but as her pistol came up level with her head, she pulled the trigger, and a second target lit up.

"Is that allowed?" Laughter answered over the link and after a moment Mickey joined in. "Unlike you, I had a mother and father and they brought me up to stick to the rules." Though even as he said it

Mickey bent and jammed the barrel between his thigh stumps. He did two complete rotations before finally hitting the target, and by then Hood had nailed his.

Bells tumbled and twisted as he tried to copy them. "I'm not doing it like that, I look stupid." He tried to hit the target again and missed.

Meanwhile Les Putes gathered around their Super, 'shooting' him with the light beams as he missed again. He lost the pistol and flailed around trying to get it back. Siflis nailed his target, five each, and Les Putes ran out of patience. One grabbed their Super's helmet while two caught hold of his arm and aimed. Another turned him to get lined up and the sixth target glowed. Les Putes turned to Beebi's Basteds, arms punching up in triumph before they headed to the ladder. In their wake the Frog Super spun in a corkscrew, frantically lashing out with his one arm to try and get stabilised.

"You bledrin Homer." Magpie smacked Bells on the helmet, but not with the pistol so he just spun out of control for a moment. He turned to her, but Mickey pointed. Les Putes had stopped to watch. One of them pointed at Bells, then mimed blowing a kiss before they swam up the ladder and out.

"She loves me."

"She's found a sucker. That was thank you for letting them win, you eedjit." Bobby sighed. "Worse, they cheated better than we did. Go on Magpie, Hood, point Bells at the target." Moments later the sixth target glowed and the com chimed completion of the exercise. The six of them swam to the ladder.

Mickey hesitated. "Shouldn't we help him?" The Frog Super had slowed up but then spun again as he tried to pick up his pistol.

"Do you prefer him grateful, or those five Putes mad at you for spoiling their fun?"

"Good point Magpie." Mickey headed for the ladder. "He's got plenty of air." The Frog Super still hadn't surfaced by the time they'd clipped on their legs and left.

* * *

Bells got his revenge nine days later, because Les Putes couldn't get their Super to throw a knife accurately. Mickey wasn't good with a knife, but being trained by a woman had motivated him and he managed on his third try. "Oh yes." Bells grinned, then lost the smile. "I am not blowing a kiss to their Super."

"Nor am I before you ask. My underwear is a strategic secret." Magpie smirked. "Our Super should."

"Piss off." Mickey wore a beaming smile after hitting his mark, though it faltered. "The women, the actual Putes, were bledrin fast and accurate."

"So I'll blow a kiss to them this time." Bells looked them over. "I can't tell which one it was last time, but I'm sure the one with the red streak is interested." Les Putes had lost interest in their Super now they'd lost, and a couple of them waved. Bells pointed at his favourite and blew the kiss. The women were all laughing at him, and his target, as the rest of the Basteds dragged Bells away.

*   *   *

Bells wasn't laughing four days later after the sparring. "I'd have beat her without these things." He used his teeth to pull on the ties fastening the big floppy gloves.

Siflis sneered. "You wouldn't have beat her if she'd tied one arm behind her back. Just why do you think her shirt buttons were half undone?"

"To show she fancies me."

Magpie rolled her eyes. "She knew you'd be trying to see down there instead of watching her beat the shite out of you."

"I did see down there but she's wearing a bra. A sexy one and it's really well-filled." Bells grinned. "I tell you, she fancies me."

Hood looked embarrassed. "I got beat because I don't like hitting women. I'll shoot them, or even use a knife, but I can't beat on one. Though to be honest that blonde lass is bledrin strong and fast as well."

"If I'd been up against their Super, I might have beat him." Mickey shrugged. "Against any of you or them I've got no chance."

"True, which might be why they sent their Super against Magpie. That way the Supers would both get beaten, and it would be four against four." Bobby frowned. "Bells is supposed to be our hand to hand expert so he should have won, though we did get a draw." Bobby grinned. "At least we know our strategic weapon will work since Les Putes version did on Bells."

"But it's still a secret because I didn't need it." Magpie smirked. "Can I add the Frog Super to my score?" Mickey flinched. He still didn't like casual references about topping Supers even if he was off the target list.

"No, he's still breathing." Bobby's eyes narrowed. "Just what did she whisper after getting the handcuffs on you, Bells?"

"Nothing." Bells turned scarlet and headed towards the showers.

Despite repeated attempts to find out, Bells kept denying his opponent whispered anything. There were no more opportunities for him to get payback, because one of the Confeds crippled a Yankee in their sparring so the squads weren't allowed to meet any more. A pity, because now the Basteds hadn't got a read on the strengths of any of the other squads.

Instead each squad member spent hours talking with an armourer as an additional weapon or two were added to their metal legs or fingers. The talks always had two observers from other blocs, and the results were all checked by a different two neutral observers. Allegedly, no addition could damage a capsule, and only a proportion of the squad could have long range weapons. They all spend periods practicing with their extras, designed to be accessible if a fight broke out before the squads reached the target. If? Bobby's squad were stone certain there'd be a bloodbath, despite the lectures explaining how everyone would cooperate in this great venture.

They became more certain when their squad had their own private lecture. The Area Manager talked about prioritising and maximising return on investment, and how the contracts between the blocs didn't preclude self-defence. He also discussed the bonuses available and the relative shares depending on how many claimed them, though he did stress the benefits of an alliance with a small number of others to achieve the best result. Bobby and all the rest got the message. If they outmanoeuvred, stitched up or just plain murdered the other squads it would make them all rich, rich enough to buy legs if they were discharged. Since all the other squads had to be getting their own lectures, a bloodbath looked more and more of a certainty.

Once the limbs worked at least reasonably well, training went up a notch. Between the new weapons, the intense continual training, and the repeated drills getting into and out of the capsule, another three months slipped by. Throughout the process the capsule loading drills were held without warning, as practice in case one of the minor blocs launched an attack. One bloc at least considered the attempt to be against their God's will, or at least against their long-term interests. Others might launch missiles, or arrange for terrorists to sabotage the capsules, simply as a spoiling action to rack up costs for the major investors.

At least the long training meant Mickey toughened up, until the Basteds thought he might beat up to half of the other Supers. Especially with a knife, since having a woman teaching him spurred Mickey to try harder there. That or the number of times Magpie mentioned withdrawal symptoms and hoped she'd be able to top a Super soon. One of the others preferably, but their own would do if he didn't shape up.

*   *   *

Instead of the scheduled crawl through pipes, supposedly an Alien spaceship, an alarm hammered out. "Move it, move it, time to go. Come on quickly!" Bobby stared at the trainer, who sounded as if he meant it this time.

"Is it an attack?"

The man grinned. "How would I know? Come on, time to load up."

"Another drill? How many times are we going to load up and spend an hour staring at a metal wall." It wasn't the wait that annoyed everyone. Nobody liked having to take off their legs and stow them onto their backs, clipped to the backpacks. Worse, they all had to put on the spacesuits and fit the waste disposal and putting on the antiseptic cream and plugging in hurt them, in and out. Bells had a black eye for a while after getting to Magpie's suit and writing Bells End on her connections. He complained she had no sense of humour. The limp to go with the black eye came from Hood, not Magpie.

Bobby checked that he'd got five green lights, one from every squad member, and tripped his own. Mickey contacted Control to report the capsule ready for launch and Bobby let his mind drift. He smiled quietly as Bells flicked Magpie about the size of his connection being bigger, while she pointed out she was happy with her usual one, thanks. Then she told him that with the practice she got in barracks, hers didn't hurt much. They didn't actually say Magpie was female, not on the air, but Magpie and Hood took a certain amount of flickin now Mickey knew. They dished it out as well.

Losing their legs had only stopped Hood and Magpie for two weeks, once Mickey knew her strategic secret. Maybe having Mickey in the same quarters slowed them up a bit, but they'd both come out from behind the screen one morning with happy smiles. After that Mickey ignored their held hands, and them always helping each other when clipping and unclipping the metal. Magpie came out in a tight blouse, briefly, just to set his mind at rest she really was a woman. Then she'd given Mickey a comprehensive knife fighting lesson to stop any bright ideas about pooching. She put red paint down the edges of her practice blade and if the marks had been real, he'd have been jointed.

The radio broke Bobby out of his reverie. *"Brace for lift-off. This is not a drill. I repeat, this is not a drill."* Bobby opened his mouth to object and saved his breath. The six of them were nicely boxed up and helpless.

Instead he tongued the internal squad com. "Relax because you all know the drill. Make sure you've actually tightened and clipped everything this time. Management have done it this way to make sure nobody gets nervous and runs at the last minute. Personally I'm pleased all the training is over."

"At least we won't get cold feet." Bells sniggered. "Did you pack your short skirt and stockings, Magpie?" Bobby opened his mouth to tell him to watch it over the coms, but it didn't matter who knew now.

The packs had been sealed for months, after the contents were checked by neutral observers. "You can wonder about that for six months, Bells, and if I've brought frillies or just tight and tiny. It'll stop you pining for Les Putes."

"Coms silence for lift-off." Everyone cursed Mickey silently for being a stiff-necked dick. "Though now I'll be wondering as well, Magpie." Bobby mentally apologised for what he'd thought about the Super, because the round of giggles and sniggers settled everyone nicely. Then he found himself too busy remembering to breathe properly as the capsule shook and he found out just why that damn machine pummelling him had been training. Lift-off!

Spaced

"Please exercise strenuously. There are only four more exercise periods before final deceleration burns." The calm, polite woman's voice penetrated Bobby's drugged haze. He worked the muscles of his throat and swallowed water to ease the pain. Five or six month's experience, he'd lost count of actual time, dictated he drank as much as possible as soon as he woke. That way he could drink more before he slept. About halfway through the exercise a chime would announce mealtime, and Bobby would drink his food as well but from a different spout.

"Hrrrm." Bobby drank again to loosen his vocal chords. "Count off, Basteds."

"Basted one." Mickey coughed. "I know, drink more."

Hood's voice sounded clearly. "Basted three."

"Basted four." As usual Siflis sounded dopey.

"Basted five." Bells growled his reply, he always woke up in a foul mood. "Another bledrin headache." He also seemed to have more headaches than anyone else.

Magpie sounded sleepy. "Basted six." Since the drowsiness affected her and Siflis most, and Hood seemed least affected, Bobby thought body-weight might account for it. He'd given up worrying after a month, or maybe two. Now he didn't care why as long as everyone woke up each time.

"Basted two here, take five to get plenty to drink, and get the kinks out." Bobby took his own advice. As the acceleration increased and his body gained weight, he drank more water and eased cramped muscles. Then he flexed each joint and gently worked any that ached more than usual. Within the five minutes Bobby knew they had reached one gee, simply because he stopped getting heavier. "Start now, and count. Muscle stretches first this time."

"Please sir, one of mine won't stretch. Can Magpie give me a hand?"

His mouth muscles stretched as Bobby smiled, because sure enough Magpie came straight back. "If I could reach you Bells, I'd use a knife instead and solve your problems."

"Please sir, that's threats of violence against a fellow Trooper."

Mickey's voice cut in. "First off Magpie isn't a fellow, and secondly if I could reach with a knife I'd help her."

Bobby hoped Mickey kept this relaxation. He'd still be baggage in real strife, but at least not a distraction or interference. He smiled quietly and wondered how many would lose their bets if Beebi's Basteds brought their officer back alive. "Now we know why our weaponry is locked down. Everyone drunk enough for now?" The affirmatives rolled in. "Then give it everything because we've nearly made it. You heard Aggie, only three more chances to get fit." Siflis had complained about being nagged every time he woke up, so the electronic voice became Aggie the nag. He'd also complained bitterly that riding a spaceship didn't come anywhere close to the vids and games.

"It doesn't feel like six months?" Hood really didn't sound sure and neither did the rest, though most thought it felt like more than the planned time. They'd all lost count of the waking periods, and weren't even sure if they were woken every day.

*   *   *

The three remaining one hour sessions weren't long enough to get fit, but dragged out for ever because they all wanted the trip over. They all went to sleep after the last session with real anticipation, at least partly at a change to their routine. Aggie confirmed that as they woke up again. *"Deceleration burn starting in five minutes. Burn will maintain one gee for six hours, then cease for an eight-hour rest period. That will be repeated twice more for a total of eighteen hours deceleration. The final rest period may include capsule manoeuvring so please ignore unexpected g-forces. Be prepared for capsule separation at the end of the third rest period. These instructions will be repeated."* Bobby blinked rapidly until his eyes lubricated. Had the bledrin thing woken him early, or had the extra effort put into the exercises last time made him tired?

"Hrrrm." Bobby snapped out of his reverie and cleared his throat, then winced. He'd forgotten to drink first. He got it right the second time. "Hrrrm. Basted two alive and more or less awake. Count off."

"Basted one. Do you feel more tired? Never mind, later."

Hood hadn't been affected. "Basted three. Wakey, wakey."

"Smug Basted. I'm Basted four." Siflis yawned loudly. "Has Aggie started early?"

"Maybe, because she interrupted a wonderful dream. This Diva..." A storm of protest drowned Bells out. "All right, Basted five to all boring Basteds."

"Basted six. What did Aggie say? I missed some of it because I was having the same dream and just about to say no and laugh."

"Did you hear that, Hood, she's teasing other men."

"Just you, Bells, no men involved." Hood coughed. "I'm dry. Did we sleep longer?"

"We don't know how long we sleep normally." Mickey coughed as well. "I'm relieved. I half expected the water to run out. At least there'll be plenty at the target."

"There will? Did I miss an update?" Bobby's brain had woken up now and he cudgelled it into action. There'd be water waiting?

"Ice." Mickey paused. "I'm sure there's lots of ice in the Kuiper belt or anywhere out here. We grab a piece and use the lasers to melt it." He chuckled. "I've been worrying about water for at least two months and still haven't worked out how to get it inside my suit."

"Take the connections from here, the capsule. We can screw them back on if we ever get back." Siflis coughed. "If I don't feel better soon I won't care about dying."

"We can't put anything into the tubes in space, the pressure goes the wrong way and the air will go out." Mickey still sounded worried.

"Crush the ice. Stick a plastic bag full of it around the end of the pipe and Gaffer tape it into place. We've got plenty of tape." Magpie laughed, because they all carried half a dozen rolls of tape to repair their suits.

"I haven't got a plastic bag. Who brings a bledrin plastic bag into space? How will we get food and water?" Bells had finally realised there might be a real problem.

"I do. I brought my strategic underwear in their plastic bags." Magpie sniggered. "If you don't fancy drinking from my knicker bag, hard luck."

"I fancy it. I'm going to have dreams about your knickers and all that water."

"I'll have a laser, so be careful or I might warm up the wrong thing." Hood sounded pissed, though by now he should be used to Bells and Magpie flickin each other.

"We've all got lasers. May the power be with you." Bells had seen some space vid where the characters fought with laser swords, and expected theirs to work like that in space. Being told they wouldn't by every single instructor hadn't stopped him hoping.

"You won't have any power if you don't exercise." Bobby sighed because he didn't fancy this either. "We've got three sessions of six hours to get fit, so make the most of it. We will work like hell for the whole six hours. We'd better or the other squads will trample us. Unclip your arms properly and let's get started." By the time Aggie gave them the ten-minute warning before sleep, Bobby could barely move his arms. They really had weakened terribly despite the exercise periods. He hoped the rest of the squads were in the same position. Bobby fell asleep smiling because even if Bells got close to Les Putes, in his present physical condition he wouldn't be able to do much about it.

*　　*　　*

By the end of the last exercise period, Bobby thought he might be able to put up some sort of fight. Although shattered physically and sore from the waste connections, somehow the three long periods awake left him feeling more alive. For the first time in six months or so the drugs didn't keep him asleep. As he half-roused for the third time Bobby felt pressure as the spacecraft manoeuvred. The previous twice had been when the couch massaged his buttocks and shoulders which it must have been doing for the last six months. Bobby drifted back off and woke slowly but fairly clear-headed rather than in a haze of drugs.

At least his throat wasn't as dry. Bobby took a drink, then remembered what would happen today and drank more. "Basted Two. Remember, drink all you can. There'll be water in the packs, but we don't know when we'll get resupply."

"Eat, drink and be merry. Basted one here, and I'm not merry because it's drink, and drink. Worst still there's no hint of booze in either drink. Shite, did Aggie give us a shot, I feel buzzed?" Mickey did sound a bit over-happy.

"Maybe it's just because we slept properly, naturally without being put out." Bobby didn't want Magpie thinking that she'd been given uppers, not the way she felt about drugs. She'd go viral, and then Hood probably would. "Let's hear you, Basteds."

"Another cheerful Basted, number four. It's not an upper, just feels more like a good night's sleep." Bobby smiled, he would bet Siflis had thought exactly the same about Magpie.

"Basted three feels like shite." That surprised Bobby because Hood usually seemed most awake.

"Basted six does, but that's normal and so is Hood waking up in a shite mood."

"You should know. Basted five here and I feel up for something. Hey, do you think Les Putes woke up feeling this good?"

"They'll be putting on their sexy underwear, short skirts and fishnets just for you, Bells." Magpie sniggered. "The ones with a sheath for the gelding knife."

"Enough, warm-up exercises right away and drink, drink, drink."

"Yes Daddy." Though everyone went silent after the round of laughter so they were drinking.

"Wha...?" Bobby spluttered and then coughed to get his throat cleared. The small vid-screen at eye level had lit up for the first time since leaving Earth. It showed a huge block of ice lit by a bright light. The wall of ice continued either side as could be seen when the camera zoomed back out. The rest of the picture looked pitch black at first with tiny, hard points of light until Bobby's eyes adjusted. Then he could see a large blacker object occluding the lights as it moved slowly and ponderously across them. The black mass surrounded the circle of illuminated ice, and then tiny ripples of reflections showed it to be a stupendous iceberg.

At least Bobby assumed huge and stupendous, based on the light beam. Mickey must have wondered as well. "How big is that thing?" He cursed. "If that's the target, we are so pooched."

Bobby had opened his mouth to point out there could just be a transmitter attached someplace, when a series of bluish glows in the iceberg lit up from one end to the other and gave an impression of the true scale. A smaller block of ice tumbled between the camera and the iceberg reinforcing the idea of huge. "Those lights are under a lot of ice." Siflis had to be right because the muted, diffuse light couldn't happen out in space. As the lights grew brighter the whole exterior of the ice block turned pale blue, which concealed whatever lay underneath.

"This object is transmitting. Please dictate your impressions as report Outreach One." Aggie's impersonal tones came as a dash of cold reality.

"While you do that, systems checks and keep drinking." Bobby gave the recorder his impressions between sips. He tried the food inlet but without success.

"Capsule launch in ten minutes. All capsules will be launched together. Please remember the capsule has minimal manoeuvring fuel, and that you will be released from your habitat five minutes after breakaway. Survival inputs and voiding connections will be transferred to your suit backpacks one minute before release. Your screens will show your relative positions and the direction and dimensions of the target object. You are expected to uphold the finest traditions of the UKs Armed Forces." The anthem began to play.

"Drink but don't piss."

"I'm bursting…." Magpie stopped. "Why not?"

"Pee after we get cut off. The backpack will turn it into water again, allegedly. Remember?" Bobby didn't fancy that, but at least there'd only be his liquids in the pack. His mind shied away from what he'd just drunk and where that came from.

"I was just thinking I could murder a curry, but not second time round." Bells laughed. "Worse still, think what it would do to the air supply."

"Mickey, have you got radar yet?"

"No, it should show up in front of you as well. I hope it starts up before release because I want to get clear of the rest." Mickey had the manoeuvring controls, with a secondary set in front of Bobby in case the officer carked it.

"Try and find a chunk of ice to hide behind. I don't trust the rest."

Bobby waited for the laughter to die down. "Not like that. I don't trust their capsules either. One of them might have managed to arm the bledrin thing."

"Run, hide, watch. Then nip in and steal the silver." Everyone heard Mickey's long sigh. "No rehearsals for this bit, and no sitrep or map."

"Because it would be uneconomic to send out a camera probe. Fifty-four Troopers is cheaper." Siflis sounded bitter, but Mickey didn't pick him up on it so he probably felt the same. Some of the usual antagonism between Supers and Troopers had abated on this trip, because this one really was in the same shite.

Bobby felt the click as his weapons lock disengaged for the first time. He couldn't draw it properly, but reached his laser wrong-handed, across his body, and raised it far enough to check the charge. "Check the charge on your laser pistol. Mine's green so here's hoping." Within minutes all five reported the weapons charged. "Remember, the spacesuits are laser-proof so don't waste the charge. The face screens will darken so don't try to blind anyone. Bells, don't try sword fighting." The noise wasn't quite a worded protest, but the rest laughed. Bobby really did wonder, again, if they'd all been given an upper.

Though his mood soon darkened. Between the private lectures about grabbing the good stuff and the lack of a co-ordinated plan including all the squads Bobby still expected the next bit to be a bloodbath. The most he could plan for was to survive the initial chaos, then weigh up the situation.

*   *   *

"*Two minutes. Please stop using the inputs and outputs until the capsule is disconnected.*"

"You were right Mickey. We've been fed from the big rocket."

"But Aggie didn't say not to drink after release, so the capsule really must have some aboard." Hood sounded relieved.

"Good point Hood. Mickey, I reckon we should stash the capsule, maybe fasten it to an ice block so it doesn't drift off. Then we can find it again, just in case?" Bobby eased off giving Mickey direct instructions in case the dick started to get official.

"If we can nudge one gently, then melt the ice surface a bit?" Mickey sounded uncertain. "It'll freeze again and that might glue them together. If the block is near enough that thing, there should be a bit of gravity to keep it close."

"Could work. Good thinking." Bobby needed all six of them thinking hard, and Mickey had officer training so he might come up with solutions the others wouldn't. "Bells can use his laser for melting, just so he can see what it does."

"Yesss."

"I'm full, so I'm taking off the water connection to my backpack now. Shite, it's leaking." Three voices shouted at Magpie to use Gaffer tape. "Got it. I just wondered how we'd be released. If the bledrin thing spits us out, we might not get back to collect anything."

"Good point Magpie. I'll take mine off. One more?" Bobby twisted to reach the tube.

Siflis spoke up. "I'll do it Beebi. I'm smaller and I've got more manoeuvring room in here. What about the food connection?"

"If we find food it can come down the drink pipe. If we don't and come back this feed pipe will still be in place." Aggie interrupted Bobby.

"*Three, two, one, capsule launch.*" A click and shudder, and something gave the capsule a definite push sideways and upwards. The radar screen lit up to show one large return to the side, now falling behind, and eight smaller contacts. The centre of the screen showed a huge, solid contact, nearly two miles long! The bledrin rocket had launched them all directly at the iceberg!

"Break away, break away!" Bobby wasn't the only one shouting, because they'd all seen what happened to the probe that fired something at the original piece of wreckage. Mickey heard or reacted anyway because the capsule yawed to the side, then the rockets kicked Bobby's ass.

"Enough, don't use all the fuel."

"Will we miss it?" Mickey sounded on the edge of blind panic.

"Yes, stop boosting!" The capsule still headed towards the huge ice block, but at an angle that should take them clear. On the radar other capsules were using up fuel as well, to avoid the mass or to slow up. Two capsules continued on their way, apparently content to hit the target. Bobby read off the tags. "Who are BIVSUB?"

"Billiton-Vale-Suncor-Barrick, the top mining conglomerate in the far north of America. The Yankees." Mickey had learned all this shite, it had to be a management thing. "The others are Mining Alliance of Chinese Co-operatives. MACC or just Chinas because all the industries are combined. Communist Corporate management, only they could make that work." Mickey paused. "Are they really going to hit it?"

"Maybe, unless they do something soon. Can we hide behind one of these smaller bergs before they do, because I remember what happened to the other probes the first time?" Bobby didn't want to nudge Mickey too hard, in case he panicked and burned off the rest of the fuel. Nor did he fancy being target practice for Alien lasers.

"We've used a third of the fuel. The basteds didn't want us to avoid the target." Mickey calculated courses and burns, the lines showing up briefly on Bobby's screen. "We have enough fuel to stop by a ninety-foot-wide block almost level with the target asteroid. They're ice asteroids. You threw me when you said iceberg." Mickey sounded truly happy to get the name sorted; Bobby worried more about those two bledrin idiots heading for the illuminated whatever.

"Will we make it before Aggie spits us out?"

"Maybe. It'll be close, but we should get there about the same time those lunatics do." Bobby saw one line on his screen strengthen and a short kick from the capsule told him Mickey had refined the course.

Bobby left the driver to his job. "Basteds, you heard that. When Aggie warns us, grab hold of something and hang on tight in case we are pushed."

"Not the seat, that might be what shoves us or it might come with us."

"You heard Siflis." Bobby glanced at his timer. "Two minutes and counting." Dead silence fell as the squad watched their screens. The two capsules headed straight for the mission target, while Beebi's Basteds' capsule kept up but at an angle to close in on their own target. The screen rotated as Mickey turned them for deceleration. The rockets kicked them gently.

Another message from Aggie horrified everyone. *"Please remember there is only enough food and water for forty-eight hours and air for seventy-two in your packs. Further survival relies on access to this capsule, with another forty-eight hours of supplies. Supplies will be released on receipt of samples and evidence of progress."*

"Shite, I thought we'd be able to access what was left on the capsule at least, and there's no mention of the main rocket. What happens after that, after the capsule is used up?" Bells asked what everyone else wondered.

Aggie answered, or just got around to the second message. *"The main rocket holds sufficient air, food and water for one squad to survive until further supplies arrive. The extra consumables will be released if Control sends the codes after assessing progress."*

Bobby opened his mouth to start cursing, but didn't get chance. "Shite!" Mickey spoke but Bobby agreed. The Chinas had poured on acceleration to hit the ice harder while the Yankee capsule started decelerating as fast as possible to stop close to the ice. His own seat pressed harder on his ass as Mickey slowed them as well.

Before anyone else could speak, Aggie did. *"Ten, nine, eight, seven...."* Bobby shouted hang on over the countdown, still watching the two capsules getting nearer the ice. The Yankees had nearly stopped. *"Three, two, one, separation."*

*   *   *

Bobby hung onto the door as it flipped open and the seat gave him a solid push. He kept his eyes on the two screens, radar and camera, as the Chinas and Yankees were also ejected. The Yankees hung onto their capsule but the Chinas spread out, using jets to get away from the doomed craft.

Bobby ended up looking above his head, along his arms, to keep the view. He saw the Chinas capsule enveloped in a cloud of what looked like steam. The steam jetted from a point about ten feet to the side of the imminent impact point, glittering into ice as it billowed around the craft and spread out. The beam that followed turned the capsule into another glittering cloud. The beam also went through one Chinas squad member who burst into a smaller, redder cloud of steam and glittering fragments.

Two of the other spacesuits cartwheeled, surrounded by vapour as

251

debris ruptured their suits. The three remaining squad members used up their jets getting away from the carnage. Another jet of steam spewed out further along the illuminated asteroid before a thin rod thrust through the ice. Not thin, Bobby could see it had to be wider than the men in their bulky spacesuits. Lights flickered at the top and the last three Chinas impacted the ice with vapour jetting from multiple holes in their suits. The screen turned white.

"Knock before entering." Mickey sounded sombre. "Whatever greeting our masters programmed into the computers didn't work."

Bobby shook himself. "Count off Basteds."

"Basted three holding on."

"Basted four holding on."

"Basted five lost contact. Back now."

"Basted six back in my seat. Can we put our legs on now?"

"No Magpie, they'll just make you a bigger target." Bobby looked around, and his camera screen hadn't shut down after all. They were drifting very slowly into the side of their own target and the block of ice had cut off the capsule camera view. "Siflis, take a peek round the side of that ice and relay the view. The rest of you, let's get this thing tethered." That took a bit of doing, until they all warmed up a door edge and pushed it into the ice. As soon as the beams quit the asteroid refroze leaving Aggie tethered. Bobby allowed Bells to cross laser beams briefly with Hood, just to finally prove he couldn't sword fence.

"Shite. Knocking doesn't work even if it's polite." Siflis relayed a view of the Yankee capsule. The rod from inside the asteroid had shot out a clump of lines, the ends of which had separated to pierce their targets. Clouds of crystals, frozen vapour or air from inside, surrounded the Yankee capsule and the six still figures as they were drawn towards the alien weapon. A cloud of steam enlarged the hole before they were all pulled down out of sight.

Everyone seemed to be entranced by the sight until Bells broke the spell. "What are the rest doing?"

With a shock Bobby realised he'd lost track. "Siflis, give us a slow visual sweep." He twisted himself up and around to his seat before pulling the door far enough closed to watch the radar. Three capsules still approached the blue-lit asteroid, but slowly and all showed tiny dots around them that must be the squads. A single tiny dot slowly grew further away from one of them. As the distance grew without any attempt to stop or return, Bobby wondered if that had been bad luck or had one squad already got rid of their Super. He tried to see that dot when Siflis panned the camera across the area, but nothing showed up and he shivered. He hoped that whoever was in the suit had already carked it and wasn't fighting to make the jets work.

One of the last three capsules, the ones that had stopped, started back towards the big rocket. Everyone's radio burst into life. *"Warning. Warning. Approaching the mothership without authorisation will result in destruction of the offending party."* The warning repeated twice as the capsule, from SEPA, continued to close. The mothership, as the voice designated the rocket, didn't leave it as late as the aliens nor was the solution so emphatic. The craft launched a missile which struck the capsule and exploded. Pieces of the capsule spread in all directions.

"Can you zoom, Siflis? Try to see if any of the crew of that capsule are alive." Bobby wasn't sure if anyone could help the radar dots spreading outwards from the impact, but even as he asked two began to turn back towards the big rocket. When Siflis zoomed the vapour of jets showed up two more tumbling figures, but they were either confused or didn't have enough fuel and drifted slowly away. The first two dots settled onto courses for the mothership.

∗　∗　∗

"Beebi, the other three capsules are stopping, but further away than the Yankees were." Hood and Magpie had moved to the edge of their personal asteroid and now they relayed their camera pictures.

"Zoom on the one nearest to us, Magpie, the Krauts. What are they doing?"

"Those are legs. They're fastening their legs into a frame, maybe all of their legs." Hood fell silent for a moment. "Maybe to touch down first before risking people?"

"Nobody mentioned that in training. How do we touch down?"

"I don't know Bells, but after someone else tries for starters. Then we pick a spot well away from those holes in the ice and the bodies." Though even as Bobby spoke more of those sodin missiles on wires arced out of the second hole and began to drag the Chinas bodies away. "At least if we get to land on the ice it isn't repelling like that piece of metal did."

"No, it looks as if there's some sort of gravity. There must be to drag the bodies." Mickey put up a picture of the giant, blue-lit alien asteroid, and marked a cross on the near end. "If we land here, then perhaps we can walk across the ice to the larger hole? At least we can look down inside and see if there's a way in."

"That's a weapon! They've clipped all their hand lasers together." Bobby looked down at his laser, wondering what Magpie meant, then up again as the camera screen zoomed in on the construct. The frame and what Magpie said were the combined hand lasers were being manhandled round using suit jets. A light glowed around the end of a short tube, an answering glow lit up a capsule and vapour gushed! The lasers weren't supposed to cut into suits, let alone metal.

Bobby didn't hesitate. He didn't want to face that weapon alone so he had to help the other squads. "Can anyone hit the bledrin thing? We've got to stop them before they get round to us. Hood, what about your added extra?" Magpie pulled a leg from Hood's pack and passed it, and Hood twisted. A long tube slid out. Magpie refastened the leg and passed him the second.

"I could throw a blade?" Bells sounded doubtful. "I might come near enough to spoil their aim?"

"Too late for the Amazon capsule, it's blown. What the…? One of the Amazons had some sort of mini rocket but missed the laser. He nailed one of the Krauts but the laser is still firing." Siflis fell silent because although a second tiny missile had struck a second figure, the Kraut laser cut right through the Amazon Troopers including the one with the launcher.

Bells performed a gentle somersault backwards as he threw but Bobby reached out and snagged him before he went far. They tried to follow the glittering spark as the knife flew across the gap but lost sight. Meanwhile Hood had screwed the two tubes together. He stuck his metal forefinger in one end to give it a sharp twist, then brought the little finger across to socket into the tube side. "Try to hit the laser, Hood."

"The Frogs are trying to hide behind their capsule. They're fitting something together." Siflis sounded puzzled. "A long tube?"

Bobby pushed Bells back towards their own asteroid. "Throw again."

"I only had the two."

"You'll get the knives out of your pack if we survive. Throw it. Give your girlfriend time to put together whatever that tube is." As Bobby finished, Bells slid a section apart on his other metal leg and pulled clear the long knife. They'd all got something built in, but not for this range and there wasn't supposed to be anything powerful enough to damage a capsule.

"Firing." A tongue of flame showed briefly at the end of the tube Hood now aimed at the Krauts and a line of smoke flew towards the modified lasers. "Missed. We're too far away, they'd drifted before it got there." Hood unclipped the index finger end on his other hand and slotted it into the tube. His truncated finger slid in behind it and gave a twist.

"Be quick, because you got their attention." The souped-up laser had burned a deep hole into the Frog capsule, but it hadn't exploded. Instead a cloud of vapour and pieces gushed out, turning to glittering ice which masked the capsule and Frog squad. The Krauts abandoned that target, already turning the contraption towards Bobby. Turning it quickly, one pointing as Bells threw again. The light flashed, and the other side of the Basted's ice block jetted a cloud of steam. A few moments later the laser burned right through the edge and steam billowed past Aggie. The steam turned to ice dust as Bobby moved across the asteroid to look around the other edge.

Hood fired. The laser lashed out again but Magpie pulled Hood down and back, so if the laser came through it would miss. The laser chewed across the face of their asteroid and Bobby threw himself backwards. As the beam bit a notch out of the edge Bobby thought he'd been quick enough, until the cold and a cloud of vapour took his breath away. He tried to speak while frantically struggling to close the gash where the beam had caught his suit. The half metre long gouge, blackened at the edges, billowed briefly as all the air gushed out and Bobby felt the seals around his neck and the tops of his arms tighten.

Vaguely, as if a million miles away, Bobby heard Siflis curse. "You got the man, Hood, though it's spun the whole thing away for now. Shoot again!"

"I can't, no more ammo until we can get in the packs. Shite, Beebi!"

Bobby had the sealant out, but the hole was too long, flapping too much. He fumbled for the Gaffer tape, all the time expecting the skinsuit underneath to rupture and spill his guts out into space. What a stupid way to go. Would he feel his blood boil, because that's what the instructors said?

Hands grabbed, pulling his own away but Bobby fought. The basteds were killing him. Why? Then other hands slapped tape over the slash, sealant gushed, and two more rolls of Gaffer tape passed over his chest and gut again and again. Hands were still shaking him, his senses swam, and then Bobby remembered to breathe. He'd got rid of all his air, breathed out, because the instructors said that. Air inside his lungs would burst them. Bobby dragged down huge gulps of air as all the noises crashed back in on the coms.

"I'm all right, I'm all right." Bobby looked at the squad clustered round him with sealant all over their hands. He panted, then got out, "Hard luck."

"Shite, missed my chance." Bells turned away with a broad smile.

"Now you'll never make sergeant, Hood." Magpie elbowed the big man in the ribs even if the suit robbed the blow of any power.

"Are you all right, Sergeant?"

Bobby turned to Mickey. "Yes thanks. Have you got anything Bells can throw?" He had to get back into this fight rather than think about all that vapour, and the cold biting in.

"I've got one blade he might throw." Mickey offered a short blade with a curve. "Not a throwing knife."

"It's better than nothing, and better than Magpie's for throwing." Bells pulled himself up the ice while the rest watched. "I hope those Frog Divas get that bledrin thing working, whatever it is." As Bells looked over their asteroid the Kraut gunner, his finger still firmly on the firing button, spun far enough to draw a line of steam across the alien asteroid. "Is that basted dead?"

Afterwards none of them were sure if the weapons inside the ice reacted before the Kraut laser reached the large hole, or after the beam hit the weapon inside. Five more gouts of steam blew out elsewhere on the rugged surface, blasting free chunks of ice. Six Alien weapons tore briefly at the Krauts and their contraption before metal glowed brightly and spattered in sparkling droplets. All the space-suited Krauts, even those already hit by Hood or the Amazons, burst apart in clouds of vapour. The rocket flying over from the Frogs to blow a big hole in the Kraut capsule came as a complete anti-climax.

Silence fell as the squad looked at the scene, but this time none of the pits spawned the tiny rockets and lines. "They've got their samples." As Siflis spoke, Bobby realised that yes, the damaged capsules and Amazon squad bodies wouldn't yield any new information.

"You think they're alive? The Aliens?" Bells had ducked down as the Alien weapons lashed out. Now his faceplate turned frantically from one of the squad to another, and Bobby knew the signs. Bells going viral right now wouldn't help anyone.

"Just automatic defences Bells, so calm down." Bobby looked at the camera picture from Siflis, peeking again. "I think it's time to go, Mickey."

"Are you sure? It's just killed another squad."

"But not the capsule, and not until the laser hit either the ice or that hole. Up until then it let us fight." Bobby hoped so, and that the bledrin thing hadn't just held off to study weapons and tactics. "We should go now anyway before the other capsules arrive, or the Frogs reload."

"Same landing place, then we'll look into both the nearest holes. Take the squad in Sergeant." Mickey sighed. "I'll be with you, but I'm sending a report first to see if Aggie releases some food or air."

"Siflis? Take Bells. Bells, you must have a close-in something, or take Magpie's punch dagger."

"I've got these." Short blades slid out of the Trooper's metal finger ends. "Come on Siflis, I'd rather be fried than freeze to death."

"Hang on to me and we'll use one set of jets. Save yours for later." The pair set off on a steady trajectory for the alien asteroid. The rest of the squad, except Mickey, watched helplessly because they were out of long-range weaponry.

"Aggie has the report and it's on the way but hasn't released anything. Radar shows the Rangers and Shiva's Children are on the way now. The Confeds and Indias." Mickey had tried explaining which conglomerates sent squads from where, but the rest found the squad names were easier to remember than the strings of letters describing the companies. "The capsules are coming in very slowly, so they could take up to half an hour."

Bobby smiled, getting back on balance again now the squad were moving. "Once they see us go onto the ice they'll wait and see what happens. Magpie, what are the Frogs doing?"

"They're inspecting their capsule. One of the bledrin Amazons is alive!" Magpie moved up a bit to clear her camera lens so everyone received the view. A solitary figure had caught hold of three partial bodies and set into stripping legs and presumably weaponry. A pack came free so whoever had survived had their head screwed on, and was collecting food and water as well as weapons. "The Putes are pointing at Siflis and Bells." Magpie waited a moment. "They're not aiming that thing."

Hood chuckled. "That one with a red streak wants Bells alive, so she can keep him as a pet."

"She'll have to house train him first." Mickey had cheered up as well. That bledrin laser had been a hell of a shock for all of them. Trust the Krauts to come up with something like that. The Japanese also had some sleek gear but any SEPA survivors were still back on the mothership, the big rocket.

"Contact. Siflis and Bells are on the ice." The levity disappeared and all of them moved to the edge of the asteroid to look. After long moments Magpie sighed. "No reaction so Siflis got it right."

"He's the nearest thing we've got to a space and Alien expert. We go across in pairs." Bobby thought for a moment, but he couldn't split the couple now just in case the Aliens decided to lash out and kill the next pair to cross. The survivor would go viral. "Hood and Magpie are rearguard. Come on Mickey, let's go and knock on the door."

"But…" Mickey bit off whatever he'd started, probably a comment about both commanders being at risk together.

"We can't cover you." Hood knew the score, but the big man always tried so hard to do the right thing anyway.

"It's the principle. We should have a sniper covering us, and Magpie's your close protection. Magpie, beat it into his head for me?"

"I'll unpack my underwear if he argues. He'll not leave then." Both Hood and Mickey stared at her.

Bobby smiled, caught hold of the Super and activated his jets. He kept to the same steady speed as the first pair in case faster might be construed as a threat. As soon as they landed he waved Magpie and Hood to follow. The last two seemed to take longer, but only because Bobby had to stand waiting.

*   *   *

"Siflis, sneak over there and get a picture of what's inside." Bobby pointed to one of the big holes in the ice, then bounced with his hands on the rough surface. "You'll have to crawl since we've got no legs yet. Don't push off too hard, because the gravity isn't much." He turned to Bells. "You go and look at the next hole, just a quick peek and a picture. Crawl and don't go fast."

"We could put our legs on now?" Bobby considered the request, even if he knew Magpie had a thing about having her legs attached. This time she might be right.

"Put yours on, Magpie. Get Hood to help you since he hasn't had hands-on for six months." Magpie giggled as Bobby turned to Mickey. "This won't be as much fun for us."

"After six months I'll take what I can get." Mickey sighed. "We'd better attach yours first, because you'll be more use if it goes viral."

"Only because you all pitched in to keep me alive." Bobby twisted to sit. "It's easier with two. Stupid idea anyway, stowing our legs behind us. They'd have been better as chest armour." He unclipped the cover on the end of his stump to present the metal interface jutting from the suit seal.

"For you maybe, but then Hood's shot might have just bounced off the Kraut." Mickey held the leg more or less right while Bobby slid the connections home and felt them click into place. Moments later the nerve and muscle interfaces fired up with the usual couple of seconds of irritation and confusion. "The Kraut legs must have held extra batteries to power a weapon like that."

"Probably. Risky because we were only allowed limited extras in the metal, and they can't have had much else." Bobby frowned as he clicked the second leg into place. "The Frog missile looked to be a bit more powerful than what's allowed." He pulled Mickey's legs from the clips on the Super's pack. "You next."

"Somebody got rich or the pieces looked relatively harmless spread among all the legs. That's how the krauts did it." Mickey raised his leg and tapped the heel on the ice. "That feels better, even if I can't feel it."

"Too true it does." A smiling Magpie stood above them and stamped gently.

"That was quick." Mickey's second leg clicked into place and Bobby stood before helping the Super up.

"I've told Hood we can rerun once I can get at the sexy underwear." Magpie really had lost any last vestiges of shyness about her relationship, maybe because of all the flickin on the trip or maybe survival gave her a buzz. "Bells is waving."

Bobby looked at the relayed views and waved to the scout. "Siflis, come and look at this." Both pictures showed a turret with a stubby tube, but the one from Bells revealed half an access hatch in the metal to one side. With legs, it took no time to reach Bells. Bobby looked over towards the Putes, still clustered around their capsule. As he did, a single figure, heavily laden, dropped out of sight around the curve of the asteroid. "The Amazon is down. Hood, keep an eye on the Putes."

Mickey looked over the edge. "About six metres, not too deep. In this gravity we could jump down, and up again." Siflis crawled up to them. "Better yet, Siflis could lower something first."

"Is your wire long enough to reach the bottom, Siflis?"

"I had extra put on the reel, Beebi, for a trip wire if we needed one." Siflis twisted off the top of a finger, pulled out a length of wire and tied it around the Super's knife. Siflis used the steel finger nail on his little finger to turn a slot, unreeling the wire until the knife hit the bottom. Siflis turned the slot again, and the wire reeled back up. Bells untied the knife and hesitated.

"Keep it, Bells. You'll make more use of it." Mickey crooked a metal finger. "I'll scratch someone's eyes out."

"Put on your legs Bells, Siflis. That knife is metal, so our feet shouldn't cause any reaction." Bobby would have crossed something for luck, but everyone would have seen. As soon as the last two had legs again Bobby didn't hesitate, he jumped down the hole before he could talk himself out of it. "Better send another report Mickey. If we get inside the radio might be cut off."

"I will. Any idea how to open that?"

"Simple, there's a handle." Five versions of what or you are joking came back. "Seriously, just behind the edge of the ice. I can see it and the other edge of the hatch further in. I'll use my laser." After a moment's thought Bobby cut out wedge shaped sections of ice rather than melt his way in or let the beam hit metal, in case the alien construct reacted. After all, it hadn't liked the Kraut laser much.

"Aggie has acknowledged the report. She relayed the radar picture and the other two capsules are ten minutes out at present progress." Mickey looked over the edge. "Do you need help?"

"Not yet. Stand clear." Bobby tried twisting left then right, then pulling one end up. The handle moved a little. He took hold of the middle and tried to lift straight out from the door, not easy from his angle but Bobby felt a distinct click. Quickly stifling his thought about spiders welcoming flies, Bobby pulled up harder and the edge of the door lifted. "Its opening. Someone bring a wedge in case I lose my grip."

An arm came past with the knife Mickey had given Bells and Hood spoke. "We're a bit short of loose equipment. I'm here because I'm strong enough to take over." Hood chuckled. "We heard you grunt when it moved." They shuffled until Hood got a grip, and he swung the door up and open. Bobby concentrated on slicing away any ice still fouling the door's path.

Bobby looked into the wide tube with one flat side and a door at the other end. "We're in. Everyone come down and we all pile in fast."

"What if the door closes but doesn't let us out again?"

"Then we're all together Bells. Unless you fancy running about up here on your own?"

"Coming down."

"The Putes are coming down but well away from here." Magpie paused. "I can't see the other two capsules yet."

"The radar relay from Aggie shows them stopped. One is moving sideways, this way." Mickey cursed. "They'll use this door."

"We can't stop them unless we find a bolt inside. Everyone down and in sharpish. We need a lead to get clear and unpack weapons. Those with the capsules still have their extras." Bobby barely finished before the last two of his squad came down into the hole. "Everyone pick up a chunk of ice and stick it behind your belt, for later. We all cram in and shut this door, then I'll try the door at the other end. This should be an air lock even if there's no air."

"Go for it, sergeant." The six of them crammed in, which meant they were crowded with the spacesuits and packs. Bobby waited until Mickey pulled the door closed and reported the catch engaged. A set of yellow lights glowed before turning to purple, one at a time. As they did gravity tugged until the flat portion became a floor. It felt close to Earth gravity, Bobby thought. He pulled at the handle in the door ahead. Nothing.

"Push. It won't open into the airlock in case it's full." Siflis had it right because the handle slid in, Bobby felt the catch click, and the door swung out. Wasting no time, he took one quick look each way down the corridor outside, and beckoned.

Once everyone came out Siflis spoke first, while the rest gawked at the blue-lit corridor stretching each way. "I'd like to jam this door. I don't think the outside door will open with the inner one not sealed." Siflis shrugged, barely visible inside his spacesuit. "That seems like a basic safety precaution on an airlock."

"Good idea but I'd rather not lose another weapon." Bobby frowned. "Unless someone has something else to jam it with?"

"Hang on." Mickey sat and raised his left foot. "Unscrew the bottom. Use a steel fingernail. I can do it but you'll be quicker." Magpie did it while Hood held the foot, and Mickey stood back up. "My balance is off but I can't fight properly anyway. Now jam the door and let's go." Hood closed the door until it jammed the steel strip in place.

Bobby looked at Mickey, in case he wanted to take over now they were inside. "We'll go right? Towards the end? This might be a spaceship so we'll find engines or the controls." Bobby's said that without thinking as his mind registered they'd come through an airlock, a real airlock, into a corridor. Which meant this whole asteroid had to be a spaceship or space station, one over half a mile wide and two miles long!

"Engines? Control room? Shite, there must be. Yes, go, quick. All the other holes in the ice are the other way." Mickey sounded just as shocked.

"Siflis, we are on patrol so scout. Hood, can you get at your ammo yet?"

"Not yet, it will take time to get into the pack because the basteds didn't want me using it out there. The rest are all frangible but they might go through a spacesuit." Hood moved in behind Siflis with his hand laser out, while Magpie positioned herself on his flank with a punch dagger on her fist. Bells moved back as rearguard with his laser and Mickey's knife.

"Come on Mickey, we stay just behind Hood and Magpie. Don't get in her way if it goes viral." Bobby drew his laser pistol. "Basteds, move out." The corridor stretched away ahead, very slowly curving away to their left. There were cracks in the wall with a dimple plate beside them, outlining occasional doors, but the squad had no time to investigate.

*   *   *

The squad moved quickly, looking for a break in the five-metre-wide, four-metre-high corridor, an intersection to leave some doubt about which way they'd gone. The hatches to their right, towards the skin and space, looked utilitarian; big steel ovals bolted and clipped into place. The inboard doors were only cracks in the light blue material covering walls and ceiling, and all those had the small dimpled bulges. Bobby noticed that although still lethally cold, the temperature inside seemed to be creeping up.

"Oxygen trace! Somebody is leaking." Mickey pointed at the small probe protruding from his suit. All eyes turned to Bobby and the mess of sealant and tape across his chest and belly. "Let me check you over Beebi." Mickey pulled the probe out until it became a wand on a wire, and passed it slowly over the repair and then the rest of Bobby's suit. "It's not you," he concluded.

The rest looked at each other, alarmed, but a quick visual showed no obvious leaks, no vapour around anyone. "We keep going, then at the first chance Mickey will check everyone with the probe. Come on, we need a base." Bobby waved Siflis forward again. A brisk five minutes later Siflis slowed while the rest caught up.

"Looks like we'll have to learn how to open a door anyway." The uncompromising slab of steel barring progress had the usual bulge and dimples on the wall nearby. Mickey peered at it. "I remember dimples, tiny hollows like this, shooting lasers on the vids showing the original find."

"Not on a door lock inside a spacecraft." Bobby tried to sound confident. "If a crewman had a hangover and poked the wrong dimple, he wouldn't get diced and sliced." Bobby glanced back, but he didn't think anyone would be chasing yet. "Mickey, will you help Siflis to open this door and check him for leaks? Hood and Magpie, have a go at that smaller door. I'll take Bells and try one further back. Vid what you do, then if a door opens that might work for the rest." The squad split up.

Bells kept glancing back the way they'd come. "I need my guns and knives, Beebi."

"I know but we have to get off this corridor first or we're sitting ducks. Just keep watch and I'll have a go at this." Bobby looked helplessly at the bulge. Thirteen dimples, five in the middle and eight in a circle around them. He tried fitting the ends of his fingers and thumb into the five.

"Maybe they've got lots of fingers. Tentacles. I saw a vid where the aliens had tentacles." Bells sounded terrified at just the thought.

"That's because vids try to be scary. This lot might have been cute little Teddy Bears."

"Or three metre Demon Teddy Bears with tentacles, look at the height of the ceiling."

"Shut up Bells or I'll punch you." The fist Magpie raised had a punch dagger on it. "I'm crapping myself without any help." She snorted. "That's if the liquid diet had left me able to crap." The squad worked in silence for a while until Mickey came back up the corridor with his atmosphere wand.

"The oxygen levels are rising, just a bit. We had pure vacuum, or nearly pure, when we came in. Now there's a five percent mix of gases, the right sort to be air." He waved the wand. "I've checked Siflis and he's clear."

Bobby continued trying different numbers of fingers in different dimples without result until Mickey finished with Bells. Then he used the wand to check Mickey. "Anything?"

"No. The levels stayed exactly the same so the atmosphere is background. The temperature is up to minus ten." Mickey took back the wand and looked up and down the corridor, baffled.

Bells sniggered. "It'll be Hood's heavy breathing now that he's holding hands again."

"It's definitely warming me up." Hood laughed and it cut off suddenly. "Got it!"

"What?" Though Bobby needn't have bothered to ask as the door in front of the couple moved back a little and slid smoothly to the side. "What's in there?"

"Bins and racks with weird bits of metal and possibly plastic. Those are nuts and bolts." Hood laughed again. "Spares. We've found a storeroom full of spare parts."

"Never mind that, how did you open the door?" Mickey moved closer and peered at the bulge and dimples. "Nothing has lit up."

"It doesn't need to with the corridor light on." Bobby pointed up at the glowing blue strip along the middle of the ceiling. "So, how did you open it?"

"Not on coms!" Mickey sounded really worried.

"Why?" Bobby frowned. "How do we talk without coms in a vacuum. Sound won't travel."

Bobby's leg tapper started up, a message from Siflis in squad code. *"Touch helmets. The sound will travel that way."* Bobby turned off his coms and touched helmets to let Mickey know. The rest would have heard the message from Siflis and turned their coms off.

Mickey thought a moment, then turned off his coms. "I can hear the other squads on my receiver and their Supers will hear you. We don't want them to know how to open doors."

"Shite! You might have mentioned it!" Bobby held up his hands, "I know, Supervisor shite. You've got to forget that now."

"I just realised that. They'll hear the tapper as well, but that was a code that's not in my databank."

"Squad code, we made it up. We'll save it for emergencies." Bobby broke contact.

Hood explained the door with his helmet touching Bobby's. "Magpie tried to elbow me like she usually does, and I twisted away. I'd got my fingers in the dimples, and the bulge rotated a bit and slid up. I twisted a bit more and felt the click through my hands as it slid up further." Hood put his hands on the bulge, both of them, twisted and lifted. The door slid smoothly back into place.

"Siflis didn't hear that so I'll nip and tell him. Wait for me." Bobby headed up the passage to a puzzled Siflis, and touched helmets to explain. "We'll just step inside that storeroom while you do the same with this bulge and see if the corridor opens up." Bobby chuckled. "Lucky you, being the scout."

"Bledrin comedian. How many fingers and where do I put them?"

"Hood said like this, but I don't want to transmit the vid." Bobby showed him. "We'll experiment a bit once you've got us through and that big door is shut behind us." Bobby looked at the chunk of ice tucked behind his belt. It had started to drip though the droplets turned to vapour and disappeared short of the floor. "Then Magpie can unpack her underwear so we can fill the plastic bags before the water melts. Use the tapper to tell me, squad extra code." The squad changed that at random and never told anyone else, even the Bigger Basteds. Bobby ran back, this touching helmets would be a real pain. "Open up, Hood."

As Hood stepped through the door, blue strips in the ceiling glowed, lighting up a room about six metres wide by ten deep. The racks of strange objects definitely looked like spares rather than complete somethings, and some of the clips, bolts, holes and flanges looked almost familiar. Mickey's helmet clicked as it connected. "That's handy, the lights."

"Makes sense." Bobby followed Hood in and beckoned to the rest. "Hood, shut the door, then we'll unpack anything that will hold the ice." Hood turned and slid the bulge on the inside and the door closed. Bobby used his tapper and squad code. *"Siflis?"*

"Some crackle, but yes. Try now?"

"Do it."

A helmet touched Bobby's. "This might help with the ice." Bells waved a large metal dish shape. "Sort of like a bowl. An alien dog bowl." He held it to his chest. "Or maybe Magpie is totally outclassed." He moved off and passed that on to Hood, grinning happily behind his faceplate.

"Or an alien hubcap. Put two together and tape them or the water will dissipate into the vacuum. Near vacuum." Puzzlement sounded clear in Mickey's voice. "This place is colder and the oxygen traces have almost gone." Once again it took a while for the comment and reply to work round the group, until they stood in a tight group with helmets touching at least two others.

"Definitely colder. My ice dripped into here and then froze again." Magpie didn't quite laugh but Bobby could hear the humour. "Hard luck Bells, no knicker bag."

The humour stopped as the tapper started. *"It's open. The corridor curves more. No lights."*

Bobby translated for Mickey and then replied. *"Step through. See if lights work."*

"No way Beebi. Might close?"

"Oke. Sealing up water. Will bring bowls." Mickey wanted to talk privately when Siflis said no, but Bobby wouldn't break contact with the rest. Bobby could see the scout's point; he wouldn't fancy being stuck on his own.

Mickey sighed and spoke where the rest could hear. "What if it seals us all in with no lights?"

"Then we're together and we've got suit lights. No big deal, and better than being slowly whittled down." Siflis rarely argued a direct order so the dark corridor must have really spooked him. Bobby wouldn't force Siflis through just to prove who was in charge. Bells gave in to his nerves,

267

filling a bowl with bolts to chuck at an enemy. He also picked up a length rod, swishing it experimentally with a big grin. The rest shook their heads and smiled at him, they'd get to their real weapons in a couple of minutes.

The six of them stepped across the deep groove in the corridor floor in a tight group, the lights came on, and Siflis closed the sliding door again. The whole group sagged as they relaxed just a bit.

*   *   *

Helmets touched together again so they could hear Bobby. "Time to get out the carbins, shotguns and extra blades. Help each other to get them out because we can't spend the time taking packs off here." The packs were married to the life support backpack, and difficult to fix back into position without fouling the connections.

"Come to Daddy." Bells ditched the iron bar and the bolts, waving his Kraut. That had been allowed as well as his carbin because the plastic ammunition wouldn't damage property. The rest loaded their carbins and shotguns. The carbins and Kraut had been modified to use compressed air. Both Mickey and Bobby carried carbins as well as shotguns in case the shotgun shells didn't work.

"Siflis, move ahead just out of sight. The rest of us will open every door this side from now on but don't go through any. Leave those big ones on the other wall for later. Use the tappers but as little as possible. The curve is tighter, so we're near this end of the spacecraft." Bobby gestured towards the corridor ahead. "Now we'll find a room for a base, and hopefully some water at least. We've got forty-two hours of food and water, and sixty-six hours of air left. Maybe."

"I should report. If we can find a way out for that, maybe we can get more food and water from the capsule." Mickey paused. "You could do with some air to make up for what you lost?"

"I can hope. Until then, let's go. We'll find a room to rest, something defensible." Bobby looked at the door sealing the corridor. "I wish we could lock that, or fix an alarm."

When that reached Hood he moved to speak directly to Bobby. "I can fix an alarm with rope, sealant and some ironmongery. Shite, no bledrin air so we'll not hear." Hood scowled at the door.

Magpie stayed in touch with Hood, of course. "We've all got thirty metres of line in our packs. We can run that from here instead of the ironmongery, since we don't need it to rope together or climb up or down? If the rope tugs, the door has opened. Start with mine." Magpie turned so Hood could get at her backpack.

"Can you do that, Hood?" A raised thumb as Hood started on Magpie's pack answered Bobby, and he pointed at an outside wall hatch. "We should also watch out for another airlock hatch, so Mickey can report. We'd better keep mothership happy or the basted might blow the capsule." The succession of glowers and glares showed everyone agreed. Command probably would put in a self-destruct in case anyone tried to get food without permission.

The first four rooms held spares or mystery machinery that appeared to be dead. The machinery rooms were warmer, though still below freezing. "Beebi." Mickey had touched helmets again. "When we came through the corridor door, most of the oxygen trace disappeared and the temperature dropped to minus seventy. Now it's rising again, and so is the air concentration. Do you think it's deliberate?" Mickey sounded a bit tentative, and definitely nervous.

For once Bobby had no qualms about keeping the rest out of the exchange. "You mean the ship? How would it know?" As he finished speaking Bobby knew the answer. "It analysed the bodies and wreckage. Is this good or bad?" Good if it provided air, part of Bobby insisted. The rest of him worried about why an alien spaceship would take so much trouble, except to get live specimens.

"Good for us in the short term. We should find a place to stop and let the air build up." Mickey sounded really worried now. "Do you think there's anything still alive?"

"Aliens? No. The briefings were very clear. That wreckage, whatever, transmitted a shot of the starfield when it arrived and now, side by side." Bobby knew he sounded worried now. "Though this doesn't look as if it survived a million years."

Bobby didn't expect the sharp retort. "The dating wasn't exact!" Mickey looked around. "Sorry, it worries me as well. Either the starfield picture lied, or the calculations were wrong, because a thing this size can't have stayed out here fully functional for that long. The power would fail."

"Doorbell rigged, Beebi. We've tied our ropes together, but we'll need another soon." Hood's report came as a welcome interruption.

"Good work. Let's catch up a bit." Bobby tapped. "*Siflis?*" The scout had moved out of sight a few minutes earlier and stopped reporting on the rooms opened. Four taps replied on Bobby's tapper, the scout's call-sign so Siflis had gone silent on purpose. Bobby used hand signals and they all crept forward, tight against the inside of the curve. Siflis had left a knife in the passage, pointing back the way they'd come. Bobby put a hand on Mickey's arm and when the Super turned he motioned for silence and to stop. The rest recognised one of their squad's unofficial signals. Stay here.

The tapper started giving Bobby a message, just Bobby and the squad because Mickey didn't understand. "*Side passage. This passage ends 10 mtrs past. BB forward.*"

A quick helmet contact to tell Mickey, and Bobby moved forward. Siflis crouched low and tight against the wall waving Bobby to do the same, then showed a taped patch on his suit. He tapped code onto Bobby's helmet. "*Lasers. Only one active.*" The scout held up a dagger tied to his finger wire and slid it across the floor. The pale flicker of a laser beam nailed it halfway across, then repeated the hit with more power as the knife slid further. After the second hit the blade glowed.

Bobby tapped on Siflis's helmet. "*Where is laser?*" Siflis pointed up and towards a point out of sight well down the passage. Bobby tapped again. "*Jerk dagger in a moment so I can look.*" Siflis handed over his mirror on a stick, let Bobby move forward, and gave the wire a tug. The laser spat so Bobby peeked and pulled the mirror straight back. Four weapons on wall mounts covered the corridor but only one reacted. Bobby looked at the dagger. This time the blade still glowed dull red and had a distinct mark in the middle. He moved back to tap on Siflis's helmet. "*Ask rest if any solid rounds.*"

Bobby couldn't because a sergeant's coms were rigged to make sure the Super heard every message. Bobby didn't want Mickey involved or he'd start bleating about damaging property. With luck Hood had another solid round or Bells had managed to smuggle a clip of solids. Bobby only had two solid rounds in his index fingers, for emergencies when breaking in. While Siflis tapped and waited, Bobby rotated his forefinger to activate the weapon, and brought the metal little finger across to clip into the revealed slot. A one shot pistol on each hand. Forty feet wasn't all that far, except if he missed the bledrin laser would kill him. Siflis tapped *"No."*

"Keep tugging a bit at a time to keep the laser occupied." Tapping that on a helmet took a while, but Bobby needed it to screw up his nerve because of the other three weapons. Siflis nodded. At the first tug molten metal spat from the dagger as Bobby moved out a bit and froze. A chill ran up his spine because two other weapons tracked him, but they didn't fire. The operating laser spat again and Bobby came out far enough to clear his finger pistol. Now three weapons on wall mounts tracked him but still none fired. Siflis must have tugged again because one weapon, the same one, spat a pale beam and Bobby brought his finger on target. Almost, but he daren't move the extra fraction.

"Next might be last." That came on his tapper and Bobby almost jumped. Crap, if he missed, he was so pooched. The laser spat, Bobby corrected and fired, then scrambled back out of sight. *"Get it?"*

At least Siflis tapped that on his helmet again. Bobby turned and reached back. *"Maybe."* He stopped there because Siflis had been right. The dagger had been mostly splashed across the floor, which had scorched around the molten metal, and the end of the wire had been cut. Wordlessly Bobby held out a small knife as Siflis rewound the wire. The new bait bounced across the corridor and the laser glittered but it missed! Though it hit the pale blue floor which bubbled and smoked briefly. Bobby gestured, again, and Siflis tugged to move the knife. Again the laser missed the knife but hit the floor, in the same place again, and metal showed beneath the covering!

"It's jammed." Bobby waved his carbin out past the curve, where the laser would see it, and nothing happened. Siflis jerked the wire and the laser gouged the floor metal at least a metre clear of the target, in the same place as before.

"What's jammed? What happened?" Mickey's voice broke in, and Bobby realised he'd spoken on coms.

"Ask Hood." Bobby tapped. *"Laser on auto. Maybe jammed now. Got a cross corridor. Come up slow. Stick to inside of curve. Check doors on the way."* Bobby sat back against the wall and sucked a slow drink from the tube while his nerves settled. He ran through it all again, and realised the air must be a lot thicker if the laser showed. Outside in space the beams were only visible where they went through annihilated space debris or the clouds of ice crystals, and when they hit the targets of course. *"Ask Mickey, how thick is the air?"*

"Wait three he's coming."

Mickey arrived and touched helmets. "Fifteen percent and rising, and it is air in the right proportions." The Super chuckled. "But without any pollutants." He paused. "Hang on, there's a hint of something nasty now."

"Burnt flooring. It's stopped now."

"Property damage?" Mickey sighed. "Sorry, automatic reaction."

"The ship did it and I'd like to see some legal Manager try to sue this bledrin thing. Better yet I'd like to see him try and collect the fine." Mickey's laughter seemed to agree. The squad caught up, reporting that two rooms contained dead machinery, and one was full of locked storage bins. Judging by the lights and handle, Mickey thought one of the doors they passed on the opposite wall looked like an airlock. After Bobby explained what had happened, Mickey no longer seemed worried about shooting up equipment. They all had a drink and a break and took it in turns to use Siflis's mirror to look at the lasers around the bend.

*   *   *

As Bobby sat resting, Mickey came across and touched helmets. "There's a lot of chatter from different squads, French, Anglic and something else. Probably the Shivas. We should keep trying to talk without coms most of the time."

"Oke. I'll tell the others." Bobby touched helmets and passed the message. Hood and Magpie moved so they could put their arms around each other and talk privately. By the time the squad were ready to move, the light above the active laser had gone out.

Siflis reported that by touching helmets after another peek around the bend with his mirror. "Either you shot something vital out, or the ship doesn't like property damage. The laser did crank up the power a bit at a time until it destroyed the dagger, and then the floor." Siflis sighed. "I don't fancy going past the other three."

"We won't. We'll turn left up the passage. If someone gets through the door back there we'll be ready when they try to follow, and with luck those lasers will join in." Bobby leaned out and waved his carbin slowly up and down, then touched helmets again. "See, they won't fire. Don't point weapons at them or the programming might decide we're a threat." He stood up and the rest did. "Let's go. I'll go first because to be brutal, I've got less air so I'm more expendable. Pass the word helmet to helmet." The arms waved in protest were gratifying but everyone understood the truth.

Mickey had the last word. "You might be expendable now, but if the air keeps building up, that might alter."

"If the air is breathable, I agree." Bobby put out an arm, waved it, and felt relieved to get it back without a laser hole in his hand. He walked round the corner very slowly, with his carbin and shotgun slung and his hands wide open and out to the sides. As he came closer a band of bright yellow glowed across the floor at his end of the short corridor leading to the doors and lasers. He took another step and light went up both walls to meet on the ceiling. Bobby stopped a moment to tap so the others would know, in case the bledrin thing meant don't come closer and shot him. *"I'm being warned. Yellow lights."* The three remaining weapons tracked him, but the fourth remained dead and silent.

Bobby heaved a sigh of relief once he turned the corner and moved far enough so the weapons couldn't see him. Mickey heard the sigh and understood why. "What's there?"

Bobby only needed one glance up the corridor before tapping back. *"Long corridor. More junctions and rooms. Come one at a time."*

Bells passed a tapper message. *"Mickey will try the airlock first. I can stay as guard."* Mickey had a good point. Bobby certainly didn't want to go back past the corner more times than necessary.

Bobby opened two doors while he waited. The first room contained stacked rows of locked bins while the second held padded shelves, possibly beds or seats. Bobby waved Hood inside the first room and touched helmets. "Wait in here and watch the corner. Siflis can watch my back. When Magpie gets here she's to open doors." He carried on down the corridor to the next junction. A narrower corridor ran back down the ship about thirty metres, ending in double doors. So did the next one and Bobby relaxed a bit. They wouldn't be suddenly surrounded.

"Beebi?" Bobby turned back to the rooms between the corridors, which he'd left for Magpie. He looked inside as Magpie's helmet touched. "I've got a canteen, or bogs, or something with what might be water?"

"This area will do for now. One guard can hold the rope back where Siflis is, with the rest of us in where Hood is to use those seats or beds. I'll ask Mickey to stick his probe in some of that." The clear liquid in a dished receptacle had probably come out of the thin pipe above. Jabbing and twisting at any possible controls produced a stream of the liquid on demand. Bobby jabbed and poked and twisted some more, until the liquid disappeared through the bottom or sides of the sink or bowl, somehow. "Maybe a bog as well." Bobby activated the flow again and the bowl held it. He looked at the row of seven. "That'll do for now."

He went out to meet Mickey and Bells, and asked Mickey to check the water. *"Here Beebi."* Bobby joined Siflis but looked around before going into the room because the corridor opened out into a large circular space over twenty metres across. Five metres up a balcony went all the way round, with another a further five metres up, both with doors leading into the walls behind. A domed ceiling rose from five metres above the last balcony, a ceiling with a starfield painted across it. Bobby didn't fancy climbing the only way up, poles with a series of short bars jutting out as they spiralled upwards, alien ladders.

A click, as Siflis touched helmets, disturbed Bobby's sightseeing. "There's ladders of sorts going up and down through holes." Siflis had opened the only ground floor door in the circular area. Two of the poles with bars went both up and down through holes in the floor and ceiling. At the rear of the room were three alcoves with just the holes and no ladders.

"Siflis, tie something to your wire and toss it down there."

Moments later both stared in disbelief. "Shite. We are so pooched. If this ship don't swat us, we'll make a mistake." Siflis barely whispered, but the sight of his knife bobbing gently in mid-air instead of falling down the hole had that effect.

Bobby agreed, but would make sure the mistake didn't leave them hovering in there. "Leave it there for the rest to see. Nobody goes near those bledrin holes." He activated the command channel. "Mickey? Here."

"What?"

"Central area, come and see, Mickey." Bobby turned as Magpie came in. He pointed and gestured 'keep away.'

Her helmet clicked on his. "Oh yes. I'm not going near that even if you order me to."

Bobby laughed. "Good, go and relieve Hood or Bells to look."

Mickey arrived as she left. He looked at the knife for long moments before connecting helmets to talk. "I should go and report this, but those bledrin lasers creep me out."

"Did you get through?"

"Yes, and Aggie acknowledged. Those other two capsules are deserted according to radar." Mickey sighed. "I couldn't get right outside to see. The door hesitated when I tried to open it, and water ran in when it did so I reckon the ship melted a way out. The trouble is the hole didn't go out to the surface, just made a bubble in the ice."

"Leave it then. Give it twenty-four hours before you report unless something happens." Bobby looked at the floating weapon. "Yeah, I mean vital something. Did the liquid test out?"

"Pure water and the air is thick enough so it'll stay there, not evaporate. Better still, the temperature is up to ten above freezing, so the suit power packs will last longer." Mickey looked down a ladder and then up. "I'll wait here until everyone has seen what the holes do. We'll need a guard in here."

"Not yet. We should explore to the end of this cross corridor first, to the other side of the ship. Then we can set up a defensible point, the same as we have at this end."

"You push on with Siflis. I'll check rooms with the rest." Bobby lifted a hand to agree and as soon as Siflis could retrieve his wire, they set off.

The circular area was four hundred metres from the lasers, and the corridor stretched onwards about the same so right across the spaceship. All six side corridors led back into the ship and all ended in doors after thirty metres, while the corridor wall that faced the end of the ship had no openings or doors at all except a few up on the balconies. The only way further forward, or back if this was the rear of the ship, had to be through the doors guarded by lasers.

Nobody checked around the next corner, because a strip of floor up one side of the junction glowed yellow when they came near. If a laser opened up like it had at the other end, anyone looking would out be a sitting duck. Siflis waited in the second room along, another with the padded beds. He would watch for the yellow glow, a very good early warning. Coming back Bobby checked more rooms, and found more water spouts and sinks.

"We have bunks unless the aliens sat above each other and were very short. First door down the second side corridor." Magpie had been door opening and come to report. This running back and forth to touch helmets ate up time, but they had no real alternative without risking the other squads listening in.

All the doors opened but two, the double doors at the end of each of the central short side corridors. None of the rooms investigated held anything other than dead machinery, the water and disposal units, more padded surfaces or locked bins, and some silent consoles. The screens and what were probably lights on the latter stayed dark even after some cautious pushing and twisting of possible controls. Bobby went to find Mickey, knowing he would argue. "We check up on the balconies after sleeping, then unless we've found something more exciting we break into those locked rooms."

"The ship might not like the damage." Mickey really did sound reluctant to break things. The Supers and Managers must be nearly brainwashed about that. "Maybe if we try some other way to open them?"

"We will. We'll try everything you can think of, then break in." Bobby chuckled. "Report the rest to Aggie before we start, then you don't have to mention breaking things. If we find something of real value it won't matter what we did."

"And if we don't?"

"Ooh, those naughty Rangers and Putes, or maybe the Shiva's. After all, they are children."

Mickey still seemed reluctant, then sniggered. "Your lot are corrupting me but yes, that's what we'll do. But still as a last resort."

"No problem." Bobby set off to let the rest know, helmet to helmet. Mickey reported the coms traffic among the other squads had dropped away so they were doing something similar.

*   *   *

The squad slept in shifts, then sucked food and water. Mickey kept pacing as Siflis and Bells stretched and drank before going back on lookout. As soon as they'd gone he wanted to talk. "Beebi, how much do you trust this ship?"

"I don't even know it's a ship so not much. Why?"

"The air is fit to breath and the temperature is up to nineteen C, sixty-four F. We could take off the suits." Mickey hesitated. "I could get that connection out of my ass!"

"I'm more worried about the state of the rest of my tackle, but I understand completely." Bobby really liked the idea, though he liked the idea of being able to breath without using up tank air even more. He actually worried if finding out the damage from the suit connections might be worse than imagination. "We daren't take the spacesuits off yet for two reasons. Firstly, the ship might stop being friendly if we break into those rooms."

"Good point, though we can take off the helmets at least. Just put them back on before breaking anything?" A night's sleep had settled Mickey's qualms about property damage. "When we do that, we should also break open those storage bins. All one operation. We can jam the room doors open while we do. What's the second reason?"

"We don't know if the rest of the whole ship is aired up. If someone opens that corridor door, or the one at the other end, whoosh. We're freezing and breathing vacuum." Bobby chuckled. "Though I'll risk that to get this helmet off. The first sign of a breeze and everyone gets their hats on."

"Done."

Bobby went to let the rest know. One by one they all took a deep breath of clean, warm air and broke into huge smiles. Bobby hadn't really noticed before but the suit air had a definite smell, not definable beyond old or maybe used. Almost as good, Bobby had his peripheral vision back. The restrictions of the helmet made him nervous and he'd spent most of his time moving his head side to side. Magpie and Hood came back from guard duty, and Bobby found them celebrating.

"Put her down. You know exactly where she's been, and should be ashamed of yourself." They broke the kiss and turned, both grinning and unrepentant.

"Yes your highness. Where's this door that needs breaking?"

"Just wait a bit, Magpie. I think Hood had better escort Mickey to the airlock, because I can't trust you alone with him if you're feeling like that. We'll go and try the doors on the balconies in the round room." Magpie pulled a face and kissed Hood again. The pair were going to have a lot of trouble getting back to normal once more Troopers arrived. Maybe the danger had done it, or knowing they were well away from prying eyes, but neither had any reservations about holding hands and now kissing even with others about.

By the time Mickey came back, Bobby and Magpie had explored the top balcony and knew they were in a spaceship. Bobby came down to let Mickey know rather than broadcast even on a tapper. At least with the helmets off nobody could overhear if they talked normally. Better yet they could all hear at once instead of passing information helmet to helmet though Mickey still spoke quietly. "Aggie has reported there are no supplies available in the capsule because the trip took longer than expected. I only reported we'd found air, because I don't want Control to give our water and food to someone else. All Control says is to explore and report. They'll assess what we tell them before releasing supplies from the mothership. We should mark a way in for reinforcements. I'm not to agree alliances, but there's no hint of just what information will get us the food and water." Mickey scowled. "Maybe we are supposed to tether the first one of us to cark it outside to mark the entrance? Basteds!"

Bobby held his smile. "We might get allies once they know we've found the bridge, control room, or whatever steers this basted great thing. That rocket that brought us has no idea what a mother the real mothership is. With luck our mothership will give us food for that information, and that's all we need now to survive."

Mickey's head came up with an incredulous stare. "We have?" A glimmer of hope showed, then humour. "Can we move it, the ship? Take the basted thing home? That would pooch the bledrin lot of them!"

"We can't get in. It's through those doors with the lasers but you can see it, and if we really get desperate maybe we can break in through the window?" Bobby stood up. "Come on, this you have got to see." A grinning Hood and Magpie met them outside so she'd told him, and all four went up.

"This has to be the captain's cabin or day office. Depends if that's a bed or a seat." Mickey shook his head. "With this view, this is definitely the captain's. One glance and he can see every screen, every crew member." The ten-metre-long curved window in one wall of this room, floor to ceiling, jutted out from the rear of the bridge so the view overlooked the entire space. The bridge curved gently away either side, and every bit of the front wall at ground level seemed to be full of screens and controls. Above the controls, across the entire hundred metre width, stretched a blank screen.

"That screen has to be a view out, or a star map." Hood whispered, and the scene really did humble them all. "It's all dead, all the screens, all the instruments. This thing needs a crew of hundreds, thousands."

"There's no more than a score of seats." Magpie shaded her eyes. "There are lights. Some are reflections from here, but some of those are winking on and off." She sighed. "Not many though."

"That's why those doors are guarded, to protect the bridge." Bobby looked around. "There has to be another way in, from here. The captain won't have run down the corridor in an emergency."

"Here, and you won't like it." Mickey had opened one of the doors off the main room disclosing another shaft without any controls, though this one only led down.

The four of them tore themselves away from that view, and looked through the other rooms leading off the top balcony. These had to be senior officer's quarters. They all had the mystery holes leading downwards. So did the rooms off the lower balcony. "We should move in here." Bobby looked down. "This would be easier to defend, and there's water in these rooms."

"Possibly food as well, if we can work out how to get it." Mickey looked down at a console that refused to do anything even if the controls moved, and frowned. "We might be trapped in here if another squad come up the corridor."

Bobby shook his head. "Magpie can give us a back door with a thermal strip if we need to get out and we'll be impossible to take by storm, up those poles. Do you want to open storage bins or the mystery rooms?"

"Bins, definitely bins." Mickey looked towards the passages with locked doors. "Let's see how the ship takes to minor property damage first."

*   *   *

The ship didn't allow property damage, or not easily. "Shite, what is that thing made of?" Bells waved a short, broad knife in disgust. The blade now had a definite bend. "I'll straighten it again the same way, but don't see that opening a bin either." He jammed the blade into a crack and then stamped on the hilt until the curve had gone. As expected, the bin remained stubbornly unmoved.

"Maybe we can use ship metal, something from the spares in the outside corridor?" Hood shrugged at the looks. "I don't fancy trotting back and forth past those lasers, but neither do I fancy bending the barrel on my carbin."

"Magpie can burn through the lock?" Mickey looked at the number of bins. "But which ones? She's only got five metres of thermal strip, enough to make a hole that we can get through."

"More to the point, would we rather keep her thermal strip in case we need to make that hole in a wall or door to escape?" Bobby hesitated. "Or break into the bridge?"

"That's a last resort, because that could really piss off some automatic weaponry in there." Mickey stood pondering for a while. "We'll rest up now and then explore the other corridor, the big one at the far end we've never been down. We'll risk the lasers, or enough to see if any of them open fire. First thing tomorrow I'll go back to the airlock and report, and pick up spares for bashing with from a room nearby. We could move faster but I'm still worried about the ship. So far it's being helpful." He paused. "I still won't mention having a water supply, so Control think we are firmly tied to Aggie. Air can't be rationed so I'll confirm we found plenty, a big aired-up section.

Bobby thought hard as well. He'd rather push on and break at least one bin open, but a day shouldn't matter now they'd got air and water and he'd rather not clash outright with Mickey yet. "In that case don't mention the bridge either, until we've looked in the other two rooms. They might give us a way in. Not only that but if control give us a reward, I want another for finding water and another for the bridge, not just one for the lot. For the rest of today we move our gear into the officer quarters, though the first balcony not the captain's room. We'll set up some sort of barricade on the balconies, maybe see if we can move some bins up there." Bobby pushed at a bin. "Unless they are all too heavy. We'll bring shelving from the other storerooms to armour them."

"I'll go and relieve Siflis on watch so he can take a break. Let me know when you need muscle for lifting." Hood left. After some experimentation, a few of the metal bins were light enough to move so the three of them pushed one through to the central area. Another discussion led to Siflis being sent back down the corridor to the big door to detach the rope alarm, because he wasn't freaked by the lasers. They'd rely on the yellow lights for warning, because the ropes would be needed to haul anything up to the balconies. Those ladders with short rods coiling around and up the pole just weren't designed for humans to carry loads upstairs.

"Everyone remember to take it easy on the food. We need to spin it out a bit, but with plenty of water that shouldn't matter as much." Nobody muttered their complaints too loud, maybe because they understood. Unless the rocket released more and they got back to collect it, this food wouldn't last much longer even rationed.

Siflis volunteered to test the lasers at the other bridge entrance. He waved a piece of metal, then an arm, and then moved out into the corridor. The light strip glowed yellow and the four lasers tracked him, but none fired. "Told you. It stands to reason. The lasers guard the door and won't kill some unsuspecting crewman wandering past." Siflis really seemed relaxed about shite like that, maybe because of the space games he'd played. The first two doors down the other side of the ship led into rooms with more spares and more bins, the same as they'd already found so Bobby didn't go further for now.

When the clocks eventually showed another day had passed, five bins had been hauled up onto the balcony to give some protection from both flechettes and hand lasers. Mickey had agreed to try both against the corner of a bin to judge their strength, and the bin seemed unharmed. As the squad worked, Mickey reported three short broadcasts from other squads elsewhere on the ship. One a warning, one a cry for help, and one a scream. He thought the warning had been in French but only told Bobby that, not the rest and especially not Bells. Bells kept remarking on how cosy the new cabins would be with a few of Les Putes sharing.

Overnight Bobby took the opportunity to wash. He removed his spacesuit, finally, biting down on a knife hilt so he didn't cry out as the connections came free. Sore didn't cover that feeling. After washing in the cold water from a spout, using one of the alien dog bowls now they didn't need it to store water, Bobby couldn't face putting the spacesuit back on. He used one of the sinks or whatever they were and it sucked away his pee just as easily as the water. His underwear felt really strange after so long without. Bobby slept fitfully, disturbed by dreams of Aliens, Teddy Bears with tentacles and alien weapons appeared out of a storage bin as he opened it, cutting down the squad one by one.

Negotiation

In the morning Bobby looked long and hard at his spacesuit. Eventually he took his knife and cut away the waste disposals inside the suit, before putting it back on. After breakfast Bobby looked over the heap of Alien spares, including three short lengths of shelving. "We should be able to do something with these." He picked up a short section of metal with holes punched at intervals and a wedge shaped end, and a thick piece of bar. Neither seemed heavy enough for their size, but beating two together had already proved the metal had to be at least as tough as steel.

Mickey had gone to send his report, but wouldn't use the coms to tell Bobby because others would be listening. There had been four more cryptic bursts of transmission overnight, one that sounded pleading and another of considerable length. The third produced a garbled mix of panicky French and the last just said 'fire' in Anglic. Other squads were still fighting further along the ship. Mickey hurried up the corridor with his load of spares as soon as he moved past the lasers. "More transmissions. They sounded Asian, I think, so the two SEPA, South East Pacific, survivors have arrived. They were alarmed about something."

"I'd be more worried if you heard voices that weren't on coms, people approaching." Bobby looked at the bins. "Pick one."

"What?"

"To break into. Then the ship can blame you." Bobby grinned at Mickey's shocked look. "Though it's more likely to be upset at Bells for actually wielding the hammer."

"Hammer?" Bells looked at the lump of metal in his hand. "I wish." Mickey pointed. "Oke. Stick the point in that crack just under the lock, Hood." He did, and Bells swung. A clang echoed but without appreciable effect. Another five blows and everyone inspected the crack.

"Maybe it's wider? Just a bit?" Hood didn't sound convinced. "Try again." Bells swung another five times.

"No, it's not working. Maybe you can punch out the lock?" The small bulge with only three dimples also had a slit in it, they assumed for a keycard. Mickey tried twisting and sliding the opener again without

283

effect. "Still solid. Use this." He offered a length of round bar with two spikes coming from the side. "Put a spike in that slot."

Bells passed the 'hammer' over to Hood. "Here, I'll hold and you hit this time." Even as Hood braced to swing the tappers gave six taps, a warning.

*　　*　　*

Everyone froze and Bobby spoke quickly and quietly. "That's Magpie in the next room, watching the corner. Keep quiet while someone puts their mirror out to look." They'd all taken one of the brilliantly polished metal plates found in a storeroom as a spy mirror similar to the one Siflis used, though not on a stick and the image wasn't as clear. Bells moved to the open door, angling his mirror to look at the junction.

"Voices." Mickey barely murmured the warning, but Bobby had also heard a short exclamation and then hushed tones, too hushed to understand.

The volume went up just a little but Bobby couldn't hear what the man said, not even enough to work out the language. The unmistakeable tones were a Supervisor wanting a squad member to obey regardless of objections. "Dick," Bobby breathed.

Hood and Mickey nodded, Mickey with a rueful smile. Bells beckoned so the three of them moved up closer to him, carbines and shotguns ready. Bobby could see the glow of pulsing yellow warning bands in the shiny metal and leaned closer to look. One of the Putes, in a spacesuit but without her helmet, started crossing the corridor end. As she cautiously approached the yellow warning strip she glanced back and gestured up the corridor towards the Basteds.

The man's voice spoke louder. "Non, la porte." The woman took another cautious step towards the yellow band, looking up to where the three operable lasers would be tracking her.

"No! Don't!" Bobby jumped and nearly opened up but the voice came from Bells, waving frantically round the edge of the doorway. The woman dropped and brought her carbin round, hesitated, then rolled back out of sight.

"You stupid basted." Mickey ground the barrel of his shotgun into the back of Bells's head, while both Hood and Bobby brought their weapons round to centre on the Super.

"No. First we ask why." Bobby wanted to shoot Bells as well, because the lasers would have thinned out the Frogs without them even knowing the Basteds were here. Then they'd have come round the corner fat and happy, but already one down. "Well Bells? Why?"

"That was Red because I saw the red streak in her hair. I'd rather join up with them than the arses that hung back and crept in later. The Frogs have used up at least one rocket thing and anyway another might be helpful." Bells babbled a bit, probably recognising the tone of Bobby's voice. "They'll be grateful now?" The last bit definitely sounded more hopeful than confident.

"Maybe. Though the real reason is whatever she whispered. What was it?" Bells had been interested in the woman he called Red before, and obsessed after being pinned and handcuffed in training. Bobby had thought losing the sparring had burned Bells and he'd wanted payback, but now realised it must be something more.

Bells hesitated, then sighed. "She pulled a few hairs from my head then said next time the souvenir was underwear, hers or mine." He started to move his head but stopped as Mickey pushed the shotgun barrel a little.

"Move that Mickey. We can't afford to lose him." In hindsight Bobby should have insisted on knowing what Red whispered, then he would never have put Bells where he might see her unexpectedly. If Bells had one real weakness, it was Divas. "He's right about this being a good chance to make an ally. Red at least should be just a bit grateful."

"Beebi Basted?" A woman's voice with a definite Frog accent sounded from around the corner. "Talk?"

"One. Unarmed."

"Non!" A man's voice this time.

Bobby glanced at Mickey with a smile before shouting back. "We could have let Red die, then shot the next one round the corner?"

A mutter of voices followed. "I will come to talk. Hands up and empty." The woman sounded nervous but she ought to. Bobby wouldn't fancy making that offer.

"Wait a minute or two." Bobby gestured back along the corridor and lowered his voice. "Everyone else move back one room and join Magpie. Red still had some sort of loose trousers over her legs, so no smart remarks about metal or stockings from anyone." He glared at Bells. "Bells, if it goes viral and you get a shot you kill any woman including Red, even if you do fancy her. Oke?"

"Oke. Sorry Beebi." Bobby pushed Mickey's shotgun away. After a moment Bells glanced around the corner, scooped up his Kraut and left, head down. Hood left, but Bobby stopped Mickey.

"If the negotiator comes out of here without me telling you it's Oke, kill her." He sighed. "The Bells thing is over. He'll kill her now if he has to, but sometimes Bells is our squad's Homer. Another time it's him that goes viral and saves all our asses. We all owe him more than one life. Oke?" Bobby held Mickey's eyes. "All over?"

"Over, as long as he doesn't do it again, give her a break." Mickey went to join the rest.

Bobby gave them time to get into cover before calling out. "Come ahead, no helmet." Again voices spoke, quietly, before a woman answered.

"Oui, yes, I am coming. Very slowly." Bobby watched carefully and first an arm waved around the corner, with an open hand.

He smiled. He'd done that with the lasers. "I see you. Come on." Already he'd thought of one problem. None of his squad spoke Frog, unless Mickey knew some, while at least one of the Putes understood and spoke Anglic. The space-suited figure had shortish dark brown hair, longer than Magpie's grown-out Trooper cut, and a nervous smile. "Come ahead to the first room, nice and slow. No heads round the corner behind you."

She glanced at the pulsing yellow band. "Laser?"

"Safe if you move slow and don't point guns." Bobby noted she'd understood the sentence easily, or didn't query any of it. She knew more than a few words. The Frog Trooper, as he reminded himself, moved slowly forward with her arms wide and hands empty. When she'd moved well clear of the corridor end, Bobby showed himself and the shotgun. "Turn around once, nice and slow." As she did he smiled at the two knives hidden in the back of her belt in addition to the clearly displayed knife and holstered laser. His eyes narrowed at the tape and sealant on the back of her suit.

Her smile held a bit of a challenge as her face came back in view. "My hands are open?"

"Keep your hands open and wide, and go into this room."

"No. One to one." No smile, and there wasn't any give in her voice.

"Nobody else is in the room. Come and look." Bobby backed up past the door so she could look. "Stand at the back, hands up on the wall." He smiled slightly as she walked in, because despite the spacesuit she managed to swing her hips. He followed and weighed up how to disarm her. Bobby didn't really want her touching those knives to remove them, not after seeing Les Putes throw in the competition. His carbin or shotgun would get too close to her, in grabbing distance, if he disarmed her. Bobby smiled and pulled the laser pistol. "Laser aimed at your head. Don't move."

She flinched slightly. The lasers were useless against suits, but would cause agony and a terrible burn at least on her uncovered head. "Oui, yes. I will keep very still."

Bobby put his carbin and shotgun down well clear before moving in to remove the two knives and the belt weapons, one at a time and very carefully. He threw them sideways and stepped away. Her wrist seals were tight so no sleeve knife, though he didn't know what might be in her fingers or in those loose trousers. Not trousers, just leggings attached to the spacesuit and covering the seal on her thighs and the metal connector strips and legs. On the other hand, she'd never leave alive if it kicked off in here. Bells would kill her to make up for Red. "Sit down and don't point fingers."

Her eyes went to his fingers and Bobby waggled the hollow index finger, the one he'd fired. She nodded slightly. "My Adju, Super will wonder if I am all right. May I call, shout to him?"

"Make it simple." Bobby moved to the side, standing over the weapons. As she walked to the door, arms outstretched, he picked up his carbin.

She shouted down the corridor. "Il est...." Beebi cut her off.

"Anglic!"

"Oui, yes." The Frog Trooper raised her voice again. "It is Beebi. I am safe." She turned slowly and sat where indicated, arms still out wide. "I am Fleur, a two-stripe. You are Beebi, a three stripe."

"Sergeant."

"My two stripes mean sergeant. Three stripes is a sergeant-chef, the same as you." She paused. "We will not join you just to provide Divas. No pooching."

Bobby laughed. "I couldn't stand the pain." Fleur had a nice laugh, light and breathy, and Bobby reminded himself she was a Trooper who only looked like a Diva. "We will negotiate. We want allies, but we don't trust you." He shrugged. "We don't trust the others either."

Fleur gestured very slightly, her eyes aimed at the mess of tape and sealant on Bobby's front. "Allemande? The Kraut laser hit you?" Bobby nodded. "You saved us. Our Super does not like you Rosbif but we, Les Putes, think you are the best squad to join."

Bobby ignored why, because he wanted to know who had been shooting at her. "You were hit as well, on the back. Who was that?"

For a moment Bobby thought she would spit. "Rangers! They joined with the Shivas and then..." A stream of French followed and it didn't sound happy. "You don't understand?" Bobby shook his head since there wasn't any point in lying. "I will explain it all later, but they killed l'Amazon and Aigu, our scout." She sighed. "The one you wrestled. There will be no repeat match."

"A pity. Did you lose any more?" Bobby felt a bit better because Beebi's Basteds would have the numbers, especially if Mickey took on their Super if it went viral.

"Non, no. Ecarlate, Scarlet, she has arm wound but can shoot. She might not win against Bells this time." This time her grin shared a joke and Bobby reminded himself again, she's a Trooper.

Though he grinned back. "He might get a souvenir."

Fleur laughed, then sobered. "Maybe she will not mind, but not yet, not until she stops hurting." She smiled. "You take off ....?" Bobby didn't understand the words but she made a gesture with an outstretched hand, pulling down. "The spacesuit feels better without the connections." Bobby nodded agreement. "My arms are tired."

"Lower your hands flat on the floor. No I don't trust you because I know what we can do." Fleur nodded understanding, but kept her smile. "Now how do we arrange this without anyone dying?"

Her smile almost disappeared. "Your Super can kill ours. We could see that, in training. Your equip has five Troopers, we have four, so we would lose. It would be better to ally with you unless you want us for Divas, without weapons. That is what the Rangers and Shivas wanted. Together, with weapons, we can kill the Rangers."

"I'm all for that. Though Bells might have ideas about pooching as well as fighting."

"Ecarlate might as well, but not yet. She might want to say thank you for the shout, at the corner." Fleur glanced at the door. "Where do we move into, to live?"

"This room and the next. There are beds." Bobby smiled at her narrowed eyes. "We'll leave it empty. Nobody will be waiting to share."

"You don't mind us keeping this room?"

Bobby gestured at the bins. "We were just trying to open one of these so feel free to try."

"We can do that, but none of the bins contain water."

"You can open bins?" Bobby thought quickly. There could be anything in the bins, including food. Especially food because if the ship knew enough to get the air and water right, it knew what food humans needed. "We have water, plenty of water to trade for bin opening. Enough for a wash but we haven't found a bath."

Real mischief flashed in her eyes for a moment. "Maybe I will need help to reach my back?"

"Let me know. You'll be safe in here until then." Bobby thought about the practicalities of having Les Putes in here. "You can guard this end of the corridor, and we'll guard the other and the ladders. The lights are a good warning."

"Ladders? We only found holes. We had to pull Aigu back when the Adj... Super sent her down. She floated!"

Bobby nodded. "We used a knife to test after meeting the lasers. What was Red, the one you call Scarlet, doing just now?"

"We heard you." Fleur nodded at the metal that Bells and Hood had been using. "The Super thought you broke open the door and the lasers must be broken."

"No. I had to shoot out a laser to get past. The lasers will kill you if anyone goes too near." Bobby waved to her weapons. "Those will be here when you get back. Stay clear of the yellow lights."

"Mais oui! We will talk later about opening bins and water. Maybe about washing?" The mischief appeared in her eyes again.

Though that wasn't what surprised Bobby. "I'll talk to you? Not Super to Super, or me and your Sarge, er, chief, three-stripe?"

Fleur curled a lip in distain. "Our Super will not meet any of you, even the Super, and Pepee is his Diva. She is not allowed to be alone with a big nasty Beebi Trooper. Maybe you could kill our Super, then you would get Pepee?"

Bobby wasn't taking that bait. "I don't mind talking to you instead. You stay right there until I'm out the door, then call to your Putes or go back and explain. Don't point guns at us."

"Don't point guns at us." That cheeky smile appeared again. "We should shake hands. You have the laser and carbin so you will be safe from one woman?"

Bobby debated but didn't think she could take him without a hell of a racket. Even if she did, when she left the room and he didn't, she'd be shot. More to the point, if they were to work together he had to show some first bit of trust. He slung his carbin. "We'll shake hands to seal the contract. If you try anything we'll wrestle and I'll insist on a souvenir."

From her laugh, Fleur might be even more relieved about the agreement than Bobby was. "Maybe another time." She stood carefully, hands out to the side, then held one out. Bobby shook it briefly. "Now our way, you would say the Frog way?"

"Oh yeah? How?"

Fleur blew a kiss and tapped each cheek, and yes, Bobby had heard the Frogs did that. Mischief flashed in her eyes again. "No sparring."

She took a cautious step closer and then kissed each of his cheeks gently. "Voila. We have a contract. May we rest before talking? None of us has slept since Aigu was killed."

"Call out when you're ready. I'd like to know how to open a bin because we're running low on food and there might be some in there." Bobby hoped for a hint as to what the Frogs had found but Fleur wasn't giving anything away.

"In three hours I will come and show you, in return for water." She sighed. "I will tell our Super that you insist on waiting three hours, or he will not let us rest."

"Deal." Bobby backed out of the door and down the corridor to the next room, trying to work out if he'd just been played. That Fleur had a hell of a way of negotiating, especially used on a Trooper who hadn't been near a Diva for six months.

Mickey barely waited until Bobby came into the room. "Well?"

"We all move back one room so they can take these two rooms and guard this end. They've lost one, and got one wounded. Fleur can open bins, and they want water in return." Bobby gestured. "Come on, if they try anything they'll be pinned in here with no water."

"Fleur?"

"Their ranks are weird. I'll explain. Now let's get clear before she calls up the rest." Bobby needed time to make sense of the ranks, and Fleur, himself.

When the Basteds settled down in the first room across the first junction Bobby explained. Mickey would have preferred to deal with their officer but accepted that if the man didn't like Britz or the UKs there wasn't much point. He seemed really happy with the idea the Putes thought he could kill their Super. It crossed Bobby's mind one of them might persuade Mickey to try. He hadn't been near a Diva for six months either. Bobby sent Bells to relieve Siflis, pointing out that the Homer couldn't be trusted near the bledrin Putes. Bells apologised again before he went.

Once he'd gone Mickey agreed that Bells calling out turned out all right in the end. With the Shivas and Rangers allied, if the Basteds and Putes joined up the only wildcards were the two SEPA Troopers. "The Aussies in SEPA might prefer the UKs, but there's a lot of business between SEPA and North America, both parts." Mickey shrugged. "So that could go either way." He sighed. "We'll have to let the Putes see more eventually, maybe have access to a water supply rather than trade it. Allies don't restrict water."

"You just fancy a bath, maybe with a Diva to wash your back." Magpie grinned. "My back is lovely and clean."

"Do we let them know about Magpie? Seeing her with Hood, or with her longer hair and no makeup to look unshaven, its bledrin obvious really." Bobby grinned at her. "If they're serious about us killing their Super we could use you to do it?"

"No!" Mickey sighed. "Sorry, but I get twitchy when you start on about topping Supers. Though if it turns out he's a problem, and Les Putes aren't against it?" Mickey shook his head. "I'm corrupted."

"A realist." Bobby laughed. "He might get used to the idea of having allies. I'll be dealing with that Fleur so I might find out if they really will care if you or Magpie tops him. He sent Red to open that door so I can see why she might not cry if he carks it." He nodded towards Magpie. "Try not to talk to them. Put on the makeup to look a bit unshaven and pull up the neck seal on the suit to disguise your hair. Even if our hair has grown the same, yours makes you look womanish." Bobby smiled. "No kissing and hand holding in front of them." Magpie produced a magnificent pout that would have showed the Putes exactly what she was, then agreed but kissed Hood while she could.

They beat it around and around for a while, then sucked a reduced food ration. Everyone agreed the Putes didn't need to know about the bridge, or that Mickey had been in contact with Aggie and there would be no food on the capsule. If the Frog capsule had been badly damaged their Super wouldn't be able to report so they couldn't get extras from the rocket. Since the Basteds now knew the Rangers were killing off the opposition, Siflis stayed by the ladders as a guard. He did so from the doorway, so he could watch the corridor towards the Putes as well.

*   *   *

The rest went to inspect the two locked doors again. Once again everything short of physical violence had no effect at all. By the time they'd tried every idea on both doors, including some attempts at levering them open, Siflis called out for Bobby. Fleur stood in the middle of the corridor, arms outstretched and hands open.

Bobby beckoned, and she walked slowly forward with her arms open. She turned round to show there were no extras this time, just a laser pistol and a knife on her belt. Bobby waved her forward again. "There are more bins in here."

"Water first? Show me the water." Bobby took her into the washroom or bog and filled a dog bowl, then drank. Fleur drank a little, then more, and lowered the bowl with a huge smile. That disappeared as Mickey started to come into the room. "Non! Just one."

Bobby waved him back outside. "Why?"

Fleur didn't have a hint of humour or mischief in her eyes or voice. "Pooching will hurt too much now. Your Troopers haven't had a Diva for long time." A hint of her smile showed. "Maybe I can get away from one of you, or make enough noise so the rest know why you want us."

"I'd only want a souvenir just now, though I don't know how long that will last?" Bobby grinned. "Bells might put up with a bit of pain."

"I will warn Ecarlate." Fleur looked round. "Will one of your men take water back so that everyone knows? We are very worried about water. We found no food in la capsule, and the Allemande laser let the water out." She sighed. "We open la huche, a bin, but there wasn't any water or any other liquid in them."

"What's in them?"

"I will show you, once we have water. Our Super didn't let us drink before leaving the capsule, to save the water for later. Then the laser let it all out into space. We've been rationing water, but now everyone is thirsty and getting worried."

"Once we get out of this room I'll send Hood in to fill a couple of bowls. You can come and get more, one at a time. You can keep a bowl." Bobby pointed. "Don't use the end one." He didn't tell her they used it as a toilet, because a woman trying to strip and do the same might be too much for Bells's self-control. He didn't have much. Bobby called to Hood and explained, before leaving him to organise water deliveries. Bobby took Fleur into a room full of bins. "This I've got to see."

Fleur laughed. "We tried to burn the doors open but it doesn't work. We tried burning out the controls, and found if we got them really hot the doors opened. We used the trick on the bins, but they didn't open." Fleur smiled. "We used the same laser each time to keep the rest fully charged until it ran down." She took out her laser and turned it down, showing Bobby as she did. "The next bin only got a little bit warm but we tried it anyway." Fleur played the beam on a bin lock for a few moments then slid the little bulge up and pulled up the lid. "Open it while the lock is warm, or it will lock again. Doors work the same way, but must be much hotter and won't close unless they're heated again." She pulled out a container and unscrewed it, the opposite way to the usual. "This is new."

The black granules looked like black sand to Bobby. "Stop flickin me. What did you find in your bins?"

Fleur's smile blazed out. "Food." She leant forward and kissed Bobby gently on the cheek. "Lots of food. You saved us outside, from the Allemande laser, you saved Ecarlate, and you found us water. A life for a life, now we have given you plenty of food for Beebi Basted's." The mischief showed briefly. "Now we should find a bath. I could wash your back to thank you properly?"

Bobby grinned and shook his head. "Are you Divas or Troopers? You looked a lot more dangerous in training than any Diva I ever met, but then you start kissing." She really had confused Bobby because that wasn't a Diva kiss, but it sure as hell wasn't anything a bledrin Trooper would do!

"That kiss? You only kiss Divas? You haven't had an amie, girl?" Fleur seemed puzzled, then the mischief came back. "If we are allies, maybe I should teach you the difference?"

Bobby laughed. "French kissing? I know about that."

Fleur laughed as well. "I will show you amie kissing, not French kissing. It's not for Divas. I forgot there are no women in your Troopers. Units like us are all women Troopers, except our officers." Her smile became less happy. "The rest of our Troopers call us chiennes, bitches. We kill a few now and then, the ones who try to treat us like Divas, to remind the rest we are not." She smiled at Bobby's puzzled look. "I will explain later."

"That should be fun." Bobby really couldn't quite get it. They were Les Putes which he knew meant Divas, but killed who, Frog Troopers? So they weren't Divas. But their Sarge was the Super's poochy-girl? That would be some explanation. "You'd better get back or they'll think I've kidnapped you."

Fleur looked disgusted. "The Super will not care as long as he gets water. He would order us to pooch you for water if that's what you wanted. Morceau de merde! Piece of shit!" She stopped and took a breath. "Je suis desole, I am sorry. Will you let me explain another time? Just now I feel much too happy, because with water we will live." Her grin came back. "On top of that we are joining with Beebi's Basteds to kill the Rangers."

"I can live with that." Bobby hesitated. "Do you want to look in these bins, or get back and check the others?" He shrugged. "Or tell me what food looks like?"

"Some bins are cold inside and contain raw meat, and other things. Baiser, the blonde, ate a little of the meat raw and had no trouble, no bad belly. The Super used up more laser to cook his." She looked at her laser.

Beebi realised they must have used up quite a bit of charge if they also opened doors with lasers. "I'll use mine to open the bins. What about other food?" Bobby reset his laser and warmed the next bin lock.

"That's enough." Bobby stopped and sure enough the bin opened. "We only tried a few. Each one of us tried something different, something that might be food, then we waited. One made Pepee sick. Those were blue flakes, cereale?" Fleur looked in the bin. "We didn't try any of these. Another?" Three bins down she pounced. "These. I ate these." She bit the end off a light brown stick. "Not fromage, cheese, but close. Maybe from an extraterrestre cow?" She pointed. "You can eat those, and these. Then try some others."

Bobby tried the stick and it tasted like strong cheese, but not quite right. Good enough for his first real meal in six months. He grinned. "I feel really happy with these right now. This bin will do until I organise some tasting to try the rest." On impulse he tried out one of those gentle kisses on her cheek. "Ammee kiss? For the food."

"Amie, yes. If you let me go back now we will eat and drink, and rest. The Super will let me come and talk again, to work out how to kill the Rangers. He likes the Rangers less than the UKs." Bobby escorted her back to the last junction, chewing a food stick and passing a few to Siflis and Mickey on the way. Then he explained food to the rest, and that Fleur at least had a real thing about killing Rangers. After opening more bins Bobby found a cold one with meat, though the outside temperature gave no hint. The meat tasted pretty good raw but nobody ate much because as Mickey reminded them, their stomachs had only taken in liquid for six months.

* * *

Mickey used his laser for warming bin locks to keep the charges in the rest. The rest of the day passed in opening bins and moving recognisable food towards their rooms, though some meat bins were allowed to relock themselves rather than spoil. One whole stack of bins remained sealed in case the food spoiled once the lock had been opened. There were sheets of cloth in some, and substances without smell or smelling disgusting. Others held blocks of unidentifiable metals and softer materials, and a few held what might be electrical components.

Bobby had two more meetings with Fleur, and again she preferred to stay one on one. Now he wasn't sure if she preferred to get him alone to sucker him with those smiles and ammee kisses, or if Fleur still thought the Basteds might want a pooching party.

While discussing the chain of command, it became clear that Fleur's supervisor would be a major problem. Fleur had to take every decision back to him, and in combat he would insist on commanding Les Putes. Fleur warned he'd already caused one death and wasted a weapon. The Super had insisted on launching the rocket at the Kraut capsule as retaliation for the property damage to his, even though the Krauts were all dead by then.

Then, once inside the spaceship, after exploring for hours, the Putes had found the Amazon with five extra legs and two spare backpacks. He'd already been negotiating with the Rangers. The Frog Super had offered to take him in, then threatened to shoot when the man didn't agree to surrender there and then without any further negotiation. The Amazon ran down a corridor towards the Rangers. They might have thought he was attacking, because the Rangers shot him down. Fleur's Super insisted that Aigu, the scout, retrieved some of the Amazon's extra gear, and even threatened her with his shotgun when she said it would be suicide.

Aigu used a doorway to get nearer, getting inside before the Rangers realised she could open the door. Then she'd thrown her rope with a loop, trying to hook some gear. She'd hooked a pack, but as she pulled it back the Rangers sprang their trap. Suddenly the Shiva's fired on the Putes from a side corridor. The Frog Super ordered a retreat. He wouldn't allow them to lay down covering fire first for Aigu. The Rangers had been waiting when she ran, hitting her with a storm of flechettes and maybe some sort of solid shot. Ecarlate and Fleur had been hit on the retreat, Fleur claimed because the Super wouldn't let them make a fighting withdrawal. He'd run away and ordered the rest to follow. By then Bobby had his arm round Fleur and really believed at least two Putes, her and Ecarlate, Red, would celebrate if their Super carked it.

*　*　*

By the following 'morning' Bobby felt sure another Pute would be happy to top their Super. The Basteds all heard the cries of pain in the night. During their morning meeting, Bobby had to ask why. "La bitte, dick, he wanted some poochy. Pepee is still sore, we all are, so he chose Baiser, the blonde." Fleur had lost her smoother Anglic, and seemed torn between fear and anger. "He says we will all have to take turns until Pepee feels better and we can't stop him. We expected to kill him quickly, at the start, but Pepee is frightened of this place and dying out here in space. She thinks we will be deserted out here if we kill the Super, so she watches his back." Fleur shuddered and hugged herself tightly.

Bobby mentally shrugged. He could fix this if the Frog dick liked pooching and it should strengthen the alliance. "If your Super goes to see Magpie, privately, will Pepee go?"

"He won't go to a private meeting. Why would he?"

"You understand spook?" Fleur nodded. "Our spook will ask to see him about contacting home. If something happens to your Super, make sure Pepee doesn't kill Magpie afterwards."

"The Super is not stupid. If he agrees to a meeting without Pepee, he will keep his shotgun pointed at your Magpie." Now she'd started thinking, not reacting, Fleur's Anglic picked up again.

Bobby laughed, but it had no humour. "Don't worry about that part." Then Bobby refused to explain, because he didn't want any hint or change of attitude warning anyone. He had a quick word with Hood and Magpie about the cries in the night. By the time he'd finished Magpie's sleeve knife had slid into her hand and she had that dead-eyed look. The one she'd had just before she set into the drug dealer. The Frog Super was dead; it just hadn't caught up to him yet.

Though before dealing with the Frog Super, Bobby had to meet Mickey to try the lock-warming on the two big doors. Mickey hadn't reported to Aggie last night because he didn't want the Frog Super involved, especially since the Frog refused to talk to him. Beebi wondered if maybe Mickey didn't want to tell the arses in Control that Beebi's Basteds would be alive and well when the reinforcements arrived. After all, they didn't need the sodin mothership's supplies now so it wasn't essential that they kept reporting.

Bobby had just decided to say nothing to Mickey about topping Supers when the tapper on his leg rapped four times. Siflis! Bobby scooped up his carbin and space helmet as he ran through the central area then paused. "Bells, bring that Kraut notsi. Hood, tell the Putes we've got someone coming at the other end, then bring that rifle thing and your carbin. Magpie stays on the ladders." Bobby started running again.

∗   ∗   ∗

Siflis beckoned from the last door before the junction, speaking quietly as soon as Bobby came near enough. "When the yellow lights started I heard voices. I think Anglic."

"The Rangers. Move along the other wall towards the doorway so you can see down the corridor without putting your head out. If you see anyone they'll see you, but we'll have to talk to them sometime." Siflis nodded, crossing to the blank wall, the one nearest the laser-guarded doorway, before inching along sideways with his carbin ready.

Mickey arrived and Bobby brought him up to date. Mickey agreed. "At least we've got a good position here with a fall-back on that central balcony. From there we can still cover the ladders."

Bobby gestured at the room behind them. "But it'll give them food unless we close the bins. If they haven't worked out how to open those, we'd be better keeping it that way. They'll get desperate even with extra food from the Amazon and Aigu's pack, especially if they've got the happy news from the capsule. Desperate might mean careless." He looked back up the corridor. "Where are the Putes?"

"Fleur came with a message. He's keeping them there in case this is a diversion." Mickey went to spit and then swallowed. "He could have sent a couple of the Troopers even if he's too frightened. Basted!" Bobby didn't mention a certain Timer Super who hid in a back room during an assault.

"If the Rangers and Shivas are combined, we could do with one more carbin here at least. We've got a good position because they can't use that doorway for cover or the lasers will nail them, but they might have the numbers for a rush. Shite!" Siflis had thrown himself backwards as carbin flechettes rattled off the passage wall and ricocheted down the corridor towards Bobby and the rest. Siflis darted forward, loosed off a long burst, then dived back again.

Mickey picked up a spent flechette, inspecting the blunted, squashed plastic. "I wondered about bouncing these down that corridor, but look at what the wall does to the plastic."

"Beebi?" Bells sounded tentative. He brandished the Kraut automatic. "The rounds are smaller, but the plastic is tougher? I don't think the Homers back at base realised that when they adapted my notsi. Maybe these will still cause damage to the faceplates at least."

"Or heads if they're not in a helmet. Try it but be careful. If you get killed, I'll give you a kicking." Bobby grinned as Bells stuck a finger up in reply. A couple of minutes later Bells opened up with the familiar tearing noise though he didn't get as far down the passage as Siflis had. The Rangers had been creeping closer. The cries of alarm and pain from round the corner cheered them all up.

Mickey laughed. "That should back them off a bit."

Bobby shook his head. "No, they'll creep up this side and stick a carbin round the corner, because now we all know those door lasers won't join in when we start firing. After how the one at the other end reacted, we'd been relying on that. Siflis, get to the end of our corridor sharpish and stick that Kraut round the corner. Give them a full clip spread all over the place, then take a peek with your little mirror while they're ducking. Report with hand signals."

"It'll do that anyway, spray all over." Bells sighed before reluctantly handing the little automatic to Siflis with three clips. "I've only got ten more so go steady."

Siflis laughed because Bells usually let off complete clips anyway, then the scout ran towards the corner. Moments later the long ripping sound signalled another hundred plastic rounds going downrange. Bobby watched as Siflis put the weapon down before pushing his mirror on a stick forward. The scout's other hand started signalling and Bobby translated the shorthand for Mickey. "At least seven so it's no diversion. A couple are being patched. They've pulled bins out of a room to use as cover, and now they're bringing more. About twenty-five to thirty metres away." The signals stopped as flechettes rattled off the corridor wall and floor and Siflis pulled his mirror in. He kept putting it back out for a quick look, but each time a carbin tried to hit it.

"Stalemate." Mickey sighed. "If they've found food and water, this could last until the reinforcements arrive. Then it'll depend on what alliances the other blocs make."

"Worse, we can't block the airlocks so everyone can come in all over the place. Even if they don't team up, we can't guard everything. Maybe they'll bring heavy weapons, enough to blow those doors and the lasers before our own reinforcements get to us." Bobby glanced back down the corridor. "We need something extra. Fleur said the Frogs only had one rocket but we haven't been totally truthful. Maybe they've kept something back?"

"Hello there. Is that Beebi's Basteds?" Mickey and Bobby looked at each other. That accent meant a Ranger. Every Trooper had seen cowboy films and heard how the Rangers and Yankees spoke, and the Yankees were dead. Mickey indicated that Bobby should answer.

"Yes, is that the Rangers? What do you want? We've got more flechettes?"

"Luck with that because we've got our jackets on but I'm more worried about notsi. That last bledrin automatic wasn't a carbin and those aren't flechettes. We want to talk."

"What about?" Even as he spoke, Bobby gestured at the others to get into Trooper gear. They'd stayed in spacesuits in case the ship voided air but now, despite a firefight, the ship hadn't reacted. The Trooper gear wouldn't stop lasers but would slow them up while the jackets and trousers, especially their adapted ones, would stop plastic flechettes except close up.

"We've got extra packs and weapons, so we can wait you out. We've also found what we reckon are the engines even if we can't work them." The voice paused. "Has your Super dropped yet, because our Super wants to negotiate a contract? He reckons you must have the control room so between us we control the ship. The other blocs can eat shit and die."

"What other blocs?"

"There's Frogs and a couple of SEPA. The Frogs lost one, maybe two. Watch those bitches, they tried to sucker us."

Maybe Fleur's smile had got to him, because Bobby preferred her version. He grinned at Mickey and shouted again. "What about the Amazon and the Shivas?"

"The Frogs shot the Amazon but we got the body and pack." The voice paused. "You got me, we've teamed up with the Shivas. A solid contract." A carbin rattled way behind Bobby. "That will be one of them sealing the corridor at the other side."

Mickey leaned close. "Ask if their contract will stand when reinforcements arrive."

"What if the Shivas have different orders when their reinforcements get here?"

The voice in the corridor didn't hesitate. "Nope. Our Super has the authority to make contacts and alliances. I'll bet yours did and that means you have the authority now he's gone."

Bobby looked at Mickey and he shrugged. "True. I'm just not as sure as he is that Area Manager Gunnar Eriksson will stand by what I agree. I'm certain he won't stick to what you negotiate." Mickey shrugged again. "That's if he comes. He's an Area Manager so I can't see him giving up his legs."

"Guns is a realist so whoever he sends will be the same. This Ranger seems confident they'll last until someone gets here, so either he got the supplies from the main rocket or they've found food and water. We can't spend weeks on alert." Bobby raised his voice. "How do we negotiate without someone getting a clear shot?"

"Our Super will come to the front of our barricade, and you stand out in the corridor."

That sounded workable. "Give us five while we talk. The mirror will watch so you don't get cute. No shooting."

"Deal."

The talk didn't take five minutes because Bobby suggested that if the Putes weren't here helping, they could live with whatever deal he made. Mickey worried about the Frog Super not agreeing, and Bobby explained the Magpie option. Mickey didn't think that over as long as Bobby expected, but added the proviso the Frog only carked it if he became a problem. Mickey insisted on one point; he would stand out in the corridor to negotiate instead of Bobby. His Trooper gear would stop a plastic flechette even at point blank because Supers didn't really trust Timers or Troopers. The last bit came with a rueful smile.

Hood went back to tell Magpie she should get her Trooper gear on, and pass that message to the Putes. Once they were changed Bobby noticed they all seemed to have a sharper edge, were more focussed and intent. Maybe the uniform did it. Bobby finally shouted to the Ranger. "Lucky you, we've still got a Super so don't try to pooch us. You don't want your bloc sued for a breach."

"You mothers still have your Super? Bullshit."

Mickey spoke up, and all the recent relaxation had gone from his voice. "This is Supervisor Steven McKay so you button it, Trooper. Who is your Supervisor? If his name checks I'll send my ID on the command channel and he'll send his." Mickey grinned and shrugged at the faces of the Basteds because he suddenly sounded like a typical uptight dick, the sort of dick Beebi's Basteds should have topped on day one.

A long pause followed, before Siflis started with his hand signals. He could hear voices but couldn't make out words. An argument had started. Eventually another, accented voice spoke. "Supervisor Satbir Singh Barar of Shiva's Children. The Rangers have lost their Supervisor but accept my authority. Please confirm ID, Supervisor McKay. I can read that over the command channel."

"I can read yours as well. Sending, Supervisor Barar." Mickey listened, then turned his com off. "He's got the right codes for a Supervisor that name, and the ID readers are hard to fool." Mickey didn't say impossible. "I wouldn't trust a contract with a Trooper Sergeant or Corporal but one agreed with this Super, thumb printed and recorded, should stand." Mickey sighed. "Then if the Frog dick acts up, set Magpie or Bells on him." The Super shrugged. "He hasn't even given me his name and ID so I don't exactly trust him, and we have no contract."

"It'll be a relief if you get a legal contract. We'll still keep a guard watching the approaches, but the Ranger is right. Between us we have the numbers to lock the ship down and when the rest arrive we can tell the other blocs to piss off. With control of the engines and control room, our bosses should back us." Bobby grinned. "It'll probably kick off on Earth, but we're out of range." He stood and saluted formally. A crap salute, but the principle counted. "Siflis will watch them with his mirror and Hood will be ready with a carbin. Good luck sir."

"Piss off, you'll have me crying next." The rest of the Basteds saluted, all crappy salutes, while Mickey replied with the parade ground version. Taking a deep breath, Mickey turned his com on and spoke. "Let's see you, Supervisor Barar."

He'd turned the volume up far enough for Bobby to hear the reply. "I am standing on the barricade. I will step forward when I see you." Siflis's hand signals confirmed that, so Mickey moved to the corner and showed himself, cautiously.

Mickey called out loudly and turned on his squad coms so that Bobby and the rest could hear as well. "Jump down and I'll take a step. Then I'll move out further as you come forward." The reply must have been agreement, because Mickey moved to the middle of the corridor in increments. Siflis indicated the Shiva's Super had advanced three steps in reply.

*   *   *

Both Supers shouted as well as used their coms, so everyone could hear as they started to discuss terms. Mickey admitted to having the Putes as allies because the Shiva's Super wanted shares to be based on numbers of Troopers. The Shivas had lost a man, and the Rangers their Super, so they had ten to Mickey's eleven. Bobby expected that to become ten as well. He'd find an excuse because otherwise Magpie would do it anyway without orders, after what the basted did to Baiser. Mickey confirmed the Putes were here as armed Troopers, not captured as Divas. Neither knew where the two SEPA Troopers were, and they hadn't been heard on the coms after that first quick burst of speech.

Mickey asked about contact with Control and Super Barar had used the same method, opened an airlock to call the capsule. They both admitted knowing that the reinforcements were on the way and the capsules had no supplies, and agreed to share any supplies in the main rocket. The Shiva's and Rangers claimed to have plenty of spare food from their own casualties, plus two Amazon packs and one from the Putes, and they'd found water supplies. Mickey told Super Barar that the Basteds and Putes had rationed their food to last for at least an extra week.

"They've found food!" A loud crack echoed the shout from the barricade, and Mickey flipped backwards before curling up around his gut. Hood and Siflis opened up with carbins as Super Barar ran back over the barricade. Bobby darted out, snagging Mickey by the collar and towing him into cover despite the scream.

As soon as he made it into cover Bobby shouted down the corridor. "You stupid basteds. Why did you do that?"

"Some packs were shot up so our food leaked and we haven't got enough even with the captures. The basted mothership won't release any, or hasn't got any. We can't find ship food, but you must have some or you couldn't last that long." A short laugh followed. "Beebi's Basteds don't like Supers anyway so I figure you won't care about him carking it. Now we can make a deal with you instead of him. Our bloc and the Indies will pay well for the ship, then you and the rest can retire anywhere in comfort." The voice kept shouting which drowned the argument behind him, an argument behind the barricade which meant someone had gone off the script. "Top the Frog Super and we'll buy a couple of the Putes, because there's no Divas here and it'll be a long lonely wait."

Cursing wasn't going to help so Bobby thought quickly, playing for time. "You must be using different cream or enjoy pain but in any case the Putes say no, piss off. They've got a cure for your problem but it'll be bloody. As far as the deal about the ship goes, how do I know you'll keep your word?"

"You don't, but we've got a real contract and you haven't. When the reinforcements get here ours will swamp you, because we can shut off the airlocks and you can't open one for your Troopers."

"He's right. You've got to hold an airlock and if he's got a man in the other corridor we're pooched." Bobby winced as he glanced back at Mickey's pale face and bitten lips. "I'm done Beebi, gut-shot. It went right through the jacket."

"What did?"

"A toe." Siflis had left Hood with the mirror while he came to report. "I saw it when the shooter fired. He's using a detached leg, bent up at the knee and he's aiming the foot. There's three toes left." Siflis shrugged. "Someone must have taken their leg off, or maybe it's one of those the Amazon brought."

Bobby called out to Hood. "Can't you reply with that thing of yours, Hood?"

"I only had two solid rounds. The rest are frangible and might not make it through a Trooper jacket at this range, or even break a face-shield." A shot sounded. "I'm trying, but not having much effect."

"I hit that basted Super but the plastic flechettes bounced." Siflis scowled. "Whoever fired really pooched that Super, going by the look on his face. Then he started running. That argument will end with one less Super or one less shooter I reckon."

A burst of firing sounded followed by an American voice. "Oh dear. Beebi's Basteds have shot the Shiva's Super. Or maybe we can blame the SEPA if we can make a deal."

"Piss off."

"All right. We can wait. We've got extra food now the Super carked it so we might get thin, but we'll make it." The voice laughed. "I've already sent more Troopers to seal off the other side. When reinforcements come we'll tell them you killed your Super, and they'll believe me."

"Beebi." He turned to the Mickey. "Unscrew my other sole. On my foot."

"What?"

"Do it for a dying man."

Bobby unscrewed the sole, frantically thinking about what to do next. As the sole came free he gasped. "A bledrin grenade. They allowed you a grenade?"

"Yes, but where you wouldn't find it if you killed me. Now use it to pooch those arses good and proper." Mickey subsided, panting heavily as Bells did his best with a bandage and wadded clothing.

"I can't. The barricade is too far. I'll not get it over the bins throwing round the corner." Bobby grinned. "It'll come in handy if they rush."

"No, you've got to push them back. That Super might have a grenade, and if they find it you're pooched instead." Mickey stopped, panting again. "I'm going to give you an order, Sergeant Three Bobby B. I'll give you a disc." Mickey coughed and blood came up. "Don't lose this disc. Eriksson will think you topped me but the disc will be a record of up to now and he'll not try to pooch you."

"Thank you Mickey. We'll push them back somehow, enough to get to an airlock."

"No you won't, or you'll lose men doing it because they're behind cover." Mickey bit his lip until blood ran. "In my pack, pouch at the back. Two needles. Green and red. Give me the green, all of it." A quick search and Siflis held the two syringes up.

"One has to be a GV."

"Give him the green like he said." If that turned out to be a GV, well, Mickey had asked for it.

The contents weren't a GV, and the dose didn't take long to work. Mickey straightened slowly and carefully. "Not too bad. I can do this. Find me a bit of shelving and something to strap it on, Beebi."

"Why?" Though Beebi nodded to Bells to do as Mickey said.

"Because I'm going to earn my squad name, Mickey the Basted. You made me a Beebi's Basted, so I'm allowed to go out right." Mickey turned. "Get the pack off. I won't feel it much, not now." Mickey felt it enough to wince and groan a little as Siflis removed it. "Take the shotgun and the weapons, all of them. That's good stuff, I'm high as a kite." Mickey grinned through the blood. "Haven't seen a kite in years. Used to have a red and yellow one."

"Sir."

"What? Oh, yes, sort of wandered off. Dying. Here." Mickey felt inside his jacket. Something clicked and he brought out a small disc and a bit of electrical kit which he passed to Bobby. "A record for Gunnar and the radio to talk to Aggie if she needs my call-sign. Get me on my feet." His face split in a silly smile. "A shelf and a jacket to stop a toe, then I'll give them a grenade." Mickey giggled. "Special delivery. Super special."

Even if the Super didn't forget where he should be going, Bobby wasn't sure that Mickey could make it that far. If he didn't, when the bledrin grenade went off Bobby would run down that corridor with both shotguns. The arse with the toes wouldn't get chance to retarget, and at point blank the plastic buckshot would get through a Trooper jacket. Bobby reassessed when Mickey stood because the Super more or less straightened and seemed firm enough on his feet even without the soles. "I'll fire my own solid shot." Bobby twisted his finger and prepared his left hand. "I can try to shoot their shooter but I've only got one."

"Good man. Should get metal. Heh, I'll get metal for this. Supers don't earn metal. A real metal super, super metal." Mickey had started drifting again, then sharpened up when Bells and Siflis strapped a piece of shelving to his front. "Aah, didn't like that." He took the grenade in one hand, pulling the pin while holding the lever down. "Give me a knife. If I get near enough I'll try a throw at toe man. Shame to waste the training. Pretty trainer. Missed seeing strategic secret." He'd started to drift, but before Bobby could get Mickey back on track they were interrupted.

"Hey, you still there, Beebi?" The shite with the American accent was back.

"Yeah, why?"

"Goodbye, sucker." Bobby knew just what the metal bouncing down the corridor had to be and if a grenade went off opposite the corridor end the blast would get them all. Even as Bobby turned to dive for the nearest room, Mickey lurched into action. The Super staggered forward, dropping the knife, and as the grenade came into view he bent with a cry of pain and scooped it up. The gun down the corridor cracked, metal clanged, and Mickey bounced off the wall before rolling the grenade back down the corridor and staggering after it.

"Cover him!" Bobby dived, rolling out into the corridor and bringing up his finger as flechettes started to rattle on Mickey's piece of shelving and faceplate. Shooting over twenty metres with his left hand wasn't optimum, so Bobby took his time. The little Kraut automatic ripped off a clip, heads ducked at the barricade, and the incoming fire eased. By the time the arse with the toe gun put up his head again Bobby was waiting. His finger end spat flame and the basted flipped backwards. Bobby rolled back into cover as Mickey staggered past the loose grenade, lifting his own high in the air.

Siflis, Bells and Hood rolled away from the end of the corridor as well, because they could all count. The first grenade went off, and Bobby didn't need to see what happened to Mickey. The blast would throw him and his grenade forward over the barricade, regardless of what anyone fired at him. Four seconds of screaming and yelling later the second grenade exploded. "Come on!" Bells went round the corner at a full run, the Kraut sending another hundred plastic bullets downrange. As Hood, Siflis and Bobby followed, shooting from the hip with their carbins, Bells staggered and spun round. He bounced off the wall and went down.

Bobby went past him, trying to close with the figures fleeing from the barricade. Another Trooper came from the room just beyond the barricade and all three carbins zeroed in. As the man staggered Bobby let the carbin drop, lifting his shotgun instead. The packed charge picked the Trooper off his feet and then the Basteds came over the barricade, past Mickey's body. Sharp metal gleamed in Hood's hand as he finished the downed man. Siflis jumped straight over the second, lower barricade to fire a short burst downwards, then he dived back over as carbins rattled from further down the corridor. A small rocket flew towards them and Bobby dropped as well. Luckily the missile cleared the barricade, carrying on down the corridor to explode someplace behind.

"Covering fire, Hood. Short bursts." The big man raised his carbin, firing blindly down the corridor but only bursts as instructed. Bobby looked around. The only bodies between the barricades were the Trooper from inside the room and Mickey. Mickey had been shredded by the two grenade blasts, one from each direction. "Siflis, what's over the barricade?"

"Two bodies. The Super but without his jacket, and a Trooper who must have caught some of the blast. I gave him a GV." Siflis meant a burst to the head, not a syringe.

"Only three. Shite. They dived over the second barricade to escape the grenade."

"Not that bad really." Hood sounded downright cheerful. "They're down to seven now and some of those running were definitely looking rough. One was being half-carried, one was nursing his arm and one dragged a leg." He peeked over the barricade. "They've gone."

"We might be down to nine because Bells is hit, or eight if the Frog Super acts up. You two move bins and make that barricade the highest one, not this one behind us." Bobby rolled back over the taller barricade and looked up the corridor. "Bells is alive. It looks bloody but an arm so not GV bad." He crawled back on hands and knees, keeping below the barricade in case someone sprayed flechettes down the corridor. "How is it, Bells?"

"A metal job I reckon. Soon as possible?" True enough because something solid had hit his arm, tearing it open as well as breaking the bone. "Green needle please." The bared teeth in his pale face wasn't a smile.

Bobby smiled at the joke because Troopers didn't carry a green needle. He hadn't known Supers did. "Let me tie that off." He pulled out a dressing and a bandage, binding a bayonet and scabbard tight to the mess as a splint.

"Wake me when you're…." Bells fainted.

"What happened? We heard grenades and the Super sent me."

Bobby looked up and Fleur's face and carbin barrel peeked round the junction into the cross corridor. "An attack by the Rangers and Shivas. Mickey is dead and Bells is hurt bad. Can you give me a hand to shift him?"

"Merde! That means just one Super. He will be your boss." She crawled forward and hooked an arm under one armpit, then helped Bobby drag

Bells back up the corridor. Fleur glanced back at the barricade. "Someone shot flechettes up the other corridor towards the lasers. Our Super told us to get ready for attack from both sides instead of coming to help you. He said you were making a deal with the Rangers to sell us."

"We tried for a contract, one that included you as fighters. We'd be screwed if you hadn't told us about bins, because we can't get food released from the rocket. Neither can they even though they've got the engines." Fleur stared, shocked, and Bobby shrugged. "We didn't trust your Super enough to tell you we were in contact with Control, not yet."

She nodded, a quick, sharp, unhappy one. "I understand. I'm not happy but I understand. Why didn't you make a contract?"

"The Troopers changed their minds. They realised we'd got more food than them, or found food, and the arses got greedy." Bobby sighed. "They got a big solid bullet into Mickey, then an argument kicked off and the Rangers topped the Shiva's Super." Bobby laughed. "Mickey took a painkiller and went viral, ran down the corridor with a grenade. There's three bodies including their Super back there, so seven left." They pulled Bells round the corner and stood, and Bobby used his tapper com. "*Hood. Leave Siflis as guard.*" He needed the big man to help lift Bells. They could use a shelf as a stretcher. "*Bring packs. Leave ammo.*" Even if the Rangers deciphered the tapper, they'd only know the guard had plenty of ammo but the packs and food were gone. Bobby assumed the Rangers would end up in charge. Apart from the Shivas Super, the only voices negotiating had been American.

The pair turned at a stream of definitely unhappy French, and Fleur braced into attention. "My Supervisor demands you tell him what happened."

"Tell him."

After an exchange in French the Super turned to Bobby and spouted something. Bobby shrugged. The Frog shouted at Fleur. "He says he is in charge. You must show respect."

"I haven't topped him?" Fleur stared and Bobby took pity on her. "Tell him Beebi's Basteds are sloppy soldiers and this is as good as I can manage. I need medical help for the wounded."

More French, more shouting and Bobby's trigger finger twitched but

Pepee stood two metres away with a shotgun, near enough to get plastic buckshot through a Trooper jacket. "You will get the man to a bed, then report. He wants to know what ammunition and food you have, and where are the officer's quarters?"

"I'll show him in a minute, once Bells is sorted. Suggest that he sets up a barricade like that one to protect the air lock in the other corridor. Tell him why. If three or four of you head down that way there can only be one man at most so he'll run." That took two or three exchanges and then some more shouting before the Frog stalked back up the corridor, followed by Pepee. The triumphant glance from the Putes Sergeant-chef confirmed that Bobby would get no help there. Pepee had just become the senior NCO of Beebi's Basteds. Bobby watched them go. "Will he do it, the barricade?"

"Yes, Pepee will encourage him now she knows about the other Troopers wanting to stop us, and that you can talk to the rocket. What will you do?" Fleur didn't look sure about Bobby obeying her Super.

"Just what he said because I need to know about ammo anyway, especially what we captured. Is Pepee a fighter or just a Diva?" If Pepee couldn't fight Bobby didn't care if she dropped with the Super, because after that display the dick had to go.

"She is a fighter, a real Trooper, but she also protects the Super and pooches for him. That's her job. Why?"

"Just nosy. While I sort this out, can you teach Magpie some French?" Fleur looked curious but nodded. "Here's what I want Magpie to learn, then tell him that it's strategic weapon time and give him this to put on the table in his room." Bobby handed Fleur the electrical kit from inside Mickey's jacket. Fleur repeated the message and the words Magpie should learn, looking more and more puzzled, but in the end she smiled just a little and set off to do as she'd been asked.

By then Hood had arrived with three captured packs, though one had been shredded. "There's water and ammo in here, but not much food." Hood brandished carbins. "I brought two carbins to match this captured ammo, and I've got that foot-gun but there's only one toe left. Siflis is using Ranger ammo right now. A bit like old times."

"Only one toe left? Shite. The fourth one must be what hit Bells.

Someone picked the leg up after I shot the arse who used it on Mickey." Bobby frowned. "That excuse for a rifle you've got, will the frangible rounds go through a head?"

"Yeah, though maybe not through. If I pick my spot the round will go in, and then it's brain soup time. You want me to shoot the Frog Super?" Hood grinned. "I haven't shot a Frog Super for years."

"No. We've got to kill the Frog for something that seems reasonable, or we lose Pepee as well because she'll shoot back. I'd like to keep her as an extra fighter." Bobby grinned. "Magpie should deal with the Frog without any bother but if Pepee doesn't swallow it, be ready because I'd rather lose her than Magpie. Now let's get Bells onto a shelf and stretcher him to a bed."

*   *   *

Bobby took his time, both to calm down a bit and to give Magpie time to learn her lines. When he saw her climb the ladder to the room she shared with Hood, Bobby walked down the corridor to the Putes. He produced the crappiest salute he thought could still be recognised as one, but didn't bother to brace to attention. "Tell his dickship I'll take him to the officer's quarters now, and give him the report."

Fleur translated, but probably not literally since the Super smiled. Pepee frowned so she'd understood, but she didn't cause trouble. French shouting became a Fleur translation. "Your Supervisor wants you to start acting like a real Trooper. You must learn to stand to attention and salute properly. He says you must have learned in training."

"Nope. We killed a shitload of Frog Supers and were promoted to Trooper before we learned drill or saluting." That really was the truth, but he didn't think Fleur would translate exactly. Pepee's lip twitched so maybe she knew, or believed him. Beebi's Basteds did have a rep for topping Supers.

They exchanged more French, until Fleur turned back to Bobby. "You must try harder." Her eyelid flickered in a wink. "Lead us to the officer's quarters and arrange warm food."

As he turned to go Bobby noted that Pepee had her shotgun aimed in his direction, so he walked up the corridor nice and steady and unthreatening. At least Bells wouldn't go viral because he hadn't come round yet. Siflis would be on guard so he wouldn't say the wrong thing. Hood would be in place by now. Bobby breathed evenly, slowing his pulse and keeping calm, because if this went wrong he'd have to drop Pepee and then the Super. As they approached the open area in the centre, Bobby turned his head. "Do you have a spy with you, a spook?"

Fleur translated. "No, why?"

"We have a spook because our commanders don't trust me." Bobby knew when that had been translated because of the laugh.

"Who is it?"

"Magpie, and he wants to talk to your Super about contacting the reinforcements, and arranging a contract." Bobby wished he could cross something, though it had never worked yet.

Fleur's translation didn't have the same tone as the original, but the words alone were arrogant enough. "I will meet with him. There is no need for contracts because I am the only officer."

"He's an officer but not in our chain of command." Bobby started to sweat a little, and hoped this held up long enough. Stopping by the balcony, Bobby raised his voice. "Officer Magpie. The Supervisor will speak to you."

Magpie came out in her skinsuit, but kept her collar up over her hair. Bobby managed to keep his smile down to a twitch. The skinsuit wasn't tight enough to show her figure but would open all the way down the front for a strategic surprise. Magpie wore no weapons, but her sleeves weren't sealed at the cuffs. "Par toi-meme. Je suis un espion. J'ai une radio."

Bobby already knew what Magpie said. "Meet me alone. I'm a spy. I've got a radio."

The Super rattled something, and Fleur translated for Bobby, which meant Magpie didn't have to confess she didn't understand. "Not alone. You will tell me out here."

"Je suis un espion. Par toi-meme." Magpie impressed Bobby, she must have actually learned what the Frog stuff meant if she'd changed it round.

The Frog must have realised a spy might want to tell him secrets. "Pepee will check the room." The French Sergeant-chef climbed up the ladder.

Moving aside, Magpie turned around once to show Pepee she hadn't a gun or knife behind her back. The Sergeant-chef went into the room briefly, then came out smiling. Fleur translated. "He has a radio."

The Super climbed the ladder, pointing his shotgun at Magpie while instructing Pepee. Fleur translated again despite a dirty look from Pepee. "You watch everyone else." He nodded towards the door. "Go in first, Magpie, and be careful or I will shoot." This glance from Pepee as Fleur translated seemed more puzzled than annoyed. The pair went inside and the Frog closed the door. Bobby ignored the surreptitious glances from Fleur, keeping himself loose but ready to move. If the shotgun went off in there he'd leave Pepee to Hood, and point his shotgun at the door.

A piercing scream rang out, high-pitched, a woman, then a second. The third cut off short and Bobby raised the shotgun, ready to kill the basted Super. But when the door opened Magpie stood there. Bobby tried not to smile because her skinsuit hung wide open all the way down the front, and everyone finally got to see Magpie's strategic underwear. Bells would be really pissed that he'd missed it though Magpie wasn't smiling, she looked furious and brandished a bloody knife. "I am not some Frog Super's poochy!" She gestured away down the corridor. "Only Hood gets into my underwear, once we're up to it."

Fleur's shocked face broke into a huge smile, which she quickly stifled. She would be realising why a Trooper had learned to say, "Vous me donnez Beebi trois bandes? Bien Poochy? J'aime le douleur." A man might ask for Beebi's three stripes, but wouldn't offer a good pooching because he liked the pain. That and flashing her strategic underwear had got Magpie inside the shotgun, where her sleeve knife did the rest. Pepee hesitated for long moments, until Bobby half expected Hood to top her just to be safe, but her shotgun barrels dropped at last. Magpie turned towards her. "I thought you were supposed to pooch the basted whenever he felt randy?"

Pepee looked away and down and probably would have blushed if she'd been lighter coloured as laughter rang out from behind Bobby. Baiser de la Mort, Kiss of Death, the blonde usually called Baiser, looked and sounded delighted. Turning to Bobby, Fleur laughed at last. "A woman? All Rosbif Troopers are men! I thought Magpie might be a pede, one who likes the men. He is a pretty boy."

"Strategic weapon." Bobby grinned back at her.

Mischief sparkled in her eyes. "Eh, Pepee, maybe we should show Beebi our strategic weapon?" Fleur didn't wait for a reply; she reached down and undid her Trooper leggings, then dropped them. Bobby stared because she wore shorts, and the legs below the metal connector band looked real. Bobby almost reached out to touch, because the curves and the stockings couldn't be real. They had to be metal because he'd seen the Frogs in space and in training without legs.

"Hrrrm." He cleared his throat. "Are the stockings real?"

"Some are, and some of us have them etched in the metal. Which do you want?"

Bobby laughed. "I really don't care." He dragged his eyes up and met Fleur's laughing brown ones. "Bells will have a heart attack."

"Bledrin wonderful. They get real legs and I'm stuck with these." Magpie pointed at her generic legs, definitely not female even if hers were slim to match her build. "If one of you carks it, I want her metal."

"They won't fit. I'll bet the Frog connections are different." Bobby didn't want Magpie arranging an accident to get better looking legs.

"I can dream." Magpie raised her voice. "Hood, come and help me with the trash. Then you can adjust my underwear where that Frog got a bit handy." From the look on Hood's face the Super might be lucky to be already dead, though Bobby doubted the Frog got hands-on. Pepee moved forward, looked in the door, winced, and turned to climb slowly down the ladder.

She moved over to talk quietly to the other two. Fleur shook her head, but Pepee insisted until the pair produced small knives, cut off their rank badges, and exchanged them. Fleur saw Bobby watching and came across to explain. "Pepee says she is not a proper sergeant-chef, that she is the Super's poochy like your Magpie said. I usually run our equipe, our squad. That is how we always work, Les Putes, but now she says we need a proper sergeant-chef to deal with Beebi Basted. I have been dealing with you up to now, so it is my job. Oui?"

"I'm good with that." Bobby did feel relieved, because dealing with Pepee might have been a bit awkward now. "Can you all speak Anglic?"

315

"Yes. Some speak Anglic better than others, and others speak better Allemande. One of our jobs is to go over the border, find a Diva bar and try to get an officer on his own. Then we do the same as Magpie but without the screaming. Though I think Baiser liked the screams." Bobby glanced at a smiling Baiser, now displaying a pair of real-looking legs, and remembered. She'd been the one crying out last night. Last night? This had all happened in no time, before they'd done much more than have breakfast.

"I'd better go and let Siflis know what happened, then we can sit down and decide how to organise the place." He turned to go. "Ah, right. There's another secret we were working up to. You'd better know now because you'll be wandering all over, in fact you may as well move into these rooms." Bobby only had three fit Troopers, and so did Fleur, so keeping the eight of them separate while guarding and looking after wounded just wasn't practical. "Follow me up to the top balcony."

*   *   *

Fleur stared out of the captain's room. "Merde! When were you going to tell me?"

"As soon as your Super had carked it?" Bobby shrugged. "He didn't tell Mickey his name or make a proper contract so we weren't really trusting."

"Oui. I understand." She waved a hand at the view of the bridge from the captain's window. "C'est magnifique. Is there no way to get in?"

"Only past those lasers or probably through that hole in the floor, and I'd rather have reinforcements first. The marks on the corridor floor back there were from a laser and it melted a knife." Bobby raised his hand to scratch at a tiny mark on the window but it seemed to be on the other side. "What the?" A fluorescent green lizard with gold flecks and a red stripe under its throat ran across the glass, paused to eat the speck, and darted away. "Pets? Pests? No, the place had no air or heat."

"They must have lived somewhere and the dirt must be food. That might be a way of keeping the house clean?" Fleur shook her head, her eyes wide with wonder. "I could believe anything just now." She looked around the room. "Will this be your room now?"

"No, none of us wanted to be stranded up here. It made more sense to be on the first balcony with those bins for defence."

"Le bitte would have moved in here. We don't know his name, just Adjutant-chef. Maybe Pepee does." Fleur frowned in thought. "You called your Supervisor Mickey. Why not his last name, or Super?"

"He was called Steven McKay. Mickey is his squad name." Bobby chuckled. "He was really proud about that, having a squad name and being a part of Beebi's Basteds. I think that's why he did it, took a Gaza Taxi. He would have carked it anyway but wanted to die properly like a Beebi's Basted." Bobby jumped as Fleur gave him one of those quick ammee kisses but on the lips.

"Then he earned it, the name." She sighed, then looked down at her legs and grinned. "You didn't show me this until I showed you my secret. Have you any more secrets?"

Bobby relaxed because Fleur had gone back to her old self, teasing a bit. "Show me something else and find out."

She raised a leg, and inspected it. "Maybe, but this is enough for one day."

"Oh yes, those legs are definitely enough for one day." As Bobby went to tell Siflis and Bells, and while sorting through the captured gear, those legs kept surprising him as they went by. They just looked so bledrin wrong, especially covered in some sort of coloured coating that looked a lot like skin, in skin tones that matched the women. When Pepee finally took off her leggings hers were the same chocolate brown as her skin, with white stockings. Shapely legs in stockings shouldn't be wandering around a war zone, or topped by serious, professional Troopers even if they were also seriously sleek Troopers. Perhaps Bells being laid up wasn't such a bad thing. He nearly had a heart attack when he woke up and called out and Baiser went in to check on him. Magpie kept scowling at the legs, not Les Putes. The Putes made no effort to cover up again, and practically speaking the metal legs were as warm and tougher than anything they could put over them.

*   *   *

Bobby blamed the legs for distracting him when he finally remembered what he'd been going to do today. He'd been eating a few more cheese sticks, wondering if he should open more bins, and how many more the lasers would open, when he remembered. Bobby smiled as he stood because this would be a new secret for both him and Fleur so he wouldn't get a secret from her in return. "Fleur, do you want to see a secret?"

"Another? Today? What you expect to see in return?" Her smile teased, suggesting she might not mind.

"I don't know. After all, I don't know what this secret is." On the way he explained. Standing outside the double doors, Fleur inspected the marks where they'd tried to force them apart. Serious hammering had only caused a few scratches in the plastic-like covering around the crack in the middle.

"We tried this first, with the other doors and bins."

"We tried with bins as well. Stand back." Bobby set his laser and warmed up the panel against the door. Periodically he tried the door, but when it worked there was no need as the doors slid apart without twisting the control. Fleur put a knife across the groove to stop them closing again, and they stood and looked. "Is that a kitchen or an operating table?"

"Abattoir, for the meat in the bins?" The object in question looked like a steel table but with grooves and holes, probably to drain fluids. A dome hanging down just above it sported a frightening array of blades, drills, syringes, probes, tweezers and pincers. "Maybe Magpie should have put la bitte on here. Maybe he would have screamed a bit more."

"I asked. Magpie said she daren't let him scream more in case Pepee came in, but she wanted Baiser to hear him die." Magpie had been a little bit more graphic about what she'd wanted to do, but that covered it.

"Baiser liked the screaming a lot. Any time Magpie needs a friend, Baiser will be there. She is sorry Magpie is a woman, and has a man, so she can't say thank you now." They'd been walking forward as they spoke, walking around the table, and now Fleur pointed. "In there would be a better place. He could scream a long time in there."

Bobby looked at the box with the heavy-looking raised lid. "If these are for injured crew they were wider and taller than us, humans." He sniggered. "Who knows how he would have come out? Six eyes, three legs, tentacles?"

Fleur shuddered and then punched his arm. "Non, stop." She paused.

"Maybe not. The ship took bodies so maybe it can repair humans. Maybe it would have put new legs on him." She flinched. "Legs from a dead Chinois or Yankee?"

"I prefer the metal ones to that, or yours anyway." Bobby looked around the banks of dead machinery and the blank screens. Marks and painted symbols showed where either drawers or maybe hatches opened. Another four tables and seven boxes were arranged around the floor space, with one couch-type seat scaled for a creature over a metre wide and nearly three metres long or tall. "Unless we can persuade Bells or Ecarlate to try a box or table, we'd better go and look at the other room."

"Maybe the second secret will help us more?" Fleur glanced towards the room with the holes and ladders. "We can try up or down next."

"Just to look, because there aren't enough of us to hold a bigger area. I'm hoping the Rangers have enough food now and will call it quits." Bobby shrugged. "They will think your Super is still alive so we could have ten to their seven, instead of eight."

"Bells will fight one handed so we have nine. He is like Ecarlate and Baiser, he will fight any way he can because he likes it." Fleur gestured at the door. "Do you want me to use my laser?"

"No, this one was Mickey's. We've used it for everything else so it's nearly done, but the rest have nearly full charges." Bobby played the beam gently on the control bulge. He began to think this lock wouldn't react, but the doors finally slid apart. This time Bobby put a knife in the groove, and as he did so movement caught his eye. A laser in the gloom tracked his movement, one like those by the two big doors. "Careful. Lasers."

Fleur peered into the room, which seemed much smaller than the last one with bars all around the walls. She leaned a bit further. Even as Bobby reached out a hand to stop her, because the laser twitched, the room lights came on. They both gasped and stood very still. "L'armurerie. We have found the weapons."

"We also found a lot of lasers, live ones." The bars surrounded a small entrance space, with doors leading off on three sides, but beyond that stretched a room every bit as big as the last one. Each of the doors had a dimpled bulge, but Bobby didn't think those big lasers would like him using his hand laser on one. "That looks like body armour, better than

319

Trooper gear."

Fleur giggled. "Better than le blinde, a tank, maybe." She pointed, then froze but although three lasers now aimed at her outstretched arm, none fired. The suit, scaled for the same size creature as the couch, must have provided complete protection. "Maybe that is a spacesuit?"

"Maybe pull your arm back? Slowly?"

"Probably as dangerous to move back as forward." Fleur moved forward a little and stopped again. Lasers tracked her hand, but only two of them. "See?" She moved further and slid a foot over the threshold. "We are no threat. No flashing yellow lights so if I do not point a weapon, I will be safe."

"How about not carrying a weapon, none at all, and moving slow?"

Fleur smiled nervously. "Oui. Very slow." She passed her weapons back to Bobby before easing forward a bit at a time until she stood inside. The French Trooper released her pent-up breath. "Come and look."

"Why not?" Because a laser might turn him into a grease spot, Bobby thought, but put his weapons on the floor with hers and moved slowly to come alongside Fleur. The lasers followed every movement but didn't fire. "They are guards to stop someone who tries to break in, not to stop someone trying the door controls."

"Unless we get the controls wrong, give the wrong command." Fleur sighed. "Just one of those carbins might be enough to kill all the Rangers and Shiva's." Bobby thought she might be right. The rifle or laser just looked the part, gleaming, lethal, Alien perfection. Somehow he just knew even a Super's jacket wouldn't slow it up.

Bobby sighed as well. "Perhaps we'll pull back slowly before I stick my arm through the bars and try to grab something, even a pistol?"

"Ha, yes. I really want to try." They both retreated, reluctantly.

Once outside they looked into the room until the light went out, then Bobby retrieved his knife. He played his laser on the control until the doors slid together. "I daren't leave it open. Somebody would have to try."

"What about the hospital?" Fleur scowled. "Or abattoir."

"We'll let them all look at that. Maybe someone will work out what it does or how to start it up if that's a hospital because we need help. Perhaps

Siflis can help because he seems to understand this stuff a bit better than the rest of us. Bells needs more than first aid for his arm, and I doubt the reinforcements will bring a surgeon." Bobby's face twisted in disgust. "They probably expect us all to be dead." He looked around the central area and the corridor leading away in both directions. "I doubt they'll bring engineers and electricians or code breakers either."

"At least Bells will have a nurse soon." Fleur sniggered. "Ecarlate volunteered to sit with him after she sleeps and before she goes on guard duty."

"Has she taken off her leggings as well?"

"Yes. Though Bells only gets to look just now, not check if her stockings are real. Do you think he will feel better?" Since Fleur had started giggling she already knew.

Bobby gave up and let the laughter come. "He'll be reporting for duty and offering to go on patrol with her."

*　*　*

Unfortunately for Bells, doubling up on a shift with anyone else wasn't an option. Mickey had divided time into six periods of four hours, because the light never altered and they all needed downtime and sleep. Now everyone spent two periods on guard, with each shift needing three Troopers. One had to guard the ladders with another guard at each barricade, which meant Bells had to stand his shift but on his own, though he did get to sleep the same time as Ecarlate. They all worked for at least part of their other eight hours' downtime, simply because there wasn't much else to do and food and defences had to be organised as soon as possible. A low barricade at the end of the cross passageway ensured that a grenade thrown up the corridor would have little effect. All edible food stocks they'd found so far were transferred to the sleeping quarters on the lower balcony in case they had to retreat that far, and the remaining bins were relocked.

This first evening without a Super, Fleur put her spacesuit back on and Bobby took her to make contact with Aggie and the rocket. He could now make the trip in relative safety because storage bins had been used to build a high barricade two bins thick right across the corridor, with a guard behind it. Borrowing the idea from the Rangers a second, lower barricade went across four metres feet behind the first. The airlock entrance now lay safely behind the second barricade. "Do you want to come in while I report?"

Fleur didn't answer straight away. "Yes, but not because I do not trust you. I want you to hear when I report, so you can be sure of what I said. Are you sure your capsule will report what I say?" Bobby noticed again how good her Anglic became when Fleur really thought about it.

"I don't know but if we tell them about the bridge they'll want us to hold it any way possible. Providing we really are allowed to negotiate contracts, then when Aggie reports what we agreed the UKs will have a legal contract with FAC. That's what we call you, Franco-African Combine." Bobby had never thought about the next part. "What do you call your bloc?"

"Francais-Africaine Combinez, so still FAC." Mischief showed in her smile. "You are UR, Unis Royaumes, or Rosbif which means roast beef. I don't know why. Why are we, les Francais, called Frogs?"

"I don't know. Everyone says that even on the news viewers and vids." Bobby gestured at the outer airlock door. "Once we've put our helmets on we can only talk by touching them, because my coms won't talk to Fr... Francais. My command link for contacting Mickey also lets me talk to Aggie."

"I know. You already told me three times. I have Pepee's coms but we have no capsule to contact." Fleur sighed. "For luck, ami."

Bobby smiled when she gave him another of those ammee kisses on the lips before he clipped his helmet on. Once locked in he pushed the handle to open the outside door but, as Mickey had reported, the door didn't move at first. The purple lights changed one by one to yellow, danger, and his suit inflated as the ship sucked air from the airlock. Once the fifth light glowed yellow Bobby pushed on the handle and the door opened.

Bobby flinched for a moment as two sections of his faceplate lit up with the radar and camera views from Aggie. He'd forgotten about those. He put his helmet to Fleur's as she followed him into the bubble created in the ice when the door opened. "Are you receiving radar and camera pictures from your capsule?"

"Non. There is nothing from our radio. Les Allemandes laser destroyed the radio or computer on our capsule. Will Aggie hear me?"

"One moment. Keep your helmet in contact so you can hear." Bobby tongued the com. "Trooper Sergeant Three Bobby B reporting to Aggie. Supervisor McKay has been killed in action, report follows." Bobby gave a short account of the fight. "The FAC Supervisor has also been killed, and as the senior remaining UKs member in the spaceship, I have negotiated a treaty with the senior FAC member. We have agreed to defend access to the bridge of the Alien spaceship and an entry point for UKs and FAC reinforcements. We have sufficient food and water to last for a while. End report and send."

"Report received and stored for transmission. Two messages for Supervisor McKay. Please record."

"Recording."

"Message one: Area Manager Gunnar Eriksson for Supervisor McKay. Maintain defence of an access point at all costs. Negotiate contract with other blocs to achieve objective if necessary. Attempt contract for access to engines or any controls. We are six or seven sleep periods from contact, depending on deceleration timing. Each bloc has sent a rocket with nine capsules. Our capsules contain all the Basteds, auxiliaries and heavy weapons. We are assured that this rocket holds manoeuvring fuel, and supplies for two months, and a re-supply rocket is following. Out."

"Message received." Bobby's mind whirled. Guns would be here in another six or seven days? Why hadn't the basteds in Control said so? Because there wasn't enough air, food or water to last even that long. If the Basteds hadn't found extra, they'd be dying or dead by now and never get the message because that sodin mothership rocket hadn't even given up food now, after finding the sodin bridge. Unless it waited for Control to send a message, but Bobby didn't have much faith in that.

"Message two: UKs Control. Vital maintain control of airlock by any means. Out. End of messages."

"Message received." Bobby paused. "Can you relay a message from the FAC representative to Area Manager Eriksson, UKs Control and the FAC Control?"

"All transmissions from any bloc are recorded and forwarded to UKs

Control. Messages for Area Supervisor Gunnar Eriksson will also be transmitted to Control."

"What have the Shivas and Rangers been saying?" Bobby spoke in pure reflex, then tried to remember the proper letters for the two blocs.

"This software cannot read the content of messages from other blocs." Bobby cursed softly. He'd tried Mickey's coms but there must be some biometrics in the contacts, since he detected a short burst of transmission but didn't get the words.

Fleur disturbed his thoughts. "I will transmit, and your Aggie will forward it to your Control. The message will record that we have a contract. Your Control should honour that, as they have told you to negotiate. Then we decide what to tell them about how we survived." Bobby wasn't so sure that would work, but kept quiet. "I will transmit now, but in Anglic and will tell them it is so that you know I am honouring that contract." Fleur paused and then began to speak formally in Anglic.

She gave details of the death of Aigu and the wounds to herself and Ecarlate, and blamed the death of her Supervisor on enemy action. That meant adapting everyone's recollection of what had really happened at the Putes end of the corridor, and would mean using up some captured ammo to shred the knife wounds. At the end she paused, and presumably stopped the transmission. "All done. Merde, I hope your Control agree."

"All finished?"

"Oui, but I would like to stay here for a little while. To see the stars." The blue ship lights still suffused the ice and tinted the sharp points of interstellar light, but the stars were visible. With a shock Bobby realised the brightest must be the sun, his sun! A much brighter star, but not bright enough to activate the darkening in his faceplate. Until then Bobby hadn't really processed how far he'd come from home. His arm tightened around Fleur. Hers returned the pressure through the thick suit.

They crouched there for a while, arms around each other, until Bobby sighed. "We should save the air in the suits." He waved a hand up at the view. "We should let everyone see this. Though maybe we should not tell them just how close help is, since they will all work out it isn't close enough."

"We should let them come and see, and talk about the rest later. All of us should realise we are on our own even when reinforcements get here, that nobody will come quickly if we need help." Fleur broke the helmet contract and turned away to re-enter the ship. When the lights inside glowed yellow and she removed her helmet, she rubbed at her eyes before turning to face Bobby. "We need each other now." A few moments later Bobby wondered if that ammee kiss might be reassurance for Fleur as well as him, and reminded himself that Les Putes were trained to fool men. Though a part of him stayed fooled.

As each trio came back from the airlock they walked closer together, and in deep thought. Bobby and Fleur explained the new version of the fight. Pepee looked unhappy but agreed to it after Fleur reminded her that otherwise Control would blame the Sergeant-chef for not protecting her Super. Fleur and Bobby fired half a clip of Ranger flechettes into the Frog Super at point blank range, split between the knife wounds. Magpie had more or less gelded him which explained the high pitch of his scream, then opened his belly, then finished him by cutting his throat. The body went into an emptied storage bin, as had the others, sealed away where it wouldn't smell when Fleur closed the lid properly.

As they loaded the body a small metallic object came out of the wall and scooted across the floor, cleaning up the spent flechettes and shredded cloth and meat. They had appeared after the battle, and then to clean up the spillage when the French Super died. The little machines disappeared afterwards into hatches close to the floor though they could also clean walls and the ceiling. This time, for the first time, one of the little lizards appeared and worked over the area. From the number of times the little creature stopped and licked, the robot missed some.

Bobby watched the lizard scuttle away along the wall. "There must be a way out of the bridge."

"Or a way in, one big enough for them." Fleur chuckled. "Maybe we've just started to make enough mess to attract them?"

"That's us, sloppy Troopers." Bobby thought a moment. "Can we talk privately now, about the message? About how close the reinforcements are?"

"Oui." A hint of mischief showed. "In your room or mine, or have you found a bath?"

Bobby grinned. "You would still be safe. Though in a few days? We could empty a bin and fill it with water, though I'd want to heat it up with a laser before getting in." They both laughed, because Fleur hadn't actually said she would be interested. In fact, she kept emphasising the Putes were fighters, not Divas, even if those kisses and leaving her legs uncovered kept arguing the other way.

"My room then, or I might stay in yours until you feel better." The mischief showed in her eyes now. "Maybe that would make Pepee jealous."

"I'm not sure I can manage more than one amie." Especially since Pepee might stick a knife in him to even up for the Super. Though once in Fleur's room, both of them sobered. "Guns is on a bigger Gaza Taxi, because they must have left soon after us. The Basteds must have been training before we took off, even when we lost our legs. Control had no idea what would be waiting."

"There must be rocket full of women like us, more squads of Trooper women, Chiennes. Our squad is Les Putes, like yours are Beebi's Basteds, but all the women who are Troopers are called the Chiennes. Maybe because we haven't got a bad enough Basted or bitch to boss them." She sat and stared at the floor, all hint of humour gone. "Nine rockets, all Gaza Taxis. We say bateau a Douvres, boat to Dover. Why didn't they send them quicker, to help us?" Fleur seemed hesitant, as if maybe she had an answer but hoped Bobby had a better one.

"So they get our reports in time for everyone to make their alliances. I'll bet there never was enough air on our capsules or rockets. Shite! Is there a supply rocket really coming for them, or are they all expected to die as well?" Bobby paled, someone had found a way to deal with the Basteds and the Duchess had gone with it. Maybe they'd finished the jobs management had needed them for.

"Some will live even if most of them die. They have two months air and supplies. If most of them die, the rest will have enough for six months." Fleur had paled as well and they had their arms around each other. "If the Chiennes or your Guns realise they will attack the others, to steal supplies. They'll all do it, attack the rest."

"This time with auxiliaries and heavy weapons, not a few extras hidden in the metal legs. There'll be a full scale war in here." Bobby frowned, thinking fast. "We have to hold one airlock, so that our people can hold this end. The bridge is a good bargaining point and will bring allies."

"We are already allies." Fleur sighed. "By then some of us might be very close allies, and that might cause trouble." Her sigh became a small smile. "It will be too late by the time the others arrive."

Bobby grinned. "If another two dozen arrive with legs like yours Bells will burst something. He'll want to check all of them to find out which ones have real stockings."

"You haven't checked yet, about my stockings." Mischief sparkled in Fleur's eyes. "That might take your mind off rockets and taxis."

"When I check those, I might want to check other secrets. Then you'll say no, and I'll beat my head on a wall." Bobby smiled. "Though you have taken my mind off rocket taxis, maybe because I can't do anything about them. Do we tell the rest that Control really did send help but timed so we would all be dead?"

"I want to think about that. We should sleep first, then we can decide. Maybe our people will fight harder to help friends, or maybe they won't care because nobody cares about us." Fleur removed her arms. "Now you must leave before we wrestle and I handcuff you and keep you here."

"You won't need handcuffs if that's what you want." Bobby yawned. "Enough for today." He went to the door and Fleur followed.

She kissed him on the cheek. "Dormez bien," Fleur smiled. "That means sleep well."

"Dormey been, Fleur." She laughed and waved as he left, and Bobby grinned and shook his head. He'd end up speaking Frog before he'd done. Fransey, not Frog. Though if the contract held, that might be a good thing. It would be harder for them to keep secrets if he understood his allies. Bobby decided to try harder with this French thing, since Fleur kept translating when she used it.

He headed for bed, nodding to Bells on his four-hour guard duty by the ladders, sat on a bin. They hadn't enough Troopers for anyone to stay in a sick bay even if Bells and Ecarlate, Red, had to sleep in a ground floor room because they couldn't climb these ladders one-handed. Siflis had the job of stopping those two from going viral or pooching on duty, because the whole group had now split into three shifts.

Bobby stripped and washed, then put on the antiseptic cream. He smiled quietly, wondering how long Ecarlate and Bells would leave it. The French Trooper had decided that because she had a wound she should sleep in sick bay as well, and Bells would certainly try to persuade her into his bed once he could stand the pain. Bobby laid on the padded oblong, which made a comfortable bed, and covered himself with a thin sheet. The sheets of fabric found in a bin could be anything, but seemed to be insulated and everyone claimed one as a blanket so they could get rid of their uniforms at night.

*   *   *

Bobby's eyes flew open because someone had come into the room. He cursed silently because he'd turned in his sleep and couldn't see in the door. He tensed, ready to dive over the edge of the padding, but someone giggled. "I am not aiming a weapon, Beebi."

Fleur! He turned over to see her stood in the doorway, looking a little embarrassed or unsure. "Come in. I'd get up but that might frighten you." Bobby glanced at his uniform on the floor.

"Maybe not." Fleur sat on the edge of his bed. "But I don't want poochy."

"I know, you said."

Fleur sighed. "But I do want to hold someone tonight." She sighed again. "All the stars, and la Soleil, and Terre, Earth, all so far away. All the Troopers out there in taxis. So many sent out to die, supposed to die, and now we will live." Fleur suddenly giggled again. "What are you wearing?"

"My shorts." Bobby thought furiously. He could do this, just hold. Maybe. Another part of him pointed out if Fleur slept in here, she could kill him if her Control told her to break the contract. Though if Guns told him the same, to kill her? Bobby sighed. "No poochy, just hold?" Because bottom and last he felt bledrin lonely himself after seeing that big bright star.

Fleur giggled again, and still looked unsure, which really did seem out of character. Considering what she'd said about how Les Putes killed enemy Supers she must have got into strange beds before. Bobby smiled a little, though not as strange a bed as this. Fleur took a breath. "Then you will get to see another strategic secret."

"I could turn around?" Though he didn't want to.

Fleur laughed. "But you will know anyway when I get into the bed." She opened the seam on her jacket. "Nothing like Magpie's." No, but Bobby thought the silky bra and the brief silky shorts under her Trooper gear looked every bit as sexy. More so, because after all Magpie was the squad sister, a Trooper, a Beebi's Basted. Then he stopped thinking clearly because Fleur got into the bed and cuddled up.

"This might be bledrin difficult. Holding without touching?"

"Non. I didn't say you couldn't touch." Fleur pulled his arm round her and laid on it. "Just no poochy, or that sort of touching. Oke? You are Oke doing that?" Fleur still seemed hesitant, unsure about that.

"Oke, no poochy and careful holding." Bobby kept trying to ignore the fact that he hadn't been near a Diva for over six months. That became harder as Fleur wriggled an arm down his side and threw the other over his chest, then rested her head on his shoulder.

"Hold me tight Beebi Basted. Keep me safe." She sniggered. "Tomorrow or maybe the next night we can compare scars, but just now I need sleep." With that Fleur gave him one of those ammee kisses on his lips, wriggled in a bit more and relaxed. Bobby laid for a bit thinking about how an ammee kiss seemed a lot more Diva undressed like this, then drifted off as well.

*　　*　　*

When he woke up Bobby found that the shorts felt silky as well as looking that way since he'd put his hand on her ass in his sleep, though Fleur's slow stretch and smile didn't seem to mind. In fact, the stretch confirmed the bra also felt silky since she rubbed it over his chest. "A good sleep, much better. Merci, Beebi ami."

"Mercy?"

"That means thank you. Bonjour is good morning."

This was a hell of a way to have a French lesson! "Bonjour, amie Fleur." Bobby returned the amie kiss from last night, on her lips, and removed his hand. Then he admired the view as Fleur stood, stretched again, and put on her uniform. She turned with a grin.

"Now you. That is only fair?" She held out his pants. Bobby laughed and threw off the covers. He felt self-conscious about his metal legs as he got dressed, because although he hadn't cared before they were crude attempts compared to Fleur's. He put on his weapons, realising that Fleur had brought none at all. She must have understood the look. "Maybe I can bring some weapons tonight?"

Bobby didn't even hesitate. Fleur could have made it out of his bed and to his carbin or shotgun in the night any time she'd wanted. He'd have woken up, but much too late to stop her. Not only that but he'd liked waking up with a silky ass under his hand, and the smile that came with it. "Bring them all. It will save you going to get them in the morning." Bobby laughed. "We aren't supposed to share beds with other Troopers but the rules don't mention foreign Troopers. I'll risk it if you will."

"It's a bit too late to say no. Maybe this is a part of our contract?" They walked out laughing. Pepee stopped dead halfway around the balcony, mouth open, then frowned and turned away.

"Will she be a problem? Pepee?" Bobby watched her stalk back into a room. Down below Bells, sat by the ladders on his second four-hour shift, grinned and rolled his eyes at Bobby and Fleur.

"I will speak to her." Fleur sighed. "Ecarlate and Bells are sharing a room already even if it is the sick room, and maybe Baiser and Siflis will get closer once they know each other better. We all watched Pepee come out of the Super's room every morning, so she should understand. Unless she gets to Siflis before Baiser." Fleur grinned and patted Bobby's shoulder. "Maybe she will move in with Bells and Ecarlate?" The Putes all knew nobody would be splitting Hood and Magpie, because now her secret was out the pair had gone back to hand holding and kissing.

"May the ultimate CEO and his blessed minions help us all if that happens. I'll end up shooting Bells to stop the bragging if he gets two women." Bobby set off down a ladder to check the guards. "I'll be back soon and we can work out what to do next. I really worry about those ladders and floating holes." Bobby also wanted to work through the Putes sharing out the men and Fleur choosing to sleep with him. Poochy or not, that was some thought.

After checking on Siflis and Ecarlate at the barricades, Bobby talked with Fleur while they ate. The breakfast now consisted of well over half ship food, with a lot of meat because everyone thought that might produce less solids. Three new types of food might be fruit, and might help with the solids problem, so Hood's shift had tried them. If nobody reacted in another eight hours everyone would include them in meals. Everyone's stomachs were gurgling and most were passing wind, but nobody felt really ill yet. That might happen in another two days when the last drops of liquid food were gone.

Both agreed they should tell the rest about Guns and the rest. After all the worrying by Bobby and Fleur, the Troopers didn't even seem surprised about the reinforcements and that they would have arrived too late. "Can you imagine the look on the faces in Control, when they know Beebi's Basteds will be looking for payback?" Bells wore a huge smile in spite of the pain from his arm. "Better still, they'll have to pay us those lovely bonuses."

Baiser cracked her knuckles and smiled back. "Some might have to eat a bullet because when we collect our pay and bonuses it will ruin the budgets."

"We might have some help when we go for payback." Everyone looked at Pepee. "I don't believe there will a supply rocket following the reinforcements, so the survivors will be as unhappy as we are."

"True, especially if we can get our people in here without a big fight. We'll have a good position with food and water." Bobby frowned. "They'll have to send someone they trust in the end, to take control of the ship."

"But not Troopers like us. Control will want picked men or women in charge out here, not the survivors of the rough, nasty Troopers they've sent first." Fleur's face twisted in anger and she spat. "Legion!" From the looks around her, the survivors were working up a good hate for Control.

"I hope the third rocket, the one sent after Guns is supposed to have carked it, brings some senior management to take over." Magpie's blissful smile didn't fool anyone. "Someone we can throw out of an airlock so they can try surviving without enough air and food."

Siflis scowled. "They'll send someone to stop us doing that. Squaddies and Legion, that sort of somebody."

"We'll want to get our reinforcements inside the ship as soon as possible, and keep down casualties, because we'll need every fighter. Squaddies and Legion are better trained and will come equipped to deal with us." Fleur put a hand on Bobby's. "But they can only get through airlock doors one at a time, so if we stick together we can stop them."

Bobby had the last word. "If the Rangers will talk before starting a fight again, I'll explain it all. There's enough to share, and that way we all stand a better chance of surviving." Everyone seemed determined but confident after the talk. They broke up to work or take rest breaks, talking together in pairs or trios as they went.

Fleur and Bobby went exploring, up and down one floor with their weapons ready but the corridors at each end of the ladders were empty. Unfortunately, they were also indefensible because someone could come from a higher or lower floor. The Basteds and Putes simply didn't have enough Troopers to push out further. The pair climbed six floors but the ladders just kept going up, though every three floors the next hole and ladder were offset so anything dropped could only go down that far. If the floors were all five metres feet apart, and went all the way to the top and bottom, there could be up to forty floors each way.

The day passed in strengthening barricades and moving supplies as more proven food went into bins nearer or inside their sleeping quarters. The rest, which hadn't been tested or stank that badly nobody fancied it, went into resealed bins left in storerooms or used for barricades. Other bins had more of the bedsheets and some smaller versions, and items that made no sense at all. Those bins were all in rooms without food. Some were used to thicken the forward barricades in case the Rangers had more of those rockets. Bobby skipped the evening message to Aggie since he didn't want to know if Control had rejected an alliance and expected him to kill the Putes. He'd begun to wonder if he could, in cold blood.

Alien Metal

The second night both were a lot more relaxed about sharing a bed, and Bobby could enjoy the view because Fleur wasn't at all shy about showing her underwear. They laughed and joked about scars because both had plenty though Fleur admitted defeat, Bobby had more. Then after finding out Bobby had been collecting them for over ten years she stopped laughing and inspected him. "How old are you, Beebi?"

"Twenty-six. Just."

Fleur looked shocked. "You were a Timer at what age? Fourteen, fifteen?"

"Fifteen." Bobby had stopped smiling now. "A friend wanted another body to back off any other gangs at a demonstration and I already looked big enough and old enough. I said 'yes' for the extra creds to help out my Ma. Then it kicked off, and went viral, and the Troopers netted us all. I came in near enough sixteen to be offered the choice. The deep mines, death penalty or join up."

"Death? For what?"

"Someone shot a Trooper when they came to break up the demonstration. That made us all guilty, even if we had no gun and were three blocks away." Bobby took a deep breath and let the bitterness go again. He'd buried that long ago, or thought he had. "I was no innocent, nobody is in a Britmine complex, but I never killed anyone. Not until I joined up." He forced a smile. "So how old are you?"

She laughed. "Non, no, la femme never says." Fleur stopped laughing, sighed and cuddled in a little. "I said no to an offer for stolen goods, and he didn't like it. The next time I sold something black market the Troopers were waiting, and arrested me as a pute, a Diva, and a thief. My choice was between what you call a spam palace or the Army. The justice, judge, sentenced me to a spam palace because someone told them I was already a Diva. He offered me the Army because I was a Diva with a knife. I wasn't a Diva but I had already used a knife a few times, a girl has to if she sells black market, so I chose Les Chiennes. They taught me to use a knife properly." Fleur shivered.

"It doesn't matter. You don't have to tell me."

"I want you to understand why we are like this, Les Putes and the rest of the Chiennes." Fleur sighed. "We are all taught to fight." She hesitated a moment before continuing. "But we also have to learn to be Divas. Though not putain, cheap ones. I had three months training in la bagnio. I had to pooch the officers, and learn to do it properly to be a courtisane, high class Diva. We use the training to help us go undercover. That is why our bloc has some women Troopers, the Chiennes. We are Divas who kill, sent out to infiltrate and assassinate or just cause confusion and unrest. I have served seven years with Les Chiennes, the last three in this squad, Les Putes. We called our squad that because officers always think we are only good for pooching anyway."

"Shite. So you had no choice, you get to be a Diva anyway?" Bobby wondered how the women he'd visited had ended up as Divas or spam. He'd always thought they did it to get out of the complexes, if he thought at all. Maybe they'd stood in a court and been given a choice of bad futures, and Diva had been the best?

"This is the best of two bad choices. In a spam palace the girl cannot say no, but as Chiennes we get to kill some of them, the men, and can say no most times. Though our officers all have a poochy girl, and sometimes the Legion officers come to visit. We are allowed to kill any others if they try but if we can't stop them, that is called training." This time Fleur hugged Bobby really hard and from her voice she also had a lot of bitterness hidden inside someplace. "If all the Basteds had been waiting for a poochy party, it would have been my fault if I didn't escape."

Something suddenly hit Bobby, because he'd never really thought of it that way. "Magpie might have ended up with those choices if she'd ended up in a court." Bobby explained Magpie and how she ended up sort of his squad sister. "Maybe our squad treat women a bit different because of Magpie though we still go to Divas, except Hood. Actually Bells is still obsessed with pooching, so maybe Magpie is just a special case to him." Bobby sniggered. "Magpie is really pissed about your legs."

"You haven't checked if my stockings are real yet?" Fleur lifted the cover and looked down. "Can you tell?"

"I'm not sure, and I want it to come as a nice surprise if you let me find out. I wouldn't want to try something and lose the amie thing, the friend bit." Bobby gave her an amie kiss. "Like that."

Fleur laughed. "Maybe it is time I told you what ami really means. Friend." She gave him a small kiss on the cheek, smaller than recent ones. "Or boyfriend." This one, on his lips, felt a lot more like the recent versions, maybe even longer and Bobby kissed back. Still not Diva though, and that confused him.

"So is it amie or boyfriend, you and me?"

"Amie means girlfriend if you say it. You never had a girlfriend?" Bobby didn't answer. "Ah, a Timer at fifteen so just the Divas?"

Bobby sighed. "Yes."

Fleur giggled. "This is an ami kiss, boyfriend ami." Another longish soft kiss followed, and Bobby began to think more about Divas. "This is Diva."

By the time she'd done Bobby had her held tight and close with a hand gripping her ass. "Shite! Don't do that again unless you mean it. I've not been near a Diva for over six months!" He released his grip and took his hand off the silky shorts. "Sorry."

"Boyfriends get to stroke there, gently." Bobby realised that Fleur still held him tightly. "Sometimes a boyfriend gets more, but then it isn't poochy. With a boyfriend it is faire l'amour, and definitely not Trooper and Diva poochy."

"I get it, no poochy. Just a cuddle at night." Bobby wondered if he could keep to that, though right now pain would stop any attempt at anything. Maybe if he healed too well, Pepee might be interested in poochy to take the pressure off?

"No poochy and no l'amour, not just now." Fleur chuckled. "But if you stay good until I feel better, maybe you will find out which I want?" The young woman hesitated. "Because I have decided that this time it will be what I want, not as a job. I will tell the rest tomorrow." She pulled Bobby's hand back onto her shorts. "Hold me tight tonight, Beebi." Her head came down on his shoulder, she sighed, and was asleep. Bobby had no idea how Fleur did that, relaxed and went to sleep in moments. He spent a long time getting his head round what she'd said, and thought he might not need Pepee after all. Providing he only stroked Fleur's shorts gently. Confusion gradually blended into sleep.

*   *   *

Bonjour ami kissing involved Fleur giving his ass a little squeeze, which startled Bobby and made her laugh. As they came out, settling their weapons and still laughing about Bobby's attempts at French, Pepee had her back to them. She climbed down a ladder and set off down the corridor to the bog without looking back. Before they could climb down Bobby's tapper signalled four times. An alarm from Siflis! Bells stiffened, then stood up from his position by the ladders and looked up at Bobby. Bobby gestured. "Go and back him up."

Bells started jogging up the corridor, the little Kraut automatic swinging from a sling as he cradled his injured arm with his free hand. Fleur turned to Bobby but before she spoke Hood and Magpie burst out of their room, still sealing their jackets but with weapons already slung. "Is it an attack?" Even as Hood asked they all heard a carbin rattling down the corridor.

"Go on, back up Siflis while I tell Fleur." Bobby turned to Fleur. "Siflis sounded the alarm with his tapper. Let the Putes know what's happening and send who you can." A shotgun boomed. "They're getting close if he's used the shotgun."

Fleur pushed. "Go, l will send the others." Bobby climbed down as fast as he could, cursing the strange ladders with their weird spacing, then set off running. Ahead he heard more carbin fire and saw Hood and Magpie pause at the corner, look, and then run out of sight. An explosion echoed followed by the ripping sound of Bells's Kraut.

By the time Bobby reached the corner, Hood came back round, towing Siflis by his collar. Carbin fire sounded then Magpie backed around the corner, festooned with the weapons kept at the barricade and shooting as she came. "A rocket blew a hole in the barricade. There's no blood on Siflis, or not a lot so he's not shot." Bells followed, firing off another clip with the Kraut. Not aimed shots because one-handed the thing threw rounds everywhere.

Magpie put her head round the corner but pulled back when a carbin tried to shoot her. She put her carbin round to let off half a clip. "There's four still coming and they've got a shield, a piece of metal to stop plastic flechettes even close up."

"Bells, get back and cover the ladders to free up someone who can go hand to hand." Bells glared but set off back up the corridor. Siflis groaned and tried to sit up, then fell back. He had no helmet now so something had hit him hard. "Lie still Siflis, and let Hood drag you because it's quicker. Hood, get him back to the centre. With that metal shield they'll get right up close and then stick carbins or shotguns round this corner. Set up behind a few bins this side of the hospital corridor." That would allow Hood to cover Bobby's retreat. "Ask someone to throw you the toe gun." With luck that would go through the shelving. Magpie fired another short burst, pulling her head back as a carbin replied.

"Where do you want help?" Baiser had her carbin ready.

"We've lost the barricade and they've got a shield. Help Hood to get Siflis back there." The pair set off at a run, dragging the scout. Bobby moved forward, stuck his shotgun round the corner, let both barrels go and peeked. The attackers had fastened two shelves together so nothing showed around the edges. "Come on Magpie, run like hell." Ahead of them Hood and Baiser tumbled Siflis over the bins and followed. Pepee had taken up a position in the nearest junction but as Bobby and Magpie ran past he waved Pepee to follow. "Come on, back to the others." Pepee let off half a clip towards the corner, then joined him and Magpie in their dash.

Either they ran fast enough or Pepee's flechettes slowed the attack, but either way everyone got over the bins and dropped flat before the attack reached the corner. At least three carbins and a shotgun poked around the corner and ripped off half clips but at over three hundred metres the hail of flechettes hadn't the power to bother a Trooper jacket. Hood grinned, brandishing the leg with one toe attached. "This made a hole in that shelf Mickey carried, so get ready with the shotgun."

Bells waved the Kraut. "Knock the bledrin shelf out of the way and this'll sort it."

"Why are you here, Bells? Where's Fleur and Ecarlate? Is there another attack?" Bobby looked back towards the other guard post and Fleur showed her head around the door from the ladder room.

She showed her shotgun, briefly. "Ecarlate is watching for an attack the other way and I am guarding the ladders. I can shoot from here if they charge you. How many are coming?"

"I saw four. Two of them were bandaged but shooting well enough. Then they put that shield up." Magpie sounded frustrated. "The flechettes just bounce off it and won't go through jackets anyway except close up."

"There were five. I dropped one with the shotgun but then that bledrin rocket came in." Siflis sat up, but Baiser pushed him flat.

"Stay down. We are behind bins." Siflis jerked his head round, startled, then smiled at her.

"Last I remember was the barricade." He patted himself. "Someone give me a carbin. Where's my helmet?"

"Back there. If you saw five, we've got some missing." Bobby turned round and shouted. "Fleur, warn Ecarlate there's two missing." He paused. "Use coms because it doesn't matter now. Everyone is here."

"Except the two SEPA. If they joined up, we've got a problem." Bells glared at the carbins. "Plastic ammo! The basteds sent us out here to fight aliens with plastic ammo!"

Magpie glared. "These aren't aliens and plastic is all they've got as well. We can't hurt each other seriously except close up where it gets bloody, but we can't hurt property either. Which bit do you think matters to Control?" She paused. "Beebi, you hit one with a solid finger shot when Mickey carked it?" Bobby nodded and Magpie frowned. "Maybe one of the others got hurt by Mickey's grenade." Baiser put her head up and fired a short burst.

Pepee moved a bin and looked through the gap she'd made. "They are coming behind the shield."

"Let them get nearly to the next junction, the nearest one, and then tell us." Bobby glanced at the leg with one toe laid by Hood. "Will that solid toe really go through a shelf from here, Hood?"

"It should when they get a bit nearer, Beebi. That corridor isn't much over fifty metres away." Hood sniggered. "That'll be a shock for the basteds. Be ready with the carbins."

"Yeah, but we've only got plastic flechettes, no notsi ammo. I wish

338

we'd found the Frog Super's grenade. It wasn't in his feet." Bobby caught Baiser staring. "Sorry, Francais Super."

She smiled. "I didn't know about the foot, only that your Super had a grenade. Frog doesn't bother me, if Rosbif is Oke with you?"

Siflis sniggered. "I don't care what you call me, just smile when you do it."

Baiser smiled wider at Siflis. "Oke, Rosbif."

"Nearly there." Pepee didn't sound happy, but that might be the people coming to try and kill her. "Now."

Hood must have been waiting because the shot echoed her words, knocking the shield back before it twisted and dropped down. Baiser, Siflis and Pepee emptied their carbins, while Bobby and Magpie fired shotguns before adding their flechettes. Men were down and rolling about yelling, someone started screaming, and for a moment Bobby thought they'd done it. Then a storm of gunfire burst out behind!

"Beebi!" The shooting came from inside the ladder room, carbins and a shotgun. Fleur staggered back out of the doors, frantically trying to get her carbin up and backing towards Bobby. She turned as another burst hit her, chewing into her arm and throwing her sideways. Fleur staggered a few more steps towards the rest of them before crumpling. Bobby leapt to his feet, cramming more shells into the shotgun and running forward. He dropped, rolling sideways as a carbin barrel came round the edge of the door from the ladders and opened up with a long burst. Behind him someone cried out as Bobby fired a shotgun barrel, came back onto his feet and kept running.

"Keep shooting at them. I'll cover Beebi." Hood would need time to get set so as a head showed from the ladder room Bobby let go the other barrel and kept running. The head moved back too quickly for a hit he thought, but it would keep the basted cautious. Bobby bent to grab Fleur's collar and started dragging her, shocked by the amount of blood because she wore the Frog Super's jacket. Flechettes shouldn't go through!

"Beebi!" Flechettes flew past from the ladder room as Hood shouted. Bobby glanced up, firing the carbin one-handed. He kept dragging Fleur as the Trooper in the doorway threw himself sideways inside again.

"Into the corridor, come on, quick." Bobby glanced back to see Baiser crumpled up behind the bins. Bells sat hunched over his arm, the Kraut on the floor nearby, while Pepee blazed away wildly down the corridor. "Magpie, bring Baiser with you then give cover." Hood lay flat, aiming his carbin past Bobby at the ladder room. Bobby left him to it, because at this range Hood could shoot the nuts off a bat so he'd hit a head. Beyond the low line of bins one of the attackers lay still while four were crawling or staggering into the nearby corridor, trying to get away from Pepee's hail of flechettes. Their wounded man had caught up but it hadn't done him much good.

Bobby took it all in at a glance then concentrated on dragging Fleur, with his free hand on the slung carbin. He wouldn't hit anything, but might make the other bloke flinch and miss. At the last minute Bobby swerved in towards the corridor, so he only blocked Hood's line of fire for a few seconds. Hood followed him into cover, dragging a startled Pepee with him. For a moment Bobby thought she'd swing the carbin towards him, then she snapped out of it. From the litter of clips she left, it might be empty anyway.

"Bells?" He looked up as Bobby shouted, face sheet white.

"Same arm. Hurts." Though he'd picked up his Kraut before staggering into cover.

"Baiser?" Magpie looked up while wrapping a bandage around the woman's head.

"A solid round hit her helmet. She'll live but she's out for now." Magpie glanced back at the end of the corridor. "A solid hit my leg, maybe two." Bobby looked down at Fleur in sudden understanding. Someone in the ladder room had steel flechettes!

Fleur's eyes flickered open. "Two on ropes. Down ladders." She spat blood. "Super jackets but got one." Her eyes closed again and Bobby tried to see how bad she'd been hit. Then he sighed.

"Hood? You got a GV?"

Fleur's eyes flicked open again. "No. Hospital." Bobby opened his mouth to say there wasn't one, then realised what she meant. He waved away the hypodermic Hood offered.

"Hey, Beebi Basted. You still alive?" Beebi recognised the American voice.

"Waiting to carve you a new one."

"No chance. You lost one at least, three wounded bad and maybe dead." Flechettes whined down the corridor. "One is stranded down the other end and you're cut off from food and water. At most you've got three up for hand to hand and I've got twice that."

"Bulsh. We can count and you just lost three more." Bobby forced a laugh. "We've got enough food and water, and the one at that end can let in our reinforcements. Game over, Ranger boy."

"Sound off SEPA." Two voices sounded speaking with what might be an Australian accent. "Your count is off and they brought solid flechettes. I'll send one of them off to come up behind that Frog dame all on her own."

"Luck with that. Your count is off and your man will run into the Frog Super. Better yet, he knows about the solid rounds now, and he's got his own surprise." Bobby kept talking but his brain worked on the problem, and it didn't look good. He'd got four if it came to close up, but those solid rounds had pooched him completely. They'd go through a Trooper or even a Super jacket at these ranges, and even knock a metal leg out temporarily.

At least he'd made the basted Ranger slow up, because he didn't sound so sure now. Not beaten though. "I didn't hear that Frog Super shouting, so I reckon you dealt with him. No problem in any case. The one at the other end will have to be lucky with flechettes at this range so we'll sort you out and give her the option. She can shoot the Super or we get her from both sides." The Ranger sounded more confident as he spoke. "We can get close enough here to hit you from both sides with all seven of us. Give it up, Beebi."

Bobby kept his voice down. "Pepee?" She looked round, startled. "Tell Ecarlate to loose off a short burst at anyone trying to sneak up. Just a few to let us know, then we'll stick a shotgun round the corner. Use the tapper so they don't realise." Pepee looked back blankly for a moment, then nodded sharply and concentrated on sending the message. Bobby raised his voice. "Why give it up? You'll top us anyway."

"Not the Divas. You can save them." He laughed. "We really do want them alive."

"Maybe I'm the greedy type." Even if he wasn't both Magpie and Pepee were wide-eyed and shaking their heads. "We'll just sit here until a few of your wounded bleed out, then nip out and top the rest."

"You had your chance." Silence fell.

Bobby spoke quietly. "There's some bins left in that room behind us, the one halfway down. I'll drag them out and make some sort of barrier. Then if they get close, we fall back and make them come the last bit in the open."

Hood hesitated, then asked. "What about Fleur?"

"She wants to go in there, the hospital." Bobby looked round and sighed. "Find out who else isn't up for a hand to hand fight and they can go in there. I'll shut the door on the way out so they have a chance because that one locks. I'll put some food and water in there in case." If the Rangers didn't know the warming trick, they wouldn't get in. Hood went round the rest. Siflis said no, while Baiser shook her head when Pepee asked her even though she couldn't sit up yet. Bells just snarled and waved the little automatic. Pepee spoke to Siflis and he looked startled, then when she dropped her shorts he got out a dressing and started on the wound in her ass. She'd collected a solid round in her metal leg as well.

"Just Fleur, Beebi. Are you sure?"

"She asked, Hood." Bobby knelt and picked her up and Fleur roused enough to get her good arm round his neck. "You're going to the hospital."

Her eyes closed again when Bobby stood. The amount of blood left on the floor startled him again. He carried Fleur through and as he entered the room and the lights came on, her eyes opened again. "Triste. Sad. No l'amour." Her eyes closed again, blood trickling from her mouth.

Bobby laid her on the table. He'd considered a box, but they looked too much like coffins. "I'm sorry. Au revoir." She'd taught him that, and "Fleur amie." He kissed her on the forehead but Fleur didn't respond. Bobby turned away, taking the dagger from the doorway. He was going to ram this down Ranger Boy's bledrin throat. He played the laser on the controls until the door closed. The bledrin lasers were useless as weapons. There wouldn't be time for the lasers to burn through a jacket over this distance, and the Trooper face-shields would protect eyes.

Inside the room the main lights went out leaving half a dozen yellow pinpricks gleaming brightly. Blood trickled down the grooves in the table, and dripped into the drain. In the darkness a tiny purple light came on, then three blue ones. Something stirred, and metal whirred.

*   *   *

Bobby pulled out the seven bins in the side room to make a barrier across half the corridor, mostly two high. They could thin the basteds in the corridor, then at the last minute nip into the room and open up as the bledrin Rangers or whoever came round or over the bins. Three times while he worked Ecarlate sent a short burst down the main corridor. Each time Hood and Magpie emptied a shotgun apiece, one each way and down low to catch crawlers. The first time they got a scream, then silence.

The ship must have calculated the action had finished. A hatch opened to let one of the little robots get started on cleaning up the long smear of blood left by Fleur. Moments later solid flechettes lashed it, punching holes in the metal. The little machine stopped in a shower of sparks and a puff of smoke, while Ranger Boy screamed at some bledrin fool to stop wasting solids. At least that meant there couldn't be many. "We could try to take out one group?" Magpie must be getting impatient. "Baiser will be up for it soon so that's six of us with Bells to watch our backs."

"If there's only one clip of solids left, one burst will make our six into three or less. Remember how hard a solid round hit your leg?" Magpie nodded, scowling because she couldn't use it properly now. Two rounds had gone in and the leg stayed stiff so she limped. "A solid will knock your other leg away and you'll fall, or you'll get hand to hand and lose your balance. Siflis and Baiser are concussed, and Pepee is limping because she's got a bullet in the ass and one in her metal leg. That means me and Hood arrive first, and they kill us with solids then kill the rest of you."

"So we just wait." Magpie still didn't like the option.

"We wait because some of those flechettes we threw down the corridor have caused injuries. The jackets mean most that get through will only be flesh wounds like most of ours but each wound bleeds, and we hit them a lot so injuries will be adding up. He's got wounded, some of them hit badly, and they keep getting flicked by a few more injuries. Ranger Boy sounds the impatient type." Bobby brandished his shotgun. "Up close we can get through all the jackets except for the two from Supers." He nodded towards the sniper. "Hood is good enough to get them through the bledrin gap between jacket and helmet, or where the glove meets the sleeve."

"If he cannot?"

Bobby smiled at Pepee and showed her the dagger. "They'll be the only two left, and we'll use steel." Pepee really smiled for the first time. She liked the idea of finishing the fight with steel. The corporal leant against a wall and took out a long knife and stone, and the sound as she freshened the edge seemed quite homely. Magpie and Bells both spent a fair amount of time doing the same back in the barracks.

Bobby told them to lie down in turn and close their eyes, to get some rest if they couldn't sleep. Hood seemed to actually sleep and so did Baiser, though her head wound might be responsible for her going out for a while. Bobby began to worry that Ranger boy had sent someone after Ecarlate, so Pepee warned her again by tapper. When his turn came, Bobby couldn't sleep because the Ranger had already taken longer than expected, well over two hours longer.

∗   ∗   ∗

Flechettes whined past, so Ecarlate had stayed awake. That had been another worry. Bobby fired a shotgun towards the ladder room while Hood fired one the other way, and metal clanged and clattered! The shield! Bobby almost looked but they'd be waiting for that, and Siflis lost his mirror back at the barricade. Ecarlate fired a longer burst and Bobby heard a scuffle towards the ladder room. The jackets! They were using those and the shield to come from both ways. He frantically waved for everyone to fall back.

They looked baffled and then Magpie turned and pushed at Siflis. "Coming both ways, run." She kept her voice down but Bells and Pepee heard and started back. That caught Baiser halfway between the barricade and corridor entrance, where she hesitated and levelled her carbin. The blonde backed up but stumbled and went over, probably because of her concussion. Almost everyone else dived or rolled behind the bins, but Hood and Bobby didn't quite make it. A burst of solid rounds knocked Bobby's legs out from under him and he heard Hood grunt as the big man went down. Bobby turned as he fell, emptying his carbin at the figure shooting at him. A hail of flechettes flew over his head once he cleared the line of sight for Pepee and Magpie.

Magpie screamed "Hood!" As Bobby rolled he saw that the big man had fallen forward into the bins, and now Magpie and Pepee pulled him over the low end of the barrier. Bobby frantically rolled again. He started to try and get up, then flinched as Bells emptied the Kraut just above his head. Solid rounds hit the bins before some knocked Bells over backwards. The little automatic bounced away towards the hospital leaving the Trooper in a heap, bleeding badly.

Bobby lurched up, glancing back as he tried to get around the barricade, then tried to stop and turn because a Trooper had almost reached him! He half-turned, bringing up his carbin but that and his bledrin shotgun were empty, and his legs wouldn't turn him properly. He jabbed with the barrel and the Trooper flinched then grabbed at the carbin barrel, pushing it wide as Bobby did the same to the Trooper's carbin.

Bobby tried for a head butt as they swung each other around, but missed and the man let go of his carbin to pull a knife. Bobby grabbed hold of that wrist, trying to get at his own knife, but he couldn't get his balance because of the bullets in his legs. He tried to turn his opponent so the basted with solid rounds couldn't get a clear target but only tottered. Bobby swore as plastic buckshot bit into his arm, but most of it tore his attacker away, throwing him across into the corridor wall.

"Thanks." Bobby didn't think Magpie heard him as she dropped the shotgun, aimed her carbin up the corridor and let off two long bursts. Bobby tried to cram shells into his shotgun, but before he could close it another Trooper crashed into him. They cannoned into the wall, with Bobby's wounded arm and open shotgun trapped between them as the Trooper's forearm went across Bobby's throat and pushed. Bobby used his other hand to grab at the Trooper's knife arm as it came down, though the point bit into his shoulder.

As they struggled, locked together, the Trooper grinned. "Got you,

Beebi."

It was the voice, the Ranger! Bobby struggled, but his legs wouldn't knee or even push properly. He let go of the useless shotgun, trying to free his arm, but couldn't. Beyond the Trooper, Bobby saw Baiser get a knife into a man but he smashed her back into the wall and her eyes rolled up. She dropped and he turned, holding his side but picking up a carbin with the other hand. Magpie still fired bursts up the corridor, and the bright marks on the bins and walls showed she'd got the attention of the basted using solid rounds.

Pepee struggled with another Trooper but Baiser's erstwhile opponent closed on the sergeant and Bobby couldn't call to warn her. Siflis rolled around the floor, trying to get a knife into a Trooper and kicking, kneeing, elbowing and head-butting. He'd wrapped his wire around his opponent's knife hand, pulling back and forth to try and cut into it.

Bobby's trapped hand couldn't reach his knife or bayonet but his fingers touched something. The dagger! Bobby pushed even as his lungs fought for air, and got two fingertips below the boss. Without the strength in his metal finger he would never have got it clear enough to grasp. Even then Bobby felt his senses reeling as he slowly twisted the short blade and then started to work the point through the Trooper's Supervisor jacket. His vision faded in and out.

A scream brought his eyes to Siflis, who'd lost his knife but got his laser up under a face-shield to burn out one of his opponent's eyes. Beyond Siflis, Pepee got her knife into her Trooper but the other hit her in the gut with his carbin butt and she went down. He raised the weapon to finish her but froze, staring beyond Bobby.

The pale blue eyes looking into Bobby's widened in surprise as the Ranger felt the dagger point finally get through his jacket and start into his gut. Maybe too late as his forearm crushed harder. Then a hand came over Bobby's shoulder, grabbed a handful of the Ranger's jacket, and threw him backwards! The Ranger flew back and toppled over, leaving Bobby staring at a Trooper with a levelled carbin. The Trooper aimed but hesitated and moved the barrel across as someone came past Bobby. Bobby tried to move forward but a leg gave way and he went over backwards. "Stay there." He knew that voice. Fleur!

Bobby sat, stunned as he watched Fleur walk up the corridor. A stark naked Fleur without even her stockings, and even with the other shite going on Bobby couldn't help but notice how bledrin gorgeous she looked. He flinched and tried to cry out as the carbin fired again but his throat wouldn't work. Bobby closed his shotgun, bringing it up but too late because he saw her judder when the rounds bit home. Instead of falling Fleur, it had to be Fleur, raised her hand. Blue lightning played around her fingertips before electric blue light blazed out. A man screamed briefly and the carbin stopped firing. Her other hand reached down to seize a Ranger by the throat, the one she'd plucked off Bobby. She picked him up clear of the ground and rammed his head into the wall then dropped him.

The man wrestling with Siflis broke free and limped away trailing blood, leaving the scout on his hands and knees, panting and shaking his head. The one standing over Pepee dropped his carbin and ran, clutching his side. Another tottered to his feet, his arm and shoulder shredded, bounced off the wall and staggered away. Bobby sat stunned as the survivors fled, forgetting the shotgun as he stared at Fleur. The one with the ruined arm reached the end of the corridor, before reeling back. Ecarlate followed her carbin butt round the corner with a savage grin on her face, reversing the weapon to fire a burst through the Trooper's shattered faceplate. Then she stopped, shock replacing the glee. "Fleur?"

The naked woman turned and Bobby gasped through the pain in his throat. Despite the calm smile on her face, the flechettes had torn Fleur's chest to pieces. Then she brushed the flechettes away and Bobby saw that although her upper body dripped crimson, the missiles were barely stuck in. That made no sense because the flechettes bouncing on the floor in front of Bobby were razor sharp steel, not plastic. He tried again and croaked "Fleur?" Now Bobby wondered what the table had done, had it created a monster, a robot who looked like his ami?

"It's me Beebi." Her smile certainly looked like Fleur. Then her face sobered. "Who can run quickly? The two who left have no carbins, and are wounded and bleeding badly. I can send you a quicker way." She concentrated. "There are two more waiting by the engines, but you will come out behind them. Quickly, or they might close the engine room and burn out the locks."

"What about Hood?" Magpie knelt by the big man, trying to turn him over to get at his wounds.

"I can fix him. Better than new, like me. But to save them I must stay, so you must kill those men."

Magpie looked up at Fleur and her face hardened. "I've got a limp but I'll try."

Fleur smiled reassuringly. "You will be quick enough."

Magpie stood up, limping forward with her carbin and a shotgun. Ecarlate looked beyond her, at Baiser and Pepee curled up on the floor and the still figure of Bells beyond. "Je peux courir." She shook her head as if clearing it. "I can run."

"Follow me." Fleur strode off round the corner towards the ladders, followed by the two women. Shortly afterwards Bobby heard a swoosh, then after a long pause another, and Fleur came back alone. She smiled, looking down at herself. "I have no secrets left." She bent, picked up Hood as if he were made of feathers, and strode off out of sight. Bobby struggled round, watching as she placed him on one of the tables before pressing what must be controls. A field formed round the whole table. As it thickened to block the view Bobby saw the nightmare of knives, probes and drills stir into action. He struggled up the wall until he could stand propped against it, while Fleur picked up Bells and did the same on another table.

Fleur, maybe Fleur, came back again. "Non, non." Baiser looked drunk, couldn't sit up, and probably wasn't quite thinking straight yet, but she wasn't going on a table! Fleur shrugged and turned to Pepee, who held out her hands to ward the naked woman off.

Siflis glanced up, still on his hands and knees. "No thanks, not until I know what you are."

Fleur turned to Bobby. "I'm not wounded, not properly." Bobby croaked it, but told the truth because nothing had gone in deep. "Metal legs are pooched."

Fleur smiled as she came towards him, but Bobby tensed a little. Her face fell. "I wanted to hold you, mon ami."

Bobby held out his arms, because even if she did seem to be flechette proof the hurt in her eyes looked like Fleur. So did the joy as she closed the distance. A few moments later Bobby could confirm that the amie kiss, or possibly Diva, felt exactly like Fleur. He looked down at her bloody chest. "Don't you need more time in there?"

"Not for that." Fleur wiped blood away with a hand, showing that the flechette holes were barely pinpricks now. "The other two will heal now, heal like me. If those two basteds double back, can you kill them?" Her eyes dropped and Fleur looked shy for a moment. "I need to wash, and find clothes."

"Go on then, though I wouldn't say you really need the clothes. Not from where I am."

"Hah. Typical Trooper! Likes any woman with no clothes." But Bobby saw real happiness in her smile as she turned away. He pulled his eyes away from the view as Fleur headed for their room, to find Siflis, Pepee and Baiser staring at her as well.

Pepee looked over. "Ses jambes. Aucun metal." She smiled but then it faltered. "Her legs. Fleur has no metal legs. Or maybe Fleur is all metal?"

The shock hit him because yes, no matter how well made the metal, the Putes wore their Trooper shorts to cover the bright band of the bio-metal interface where steel knitted with flesh. Fleur had no join, not even the garters Ecarlate used with her briefer shorts. "Fleur doesn't feel all metal, she feels all woman." Bobby felt his face heat up and waited for Siflis to flick him about it. Troopers didn't blush. Instead all three laughed.

Baiser glanced towards the hospital room, now closed off again. "Will they be like that afterwards, no metal legs?"

"I don't know." Bobby frowned. "Maybe there's more metal because Fleur's arm took a burst of solid flechettes, and so did her hip and some of her gut." He daren't say the next bit, that he'd thought she died.

"Ecarlate might be happy if Bells gets the metal he wanted." Siflis sniggered. "I wonder if he gets hydraulics." The two women caught on and then they were all laughing at the idea, or maybe they were all just glad to be alive.

Baiser put a hand on the wall before resting her head on it, holding her stomach with the other hand. "I feel sick." Moments later vomit splattered on the wall and floor. "Sorry."

"Concussion. Siflis will probably do the same." Bobby grinned. "You should both go and lie down." He nodded towards the hospital room.

"Not in there, but lying down is good." Baiser stood up straighter, helped by Pepee. She tried to walk and staggered. "I cannot climb a ladder like this, so sick room."

Bobby shrugged, gesturing to the dead Trooper by the end of the passageway. "I'll sit by the ladder room in case those two come back. I doubt it, but if they do that carbin has got solid flechettes, and I've got my shotgun." They all looked at the charred hole in the Trooper's jacket and chest, a Supervisor jacket.

"How did Fleur do that?" Baiser frowned and swayed again. "What can do that?"

"With her hand. Like this. With la foudre, electricite, zap!" Pepee held up her hand just as Fleur had. She looked over at Bobby. "Fleur really feels like woman? Not metal under the skin? Your hand on her ass felt right?"

The answer came without thought. "Oh yes, very!" As they laughed Bobby blushed again because yes, when a naked Fleur kissed him he had stroked her ass. He paused, and thought this time. "She felt just the same as the last two nights, but without clothes."

Pepee smiled. "Good." She helped Baiser away, followed by a sniggering, staggering Siflis.

Bobby shuffled along the wall, carefully because his legs were really pooched, and bent enough to pick up the carbin. He checked the weapon over, finding it had half a clip of solids left, and put a new clip of plastics in his own carbin. Bobby worked his way carefully round the corner to lean against the wall by the ladder room. Relief swept through him. They'd made it. Bobby stuffed dressings down his jacket sleeve to stop the bleeding until he had chance to fix it properly. He injected himself with Kwikheal, then concentrated on staying upright and checking each way along the corridor now and then, rather than collapsing from sheer exhaustion.

*　　*　　*

His tapper made him jump. A very short message followed, preceded by Magpie's six rapid taps, but the brief shorthand code told him everything he needed. *"Contact. Taken objective. Waiting in ambush."* Bobby acknowledged. He would have liked to ask how the two Troopers had run nearly two miles and won a fight in under ten minutes, especially with Magpie dragging her bledrin leg, but didn't want to warn whoever the ambush had been set for. He wondered if the engine room were nearer, in the middle of the ship. The tapper had jerked him awake again, but then despite Bobby feeling every cut, bruise and ache, his eyelids drooped.

He forced them open, moving a little now and then, turning to inspect the corridor each way and the ladder room. Ropes still hung from the ladder holes. A crumpled body below one showed where Fleur's plastic buckshot had smashed through his faceplate at point-blank range. The Trooper's comrades had stripped away the Supervisor jacket and his weapons and clips. Fleur didn't need a jacket for protection now. Bobby shied away from that thought. Instead he watched the lizards run along the ceiling before coming down to start cleaning up the bloodstains. A different little robot came from a hatch to drag away the damaged one, then three cleaner robots arrived.

"Pepee? Are you fit enough to round up weapons before the cleaners take them?" Down the corridor a robot dragged a carbin into a hatch in the wall. Pepee limped out of the sick bay, cursed in French and began to throw weapons away from the robots. She moved up the corridor, picking up knives, carbins and shotguns and scooting them along the floor towards Bobby. He leant carefully sideways to pick them up, putting them on the bin Bells had used as a seat.

"Sorry, I can't move away from the wall." Bobby snorted. "I can't even bend forwards or I'll fall."

"Sit down then. I can't because I have a solid flechette in mon cul. Siflis put on a dressing but it's still in there." Pepee sighed. "I can go on a table, and maybe come out like Fleur, but..." She shrugged.

"I know. I'm still worried about what happened. Look on the bright side, she saved us so whatever she is Fleur is still one of Les Putes."

"She came to you, not us, to be held. She came for a kiss. That is a better sign, I think." Pepee looked down, abashed. "I am sorry. You and

Fleur, after Magpie killed Raymonde? I wanted to kill you both." Pepee glanced up to where Fleur had gone into her room. "Now, maybe that was the best thing. She likes you, not for poochy and not for the job, not to kill you easier."

Bobby tried to keep shock from his face. The women had been friendly to help them kill the Basteds? Then smiled because what Fleur said about doing what she wanted suddenly made sense. "Fleur was going to tell you there was no need now. She told me she wanted an ami but not for the job. A boyfriend."

"She said boyfriend?" Pepee looked surprised. "Or just ami?"

"She said boyfriend, but not Diva or poochy." Bobby wondered, then asked. "You and the Super, Raymonde?" Pepee nodded. "Ami?"

Pepee curled her lip and almost spat. "Non. Cochon, pig. But that is how Trooper Chiennes are treated by our officers. For one of each squad, that is a part of our job." She looked down then away, obviously embarrassed, before moving off quickly to get more weapons. Bobby moved the weapons off the bin and put them inside the ladder room, then sat on the box.

"Beebi?" He looked round and up to the balcony, then kept looking. Fleur hadn't put on her uniform. Some part of Bobby remembered her Trooper uniform must be in that room with tables, shredded, but most of him just looked. Fleur looked down at herself and smiled, a cautious smile. "You like it?"

"Oh yes." Bobby wanted to say a few more things but reminded himself Fleur wasn't a Diva. The short skirt and tight blouse looked very Diva, but the way she swung quickly down the ladder wasn't. She moved quickly, efficiently, as if she'd climbed the bledrin thing every day of her life, barefoot.

Fleur started forward and then stopped, unsure again. "We brought these clothes for fooling Troopers, a strategic secret, but I am wearing them now so that you remember. I am Fleur, not..." She waved a hand helplessly, unable to find a word she wanted to use.

"A woman who catches flechettes and throws lightning?" Bobby smiled, though it felt a bit forced. "You feel like a woman." Then he smirked. "That kiss went a bit Diva."

Her face lit up, and Fleur closed the distance in swift strides. "Maybe my kiss will be more ami now I have clothes?" She bent and yes, Bobby agreed the kiss felt more ami than Diva, but not much more, not in a skirt. He'd never kissed a woman in a skirt, well he had but only a Diva. Though Divas didn't do much kissing because a Trooper went for the pooching and there'd be other Troopers waiting outside.

Bobby shook himself. Fatigue and Fleur in a skirt with real legs had really messed up his concentration. "Magpie says they've got there. Where did they go?"

"To the main engine rooms, at the other end of the ship. There were two waiting there, and the other two were moving as fast as they could to join up." Fleur cocked her head slightly to one side as if listening. "One enemy is dead. The last two are getting close to Ecarlate and Magpie."

"How do you know?"

Fleur looked almost guilty, and definitely worried. "The ship, it showed me. Not the people, but a map with dots. Purple for us, yellow for the enemy." She frowned. "One dot is blue, the one with Magpie and Ecarlate and still alive."

Bobby skipped past the ship talking to her, in her head. If a woman could throw lightning that seemed almost reasonable. "So how did Magpie and Ecarlate get there so fast? Are there cars?"

Fleur giggled. "No. Better." She started to bend and stopped. "Let me bind your arm first. Then I can show you, if you trust me?"

"You saved my life then kissed me, all while you were stark naked. I can manage trust." Fleur laughed and bent helped him off with his jacket. The uniform looked fairly ragged and spattered in blood but he put it back on afterwards because it would still help to stop plastic. Bobby managed not to tense as she bent and picked him up before walking into the ladder room. He did tense as she kept walking, towards the hole in the middle of the floor at the back. "Fleur?"

"Instant, a moment." Fleur stepped into the hole, Bobby heard the whoosh from before but louder, and the walls blurred. He thought they were falling and held tighter but they slowed, coming up through a hole into what must be the floor above. "We have a lift." She stepped forward, off thin air onto the floor.

"How did you do that?"

"In my head. I asked the ship, or maybe the lift." Her voice dropped to a whisper. "I'm not sure. I am frightened, Beebi."

Bobby smiled. "No, the Rangers and Shivas are frightened, scared shiteless. You were going to show me how to run two miles with a stiff leg in about five minutes?"

She set him down and giggled. "They didn't run." A door in the wall opened as Fleur approached to reveal a wide walkway, two walkways when Bobby looked properly. His eyes tried again because now each part seemed to move faster than the one next to it, with the slowest next to the door. "The further across the strip, the faster the floor goes. Ecarlate and Magpie stood on there, moved across to the faster part and went most of the way very quickly. They came out behind the enemy, around three corners from them." Fleur shrugged. "I told them exactly where to go."

"That door opened without using the controls. Did you ask it?"

"I might have, or the ship might. I don't know." The last came out plaintive, a cry of bewilderment and maybe fear. "What am I Beebi?"

"One bledrin sleek amie from where I'm standing." Bobby started forward, tottered, and Fleur leapt to catch him. "Fast and strong as well. It's a pity that table can't repair metal." Bobby reached down to tap his leg.

"I will ask." Fleur's head tilted slightly in the listening posture, her forehead furrowed a little. "Ship says no. The table will replace your legs and mend everything to make you like me, but not repair your metal." She fell silent again while Bobby tried to decide if he should risk the table. He couldn't even walk right now. "Ship says if we open your metal legs, maybe I can fix them so they work better?"

Bobby sighed in relief. "That will do for now. Sorry Fleur but I don't want ship in my head until the reinforcements get here. Can the ship give me coms, so I can talk to it?"

"Not yet because ship says most of it is still asleep. The ship will not wake properly until the captain comes." She listened again. "I am an emergency Internal Security Officer? Oh." Fleur looked shocked as she kept listening. "My job is to stop further damage inside the ship." She swallowed. "One of the other operatives will assist me, and one will operate ship defences against the fleet of spacecraft closing with us."

"Other operatives?" Then Bobby realised, ship must mean Hood and Bells. Bells with blue lighting? Shite!

"I must mend your legs quickly before Hood and Bells are fixed." She held out her arms and Bobby nodded, he didn't mind being carried now. Moments later, after another dizzy ride, Fleur stepped out into the ladder room. A cleaner robot tugged at the pile of weaponry.

"No, stop." Fleur raised a hand, then stopped because as she did so a line of lights ran down the robot and it backed away.

Bobby laughed, "Did you tell it bad dog?"

Fleur sniggered. "No, I meant to stop it but then it knew. Should I tell it good dog?" The robot turned and set off out of sight. "My Anglic is much better."

"Don't lose your accent, I like that." That seemed to call for an ami kiss as Fleur set him down on the bin at the entrance. Then she set off purposefully down the corridor at the opposite side of the ladders to the hospital, towards the armoury. Bobby listened intently but heard nothing until Fleur strode back round the corner. She wore a belt with a holstered weapon. "The lasers let you in?"

"I am security." Fleur pulled the weapon and as she did so two small wires or tentacles extruded from her wrist and plugged into the sides. Lights rippled on the weapon and a small screen lit up. "Oh." Fleur seemed taken aback, then she concentrated. "This is more powerful than my hand, or will do less, just stun. I wondered what to do if Bells wakes up and goes viral because a carbin won't stop him. The ship says this will, and we can fix him again if he is damaged." She listened for a moment. "There is time to mend your legs, or the ship will keep him asleep until then. I'm not sure which."

"So where do you start?" Bobby looked at the jagged holes in his calves and lower thighs, four in one leg and three in the other. "It'll have to be here because you can't climb ladders and carry me at the same time."

"No need." Fleur didn't even look down to slip the weapon back into the holster. As she did so the two wires disengaged and retracted. She showed Bobby her wrist and there wasn't a trace. "I am worried, Beebi."

"Concentrate on fixing my legs, and we can talk about your new talents at the same time. Your mind is still Fleur, or the bit that counts." I hope, Bobby added mentally. "Your body feels like Fleur, especially your lips." This time Fleur managed a smile. "We can work the rest out." Her smile strengthened as Fleur plucked him off the bin and set off towards the wall underneath their room. As she approached a hidden door slid aside. Fleur stepped into the hole inside without hesitation, then whoosh and she stepped out into their room. "Sleek. That saves climbing."

"The ship only told me when I thought of coming up here. It doesn't seem to know what to do, not until I want to do it." Fleur put him down on the bed, then sat beside him. "Am I still human, Beebi?"

Bobby didn't think words would do it, and anyway she'd sat on the bed next to him. The ami kiss deepened a bit as Fleur clung to him which reminded Bobby of what a boyfriend could stroke. When the kiss ended she smiled, a really bright happy smile. "Merci, Beebi, mon ami." She knelt to pull Bobby's legs round onto the bed. "Now I will mend you, and talk."

The talk turned out to be about how worried Fleur felt about what happened in her head, and the things her body did. She felt normal, human, the same as before she had any metal at all, but then her body did strange things. Bobby tried to reassure her, but found that touch, even holding or stroking her hands or shoulders, worked best. Being treated as something weird, deadly and untouchable frightened Fleur more than what the ship had done. The talking and touching helped Bobby as well because Fleur looked, sounded and felt like a woman, not an alien machine that threw lightning.

The talking came in bursts in between Fleur 'talking' to the ship. She did that in silence, then explained to Bobby, then tried to carry out her instructions. He found out how bledrin strong her fingers were when she peeled off the damaged plates on his legs and used both hands to smooth the ragged edges of the holes. Bobby stared at the insides of his legs, at the wires and rods and motors, none of which he understood.

Fleur touched various parts inside the metal legs, as instructed, and Bobby's legs flexed obediently or in some cases jerkily or not at all. Fleur used her fingers to straighten metal rods, and Bobby felt sure he saw the metal glow cherry red at least twice. Then she twisted steel wires together and this time Bobby saw her finger ends, held just apart, glow with the blue lightning to melt the frayed ends into one. Fleur also stripped the covering from electrical wires before melting broken ends together. Finally, she smeared sealant, the suit repair stuff, over the bare copper.

Midway through the repair Bobby's tapper started up when Magpie reported mission accomplished, one prisoner. Fleur surfaced from her latest talk with the ship to report that all the yellow dots were dead, Magpie and Ecarlate were alive, and the blue dot still lived. Bobby sent back a consolidate and hold order, while Fleur carried on with her repairs.

At the last she went to an invisible hatch, the small one for the cleaners, waiting until a robot came out carrying two components. Fleur clipped those into Bobby's legs, ran through some tests, and announced that the legs were mended. She clipped the cover plates back on, and Bobby stood.

"Stiff, not quite right, but bledrin sleek. You could get a job fixing cars and washing machines with hands like that." Bobby held out his hands and Fleur reluctantly put hers in them. He inspected her fingers. "No, these are much too soft and delicate to get dirty and calloused fixing motors." Bobby had wondered if he could see where the lightning came from but her hand looked human, even down to the fingerprints. Though the callouses she should have from using weapons had disappeared, as had any trace of sealant or the melted insulation.

Fleur looked relieved. "Are you ready to meet Bells and Hood?"

"Can we talk to Hood first?" Fleur consulted with the ship.

"Yes. Can you climb, or shall we?" She gestured at the hole in the floor inside the alcove.

"Hold me tight."

"Always, mi copain." Bobby wondered what difference copain made, then gulped as he shot down the tube.

*   *   *

Hood climbed off the table in a daze and sat on a small padded seat that had been extruded or uncovered by the room. He shook his head as if just waking up, sharpening up suddenly to look around with real alarm. "Where is Magpie?"

"Calm down. She's got a stiff leg from a bullet in the metal and the usual flesh wounds but otherwise she's Oke. Maybe you should get dressed first, before going to look?" Bobby frowned. "Can't you tell where she is? Fleur can."

Hood looked around baffled. "How, where?"

"In my head Hood." Fleur fell silent, and then Hood jumped.

"How did you do that in my head?" He looked at Fleur properly. "I thought you were, that the flechettes, there was so much blood...." He took a deep breath, then looked at the tables and the one still hidden behind some sort of screen. "This fixed you?" Fleur nodded and Hood looked down at himself, shock on his face. "How bad was I?"

"At least two solid flechettes in the back, and a lot of blood, and we didn't look closer. Fleur told the machine to fix you." Bobby debated then pushed on. "Ask the ship."

"Ask the ship? Oh." Hood looked panicky, then he froze before listening intently. "Nine spacecraft approaching." An expression of pure wonder spread across Hood's face. "I can see them and the asteroids all around, and the first rocket and capsules and Aggie. Oh man, I tell you, this is so sleek. Rifle?" He paused. "Ooh, someone is pooched. That is one hell of a bledrin rifle! Let me know if they don't play nice, Beebi." Hood shook himself and grinned. "I can use some of those beams, the ones we saw, and bullets the size of Aggie. Ship wants to me to protect us. Ship?" The grin disappeared and Hood looked stricken with sheer terror. "Immortal CEO protect us; I've got a computer in my head!"

"No, no, just coms. No computer." Fleur looked at Bobby and shrugged, so she wasn't that sure.

Bobby reverted to Trooper, using his best sergeant voice. "Hood!"

"What?" Hood leapt to his feet, his eyes centred on Bobby.

"Welcome back, Hood. Put on your pants, then go and get a weapon in case Bells goes viral." Hood spun, looking for his weapons.

Fleur pointed at her gun, then crooked a finger and Hood followed. Bobby walked around the room marvelling at all the lights and screens, about half of which were alight and not one of which he understood. It didn't seem long before a bemused Hood followed Fleur back into the hospital room, dressed in shorts and a tee. "Hey Beebi, look at this." Hood drew his new sidearm and by the time it cleared the holster the two wires had slotted home.

"What are those wires for?" The weapon looked lethal, the beautiful sort of deadly, but those wires flicked something in Bobby and made him uneasy. He hoped they were wires, then wasn't so sure because that meant Fleur's arm had wiring.

"Fleur tells me I can change the settings by thinking about it." Lights flickered on the weapon and Hood stared at it. "It talks, sort of." He lifted his head, listening just as Fleur did. "Ship wants me to hurry, because the fleet is only fifty-one hours out if they intend to decelerate for a docking at the same rate as our ship did. Ship wants me to train, and to test the exterior armament." Hood stared at Bobby. "I'm learning words and other stuff all the time, pouring into my head. Bledrin hellfire Beebi, what did we do?"

"We lived, Hood. If Fleur and Ship agree, I'd like to get Bells out of there." Bobby added ship in because the sodin thing already dished out orders. He'd best treat it like some sort of invisible Super for now, act as if it had some say but don't ask an opinion. The amount of influence that ship might have worried Bobby since he hadn't a grenade, or the faintest idea where the ship went to shite. "This time I'd like ship to keep out of his head until we can talk to the bledrin Homer."

"Ship agrees." Fleur and Hood stood either side of the hidden table as the barrier flickered, then died. Bells lay naked but without a blemish as far as Bobby could see. His eyes snapped open and he sat up. "No!" Bells twisted his hand before pausing for a moment, staring at both hands. Bobby knew why. That twist should have activated the knives in his metal fingers, fingers that weren't metal any longer.

"Bells."

The Trooper looked around, taking in Fleur in a skirt with a weird weapon in a holster, Hood in shorts with another, and Bobby still in his bloody, tattered Trooper uniform. He came off the table in a smooth roll. Bobby gaped at the sheer speed of the move, and the dexterity as Bells twisted in mid-air to pluck the weapon from Hood's holster. Fast though Bells was, Fleur had her own weapon levelled as the man rolled to his feet and lined his capture up on Bobby. "What did you do to me!"

"Saved your worthless life, you bledrin Homer. Now put that down." Bells stared, hearing the words but not really making sense of them.

Hood grinned. "It won't work for you, not until Fleur tells it to." But Bells wasn't listening to reason. He turned and pulled the trigger, trying to beat Fleur to the shot. Nothing happened.

Fleur smiled and blue lightning writhed and glowed around the muzzle of her weapon. "Mine works." Bells stared at hers, then his. "Now give Hood his weapon back, listen to Beebi, and you can have one that works."

"Beebi?" Bells wanted to do something, attack, run, break things, but that lightning looked creepy, wrong, and it held him in place for long moments.

Beebi smiled. "Seriously Bells, do it. She doesn't need the weapon, not now."

"What is she, what is Hood? They aren't right; they're different. What happened when I went down?" Bells looked down. "Where's my gear?" He looked around wildly. "Where's Red?"

"She went to finish the Rangers and Shivas. Now give Hood the gun you prat and get dressed, though Ecarlate might like what she sees if you don't." That worked.

Bells looked at himself again and a big grin broke over his face. "You reckon?" He looked at the weapon and threw it to Hood. "Here. It's broke anyway." Bobby relaxed because Bells had snapped out of it again though it usually took a lot more once he'd gone viral. Though this time he hadn't actually got started on the fighting part.

Hood caught the weapon and the wires snapped into place. The blue nimbus formed. "Seems fine to me."

Bobby cut in before Bells could react to that. "Now get some clothes on and we'll explain. For now we won, the table fixed you, and we all lived."

"But Hood and Fleur?" Bells looked down at himself and moved the arm he'd had bound up, the one shot twice and broken. "This has to be a plus. Hey, where's my metal?" His head came up, eyes wide in alarm again.

"Calm, Bells, remember calm?" Bells stared at Bobby but this time he listened, and gradually did lose the wild-eyed look again. He seemed to rally better when Bobby said he should visit Siflis and Baiser because they were injured, though first he should get some pants on in case Baiser couldn't restrain herself. Bells grinned and pointed out he'd have to risk it since his pack and pants were in the sick bay anyway.

*   *   *

As they escorted Bells, Bobby told Pepee to take a break from guard duty and get some rest because there were no more enemies on the ship. Fleur seemed certain of that, and since she'd known about a mystery man two miles away Bobby believed her. Bobby used the delay while Bells got dressed to contact Magpie. He figured if everyone else had died, he may as well go back to using coms.

The mystery blue spot had been found tied up, apparently a captive of the Rangers' alliance even if he wore a SEPA uniform. Neither Ecarlate nor Magpie could understand a word he said. Magpie hesitated before asking about Hood, and then wanted to come back to see him when Bobby confirmed her lover would live. She reluctantly agreed it might be best to stay put until Bells came to stand guard on the engines, though how Bells could do that confused her.

Bobby didn't want to go into that at long range, so he asked about the fight. The Ranger waiting by the engines had been the one Bobby shot with his finger, in a bad way but alive and armed so the women took no chances. The other two, running from Fleur, had died before even realising they'd been ambushed. The women found very little food in the spacesuit backpacks so impending starvation might have prompted the attack. Magpie reported that Ecarlate seemed to be fine. She kept playing with some swords she'd found and fancied keeping them.

Bobby promised Bells would relieve them both, soon, and assured Magpie again that Hood had survived. By then Bells had put on clean shorts and a tee-shirt because he'd lost his uniform on the table. He didn't seem bothered about not having more clothes, more interested in touching the places his metal had been joined on. Like most of the Basteds he'd not worn civvie clothes except as disguises for ten years so didn't bring any on the mission. After enough explanation Fleur spoke to Bells in his head, or so she told Bobby. Bells tensed, but listened to her and then Hood as ship connected them. Finally, ship spoke to him.

"I'm heavy muscle for Fleur. The, er, ship is worried about the fighting in here and wants it all stopped." Bells frowned. "I thought it was all stopped? You said everyone else is dead."

"We're done for now but there's the best part of three hundred Troopers on the way. If they're anything like the rest of Beebi's Basteds they'll be expecting a ruck." Bobby sighed. "Are you all right now, because Magpie wants to come and check on Hood?" Bobby grinned. "Ecarlate might want to stay there with you when she sees you dressed like that."

Bells grinned back. "Yeah, I'm Oke. Just as long as it's like Fleur says, and ship stays outta my head most of the time. I don't mind Fleur because that's like coms talking, sort of, and she's a sarge anyway so she's in charge. Or she is if you say so, Beebi?"

"I do. Now go and get some of that fancy gear and sod off so I can rest."

"Wimp."

"I am among you three, but you're still the Homer." Hood left to sort out the bodies and put the captured weapons in a bin out of the way, since he felt fine now. Opening bins wasn't a problem for Hood now because he could ask the bledrin things to unlock. Bobby watched Bells follow Fleur and thought about that, and the wimp thing. The three of them could talk to each other without speaking, anyplace on the ship, and were all fitter and stronger than any man Bobby had met. Bobby considered getting an upgrade himself, but still didn't fancy it unless he ended up wounded. He sat on the bin by the ladder room and checked his various aches, pains and numerous flesh wounds while sipping water for his throat.

"What is that?" Bobby stared at the apparition that had to be Bells, until the visor slid up and disappeared.

Bells grinned. "Muscle." He rapped the bronze, scaled, articulated armour with a gauntleted knuckle. "Those rockets will bounce off this and so will solid rounds. I've got my own gun, and the knives and the rest, and then there's this." He clenched his gauntlet and spikes grew from the knuckles. "What do you think? Will Red like it?"

Bobby rolled his eyes. "It won't help if she does. She'll never get through that to do anything about it unless she's got a hacksaw."

"Watch and learn." Bobby concentrated. The armour seemed to flow until it disappeared into thick wrist and ankle bands, a collar and a belt. He concentrated again and the armour flowed back out. "Can I go and show Red?"

Bobby nodded. "You can relieve her and Magpie if your new boss says so, and Ecarlate can stay and admire you if she wants." Bells frowned, opened his mouth to answer and stopped, listening.

He turned to Fleur. "Yes Sarge." The Trooper strode into the lift tube and shot upwards.

Bobby shook his head. "Is all that necessary? That gun alone should deal with anything coming on the rockets from Earth. That machete or sword thing, all those knives and a bledrin great axe seem a bit over the top? A whole bandolier of throwing knives is excessive even for Bells." Though Bobby thought Magpie might want one.

"Ship doesn't want any more damage if we can avoid it. The armour will stop any weapon he'll face, and then Bells can walk up to the Trooper firing it and kill them without tearing pieces from the walls." Fleur sniggered. "Anyway, Bells likes all that sharp steel. It makes him feel properly armed."

"What about you? Don't you get armour and a lot of sharp stuff since you're the security officer?" Bobby laughed. "You sound like a Super, on about stopping property damage. Do I call you sluur?"

"No." Fleur whispered her reply, soft and uncertain. "I don't want armour, or to be a Super. I want you to remember Fleur amie, your copine?"

"I can hardly forget Fleur amie, or copine, dressed like that. Though you'll have to explain the difference if you're a copine now."

This smile seemed stronger, and her voice more certain. "I can do that later, after you rest. I can carry on because I had a long sleep when you saved me, or it seemed like I did. I must check that the weapons are stowed and the rest of our people are all right." She moved closer. "Will you check I am still femme, a woman? Hold me a moment?"

Bobby did, and kept holding as she took him up the lift to get his rest, then assured her she still felt like a woman. Her speed startled Bobby when she shot down the hole and he worried about what else Fleur might be. Fleur really worried about being human and a woman, worried enough that he wondered what it felt like inside her skin. Did she have a pulse, or a heartbeat? He hadn't dare check if she still lived when he'd left her on that table, and Bells had looked dead when Fleur carried him in. What happened if Bobby told her one thing, and ship said another? Then exhaustion crashed back in and Bobby lay down and slept.

Breach of Contract

Bobby half-roused when Fleur came back to help him up, then out of his clothes. Giggling, she gestured and a panel slid aside. The alcove probably wasn't made for two, and the shower didn't seem quite right without water, but whatever flowed over him seemed to leave Bobby's skin fresh and tingling. It definitely woke him up. So did Fleur, pressed against him and murmuring French words as she rubbed away at the scratches. Fleur giggled again as she felt him against her, and began to kiss his neck.

They left the alcove still entwined, though Bobby thought she half carried him to the bed. "You want some poochy now, Beebi Basted?" Her voice sounded low and throaty, and her accent thickened, and yes, Bobby really wanted some poochy even if it hurt like hell.

Though he hesitated because he'd got to like the other stuff, the ami stuff and didn't want to lose it. "I thought you said l'amoor for an ami, boyfriend? You said you didn't want to pooch, that you'd show me what the l'amoor thing means?"

Fleur stopped kissing, and froze for a moment. "Even though, I am… Even after what happened. In spite of what I am now?" She sighed and melted into him. "Mais oui, Beebi copain. I will show you l'amour." She giggled. "But first, Pepee gave me la capote, a sheath and cream so I won't hurt you. Then I can teach you l'amour, properly." Fleur's new, better Anglic had disappeared at the thought of l'amour.

"I'm already sure I'll enjoy the French lesson, even if it does hurt."

It had been over six months, so l'amour didn't take long even if the build-up seemed a lot longer and a lot more fun than the usual Diva poochy. Laying together afterwards, talking and stroking and cuddling, felt nothing like Diva pooching. "Did you like l'amour? Did I feel right, like a Diva?"

"Better than any Diva, I swear. Why are you so worried?" Bobby suddenly realised he might be wrong about Fleur's reactions, they might just be her training. "Didn't you feel right, or like it, the l'amoor?" He only just avoided asking if she felt anything, because Fleur hadn't felt half a clip of solid flechettes hitting her chest.

"Yes, I can feel everything. Better." Her low laugh sounded really happy and contented. "I was worried that maybe I am metal under the skin now, all metal, but metal could never feel so good. I am all new and you are my first, Beebi." Bobby laid and listened as Fleur explained how worried she'd been about the flechettes and the lightning, and talking to ship. How she'd kissed him and kept asking, and still wasn't sure. How she'd worried ship made her into another robot, like the cleaning ones. Now everything would be all right, because metal couldn't feel like this, no man could make metal feel good and metal blood run hot.

Bobby murmured words of encouragement now and again, and stroked and hugged, and let her talk. He didn't know what else to do. Divas didn't talk apart from poochy words, and Magpie certainly didn't talk about this stuff. Bobby did wonder if Hood might be having a talk like this with Magpie, or Bells with Ecarlate. Eventually Fleur wound down and told him to sleep. She might not, but would rest which would be the same. Then she closed her eyes and seemed to go to sleep the same as she had on previous nights. Bobby smiled. Not quite the same since there were no silk shorts under his hand.

* * *

In the morning Fleur seemed much more content, smiling quietly and humming something as they 'showered' and dressed. When Bobby and Fleur came out of the drop-shaft a group waited for them, but Bobby didn't have chance to ask why. "I want some of what she got." Magpie pointed at Fleur and Bobby's mind whirled. Did Magpie mean the metal upgrade or l'amour stuff? Magpie must have learned to mind-read. "Some of that as well, you smug looking basted."

"Are you sure? You'll get ship in your head."

"Ship left my head when I asked, last night." That might explain her loss of Anglic when she started on about l'amour. Bobby glanced over and yes, Fleur looked a bit smug.

"I don't care about ship or the knives table and lightning thing, I want my legs back!" Magpie's face started to crumple and the rest became almost a wail. "Hood wants my legs back."

Bobby glared at Hood and he raised both hands. "I told Magpie it's up to her because I lo… I fancy her anyway and once you know, she heals?"

Magpie pointed. "She's healed everywhere already and that's another reason."

"But I don't know what ship will do to you. It wanted internal security and someone to man the cannons, but you could end up stuck in the engine room or somewhere you'll never see Hood. Let's get the airlocks blocked first and then sort this out." Bobby wanted time to think about changing more people. He'd had visions of them being adapted to plug into drones for scouting or having hands that were spanners and screwdrivers. Worse, he felt sure the ship couldn't possible reverse what it had done if Magpie didn't like the result, not enough to put her old metal legs back on. To top it all, Bobby didn't know how Guns would react to meeting people who soaked up steel flechettes and came back with lightning bolts.

"I have locked all the airlocks. They will only open on my personal command." Fleur smirked and waggled her fingers. "Internal Security Officer."

Bobby stared. "How do I contact Guns or Control?"

Fleur wiggled her fingers again. "I will open one." She frowned, thinking. "Maybe ship can send the message, to save going outside?"

"That's better coming from my transmitter, or Aggie might not accept it."

"So that's sorted. Now can I get my legs back?" Behind Magpie a pale-looking Baiser seemed really interested in repair as well. Pepee, and Ecarlate who must have returned at some time in the night, didn't seem so sure. Siflis shook his head when Bobby looked over. That meant there'd be four who were free of ship's voice, so they'd be the best four to meet Guns and whoever the Frogs, Francais, sent.

"All right. From what I just saw, Baiser and Magpie want to get the upgrade. Anyone else?" Pepee shook her head as did Siflis, though Ecarlate hesitated for a while before she shook hers. "If someone changes their mind, come and see me." Bobby looked at Baiser and Magpie as seriously as possible. "I don't think you get the option of changing your mind afterwards, the other way."

Magpie moved over to hug Hood. "Why would I?" Baiser just shrugged, then winced and swayed and put a hand to her head.

Pepee glanced up the corridor, towards one of the water and bog rooms. "What about the prisoner?"

"No." Bobby wanted to know a lot more about the man before giving him this sort of power. "I'd forgotten about him. Will he survive without?"

"He's got some cuts and grazes but his injuries are mainly bruising, though he really has been hammered. I locked him in a bog room with some food. It'll take me to let him out." Hood waggled his fingers, copying Fleur. She wiggled hers back and he lost the smirk. "Or Fleur. She has a security override."

"Fleur, will you take Magpie and Baiser to get their legs upgraded?" Bobby thought that sounded a reasonable way to put it, better than rebuilt or wired up. Fleur beckoned to the pair and headed for the hospital. "Will the table know what to do?"

Fleur hesitated and now Bobby recognised her tilted head as ship communication. "Ship would like another security operative like Bells, and a close support pilot."

"Pilot?" Bobby didn't like the idea of a pilot being someone ship had rebuilt, someone the ship might control. His mind flitted back to people being rebuilt to plug into machinery. "What will it do to them? Will they still be the same?" He didn't want to mention anything specific, just yet. Hood and Magpie would go viral if they couldn't get into each other's underwear afterwards.

"Pilot will fly small ships, fighters and shuttles. The controls and seating will adapt to suit her human form." Fleur chuckled. "I am learning more new words and about new things, new machines and spaceships. I hope my head will hold it all. A shuttle will move goods and people, or collect the capsules. A fighter will...." Her words tailed off and Fleur listened, then stared at Bobby. "One fighter can destroy all the approaching fleet, unless they have really powerful weapons and shields that haven't been detected."

"I'll take the fighter, to help Hood defend the ship?" Magpie put out her arms and flapped them. "I'd like to fly."

"I would like being muscle, with strong legs." Blaise put a hand to her head again. "I would really like no headache."

"Baiser is close support in Les Putes, was close support. Like Bells." Fleur got that distracted look, briefly. "Ship understands." She headed towards the hospital again. "This will take two hours even if they are not badly wounded. Ship hurried with me, because of the fighting. That is why I felt strange afterwards."

"I'd like you at the interview with the SEPA Trooper, Fleur." Bobby hoped she might recognise a word or two because according to Magpie the prisoner spoke gibberish.

"This will take a few moments, then we can leave the tables to do the rest." Fleur flashed a smile and left.

Siflis came over with Ecarlate and Pepee. "You don't mind us not going in there, Beebi?"

"No Siflis. I'm not going in there either." Bobby debated a moment, but told them because he'd always tried to keep his squad in the loop. "I prefer some who haven't been changed. Guns might not like dealing with the others."

"You are right." Pepee frowned. "The FAC officers will not want to talk to Les Putes, any women. They will use the new metal as an excuse to break our contract, to get out of paying the bonus." She smiled. "Not talking to Fleur might be bad."

Ecarlate looked unsure. "I wonder about going in there because I would come out healed, and not just where I've been shot. Then I think, if man is interested he will wait a few days. I think maybe Bells just wants poochy, and doesn't really care who with." Her grin flashed. "Sometimes I do not care either, but Fleur explained. Just now I have no orders to pooch anyone so maybe there's no hurry. I like having no officer, no Legion." Her grin faded a little. "I liked those swords but Bells said leave them." Her smile strengthened. "I'll get them back when I can pooch."

Bobby smirked. "I only ever saw one Legion."

"Where?" Ecarlate spoke but Pepee looked interested. Siflis smiled.

"When I was a Timer, in a house near the Rotterdam refinery, just after I shot him."

"After? You shot him before seeing him? Was he dead?" Ecarlate sounded almost breathless with anticipation.

Yes meant they both wanted the story. Siflis helped to fill in, and Bobby found out Trooper Chiennes in general didn't just not like Legion, the women hated them. They liked officers less, but not by a lot, and both of them loved the idea of Bobby and Hood topping so many French ones. The dislike of Legion came from two things, the first being that Legion officers were allowed to treat the female Troopers as Divas if none were available. The second reason really burned because no matter how long they served or how good they were, female Troopers could never become Legion. Every single one of the women coming on the rocket would be like Les Putes, they'd either served long enough or killed enough enemies to be promoted to Legion if they were a man.

That worried Bobby and he said so, because Beebi's Basteds were only Troopers. Siflis laughed, pointing out the same had to be true of the Bigger Basteds. Maybe a few of the newer ones hadn't killed enough yet, but the shite jobs Beebi's Basteds did would probably get half the Squaddies killed. Half the Basteds were definitely over their ten years, and the original squad had just reached their ten and also killed enough people to be promoted early. Fleur arrived in the middle of the discussion and agreed with the conclusion. Both groups were too useful doing their job to be ever promoted. They also agreed the other blocks had probably sent their own bad boys or girls, to get round the Trooper restriction. That made upgrading Baiser to internal security muscle a bledrin good idea.

The three unmodified Troopers went with Hood to dismantle barricades and check the open bins. If the contents hadn't spoiled they'd be sealed again since the upgraded crew could open them as often as necessary. Bobby and Fleur went to see the prisoner but found exchanging ideas difficult. By the time they left him again to greet Magpie and Baiser, they'd managed a name and rank. Gocho seemed to mean corporal since he'd had two superiors and three below him in their group. Samurai, his name, seemed content to be a prisoner though he worried about a missing item. They'd work on that next time.

Baiser and Magpie were easy to deal with when they woke up because they'd known upfront. They'd undressed before getting onto the tables, and Magpie quickly put on her strategic underwear when she woke up. Baiser put on underwear when Bobby mentioned it though like the rest of those who'd been upgraded neither seemed bothered by lack of clothes. The two of them sat on a pair of the small seats the room seemed to produce to order. Baiser wanted armour like Bells. Magpie wanted to put on her short skirt for Hood instead of her uniform, now she'd got her legs back.

Neither were thrown by Fleur or ship speaking in their heads, though Magpie still worried about her thoughts being overheard. Fleur promised that she couldn't read Magpie's thoughts, and repeated that ship had disconnected when asked last night. At that Magpie smirked at Bobby and headed for her rooms and skirt, presumably before looking for Hood.

Baiser went to get armed and armoured. The scales on her sleeker armour formed intricate patterns in shades of red and gold, and her blades looked more elegant than those Bells chose but still numerous and lethal. She set off to relieve Bells but instead of taking the walkway the blonde ran the two miles, simply because she could. Fleur confided that Baiser had been a superb runner before having her legs cut off, and hadn't been able to get the same speed out of the new ones. The metal legs had thrown her balance and rhythm off but from the way she accelerated away down the corridor, ship had cured that. Bobby and Fleur went to the bog room for water, and then to a room with bins for food.

*   *   *

"You should be in command now. You can contact everyone who's been upgraded, and I can't talk to the Putes on my coms. If I give you my coms and take the ones Bells won't need, you can reach everyone and that makes more sense." Bobby glanced at Fleur, chewing one of the cheese sticks.

She finished the stick, thinking about it, then shook her head. "When the rest arrive the Chiennes will be four or five squads commanded by their officers, all men and women we never worked with before. Beebi's Basteds are one unit and used to working without an officer, with you in charge. All the corporals will take your orders, but none of the FAC officers will pay attention to me."

Bobby grinned. "The Chiennes won't pay attention to me either."

"They'll have to." Fleur picked a piece of meat out of a cold bin, held it briefly between the palms of her hands, then tore it in half. She handed one piece to Bobby. "Mi-saignant, medium rare." Real mischief showed in her smile. "I think we can show why they should listen." Then she sobered again. "We need a human in charge, in the ship."

"You are still human. You just ate a cheese stick and cooked your steak, so you're not a machine. There's other hints." Bobby grinned and Fleur grinned back, then shrugged.

"You know that, all of us here know that, but they will see the wires from my wrist and the legs with no join, and the doors that open without touching." Fleur sounded a little bitter, but she had a point. "Control cut off our legs and fingers and gave us metal, then told us we were still Troopers. They will not accept that ship made a better job of repairing their butchery. They will believe ship controls us."

"Can the ship control you?"

"I have asked because I worried, at first. When the rest of Ship wakes up, I will get a proper explanation, or so I'm told. The small part of Ship I can talk to is confused about why it would want to control crew. Crew must act under orders but without Ship controlling their minds, or they will not operate efficiently. Ship can stop the powered weapons from operating if a crew member tries to destroy or damage Ship, but cannot stop the crew member. Ship cannot kill lifeforms once inside, unless an authorised crew member orders it." She smiled. "That is why Ship couldn't stop the fighting, and why I became the Internal Security Officer."

"So you can stop any fighting now?" Bobby chuckled and waggled his fingers. "I know you can like this, but what if you aren't there?"

"I have two others to help now and I don't need my hand or this gun." Fleur pointed. "Look out of the door." Bobby did and one of those invisible, seamless wall hatches opened to let a laser on a swivel slide out. It turned smoothly to point up and down the corridor, then slid back into the wall. "When it does that, I can see what the laser does and tell it to fire. I can look around corners and inside rooms but I need to be close. About...." Her brow furrowed in concentration. "Ship is translating, and the distance is one hundred and thirty-two metres. The map in my head will show me the dots, which tell me where everyone is on the ship. They are coloured friend or enemy or unknown. Ship used to have one hundred and fifty-four internal security operatives to cover everywhere. Muscle."

"So Bells can do that with the lasers?" Bobby swung his finger back and forth as if aiming.

"No, just me." Fleur finished her meat. "I am not as hungry now, since my upgrade."

"But still human because you eat, and went into the bog?"

"I even used toilette, and have asked Ship to alter them. Using the dog bowl and then a sink for disposal is not the best way." She laughed. "Those dishes are external detector shields, to prevent any space dust leaking through the shields from abrading the instruments at light-plus." Fleur stopped, and then repeated her last words as a question. "Light-plus?"

"Beats me. I'm sure one of those space games Siflis likes said faster than light isn't possible but maybe Ship means something else?" Bobby looked around at the bins, the door panels, the sheer strangeness of the place. "I'm willing to believe?" He shrugged. "Until then, if you need food and a toilet you aren't a machine."

"But I worry, so you will not mind if sometimes I want you to tell me I am human?"

"I can do that and Magpie and Hood can reassure each other." Bobby sniggered. "I'm not sure Bells cares."

"Nor Baiser. Perhaps Siflis and Ecarlate can reassure them, or Pepee?" Fleur frowned, then a little smile appeared. "Baiser and Bells have met, but are taking a long time over changing shifts. Maybe Baiser wants to test all her new equipment?"

"Will that cause problems, with Ecarlate?" Bobby thought about the wording when Ecarlate refused an upgrade. "She seemed to think that might happen, Bells ending up with someone else."

"We, all the female Troopers, don't expect a man to want more than poochy. Ecarlate and Baiser aren't under orders any more, so they can pooch who they want to. If both want poochy with Bells they'll share. Your Hood and Magpie are lucky. Except for one or two who have the right officer we will never know a man who wants us, not just the poochy." Fleur glanced at Bobby with a shy smile. "Maybe." She stood. "Come, you must talk to your Guns if they are near enough, and Aggie will allow it."

"Good idea though maybe the main rocket won't allow direct contact. We'd best get our spacesuits." Bobby grinned. "Do you need one?"

"Yes, I need air so I am human." Fleur looked very happy about using a spacesuit, happier than Bobby felt about putting the stinking bledrin thing on again.

* * *

Once they were suited, nothing indicated that Fleur had changed in any way because the patched suit covered everything but her face. Though the suit didn't stop her opening and closing doors without needing to touch. Except the airlock, that needed a physical pull or push to avoid mistakes she told Bobby. As they waited for the airlock to cycle Fleur touched helmets. "There are airlocks big enough to take the whole mothership rocket and the capsules, according to Ship."

"No, I don't want the capsules with extra weapons or the main rockets inside here. I'm not sure what Control might have built into them." Bobby rethought his first reaction and expanded. "We'll insist the Troopers disarm out there after the capsules eject them. The Basteds and Chiennes come in unarmed for Bells and Baiser to check them over."

Fleur smirked. "The rest can go into a cargo airlock, disarmed and legless until you have met our own people and explained. Then your Guns can decide."

"Your officers as well."

Dark humour coloured Fleur's voice. "We may not have many officers once Les Chiennes know what has happened, especially if there are no carbins or shotguns for the sergeant-chef to protect them with." Her voice brightened. "The hatch is free."

Bobby pushed the handle. "Do the stars look different? Are your eyes upgraded?"

"Why? Do my eyes look different?" Fleur sounded worried again. "Did you look at them? What colour are they?"

"Dark brown, very pretty, and no I can't see any difference." Bobby turned so their touching helmets were face to face and he looked right into two definitely frightened brown eyes. "Don't be frightened, they look exactly the same." He could see her relief, though Fleur still looked worried.

"But they are different. Ship is telling me now. I didn't need to know before, but I can see different wavelengths if I need to." Her voice dropped so Bobby had difficulty hearing through the touching helmets. "I don't want to, not yet."

Bobby had a simple way to change the subject. "You don't need to if we only want to talk to Aggie."

The connection worked perfectly. Aggie accepted Bobby's message but confirmed she couldn't talk directly to the approaching rockets, only through the mothership but that would pass the messages on. *"Report received and stored for transmission. Four messages waiting for Trooper Sergeant Three Bobby B. Prepare to record messages."*

"Trooper Sergeant Bobby B recording."

"Message one: Area Manager Gunnar Eriksson. Well done Beebi. Arrival in approximately one hundred and thirty hours. Please arrange access for TRRF and auxiliaries with heavy weaponry. How large is the airlock, and can you guide us in and maintain control of the area? Out."

"Message received and recorded."

Message two: Area Manager Gunnar Eriksson. Arrival in approximately one hundred and ten hours. Please arrange access for TRRF and auxiliaries with heavy weaponry. How large is the airlock, and can you guide us in and maintain control of the area?" The message paused. *"UKs and FAC contract confirmed, depending on your continuing Alliance and control of ship bridge and access to ship. Please confirm chain of command and personnel, how long you expect food and water to last, and details of opposition with weaponry if possible. Talk to me Beebi. Out."*

The report had covered most of the last part, though Bobby had left out the upgrading or the food. He'd said they'd found a source of water that tested pure, and confirmed that all the wounded were still able to fight. He'd also left out any mention of the prisoner in case quietly topping the SEPA Trooper seemed the simplest solution. "Second message received and recorded."

"Message three: This is UKs Control. You will defend the bridge and

utilise the FAC Allies to do so. We advise keeping access to the bridge itself confined to UKs Troopers. If an opportunity occurs to take control of the engine rooms, you must do so. You will not be held responsible for damage to equipment or loss of personnel while doing so or breaking ISSCIC-COSSO-SEPA Alliance. Please preserve the remains of Supervisor McKay and FAC Superviseur Raymonde Kleber for investigation into deaths. Out."

"Third message received and recorded."

"Message four: This is UKs Control. Essential you respond to confirm Alliance and continued control of bridge and airlock. You will defend the bridge and utilise the FAC Allies to do so. We advise keeping access to the bridge itself confined to UKs Troopers. If an opportunity occurs to take control of the engine rooms, you must do so. You will not be held responsible for damage to equipment or loss of personnel while doing so or breaking ISSCIC-COSSO-SEPA Alliance. Essential you preserve the remains of Supervisor McKay and FAC Superviseur Raymonde Kleber. Out. End of messages."

"Fourth message received and recorded." Bobby cut the link. "Great, they think we killed our Supers, and want to make sure our allies don't get a fair share of the prize."

"We did kill a Super, one of them. We could lose the bodies, all the bodies if we throw them out of the airlock and say the ship took them?"

"I'd rather not lose Mickey's. He died right and deserves a proper funeral with all the bulsh." Bobby laughed. "He really will get metal. Metal Mickey."

"Maybe we won't quite seal the other bin, so our Super spoils a little. He was a stinker alive, so that would be right." Fleur didn't seem to be joking.

"Seal him in a room first because I don't fancy the smell, though three days might not be enough for him to rot." Bobby shrugged. "I'll give Mickey a space burial if you really want to lose the other body?"

"No, they will believe we killed him anyway. This way maybe they'll believe you." She sniggered. "They can't hold me anyway, and firing squad flechettes would bounce off."

"That'll be my excuse for not keeping you away from the bridge, that and your strategic clothing." Bobby frowned. "We'll have to watch out for some sort of double-cross when everyone arrives, some attempt to stop your reinforcements coming aboard."

"We would have to watch for treachery anyway. Maybe we should explain how close this alliance is." Fleur smirked, then sighed. "Now I will report and then I want to watch stars again. We have enough suit air for a few minutes each time."

Fleur's report matched Bobby's of course, though at the end she confirmed she'd placed herself under Bobby's operational command because of his longer service and time in rank. They sat for a while star watching, then walked back hand in hand. Stars had that sort of effect.

*   *   *

Bobby held a meeting to tell everyone about the timing, and that there would be an investigation into the deaths of the officers. Everyone agreed that disposing of the bodies would only increase suspicion, and Pepee made the most of that. She wanted a simple death in action with a body and the wounds visible and full of foreign flechettes, something a sergeant-chef couldn't stop. The rest of the bodies had been preserved by the bins, as Hood confirmed by looking inside, so the bodies at the other end of the ship were also put in bins and locked in.

Fleur confirmed the size of the larger airlocks, and that she had access, and the small force mapped out a plan. Hood still had a feed from Ship showing nearby targets, and four and a half days out seemed to be nearby according to Ship. While waiting for Guns to arrive, Hood started to practice with varying types of Ship weaponry including some live-fire from the side away from Earth, blowing away small asteroids. Ship had warned Magpie her fighter would take another six hours to prepare for her body proportions, but she could start training on a shuttle or salvage vessel immediately. She would start by collecting capsules and every remaining bit of wreckage except Aggie and the mother rocket, and putting it all in an airlock the opposite side of the ship. Some of the wreckage had drifted away, but Ship told her finding the pieces and bodies and retrieving them would be good practice in the fighter.

The remaining unmodified Troopers needed exercise and training to get sharp again as the Kwikheal encouraged their numerous small wounds to heal. The upgraded were incredibly strong and fit, but the increased strength and agility threw off some of their training. Bells accidentally crushed the mechanism on a carbin while putting in a clip so those were left for Troopers without leg upgrades. They all danced around saying just what they'd done.

The last day or so had been a sort of holiday but now they had to get sharp again. Up to three hundred Troopers would be a handful if they got loose, even with Ship's weapons to help subdue them. With all the captured weapons and ammo Bobby could even let the ones still using flechettes get in some live fire, shooting at shelving so Ship didn't get the paint chipped. Bobby wasn't sure even a rocket would do serious damage to the corridor walls under the blue coating, though the Ranger's missile had blown a hole in a storage bin when it hit the barricade.

Hand to hand meant splitting into upgrade and old-style, because only an upgraded Trooper could spar with another upgrade. Speed, strength and reflexes were all so much better, and watching Bells and Baiser spar full-out stopped any challenges from Siflis, Ecarlate and Pepee. Even when the two sparring Troopers misjudged and cut or hit each other too hard, the marks healed in minutes where normal human skin would have needed stitching. Bobby enjoyed sparring with someone different, with new moves. Ecarlate and even Pepee turned out to be really nasty infighters and stretched him.

* * *

During the next "day," Magpie brought Bobby a pair of headphones and a headband with numerous pads on it. "I wear one of these bands to talk to the spaceship, the big one, when I'm outside in a little one." Her face lit up. "That is unbelievable." With an obvious effort Magpie dragged her attention back to her errand. "Ship knows what I'm thinking when I wear this even when I am connected to my own spacecraft. I asked if Ship could use one to talk to you, in your head, and no because your head won't understand the input. But Ship can read your head, your thoughts with it and I heard you complain the prisoner is talking gibberish."

Bobby took the offered items. "But even if Ship reads his head, it will still be in his own language. I'll bet Fleur talks to Ship in French."

"Ship reads what you mean, not in a language. How do you think the ship talked to Fleur at the start? It didn't know French, or Anglic." Magpie tapped the headphones. "Then Ship can talk into these in Anglic, and you will understand."

"So if I wear a headband as well, and he wears headphones?" Bobby smiled as Magpie nodded. "Good thinking. Can I have another set please?"

"Will you put those on first, so Ship can check if it works? I'm no good for checking because there's a com in my head, built in. Better than com, it has vid and sound effects." She laughed. "I don't know which is better, the training vids for the fighter or being out there in the salvage tug."

Bobby smiled; her enthusiasm was infectious. "No fighter yet?"

"The fighter is ready, but I'm not." A savage note in her voice matched her curled lip. "Don't worry, I'll be ready before the others arrive. If one of the other blocs starts trouble, this time I'll finish it."

"Good." Bobby looked at the gadgets and hesitated, then put the band on his head and fitted the earphones.

"Can you hear me, Beebi?" Magpie's voice only came in the earphones, so they cut out other sounds.

"Yes. Can Ship hear me?"

"Please talk some more. Explain ranks, and who is coming because Ship seems very interested. Ship is waiting for the captain." Magpie sounded unsure about what that meant, but that happened now and then with all those who could hear Ship.

Though Ship had to mean it wanted a senior officer. Right up to then Bobby had never realised he harboured some secret longing to fly this ship, to be her captain and take her across the stars to explore or into battle. He quickly shelved that and talked through the ranks of everyone here, then those in the approaching rockets, and then his best guess about the UKs up to the Duchess and Royalty. "Is that enough?"

"Yes, Ship says it can adapt the frequencies now, so the second one will work better." Magpie paused. "Seventeen minutes thirty-seven seconds and counting."

Bobby took the headphones and band off. "That's precise."

379

"Ship is precise. We usually cut out the seconds when passing messages. Out there, Ship splits seconds into tenths for me, because things happen faster." Magpie glanced towards the bridge. "Maybe we'll get in there when the captain arrives."

"Maybe you can look in from outside if you fly round the front? Where do I pick this thing up?"

"A servitor will bring it, a little robot." Magpie turned to go. "I need more practice grabbing nuts and bolts out of space. I went around the front but it's all ice and no sign of a window anywhere. Aggie is still firmly attached to the ice because I checked, but the capsule looks very small after all this. SEPA did a lot of damage to the big rocket, maybe trying to get the air, food and water." She laughed. "The mothership keeps threatening to fire at me, but Ship won't allow it to get a targeting lock."

Bobby went to get a drink of water while he waited, because his throat still felt sore if he talked a lot. A partition now cut off half the washroom, while Ship altered the sinks and water supply behind it into toilets for humans. Once he could check the new facilities worked, Bobby wanted the other washroom sorted so he could designate one for women and one for men. When the little metal messenger arrived with his second headband and earphones, Bobby contacted Hood so he could ask Fleur to come and help with the interview. Maybe with the headband he could talk directly to Fleur's new coms?

*   *   *

Gocho Samurai sat because he couldn't stand. His legs were among the spares found near the engine rooms but he wasn't getting them back in case they held a surprise. He looked at the headband that Bobby put on and shook his head at the one Fleur offered. She pulled a knife, one of the captures, and bent it with her bare hands then handed to him. He tried to straighten it and looked startled. Then she offered the headband again.

This time the Gocho put it on, and the earphones, watching as Fleur straightened the knife again to drive the message home. Bobby left him to talk or listen for a while because Fleur claimed that Ship would be refining frequencies, though she confessed she'd no idea what that meant. Her education had been similar to a UKs Pleb's, basic except if they showed an aptitude and were trained up for a particular job. Ship, she confessed, spent at least half the time trying to explain what it had just told her.

Since neither knew when the Gocho would start to understand words, the pair talked about growing up, comparing a Britz mining complex to a French agricultural one. Fleur had lived in a farming complex but that didn't mean they ate better, just that they saw all that lovely fresh food being packed and shipped away. The shite in the company shops sounded like the same shite sold in the Britmine complex.

"Coloured and flavoured rice. No shrimps and real greens like Grandfather remembered." They both turned to the SEPA Trooper as he spoke, and he stopped, wide-eyed. "How?"

"Through this." Bobby tapped the band. "Translator." He wouldn't be mentioning Ship but though the man might be shocked, he wasn't stupid.

He looked at Fleur. "What about you? You have no translator."

"I get the translation through Beebi's coms." Fleur tapped her earbud and the speaker wand curving out. She still wore it to contact Ecarlate and Pepee.

The man assessed the reply, then suddenly turned back to Bobby. "You are Beebi Basted, I remember you." He concentrated when Bobby nodded, trying to remember as he looked at Fleur. "Not gonso, not a three stripe like Beebi. Not like Pepee de Glace." He looked relieved to finally remember names. Remembering anyone impressed Bobby. He'd not bothered with names as long as he knew which bloc a uniform belonged to because he'd expected to be fighting them, not talking.

"I am Fleur Mortelle, Deadly Blossom. I am the Putes three-stripe now but Pepee de Glace still lives. All the Basteds and all but one of Les Putes survived, though both officers died. Who are you?"

He laughed, though it came out a little bit hysterical. "All survived? Noname seemed so sure he would kill you all with the solid flechettes. I am called Samurai, because of my swords." He looked around anxiously. "Did you find them? My Grandfather gave them to me. They are not old, they have no history, but they belong to my family."

"Are you hurt, injured? Maybe a bang on the head?" Bobby shrugged. "I'd have thought you'd want legs or a carbin more than a sword."

"I have a headache, but I can fight without legs and this close

Grandfather's blades would be enough." He sighed. "But I will never get the chance to show you. Why am I alive?" He looked at Bobby's head. "I never heard of a translator like this. You have my accent, my regional accent. You both have."

"Really new and top secret. No doubt your spooks will steal it, or SEPA will buy them." Bobby thought a minute. The man seemed really thrown by the sudden translation but he had a good point about survival. Bobby didn't know why the man had been tied up, so maybe Samurai should be dead. "Why were you tied up?"

"Four of my squad are Australians, the fifth one rejected the interface when his legs were cut off." He grimaced. "Nobody told me that I would lose my legs! Just that I should feel honoured that I am chosen replace him. I am the best Trooper in 103rd Hokkutan Consolidated." His chest swelled a little. "Hokkutan is a subsidiary of BBTV Australia who are the contractors, they supplied the Roo Riders. They took away a rank, demoted me to fill the space." He stopped. "You speak perfect Japanese now, not Bahasa."

"If you were with the Australians, why don't you speak Anglic?" Bobby felt certain they spoke Anglic of some sort there, and wanted to get away from how well the translator worked.

"SEPA countries speak their own language but we all speak Bahasa. I was speaking Bahasa. Then I spoke Japanese but you still understand and reply in the same language."

"They're all in there, in the translator. Now why are you tied up?"

"Because I am not part of the plan." The bitterness bleeding into that would have been hard to fake. "BBTVA are making a bid for a controlling interest in SEPA, based on whatever is found here." He sighed. "They kept me alive to take the blame for the officers. I would be blamed for killing the SEPA officer, then the Ranger's officer, and then the Shiva's officer."

"Why go to all that trouble?"

For the first time their prisoner smiled. "Because I survived and that would stop questions. When the rocket hit the capsule with a missile, our officer was already dead. The Roos wanted to control access to the air, water and food, but the rocket, the mothership, held very little. Taking control of the coms to Earth didn't work either, they missed something or all the capsules contact Earth directly. The survivors thought I spun away into space because the explosion threw me away from the rocket, but I didn't try to get back. I changed direction enough to crash into the ice." He waved his hand around himself. "Into this. I crawled inside and joined the other two."

"Then joined the Rangers and Shivas and tried to kill us." Bobby scowled. "So let's get back to why you were tied up, if you managed to re-join your buddies."

"They were not my friends. I heard them speaking on the coms when they thought I had died. They were going to kill me anyway if I didn't agree to their plan. When they reached this spaceship I joined up, pretended I didn't hear their coms, because I thought that would be better than being alone for someone else to kill. My Sergeant, Bold Jack, needed me by then because he'd lost men. He agreed a contract with the Shiva's officer. That's why the Rangers didn't kill the Shivas officer, so that any contracts would stand."

"They told me sergeants could make contracts. Go on."

Samurai sighed, a long, sad sound. "I told the officer about the sabotage to the rocket and what I heard over the suit radios when the Roos thought I am dead. He challenged Bold Jack but the Rangers backed Bold Jack. My own sergeant hit me on the head, then took my swords and tied me up to be interrogated later. When I woke up they didn't ask questions, Noname told me I'd be blamed for the officers." Samurai shook his head. "They expected to make a contract with you, one that could be broken because your officer would be dead. They were surprised and very angry about what he did. Then they had to attack because the food was running out."

"Yeah, Mickey went out like a Trooper." Bobby didn't think this man had lied, or not much, but he'd check later with Fleur. "What will happen to their contract now?"

"Your officer died with great honour, more than I would expect from an officer. I do not know what happens to the contract because dead men cannot keep it." A savage grin split the SEPA Trooper's face. "I am the only survivor so I could negotiate a contract between you and SEPA, not BBTVA? Being tied and sentenced to death is a breach of contract, my contract, so I can do that. A contract to give SEPA a small stake here?

Then their reinforcements will ally with you. The others told me about reinforcements. They were told before they left as part of the plan to take over all the assets, whatever they were." The Trooper shrugged. "The new Troopers will not all belong to BBTVA, just be contracted. SEPA will overturn the contract for a share in the ship, even a one man share?"

Bobby laughed. The man definitely never gave up, and he seemed to have a real dislike of this BBTVA. "We'll think about it."

"My swords?"

"I'll ask and see where they are though I'm not likely to hand them over."

Samurai leant forward, intent. "You could send them to my father?"

Bobby couldn't work out why the bledrin swords were important, but sending them home wasn't much to ask. Not for a man who'd come all the way out here, been pooched twice and then captured, and still kept trying. "If I can. We'll talk over options and contact our reinforcements."

Samurai laughed. "All the blocs will get the message, or know you sent one. Even without the words they will know you survived."

Bobby chuckled. "Without a message from their own people, they'll know we won. I guess whatever agreements they had will be dead in the water. That should be enough revenge against BBTVA to keep you going."

Samurai shook his head. "I want more. It is a matter of honour."

Bobby stared but the man seemed serious. He stood and beckoned Fleur, and the door opened. "We'll see. I'll get Hood to move you to somewhere with a soft seat." That would also let Ship get started on a toilet in here. Fleur followed Bobby, closing the door behind them. He turned to her. "Did he lie?"

Fleur did the listening thing for a while, so Ship must have a lot to say. Though the translation didn't take long. "Ship doesn't know."

Bobby stared at her, perplexed. "I thought Ship read his mind to translate?"

"Samurai seemed to be saying what he thought without hesitation so he probably wasn't thinking something different. I asked and Ship doesn't read minds, just the intent behind speech. I don't understand but I'm used to that." Fleur smiled. "Not understanding reassures me I am

Fleur, and not a computer in Fleur's body."

Bobby recognised another plea for reassurance. "The person looking out of your eyes seems to be Fleur." He held her for a moment because that always helped with any reassurance, and anyway he liked doing it. "What is the deal with the swords?"

"He really seems worried about the swords, more than dying and that puzzles Ship as well." They had been walking as they talked but now Fleur swerved into a room. "What are we going to do about him?"

"Give him the swords and see who he kills?" Bobby sat on one of the flat seats.

"Give him the swords but make sure he is only with one of the upgrades?" Fleur smirked. "If he tries to chop one of us, we'll laugh and break his sword then stuff it someplace painful."

"Do we have the sword, or swords? Are those the ones Ecarlate told me about, the ones Bells kept?" Bobby had just remembered about that.

"Probably." Fleur barely hesitated. "Bells says there are three of different lengths and he kept them because they are samurai types. The same as in old vids and there is a Katana, a Wakazashi and a Tanto." She chuckled. "He even knows the names, and now we know why Samurai is called that. I'll ask Ship to make Bells a new set if Samurai keeps his, but for now Bells will bring them back on shift changeover. Unless you want them now?"

"Not until we've talked properly, you and I. Sit down here and let's go through the options." She sat, Bobby sipped water, and they talked. An alliance made sense, but a lot depended on Control or Guns and if they wanted to share with SEPA. Maybe Samurai couldn't renegotiate, maybe being tied up didn't breach a contract? Though even then the SEPA alliance had lost control of the engines because their Troopers were dead or captured. Fleur had ordered either Bells or Baiser to guard the engines day or night because she couldn't bring herself to trust the Ship sensors, not entirely.

One thing occurred to Bobby, and Fleur agreed. If tying up breached the contract, sending them all out here without enough air, water or food had to be a big breach as well. With Fleur controlling all the airlocks, maybe the survivors could negotiate a new contract? Bobby and Fleur went to talk the rest, and then to Aggie.

*   *   *

Aggie replied to the signal and accepted the reports. The one for Control gave a proposed new contract with SEPA with information about the betrayal and a request for clarification. Bobby's report to Guns told him the survivors aboard had found food as well as air and water. He included advice for the rest of the Basteds to conserve the food in their packs after leaving the capsule. That way they could start moving over to solid food immediately, but be able to take longer. Bobby's combined squad, those who hadn't been rebuilt, still suffered from stomach cramps, wind and bouts of the trots.

The capsule had updates for Bobby but only from Guns because there hadn't been time to reply from Earth. Guns reported they were already decelerating and should arrive in seventy-six hours. As usual his estimate for arrival seemed a bit too high compared to Ship's, but that could be the delay before Bobby received the message. The TRRF were awake and exercising in the first of four six hour periods.

At the end Bobby and Fleur sent one additional message, one agreed by every survivor. "Message for UKs Control, FAC Control, Area Manager Gunnar Eriksson, officer commanding FAC reinforcements and SEPA Control. We consider the lack of supplies in our capsule and rocket a breach of contract, and request a renegotiation. We can offer access to the spaceship with air, food and water for all. We will restrain all arrivals inside airlocks, including allies, pending an agreement and then a decision by the officer commanding. Out."

"Message recorded. Transmitting to mothership." Both Bobby and Fleur needed reassurance from their ami after that, because neither knew just what the response would be. After all, Bobby's steel umbrella had gone now because the Duchess had put him here. Then they went back to practice and spar, to get honed and ready, because none of them expected Control to roll over and play nice.

*   *   *

Twelve hours later they knew the worst, because Guns sent an answer. *"Message one: Area Manager Gunnar Eriksson. Reference Contract breach. Contract stated that Troopers would be sent to investigate source of alien signal and be supplied with sufficient air, food and water to do so. There is no contractual requirement to supply Troopers with any support once their objectives are achieved. Breaking your contract will mean dishonourable discharge without pension."* Guns paused and continued in an urgent voice, *"Beebi, don't go viral. Let me and the TRRF inside to talk with you face to face. Please. The SEPA contract will probably be agreed but be careful with SEPA reinforcements."*

"Message two: This is UKs Control. UKs-FAC alliance and chain of command confirmed. Bonus will be paid for breaking COSSO-ISCIC-SEPA alliance and gaining control of ship. Essential no other bloc allowed aboard. Wait for arrival of UKs forces before attempting to operate spaceship. Out."

Bobby didn't even try to explain, he played the raw messages back to the rest. "Control haven't had time to reply about the contract breach yet but we already know what it will be. If we don't roll over and play nicely, they'll throw us out into a housing complex without creds or legs. We've got three days, or seventy hours according to Ship. Go back to exercising and training but think about it while you work. We'll have a meeting in eighteen hours to decide what we are going to do, then there's still time to send the answer to Earth and get a reply. By then Ship has told Fleur we'll be able to talk to Guns with only a short lag, short enough for a conversation. Maybe we can get an idea of what the last bit from him is about." From their faces as the rest split up, Bobby didn't think they were going to roll over and play nice.

THE END

Coming Soon
Riding the Spear
The Shattered Stars - Book II

Breach of Contract - Players

Timers:

Bobby B - aka Beebi - miner's son from the Britmine complex at Swansea. 5'11" well built

Stifles - aka Siflis - ex poacher, 5'5", slim and wiry, deadly with a garrotte

Hellis - aka Bells - not a deep thinker, prone to go apeshit in a ruck. 5'10" muscular and works out continuously. Prefers edged weaponry or brass knuckles

Fenton - aka Hood - Malazan God of Death. Sniper. 6'2" tall, broad

Sarge - Bjorn Kelsey - Sergeant of the Mob of Timers - veteran with metal, steel knees

Supervisor Steven McKay - aka Mickey - Supervisor bossing Beebi as a Timer, aka dick

3914 SSAB-Tata - Unit of 100 Troopers employed by steel manufacturers

Lord Alaine Bertram Curen - Supervisor Curen - commands 3914 SSAB-Tata

Beebi's Basteds - Beebi, Bells, Hood and Siflis - sniper-scout squad

Elli Funt - Corporal Ellis - 3914

Sudden - Corporal Sidden - 3914

Magpie -Uunofficial recruit to Beebi's Basteds- Margaret (Maggie) imitates Trooper. 5'8" slim.

Nathaniel Wright - Magpie - New identity of Maggie, taken from a dead 3914 Trooper

659th Armoured Troopers - Unit utilising armoured cars. Twenty vehicles split into fours.

Sandman - Armoured Trooper Corporal with remains of Tango Squad, four armoured cars.

Attic - Attica - Armoured Trooper with Sandman

The Horseman - Traditional name used by Troopers for the UKs Spymaster. Either the Headless Horseman because nobody knows who he is, or because he is one of the Horsemen of the Apocalypse - or all of them.

Spooks - Trooper name for spies

Judge Area Manager Svend Billings - Judge in Beebi's case

Manager Jakkob Bryant - Defence lawyer assigned to Beebi

Belinda, Duchess of Ironhills - Widowed mother of Supervisor Curen

Line Supervisor Peter Varney - Officer organising rescue

TRRF - Trooper Rapid Reaction Force (Beebi's Bigger Basteds)

Guns - Area Manager Gunnar Eriksson - Commander of TRRF

Beebi's Bigger Basteds - Squad Corporals

Attic - Ex Armoured - Coms expert

Beddard - 'Ard - New man

Hood - Sniper - ex 3914

Reaper - Sniper - new man

Sandman - Heavy weapons - ex Armoured

Sudden - Two metal feet - ex 3914

FAC squad - Les Putes

Adjudant-chef - Super - La Bitte - the Dick - Raymonde Kleber

Pepee de Glace - Ice Babe - aka Pepee - Sergent-chef - sergeant - Super's poochy. Black haired, black skinned six footer - hourglass figure - likes knives

Fleur Mortelle - Deadly Bloom - aka Fleur - Sergent - corporal -

contact with Beebi - dark brown hair and eyes. 5' 9" Slim, lithe, wiry.

Ecarlate - Scarlet - 6' has a red streak in her light brown hair, and brown eyes - athletic and buxom - shooter

Baiser - Kiss - aka Baiser de la Mort - Kiss of Death - 6' blonde with green eyes. Tall, strong, well-built and athletic - close support fighter

Aigu - keen, sharp - scout

Les Chiennes - Bitches - name for all FAC female Troopers

Satbir Singh Barar - Shiva's Children Supervisor - Indies bloc

Noname - Squad sarge of Rangers - COSSO

Bold Jack - Squad sarge of Roo Riders - SEPA

Samurai - Higa Jiro - SEPA survivor. Japanese Trooper Corporal - Gocho

Blocs sending Troopers

UKs - United Kingdoms - Britz - squad called Beebi's Basteds

FAC - Franco-African Corporation - Frogs - squad called Les Putes

MEEC - Mid-European Economic Consortium - Krauts

MACC - Mining Alliance of Chinese Co-operatives - Chinas

ISCIC - Indian Sub-Continental Industrial Combine - Indies - squad called Shiva's Children

SARC - South America Resource Combine - Amazons

SEPA - South East Pacific Alliance - Squad called Roo Riders - Mainly Australian

UFIA - Union of Financial and Industrial Assets - Northern states of USA and Canada - aka Yankees

COSSO - Confederacy of Southern Silicon and Oil - Southern states of old USA and some Mexican - aka Confeds - squad called Rangers

Frogs, UKs (Britz), Krauts, Russ, Chinas, SEPA, Amazons, Mexes, Yankees, Confeds, DeBeers - All slang names of econo-military blocs

BBTVA - Barrick-Billiton-Tinto-Vale-Australia - Major mining conglomerate in SEPA

BIVSUB - Billiton-Vale-Suncor-Barrick - mining conglomerate - Yankees

Britmine - Minor mining company - UKs

CB-S - CyberBlast-Sage - UKs Computing conglomerate

DABES - Deutsche-Auto-Bayer-E.ON-Siemens - Large conglomerate in space mining - Kraut

FAGMPEG - Facebook-Apple-Google-Microsoft Petroleum & Generating - Confed space exploration

MACC - Mining Alliance of Chinese Co-operatives - Mining arm of ruling conglomerate - Chinas

THULL - Tinto - Haworth - United - LKAB - Lundin - UKs Conglomerate owning and operating majority of mining and smelting in United Kingdoms. Major shareholder - Duchy of Ironhills.

General

Supervisor - Lowest officer rank, equivalent to the old lieutenant

Line Supervisor - Officer rank, equivalent to the old captain or major

Manager - Officer rank, equivalent to the old Colonel

Corp - Corporal - commands a squad of three to six Troopers

Sarge - Sergeant - commands a file - usually of four squads

Timers - First-Timers. Criminals or recruits to the security forces, given little training or equipment until they prove they can fight or they die. Only used in contract disputes (border clashes)

Mob - Group of Timers given their basic training by being blooded against Timers from other blocs

Troopers - Blooded fighters that have completed their Timer training. They have better equipment, more training, and are allowed considerable leeway in subduing civilian unrest or criminals.

Unit - Troopers are allocated to units of 100, and are sub-divided into files of twenty to thirty and squads of four or five based on need and skills.

Squaddie - Heirs to the professional British Army. Well trained and equipped and trusted with weapons that can damage valuable assets if misused. They are used sparingly as training them is expensive.

Legion - French Foreign Legion - the Frog equivalent of the Squaddie.

(le) Bateau a Douvres - (the) Boat to Dover - Frog suicide mission

Bledrin - Stronger curse

Cark it - Die

Diva - Young good looking woman, available for sex

Gaza Taxi ride - Britz suicide mission

Homer - Homer Simpson, a really stupid person

Pooched - Screwed - Army equivalent of obscenities

Poochy, Pooching - Fornication

Prats - Ignorant or stupid - usually die quickly

Sleek - Smart, slick, as in a sleek Diva, or that was a sleek move

Sodit - Mild curse

Spam - Less attractive or older women who provide sex in Timer or Trooper bars

Vance Huxley

Vance Huxley lives out in the countryside in Lincolnshire, England. He has spent a busy life working in many different fields – including the building and rail industries, as a workshop manager, trouble-shooter for an engineering firm, accountancy, cafe proprietor, and graphic artist. He also spent time in other jobs, and is proud of never being dismissed, and only once made redundant.

Eventually he found his Noeline, but unfortunately she died much too young. To help with the aftermath, Vance tried writing though without any real structure. As an editor and beta readers explained the difference between words and books, he tried again.

Now he tries to type as often as possible in spite of the assistance of his cats, since his legs no longer work well enough to allow anything more strenuous. An avid reader of sci-fi, fantasy and adventure novels, his writing tends towards those genres.